"I found him...Lucca...bac[...] his belly. I pulled it out. I-[...]

"Smart thinking, Morty. No wonder my dad locked the gate on you in 1959. He was trying to save your neck. Show me where you found the body."

Lucca was stretched out a few yards inside the exhibit, his head resting on the cold marble floor just inches from the base of a gigantic display—the Oasis Diorama—that depicted him and the team that accompanied him on the expedition looking two-fisted and stoic in front of a patch of lush oasis greenery. Lucca seemed, at the moment, to be looking down from the wall-sized diorama onto the lifeless body of the real thing.

———————— ★ ————————

"...you'll love Donovan, who's so well-informed about everything that you'll just want to pinch him—hard."

—*Kirkus Reviews*

Forthcoming from Worldwide Mystery by
MICHAEL JAHN

MURDER ON THEATRE ROW

MICHAEL JAHN

MURDER
AT THE MUSEUM
OF NATURAL HISTORY

WⓇRLDWIDE®

TORONTO • NEW YORK • LONDON
AMSTERDAM • PARIS • SYDNEY • HAMBURG
STOCKHOLM • ATHENS • TOKYO • MILAN
MADRID • WARSAW • BUDAPEST • AUCKLAND

For Ellen

MURDER AT THE MUSEUM OF NATURAL HISTORY

A Worldwide Mystery/January 2000

First published by St. Martin's Press, Incorporated.

ISBN 0-373-26337-6

Visit us at www.worldwidemystery.com

Printed in U.S.A.

MURDER
AT THE MUSEUM
OF NATURAL HISTORY

ONE

ALONE AGAIN

IT WAS SIX on a September morning, and a freshening breeze was coming in off the Hudson River and humming slightly in the half-inch cracks, stuffed with crunched-up matchbooks and business cards, that otherwise would have kept the old wooden window frame rattling like a machine gun.

Donovan shook off the cobwebs of sleep and hoisted himself up on one elbow to squint at the pigeon whose cooing had come in on the dawn breeze to wake him up. Donovan eyeballed the bird, glaring at it with one eye shut and the other blazing with mock-evil portent. "I damn near killed your great-grandfather for waking me up in the morning," he snarled.

The fowl was unimpressed. "Poor," it seemed to say, which Donovan took as a judgment on his bank account, his early-morning demeanor, or his ability to form lasting relationships with women. All of the aforementioned were on Donovan's mind the morning of his fiftieth birthday celebration.

Ten or eleven years earlier, still brooding over the deaths of his father and a few million dreams, Donovan had been filled with Scotch and rage and occupied his many lazy moments trying to assassinate the avian adversary who had taken up residence outside the window. He failed, of course. Little he did in those days worked out as planned.

In fact, in those days Donovan acknowledged being good for little more than drinking and catching murderers, a lifestyle he defended vigorously, very nearly to the grave on more than one occasion. Little did he know, in those halcyon days of midlife crisis, that four generations of pigeons would go on to live in peace, harmony, and relative quiet a few feet from his bed. Even less did he realize how much he would come to love them.

The birds were the one constant in his life. Without them he would wake up alone...again. As he lowered his feet to the hardwood floor and stretched in the dawn, Lieutenant William Donovan of the New York Police Department was a bachelor again and facing a milestone birthday celebration accompanied only by a bird.

"Poor," said the pigeon.

"Get your own breakfast today if that's the way you feel," Donovan said, yawning and padding into the bathroom. A few minutes later he plucked a piece of stale bread from the kitchen cabinet and left it on the windowsill for the bird, then listened to the all-news radio while watching the electric coffeemaker churn out a small pot of decaf. All was constant and familiar in the Empire City, as revealed in the morning bulletins. A mild-mannered gardener was about to be sentenced for strangling a small army of prostitutes. He was the city's first serial killer since Son of Sam enlivened the 1970s, and the city's violence buffs were having a ball with it. The radio celebrated other highlights in the blood trade:

A Bronx woman had lost her fourth son to street warfare. All died innocent victims of crossfire between drug lords. Losing four children in unrelated but similar circumstances was akin to losing grandparents on both the *Titanic* and the *Lusitania*. It stretched the meaning of coincidence beyond all bounds.

Finally, down at the federal courthouse on Foley Square, reporters were lining up to cover jury deliberations in the trial of the group of Arab cab drivers accused of blowing up the World Trade Center and trying to blow the rest of the city of New York to smithereens. Donovan felt vindicated by the arrests in that case. For years he had been grousing about the Muslim cab drivers who raced about New York City, which has more Jewish citizens than does the entire state of Israel, with "Allah is great" stickers plastered on their vehicles. Donovan took the fact that they still expected good tips to mean that their engines weren't running on all cylinders.

He switched from the all-news station to the one that played American standards: at the moment, Ella Fitzgerald singing "My Funny Valentine." Donovan hoisted his coffee cup in a toast to the days when he was young and bulletproof and walking down Broadway with a beautiful woman on his arm. He set about making himself an egg-white omelet that he ate on toasted nine-grain bread. He read yesterday's unread mail. It included a prospectus sent by Myron Glass, the manager of his apartment building. The building was going co-op, and Donovan had the chance to purchase his apartment at the insider price of only $500,000. With a snicker, Donovan balled up the prospectus and tossed it into the garbage using a perfectly executed bank shot off the cupboard.

A short time later, having pulled on his blue gym shorts and a white T-shirt, he was perched somewhat precariously on his old weight bench doing chest presses with a modest eighty-pound bar. Donovan wanted a good workout, just enough to tone up, to firm here and there and keep whatever might be inclined to sag from doing so. He did not want to look either like Arnold Schwarzenegger or, worse yet, like a fifty-year-old man who was *trying* to look like the muscle-bound actor. He had, in fact, made Mosko, his current aide, promise to shoot him should he ever be seen in public wearing spandex. By exercising, Donovan just wanted to feel good and continue to fit in the size 36 pants he had been wearing since giving up drinking five years before and dropping twenty or thirty pounds.

The weight bench had been with him since adolescence. It was black where the Rust-oleum had failed to flake off the rust spots, and reddish-brown elsewhere. It squealed like an old garden gate with each pump of the iron. Donovan had long felt that half the workout was merely staying on the thing. "It improves my balance," he told Marcy when they were still living together. She scoffed at him, of course, as she was inclined to do about all his attractions for the old and quaint objects with which he filled the three-bedroom apartment on Riverside Drive.

"You can keep the *tchotchkes*," she sniffed in Yiddish-English as she loaded all her stuff into the van the day, six months earlier, when she moved out. To her, his things were gewgaws, knick-knacks. To him, his parents' old furniture and the other *stuff* he collected in secondhand shops around town were as important as the medals, awarded him periodically by a grateful City of New York, that he kept in a shoebox in the bottom of a closet. When Marcy left she took all her things, mostly snazzy European art furniture bought for exorbitant prices at SoHo and Columbus Avenue galleries, and had them loaded onto a truck. Doing the loading was a crew of Israeli immigrants, Israelis having taken over the moving business as surely as Arabs took over the taxicabs, Turks and Indians the gas stations, Afghanis the fried chicken joints, Koreans the grocery stores and fruit stands, and Pakistani doctors the emergency rooms.

The buzzer sounded. "I'll be back," Donovan said to his beloved old weights, using his best Arnold Schwarzenegger accent. Then Donovan walked to the entrance hall and picked up the intercom. The doorman announced the imminent arrival of Detective Sergeant Brian Harold Moskowitz. Indeed, Donovan had barely fetched a towel and begun to sop the perspiration off his face when the doorbell rang.

A sunny smile highlighted Moskowitz's round, almost pudgy face, which always made Donovan think of the young Mickey Rooney. The face sat beneath a wire brush of reddish-brown hair and atop a weight-lifter's body. If anyone looked like a diminutive Schwarzenegger, it was Mosko, as Donovan found it simpler to call the man.

"*Shabbat shalom,*" Donovan said, amicably and ecumenically.

"Top of the morning, Lieutenant," the man replied, in a patently phony brogue. In Donovan's world, where nearly everyone was half something else, Mosko was Jewish, Scottish, and Irish.

"You're early."

"I didn't want to miss you. Sorry to interrupt your workout."

"I'm done," Donovan said, and led the way back to the spare bedroom that he had long ago turned into a workout room. There he replaced the twenty-pound dumbbells atop the painted metal milk carton that served as their rack.

"I love that weight bench, Lieutenant. It must do wonders for your balance."

"You've been talking to my ex," Donovan said.

"Not recently, but I'll see her later. You *will* be at the party, won't you? Five o'clock at Marcy's."

"It seems to be unavoidable. I've been ducking it for three weeks, but you guys talked me into it. Will *you* be able to make it?"

Mosko blushed slightly and averted his eyes. He was embarrassed—as well he should be, Donovan thought.

"I'll be there," the man said. "Don't worry."

Donovan draped the towel over the weight bar and went to the kitchen, where he fetched a spare set of keys off the key holder, a stamped-tin affair in the shape of a piglet that he'd gotten for two bucks at the New York Society for Mental Health Thrift Shop on Amsterdam Avenue. He dropped the keys in his assistant's outstretched hand.

Donovan said, "The rules of the house are as follows: No sex on the carpet. Well, there *is* no carpet, but you know what I mean. Clean up whatever you spill on the hardwood floor."

Mosko bobbed his head in agreement, all the while continuing to avoid eye contact.

"No rock and roll. No hard liquor. There's a modest little Bordeaux in the cabinet alongside the pasta and olive oil. You're welcome to serve it to the lady afterward—or beforeward, if you find that necessary—but run out and replace the bottle before I get home. I may entertain a woman again myself some day and would like to have a bottle of wine on hand."

Mosko made eye contact, forced a smile, and said, "I'm Jewish. I don't drink."

"You're part Irish."

"Oh no, pour, and you're a wannabe. Besides, you're making this out like I'm marrying the girl. It's only a one-day thing."

"Don't play down what you're doing here," Donovan said. "You're using your boss's apartment to cheat on your wife."

Mosko looked away again, but didn't stop smiling. "You won't respect me in the morning, will you?" he asked.

"I will if you don't make a mess."

"I swear on my mother's Scottish-Irish eyes," Moskowitz said, raising the hand with the keys in it as if he were taking an oath of office.

"So when do you want me out of here?" Donovan asked.

"Nine will be okay."

"Nine! Donovan exclaimed. "Who has an affair at nine on Saturday morning?"

"You *are* getting old," Mosko said. "I said this was a one-day thing, not a one-shot thing."

"All right, all right. I don't want to hear the details. Who is she, by the way?"

"None of your business. Come on, Bill, shave and shower and get the hell out of here. Go lose yourself for a day and I'll see you at the party."

"The things I do for my friends," Donovan grumbled, then poured himself another cup of decaf. Before disappearing into the bathroom, he said, "If you need me, which of course you won't, beep me. I'll be at the museum."

"Which one?"

"The American Museum of Natural History. It's my last chance to see the exhibit on the White Temple of Uruk. It's closing tomorrow and they're setting up for some big new exhibit.

"What's the White Temple of Uruk?" Mosko asked skeptically.

"An early Sumerian ziggurat," Donovan said.

"A who what?"

"A *temple*."

"Hell, Bill, how come you always know more stuff than anyone else? You know more about Africa than Jefferson, Mr. African-American, more about Italy than Bonaci, Mr. Paesano, more about Judaism than me—"

"Mr. Body Builder," Donovan cut in. "If you spent half the time on your mind that you do on your muscles—"

"I wouldn't be getting laid today," Mosko said.

"For the past five years, reading has been my replacement for drinking," Donovan replied. "It's how I spend the money I used to waste on booze and fill the hours I used to spend on bar stools. Feel free to use my library if the joy of sex wears thin."

TWO

THE WHITE TEMPLE OF URUK

DONOVAN PONDERED the fate of Ziusudra of Shuruppak, who—so Mesopotamian legend held—was the survivor of the Flood who carried the seeds of all living things and became immortal. Donovan scrutinized the Royal Standard of Ur, which bore on one side scenes of four-wheeled war chariots and, on the other side, domestic scenes of eating, drinking, and playing the lyre. Donovan admired the design of Sumerian temples, with their stepped pyramids that inspired later, grander Egyptian efforts. The sun-dried clay-brick ziggurat had corners aimed at all four points of the compass and three ramps allowing the faithful to approach the home of the gods. The courts were decorated with brightly painted clay cones that had been formed into geometric patterns, suggesting an otherworldly sense of order. But it was Ziusudra of Shuruppak, a Sumerian city just up the river from Uruk, keeper of the seed of life through the Flood, who captured Donovan's fancy.

The Flood itself captured Donovan's fancy. He was sure from his reading that the Sumerian and Hebrew legends of that apocalyptic deluge were based on the explosion of the volcano at Thera, which occurred about 1600 B.C. That connection was now an active scientific debate, he had read recently. Donovan first thought of it when he was ten years old and heard, in Sunday school, the stories of the Flood and the plagues of Egypt. He also knew the Atlantis legend. So he ran straightaway to the American Museum of Natural History on Seventy-ninth and Central Park West, seeking a more logical explanation than the one offered by the priests and rabbis, that the tragedies of legend were caused by the hand of God.

A tidal wave, he thought at that tender age. He had seen one dramatized in a Saturday-afternoon thriller shown at the Thalia on Ninety-sixth Street. A tidal wave caused by a volcanic explosion could have caused the Flood, the parting of the Red Sea, and all that stuff, and God might have had nothing to do with it. As a child Donovan disbelieved what he heard in school and as a man of fifty he remained disinclined to accept the official or easy explanation for anything. So he became self-educated, a tireless conductor of independent (if always emotional and sometimes erratic) investigations and, along the way, the City of New York's most decorated detective. He owed much to the American Museum of Natural History, which had helped him realize his talent for making connections between seemingly unrelated events.

After exhausting the Uruk exhibition, Donovan rode the elevator to the basement of the museum, where he sought lunch. Ignoring the fast-food Diner Saurus, with its throngs of school kids and its Brontosaurus Burgers, he sat down to a restful meal in the Garden Café. The restaurant was pricey, which kept away the crowds, and Donovan read the Saturday *Times* while enjoying a tarragon chicken salad on a croissant with mint iced tea, capped by a crème brulée.

At two in the afternoon he set out for the third floor to catch the final day of yet another exhibition, the seventieth-anniversary retrospective of Roy Chapman Andrews's Outer Mongolian expedition. Donovan always had a soft spot in his heart for Andrews, like him a largely self-taught man, one who stood science and much of the informed public on its ear in the 1920s with his highly publicized camel-caravan expeditions to then virtually unvisited Central Asia and Mongolia. Andrews's big scientific achievement was the discovery, in the sandstone of the Flaming Cliffs of Shabarakh Usu, of a clutch of fossil dinosaur eggs. But it was his good looks and dashing image (not to mention the 6.5mm Mannlicher rifle often seen in his hand) that were said to have inspired the creation of the movie character Indiana Jones. The Andrews romance wasn't lost on Donovan either, who often daydreamed of himself in faraway lands with a villain to defeat, a treasure to plunder, and a nut-brown maiden to protect. The daydreams contrasted with his real life, wherein murderers were the villains, the NYPD's overtime budget was the treasure to plunder, and Marcy was his café-au-lady.

Interesting, he thought, *I've been having more of those daydreams since I turned fifty.* He smiled at his own folly. He had reached the point in life where he could really enjoy his harmless eccentricities.

Andrews's Central Asian expeditions were cut short when the Iron Curtain snapped shut and foreigners were thrown out. Seventy years went by before another Western scientific expedition could find its way along the old Silk Road into Central Asia. Before that could happen, the Soviet Union fell apart, the Berlin Wall came down, and the Iron Curtain crumbled faster than a lump of sandstone from Shabarakh Usu. Then in 1993 Paolo Lucca, a billionaire Italian industrialist and playboy who at midlife had turned his attention to philanthropy and archaeology, funded and led the famous International Expedition to Investigate the Lost Treasure of the Silk Road, the ancient caravan route between China and the near East along which Marco Polo traveled on his legendary 1271-1275 journey to find Kublai Khan.

Lucca bribed the cash-starved fledgling government of the former Soviet Central Asian republic of Pamiristan to gain extraordinary access to lands long forbidden to Western archaeologists. As a result of Lucca's largesse, the long-lost Silk Road treasure city of Chandar was found and excavated. The priceless Treasure of the Silk Road—as Lucca called his exhibit—was set to have its world premiere at the American Museum of Natural History.

As Saturday wore down and the crowds of schoolchildren and tourists thinned, the museum began its preparation for the big opening. The following day, Sunday, September 13, a black-tie banquet would kick off the Silk Road exhibit. Donovan would have killed to get in there and meet Lucca. He was so eager to be a part of the Silk Road opening that he had volunteered—to no apparent avail—to serve as bodyguard for the police commissioner on his announced visit to the banquet.

While the Italian playboy hardly sported Roy Chapman Andrews's panache, Lucca *had* succeeded in making wonderful discoveries. He, too, was self-educated and interested in the odd bits and pieces of knowledge that made life so much fun. Donovan felt a strange sort of kinship with the man. If only they could meet. Well, Donovan thought, it would never happen. You had to be connected to get invited to black-tie banquets with the crème de la crème of society. And he was just a cop.

He consoled himself by spending two hours soaking up the Andrews retrospective. At four-thirty Donovan was peering into a display case that held some stone tools and other artifacts of the Dune Dwellers, Outer Mongolian people of twenty thousand years ago who, Andrews thought, might have been the long-sought missing link between man and ape. A guard came down the hall, quietly informing visitors that the museum was closing early to set up for the Treasure of the Silk Road banquet. Donovan realized that it was time for his own, humble birthday celebration.

He retrieved his car from the museum lot. After double-parking in front of two Broadway shops to buy a packet of Fruit of the Loom boxer shorts and a can of Barbasol menthol shaving cream, Donovan drove north to his ex-lover's café.

THREE

NEVER EAT AT A PLACE CALLED MOM'S

MARCY'S HOME COOKING had the considerable distinction of occupying hallowed ground. When it opened—the grand opening would be later that week—it would inherit the cachet of Riley's Saloon, the Upper West Side bar that had been home away from home to the assemblage of cops, neighbors, and friends whom Donovan counted as family. The fact that many members of that family, including Donovan, its patriarch, had stopped drinking mattered but peripherally. They all lived to talk and tell tall stories, and the precise nature of what they consumed while doing so had proved to be entirely beside the point.

In the waning days of Riley's, the tribe gathered often to guzzle light beers, Diet Cokes, and Canada Dry Club Soda and pledge allegiance to Marcy's, whose matriarch was Donovan's on-again and, currently, off-again lover. She needed something to do after quitting her job as an undercover policewoman and walking out of Donovan's life. The lease on Riley's hallowed ground was available. Riley's regulars needed a gathering place, preferably one that offered food in addition to drink. A deal was struck and the sacred land stayed in the hands of a member of the family. So what if she had recently moved all her good furniture out of Donovan's apartment? The two of them were as famous for their fights as for their love affair, and everyone figured that this separation was a phase that would pass. At the very least, many of Donovan's friends assumed, having Donovan and Marcy in the same joint could make for some interesting fireworks.

"Five to one she poisons your pasta," said Jake Nakima as Donovan walked in the door for his fiftieth birthday party.

Jake was the local gambler, friend of bookies, placer of bets for the men and women in blue who felt somewhat constrained from doing it themselves, and for years Riley's gatekeeper—the one who was there all the time, sitting by the front. Since he had invested in Marcy's Home Cooking, it was Jake's duty to decide who qualified as a regular and thus could get in the door during Super Bowls and other ceremonial occasions. For Donovan's party he was pressed into service watching the door.

"Go find another sucker," Donovan replied. "I've been poisoned by her pasta before and can spot the tainted batch a mile off."

"This is gonna be fun," Jake said with a mischievous grin.

Over the heads of the crowd inside the not-quite-open beanery Donovan could see the raven-haired head of his ex, bobbing up and down as she carried a caldron of something-or-other from the kitchen.

"Is this the first time you've seen her since the split?" Jake asked.

Donovan sighed and mumbled the mantra he had been chanting lately: "Never eat at a place called Mom's. Never play cards with a man named Doc. Never sleep with a woman whose problems are greater than your own."

"This place ain't called Mom's, and Doc ain't here," Jake said.

"Yeah, but my third point is a gem for the ages. I spent the day praying at the ancient White Temple of Uruk and thinking of its basic truth."

"Were your prayers answered?" Jake asked idly.

"They will be if Moskowitz didn't make a mess on my floor. Where is the little bastard?"

"He ain't here either. It's the sabbath for him, isn't it? Maybe he went home to Crown Heights to pray."

"Nah, he lives in Canarsie. He's not here, you say? I'll kill him."

"Let me check." Jake cupped his hands over his mouth and yelled, "Yo! Moskowitz? The man is here!"

Up to that point, the crowd inside Marcy's had been too preoccupied with food and drink to notice that the guest of honor had arrived. But Jake's sounding the alarm, such as it was, caused every head to whip around. Then a flood of friends descended upon Donovan, calling his name, shaking his hand, pressing packages large and small upon him. They were all there, his compadres from the West Side Major Crimes Unit, the guys and girls who worked under him. Well, not all of them. Donovan's longtime aide and best friend, T. L. Jefferson, was off on a month's scuba trip to Grand Cayman Island. His replacement as Donovan's assistant was Moskowitz—who, after the last hand had been shaken and the last congratulations accepted, still was among the missing.

"I'll bet he had a heart attack and died," Donovan said. "I'll bet he did it on the floor."

Donovan thought he had been talking to himself. He was wrong, of course.

"Hello, Donovan," Marcy said, brushing a curl of black hair off her forehead as she delivered a silver chafing dish to the buffet table.

"Hiya, kid," Donovan said, a bit too jovially considering that the last time they were together she was very nearly throwing plates at him. Recalling that day, he found himself quietly humming "I Wish I Were in Love Again," the old jazz tune about ineffable romance.

"What's that?" he asked, sniffing an aroma that came up part butter, part wine, part nose-tingling spice.

"Veal paprikash. I made it myself."

"I thought the menu for this place was going to be Southern home-style. You know, like 'Eat at Mom's.'"

"Waldbaum's had veal on sale. What do you want from me, Donovan? The restaurant will be what it will be. This is your party, which means it's whatever I could lay my hands on."

"Thank you," he said, forcing a smile.

"Happy birthday," she said, and kissed him lightly on the lips. More than a peck but less than a passionate kiss, it was still intimate enough to prompt a voice from the crowd to say, "Here we go again."

That caused Donovan and Marcy to pull away from each other, and *that* inspired a twitter. "What tangled webs we weave," Donovan said with a sigh as Marcy retreated into the kitchen to get more food.

He fetched a Diet Coke from the bar and circulated for half an hour, munching on carrot sticks and dip and thanking one and all for their gifts. So far he counted two polo shirts, a tie, three pairs of socks, a Bavarian beer mug, a weightlifting belt and matching gloves, a Phillies Blunts T-shirt of the sort favored by the black teenagers who hollowed out the stubby little cigars and filled them with marijuana, a soundtrack CD from the *Guys and Dolls* revival, and a Charles Barkley signature basketball.

"You could never tell from the selection that I'm single," Donovan noted to Jake.

"You've been working at that for a long time," the man replied.

A hush went through the crowd then, all eyes were on the front windows and the door, gaping at the tall and important-looking man getting out of the chauffeured black limousine that idled by the fire hydrant out front.

"Uh-oh," Jake said, recognizing the police commissioner, Donovan's ultimate boss. "What did you do?"

"He must have heard that story about me, the archbishop's niece, and the bottle of gin," Donovan said.

"Oh, *that* old story," Jake said.

As it turned out, the commissioner had come not to fire Donovan but to praise him. The crowd parted, the cops among it preferring to let Lieutenant Donovan be the highest-ranking officer to rub shoulders. So Donovan and the commissioner found themselves a quiet table in the back.

"To what do I owe this honor?" Donovan asked. "Surely my birthday didn't drag you this far onto the wrong side of the tracks, and on a Saturday to boot."

"Happy birthday, Bill," the man smiled, handing over an envelope plucked in a swift, confident gesture from an inside jacket pocket.

"Thank you," Donovan replied, opening it with a butter knife.

"I know of your fondness for antiquities," the commissioner said.

Donovan's eyes went a bit misty as he recognized a membership card for the American Museum of Natural History. That membership, something Donovan toyed with but never got around to buying, offered unlimited free access to exhibitions, as well as a subscription to *Natural History* magazine.

"Thank you," he said again, this time with real feeling.

There was more: a four-color brochure wrapped around an expensive-looking ticket. Donovan peered at the lettering: "Treasure of the Silk Road," it read. His imagination went wild.

"The new exhibit," Donovan said excitedly. "And this ticket—"

"—is to the special opening banquet," the commissioner said.

"The opening banquet! That's great. Thanks again."

"I'm giving you my seat and my car to get there in. I can't go.

I have to be on the campaign trail with the mayor. Besides, you'll get more out of this than I would. Look, Captain, we have to talk about something."

Donovan was still thinking of the lost city of Chandar and the possibility of discussing it with Paolo Lucca, and so it took a moment for the commissioner's words to sink in. When they did, Donovan's spine froze into a block of ice. "What did you call me?" he asked, his face muscles taut.

The commissioner smiled a big politician's smile as he grasped Donovan's hand. "I wanted to see how that title fits on you. What do you think? How does Captain Donovan sound to you?"

A captain's badge was something that Donovan allowed himself to wonder about from time to time, especially this year when he was celebrating his fiftieth birthday and thirtieth anniversary on the force. But being a captain was a lot different from being a lieutenant. It was like going from a seat on the New York City Council to one in the United States Senate. Captains had to be politically aware and respectable, and until the past few years Donovan had been neither of the above.

"It sounds great, but I..."

"John O'Donnell is retiring, as you know."

"I'm going to the party. I bought him a new surf-fishing rod."

"That means that a captain's job is open. You'd be chief of special investigations. Your portfolio would include the entire City of New York. No more being limited to a relatively small jurisdiction. And, not unimportantly, no more getting shot at."

"One of my mid-life resolutions is to avoid getting shot at. Another is to avoid having to draw my weapon. But making captain would mean giving up the West Side Major Crimes Unit," Donovan said, apprehensive at the prospect of losing the command, which had been his for a very long time.

"I think you will agree with me that it is a small price to pay. Look at it this way. The city is, more than ever, a global village. We don't have just the old Irish, Jewish, Italian, black, and Hispanic groups. We have people from every culture on earth."

"I know. The other day I swear I saw a guy who was from the hill country of Borneo."

The commissioner smiled. "And no doubt you can tell me all about his native customs. Look, Bill, all these people are bringing their peculiarities with them, including their unique criminal propensities. Of all the senior detectives in New York City, only you have the breadth of knowledge needed to tangle with a serial killer from Uzbekistan.''

Donovan's eyes widened.

The commissioner read him well. ''See? You liked the sound of that, and it was only something I made up. I used to think that all the cases involving weird killers and exotic weapons found their way onto your desk by accident. Now I know better. You like them. They challenge you. They turn you on.''

Donovan nodded in acknowledgment of the truth.

The Commissioner went on: ''You're the only cop in this town who logs on the information superhighway at home, spends his spare time reading or in museums, and yet isn't afraid to draw his weapon or wear out shoe leather.''

''I'm a regular font of arcane information,'' Donovan said, a bit too self-effacingly.

''We need you in a capacity where you can use your knowledge to tackle any assignment in the whole damn city. If you had this job a year ago you would have been in on the World Trade Center bombing—''

''I think I rode in one of the perpetrators' cabs,'' Donovan said.

''And the Long Island serial killer. You would have headed up our investigation.''

Donovan's mind raced through the possibilities, which were everywhere: East Side, West Side, all around the town. The best cases in the world's most polyglot city. It was, indeed, a turn-on.

''Why now?'' he asked when his thoughts came down from the clouds.

''Your name was first proposed five or six years ago, when O'Donnell let his retirement plans be known. But you were still drinking then and, frankly, something of a loose cannon.''

Donovan looked down at the table, where his fingers were curled around his glass of Diet Coke, absent-mindedly swirling the cubes around as if the vessel contained Scotch. You can always tell a reformed drunk, he thought. He's never without a glass of one kind or another in his mitt, twirling the ice cubes as if they were a baby's rattle.

''When was the last time you had a drink?'' the commissioner asked.

''Super Bowl, 1989,'' Donovan said proudly.

"Who played that year?"

"Beats the hell out of me," Donovan said. "I was four sheets to the wind."

"Well, it's been more than five years, and we're all proud of you."

"Me, too," Donovan said.

"I'll be blunt. Your dad has been gone a long time now, rest his soul. We all miss him. There never was a cop like him. But it's time for you to move on. You stopped drinking yourself to death over his murder. Now you can stop walking his beat on the West Side."

"Is that what I was doing?"

"It's time for your reward, Bill. Join the big leagues. You'll get an office at One Police Plaza, as much support as you need and, in case you were wondering, about twenty grand a year more in your paycheck."

"I could use it," Donovan allowed. "The online charge for a full computer search is two hundred an hour."

"Jesus, and I thought sending my boy to Georgetown was expensive. The price of knowledge, right? One more thing, Captain..."

"I haven't accepted yet."

"I recommend that you buy a few new suits and maybe get around more. When you sit down in my seat at the formal banquet at the museum you will be wearing a tuxedo, won't you?"

"Of course."

"Collect allies, Bill. Make important friends. Stop insulting reporters. Take the medals out of that shoebox and put them on the mantel. Smile more. And, remember that it's an election year. For God's sake, register to vote and send a hundred bucks to the mayor's reelection campaign."

"Okay." Donovan laughed.

"You didn't really vote for Reagan, did you? I know you used to tell people that."

"It was a line I used to avoid conflict in bars," Donovan admitted.

"Well, think up a new line. This is a Democratic town."

"I'll work on it. When do you need a decision?"

"A week," the commissioner replied.

"You'll have it by Friday," Donovan said.

The commissioner leaned back in his chair and sniffed the air. Several food aromas wafted across the room from two new chafing dishes brought out by Marcy. She was standing near the buffet table, fussing around and pretending not to be staring at Donovan and the police commissioner, wondering what the secret conversation was about.

"What's that smell?" he asked. "It smells delicious."

"Veal paprikash," Donovan answered.

"I thought she was doing Southern home-style cooking."

"She's never been south of Upper Saddle River, New Jersey," Donovan said. "Furthermore..."

That was when there came a passel of shouts from the front of the restaurant. Jake Nakima burst through the crowd, his eyes as big as the Rising Sun emblem on the Japanese fighter plane he claimed, preposterously, to have flown at Pearl Harbor.

"What's the matter?" Donovan asked, startled.

"I just got a call," Nakima replied. "Moskowitz had a heart attack at your apartment."

FOUR

A BROOMSTICK AND TWO CLOROX BOTTLES

DONOVAN PULLED HIS CAR to a screeching halt in front of his building, leading a caravan of detectives' cars and cabs, and was halfway across the sidewalk with a crowd of partygoers trailing behind him when something in his peripheral vision told him he had been snookered.

No matter. He hurried up to the fifteenth floor anyway and burst into his apartment to find Michelle Paglia, the West Side Major Crimes Unit secretary, decked out in a powderpuff pink-and-blue spandex exercise outfit. She stood by the door feigning panic, pointing toward the bedrooms.

"So you're the other conspirator, huh?" Donovan said. "Where's the victim?"

"Oh God, Lieutenant," she gushed. "Will you ever forgive me? He's in the spare bedroom."

Donovan burst into the room that until a few hours ago had held his old and creaky weight bench and the other stuff of his humble workouts. Inside was a spanking new Universal-style gym machine, gleaming with stainless steel and chrome and decorated with Man Mountain Moskowitz, whose pectorals bulged from beneath a Stanley's Canarsie Gym T-shirt. He extended a stainless-steel curling bar in Donovan's direction.

"Happy birthday, Lieutenant!" he said proudly.

"Mosko, you *schmuck,* you had me going until two minutes ago."

"What did I do wrong?" the man cried out in mock anguish.

"You left the truck parked across the street."

"Oh shit, the truck!"

"What truck?" Jake asked. He was hard on Donovan's heels, followed closely by the rest of the crowd.

"The truck from his uncle's place—Stanley's Canarsie Gym Supplies," Donovan said. "We don't see that much of it here in the big city."

"Shit," Moskowitz said, blushing. "Oh well, do you like it? We all chipped in. Every man and woman in the unit and half the customers of the bar...er, restaurant."

"I love it," Donovan said, as the crowd pressed around him with pats on the back and snappy comments about him and Arnold Schwarzenegger. "I would never have bought new weight equipment. I used to do curls with a broomstick and two Clorox bottles."

"You got it all now," Mosko said. "You got your library and computer in one spare bedroom and your gym in the other spare bedroom. There's no reason to go out of the house anymore."

"Pizza can be sent out for," Michelle chimed in. She had caught up with the rest of them and, the charade having succeeded well enough to get Donovan out of the house for the day, whispered in his ear.

"You know, Lieutenant, Brian and I didn't really...you know..."

"I know."

"He's a married man, after all."

"All *right.* Thank you, Michelle." He kissed her on the cheek, and she blushed. Seeing her vulnerability, Donovan decided to tease. He whispered in her ear, "Although, come to think of it—married or not, you could do a lot worse."

"*Lieutenant,*" she said, feigning shock.

Make that "Captain," he thought, then mused: These are good people who have been my friends for years. They've been with me through thick and thin, from the time my father was shot and I fell apart but had to pull myself together enough to walk his beat on the West Side, something I swore I would do forever. But years have passed, and now they went to all that trouble to get me out of the house for the day just so they could sneak in fifteen hundred bucks' worth of birthday present. But I wouldn't have to leave them to accept that promotion. I would still live here. I could still see them around the bar, er, restaurant, on evenings and weekends. I have to do a lot of thinking in the next couple of days, Donovan concluded.

He took the curling bar from Mosko and, to the cheers of his friends, did a few pumps with fifty pounds. "Not bad for an old man," Mosko said, and Donovan thought, *No, all things considered, I'm not doing badly at all.*

FIVE

A FONDLY REGARDED IF EMBARRASSING MEMORY

DONOVAN HAD BEEN to a number of certified events in the course of his professional life. He was a uniformed officer called upon to restore order in Harlem following the assassination of Malcolm X at the Audubon Ballroom in 1965. He was on the campus of Columbia University in a similar capacity during the anti-Vietnam War demonstrations of 1968. In 1976 Donovan was a young detective assigned to an antiterrorist detail during the Democratic National Convention that nominated Jimmy Carter. In 1980, and early in his career as head of the West Side Major Crimes Unit, Donovan saw the investigation of John Lennon's assassination taken away from him and given to John O'Donnell—the man whose captain's job he had just been offered.

But nothing quite prepared him for the uproar that greeted him upon his arrival outside the American Museum of Natural History that Sunday evening in September. Central Park West had been turned into a parade route for limousines. Police barricades kept back a crowd of curious onlookers and TV cameras. Two gigantic spotlights swept the skies, illuminating the clouds. A red carpet climbed the banks of stone steps leading up to the main entrance, over which hung in solemn majesty a three-story banner reading "Treasure of the Silk Road—American Premiere—September 13-December 15."

The police commissioner's limousine was a Lincoln Town Car that picked up Donovan in front of his building at Eighty-ninth and Riverside. When he walked out to be ushered into it, wearing a rented but perfectly fitting tuxedo, Donovan wowed his doormen and several familiar faces from the neighborhood. In the back of the car he nervously adjusted his cummerbund and combed his gray-flecked but still bushy brown hair. As the limousine made the turn onto Central Park West from Seventy-second Street it cruised past the spot where Lennon was shot, reminding Donovan of the first time he had coveted a captain's badge. Once on the broad boulevard, flanked on one side by stately old apartment buildings and on the other by the lush foliage and sweeping lawns of Central Park, the limousine joined the slowly moving line of similar vehicles, all of which were discharging black-tied men and mink-draped women onto the red carpet in front of the museum.

The carpet was twelve feet wide and lined on both sides by police barricades that served to keep back a crowd of TV crews and curious onlookers. Donovan was saddened to think that the people were drawn not so much by the science as by the celebrities. He preferred to think that the romance of the Silk Road and the glamour of the lost city of Chandar would be enough to get them out on a fine September evening. No, he knew it was the lure of Madonna and her new boyfriend, who were friends of Katy Lucca, the explorer's American-born, social-climbing wife. What brought out the crowds was the appeal of Elizabeth Taylor and her young husband; of West Side celebrity couple Alec Baldwin and Kim Basinger; of Hollywood couple Bruce Willis and Demi

Moore. Donovan picked up an occasional copy of People magazine, and so he knew that Willis was the chief contender to play the lead in the movie the Luccas were said to be financing about the Silk Road expedition.

It's amazing how having a few billion in the bank can increase the quality of your friends, Donovan thought idly as his limousine finally pulled up to the red carpet.

One of a dozen liveried retainers who scurried up and down the length of the red carpet, escorting guests into the museum, swept open the car door. As Donovan stepped onto the carpet he was smacked in the face with the glare of television lights. They shined brighter with halos made in the soft, fine mist that had been falling for an hour. Half-blinded, Donovan welcomed the steadying hand of the retainer that suddenly appeared on his arm.

Donovan squinted and looked away from the lights as he heard a voice, the gruff voice of a working man, asking "Who's that guy?"

"Damn," Donovan muttered. "Anonymous again."

The retainer said, "They want to know who you are, sir."

As he started up the carpet, the retainer at his side, Donovan said, "You know, I only just found that out."

"Found what out, sir?"

"Who I am."

"Who are you?" the voice from behind the barricades asked, directing the question to the lieutenant himself that time. Donovan squinted and saw that the voice belonged to a cameraman from *Eyewitness News,* the local television operation upon which Donovan had heaped abuse for years. *Uh-oh, got to be nice to the bastards,* he thought.

"Bill Donovan," he said. "Good to see you boys again."

As he continued up into the museum, Donovan heard the man's fading voice saying to his buddy, "I got no idea. Do *you* know who he is?"

The gigantic main doors were swung open to reveal a mammoth, black-tie bash that sprawled across the floor of the Theodore Roosevelt Memorial. Known as the Rotunda, it was the museum's grand showcase hall. Its vaulted roof towered over mammoth frescoes showing scenes from the natural history of Africa and from the construction of the Panama Canal. Sitting squarely in the center of the floor was perhaps the ultimate dinosaur fight scene. The head of a gigantic but gentle plant-eating barosaurus rose five stories above the fangs and teeth of a smaller, vicious allosaurus that threatened the immense dinosaur's baby. The gigantic mama rose up on her hind legs and threatened to bring her pillarlike forelegs crashing down on the meat-eater. It was a dramatic scene, and no matter that critics carped that it probably never happened. (Such a heavyweight, rearing up on its hind legs and crashing down its forelegs, would certainly have smashed its own limbs along with those of any potential adversary, they said.) Donovan knew that drama was what the museum wanted in its crowd-pleasing centerpiece, and it got drama and glamour and more as the celebrities mingled with the rich, the scientists, and the politically connected curious below.

Well, the commissioner told me to get some friends who are connected to more than the local bookie operation, Donovan thought. *This looks like as good a place as any to start.*

Bars and hors d'oeuvres tables were set up in the four corners of the Rotunda. The rest of the floor was dotted with round banquet tables save for the central space just below the would-be descending forelegs of the barosaurus. That was where the dais sat, decorated with a New York interior designer's idea of a Silk Road scene, complete with palm trees, elephant tusks, and bamboo mats.

The dais itself was unoccupied, but waiters buzzed around it, setting up crystal goblets and twirling bottles of champagne in silver ice buckets. Off to the right was the entrance to the Silk Road exhibit and, in front of it, a knot of important-looking people. Donovan immediately recognized Katy Lucca.

Who wouldn't? She was tall and gorgeous, with hair that was a lush honey brown and fell in flowing waves over her shoulders, partly covering the straps of her shimmering black sheath, visible when her exquisite black sable jacket slipped off her shoulders. Long the darling of the gossip pages of the three New York City tabloid newspapers, Katy was a New Jersey girl who had made good as a high-profile model. Her face and body had adorned the cover of nearly every fashion magazine at one time or another. She had been on the cover of *Vogue* twice and *Vanity Fair* three times (including once wearing only body paint done by acclaimed neo-realist artist Leonard Osrick), and created a media stir by becoming the first model featured on the cover of *The New Yorker*. Katy capped this career with two Hollywood and three Italian movies, and caused a worldwide sensation when she refused to pick up her Oscar for *Questa Notte* ("Tonight"), protesting Hollywood's shabby treatment of Italian-Americans. In 1993, she was appointed the spokesperson for the Clinton administration's "Inner Strength/No More Drugs" campaign. All in all, Katy Lucca beguiled a whole generation of Americans too young to know the cliché of the small-town girl who marries a fairy-tale billionaire. The inside line on her was that she was smart and likable.

Lucca looked different in a tuxedo than he did in his Roy Chapman Andrews outfit. The battered leather boots, dark khaki jodhpurs, leather-and-brass ammo belt, tan felt shirt, and crushed felt fedora might have gotten him onto magazine covers from *National Geographic* to *Time* and on television shows from *Nature* to *Nightline,* but that outfit wouldn't get him a taxi in New York City on Sunday night. He wore a Vespucci-designed tuxedo, notable for its one wide and one narrow lapel and a cummerbund that was flecked with gold strands. Lucca's jet-black hair was, as usual, pulled back into a fashionable ponytail that curled an inch over his collar. His surprisingly pale face sported the stubble that was another of his trademarks. Donovan noted it with vague disapproval. The unshaven look worked with the khakis and the ammo belt, Donovan thought. He was disappointed that the man he'd come to meet looked, that evening, pallid, unhealthy, and fashionable, like a fashion model or someone in a music video.

A long receiving line snaked its way to the Luccas, who stood in front of what had for years been the Hall of the Asian Peoples. That old museum landmark staple had been gutted and rebuilt, with Lucca money, to house the Treasure of the Silk Road exhibit. The entrance to the new display was through a mammoth door that punched through the south face of the Rotunda, past a mural dominated by generals talking at the end of the Russo-Japanese War. The Silk Road exhibit was concealed by a red velvet curtain that was closed with a silver rope clearly designed to be pulled by Lucca in a dramatic "see it tonight on the 11 o'clock news" opening ceremony. To record that event, three television crews were set up on a wooden platform near the allosaurus.

Donovan pulled the invitation from his inside jacket pocket and read it to check the schedule. It was cocktails and hors d'oeuvres, preview of the exhibit, and dinner. He checked his watch and discovered that a half hour remained in the cocktail hour, so he got himself a copy of the expensively printed exhibition brochure, a Perrier and lime, and two toast points with beluga caviar and stood in the receiving line. There was still time for a word with Lucca before the grand opening ceremony.

Donovan read the brochure while waiting near the back of the line, and as he drew closer to the famous couple he saw another man join their immediate circle and give Katy a hug. He was Steven Clark, Lucca's partner in more than one way. A real estate developer and oil speculator from Long Island, he was a billionaire in his own right and at one time had been Katy's boyfriend. But then came gossip that Clark's financial empire was built on sand. The empire was half liquidated; yachts and estates were sold, and Clark and Katy took to going out in public in disguise to avoid the inevitable tabloid photographers. After a lot of public wrangling with bankers, the Securities and Exchange Commission, Wall Street, and the press, Clark emerged apparently solvent. Key to his newfound financial stability was the announcement of a joint venture with Paolo Lucca. The exact nature of the enterprise was a closely kept secret, but the mere fact that multibillionaire Lucca, the man with the golden touch, would go into a joint venture with Clark convinced Wall Street and the bankers. A few commentators assumed out loud that the undertaking had something to do with real estate. If so, perhaps this would be the first Clark development that didn't bear his name. The others were spread all over the metropolitan area: Clark Estates in Queens, Clark Acres in Nassau County, Clark Beach Village in Canarsie, Brooklyn (not far from Stanley's Canarsie Gym, in fact), Clark Casino International in Atlantic City, New Jersey, and Clark Tower in midtown Manhattan.

Despite, or perhaps because of, this ostentatious display of wealth and consequent skulking about in disguises, Katy shifted her allegiance to the genuinely cultured Lucca and, before long, married the man. The odd arrangement didn't shake the Lucca-Clark financial partnership, however. So it was not so unusual that Clark would show up at the grand opening bash of the Silk Road exhibit.

Donovan had met Clark once, years before, when one of his personal helicopters went down in the Hudson (the owner wasn't aboard), but doubted he would be remembered. Donovan didn't like Clark, considering him a boor whom money and the public spotlight had failed to turn into a civilized being. Maybe it was the costly out-of-court settlement of a lawsuit brought by a former maid, who charged that Clark beat her severely after flying into a rage when she touched one of her employer's personal effects. Perhaps it was the *New York Post* photos of the solid-gold bathroom fixtures in the 218-foot yacht that the man had had to sell to help solve his money problems. Donovan freely admitted that among the many prejudices instilled in him by his late father was one against the rich. "The fancy people," the elder Donovan sneered at Republicans, golfers, and, for that matter, anyone wearing a business suit.

Yet when Donovan reached the head of the receiving line, he felt a twinge of excitement. *These are the people with power in the world, he thought. Say what you will about generals and statesmen; it is the filthy rich who call the shots in this life.* There was a time—1968, as well as he could recall—when Donovan would have changed all that. But, like so many things that seemed important in 1968, the thought faded and now was just a fondly regarded if slightly embarrassing memory.

SIX

THE WORLD'S WEALTHIEST AND MOST BEAUTIFUL

"I'm PAULO LUCCA. Thank you for coming to my party," the guest of honor said as he grasped Donovan's hand. The man's handshake was firm and confident, and he looked Donovan in the eye.

"Lieutenant Bill Donovan, representing the New York Police Department."

"Ah, New York's finest. May I introduce my wife, Katy."

"Lieutenant," she said, offering her hand while fixing Donovan with eye contact that would have melted a lesser man. She was some beauty, Donovan thought. Celebrities liked eye contact, he knew. It allowed them to grant harmless favors to the lesser classes, who could then go home and tell their grandchildren, "She looked me right in the eye."

"Hi," Donovan said.

"And my partner, Steven Clark."

"Good to see you," Clark said, a bit abstractedly and without looking anyone in the eye.

Donovan decided not to bring up the helicopter.

Lucca said, "Donovan? I know that name."

"It's a common name."

"Of course, but not in the NYPD."

"Actually, there are three other Bill Donovans on the force, two white and one black."

"But you wouldn't be the same Donovan who solved the case involving ritual murders of young girls in Central Park, would you?"

Donovan beamed. "It was Riverside Park," he said. The "fancy people" didn't look so bad up close, he thought, even if they were fashionably unshaven.

Lucca smiled and grasped Donovan's arm. "I read the book about that case. I bought it in Madrid—the Spanish edition, of course—and read it in my tent in Pamiristan during the Silk Road expedition. You were wounded quite badly."

"I got better," Donovan said, his chest swelling with pride much as it had swelled with shotgun pellets toward the end of the incident in question. "Mr. Lucca, you have made my life complete."

Lucca laughed. "Lieutenant, don't sell yourself short. You're a well-respected man."

"I don't want to take up any more of your time," Donovan said, sensing the receiving line shifting its feet impatiently behind him. "So tell me one quick thing. What satellite-imaging system did you use to locate Chandar? It can't have been Cray-enhanced Landsat. Resolution is only five meters and it's no good in the far ultraviolet. The SIR-B radar on the space shuttle penetrates sand and was used to find Ubar, but doesn't do well with topography. I would say that the French SPOT satellite is out of the question."

Lucca looked astonished. "You amaze me," he said.

Donovan shrugged. "Anyone who's well read would know those things."

"Yes, but you're a *policeman*. Of course, you're not an ordinary policeman, are you? I'm sorry, Lieutenant. You're right, of course. Landsat and SPOT were no good for my purposes. SIR-B is indeed good in sand, and it did pluck the ruins of Ubar out of the sands of Oman. But I have not released details of how I found Chandar. What makes you think the city wasn't buried in sand?''

"Sandstorms aren't strong enough on that side of the Pamir Mountains to bury an entire city," Donovan said.

Lucca gasped, and Donovan swore he saw Katy giving him the eye. Lucca said, "God, where are you sitting?"

"Table eighteen, wherever that is."

"I wish I could ask you to join us, but the dais is full and *I* have my hands full with some political problems." Lucca lowered his voice and whispered in Donovan's ear. "Do you see those men behind the gold rope?"

Donovan nodded. There were six of them, all looking somewhat uncomfortable, standing in a special area marked "Mr. Lucca's party." One or two looked like politicians; another wore a morning coat, and a third looked like a kid. Donovan recognized none of them.

"To mount an expedition on the scale of my Silk Road adventure, it was necessary to ruffle some feathers. Surely you understand."

"I used to spend a lot of time ruffling feathers."

"So I assembled the birds here tonight and will stroke them a little—a first view of the exhibit and, if that doesn't work..." Lucca struggled for words, and a mischievous look took over his face. "Maybe I'll just bribe the bastards."

"That's how it's always been done in this town. Are those guys all enemies of yours?"

"No, of course not. And Steven will be there, of course. Look, Lieutenant, I was joking about the bribes. Why don't you stand with us and help me open the exhibit? Let Steven and me give them their preview; then you and I will walk through, with my wife, at the head of the crowd. We can talk a bit then."

"I'd love it," Donovan said.

"Good. You're perfectly correct about the imaging system—I used SIR-C, which was designed expressly for my purposes and flown on the space shuttle two years ago. I bought a lot of time on that flight. We *must* talk. Let me give you my phone number in case we get separated later."

He fumbled around for a pen, but found none in his custom tuxedo. Lucca looked to his wife. "Darling..."

Katy pulled a silver pen out of her handbag and scribbled a phone number on the inside of a matchbook. She handed the item to Donovan, who held it as if it were a treasure from the lost city itself before slipping it into a pocket.

"When all the fuss is over you will come to my apartment for coffee. Perhaps next week. We're at Clark Towers. Steven graciously fixed us up with a modest flat."

I'll bet it's modest, Donovan thought.

Lucca swung his attention to the next in line, and Katy took the opportunity to take Donovan's arm and guide him off to the side, behind her husband and herself and up against the red velvet curtain behind which lay the Treasure of the Silk Road. She gave his arm a squeeze before letting go of it to return her attention to greeting the dozen or so people at the end of the receiving line.

When he turned to stand proudly next to—if a little behind— the Luccas and Clark, Donovan found himself smacked again in the face by TV lights. This time he was with the Luccas, though, and couldn't help but wonder if the commissioner would see him on the news. "The man told me to make important friends," Donovan said to himself, proud at how fast he had taken that advice to heart and how well he had done at the assignment. Unconsciously he wrapped the fingers of one hand around the spot on the other arm where Katy had touched it. He imagined feeling the warmth of her touch.

This will be one to tell the boys back at Marcy's, he thought. Perhaps even to rub Marcy's nose in.

As the reception line drew to a close, another man drifted over from the vicinity of the dais, accompanied by several Lucca aides and clearly operating in some sort of official capacity. Donovan recognized him instantly—Morty Berman, the investigative reporter for Wolf Television News. He was done up in a rented tuxedo like Donovan, but Berman's fit less well.

The reporter was thick about the middle, and the bald spot that topped his head glistened in the television lights. All in all, he was an odd choice for an official role in the opening. His reputation was that of an in-your-face confrontational journalist, a man more likely to accuse a businessman of cheating his customers than to narrate the opening of a major archeological exhibition.

What's he doing here? Donovan wondered. The perplexity was increased by a family connection. In the late 1950s Berman had tried to cover the capture of a man who had used a shotgun to murder three men in as many West Side diners during a ten-hour crime spree. The arresting officer was Donovan's father, who earned Berman's hatred by trapping his camera equipment in a locked corridor of the Twenty-sixth Precinct station house and then losing the key. That was the genesis of the Donovan family feud with the press. It had continued unabated until the moment when the commissioner made peace overtures a condition of promotion.

"Evening, Morty," Donovan said to the startled newsman.

"Bill Donovan. Who died? I'm looking around and I don't see a body."

"Nobody's allowed to die on Sunday in this town. It's my day off. I came to see the exhibit."

"How'd you get in with this crowd? You a friend of Lucca's? I know you can't be chummy with the Boss."

That was how Clark was known. The Boss. The name was given him by Katy during the days they were an item, and it stuck in the tabloid press (even though it caused headline writers a lot of trouble distinguishing Clark from other celebrities with that title, namely Bruce Springsteen and George Steinbrenner). He liked it, so the story went, because it reeked of his blue-collar roots putting up single-family frame houses on the outskirts of Levittown, Long Island, and was consistent with his reputation as a tough former marine. The usage always reminded Donovan of the classic Irish put-down, referring to a self-important man as "himself." "Oh, so it's *himself* you came to see": That was the way you talked about someone who thought he was God's gift.

Donovan smiled. "No, I just came to see what Lucca found in Asia. The subject interests me, and the commissioner slipped me his ticket. How did *you* get in with this crowd?"

"Don Atherton couldn't make it, to be honest with you. I'm standing in as emcee."

"I see." The fresh-faced, all-American anchorman for Wolf was the ideal figure to emcee the opening. Much more the type than Berman.

"So we're both stand-ins," Donovan said. "Me for the commissioner and you for Atherton. That gives us something in common."

"Who would have thought it?" Berman said with a smile of his own.

"Maybe you know: Who are the guys behind the gold rope?" Donovan pointed out the group that Lucca had referred to as the birds; he noted that Clark and another man had joined them.

"I only know them from seeing them in the VIP cloakroom upstairs. I think one is a museum dignitary. The blond guy with the fancy haircut is a German corporate type. I don't know what his angle is. But I've met the slender, elegant-looking man. He's a Russian: the delegate to the United Nations of the Republic of Pamiristan. And he was a member of the Congress of Peoples' Deputies in Moscow before Yeltsin dissolved it last year. He only agreed to part with his bodyguards after Clark assured him everyone would be safe. Are you sure you weren't part of the deal to make Ambassador Lemovin feel safe and comfy in the Big Apple?"

"No way. They didn't know I was coming, I told you. I walked up and introduced myself. Lucca asked me to stick around—"

"Like I said—"

"Because he found me interesting. Don't laugh at me, Morty. I've read a lot about archaeology and can hold up my end of the conversation."

"I wasn't laughing at you. Only pointing out that they could be using you. Are you carrying a gun?"

"Uh, yeah. Always. Why?"

"You're being used, Lieutenant."

"Whatever you say. Look, I'm in a great mood tonight and anyone who feels like it can use me any way he wants. Why don't you and I go out to lunch one day and then you can use me, too. Really, it's all right."

Berman laughed and cuffed Donovan on the arm. "You're okay."

"I just turned fifty. I'm mellowing."

"*Mazel tov!* Your dad didn't make it to fifty, did he, God bless him?"

"Barely. He was fifty-three when that junkie shot him."

"A damn shame. I liked the man. I forgave him for that stunt with the camera a long time ago, even though he made me the laughingstock of the New York press."

But have you really forgotten? Donovan wondered.

"Let's be friends, you and me," Berman suggested. That seemed like a good idea to Donovan on an idyllic night. They shook on it.

Still, Berman's comments got Donovan to spend the remaining minutes before the start of the opening ceremony studying the other men. The German was in his forties at most, tall and thin-faced with nervously moving gray eyes. He stood stiffly, like a man who was unaccustomed to and didn't like being at the center of attention. But he was well-dressed, sporting a conservatively cut tuxedo that had faint pinstripes. It was his hair that was unusual. Atop such a stiff and otherwise conservative man grew a carefully and expensively styled coif. A two-hundred-dollar haircut, to be sure, Donovan noted. The man's longish hair made him look like a very successful producer of rock-and-roll records, but Berman thought he was a corporate executive of some sort. Probably a friend of Clark's, Donovan figured. The Boss also looked slightly wacky in the hair department, with long blond forelocks combed clumsily over an expanding bald spot and back-of-the-head hair that was too long and tended to bounce off his collar and stick out at strange angles. Odd, Donovan thought; for all his money the man couldn't find a good barber. *Maybe he thinks it makes him look young again, and rugged, like all those Reagan-era yuppies who walked along Columbus Avenue wearing red bandanas, Bruce Springsteen style.*

Lucca turned then and beckoned Berman, who excused himself from Donovan and hurried over to meet the explorer. Lucca and Berman shook hands and spoke briefly and a bit formally before Lucca unhooked the gold rope and urged the newsman behind it. The flock had grown, Donovan observed, entertaining himself by trying to imagine Morty Berman in feathers.

The envoy from Pamiristan went up to Lucca and the two men exchanged hugs and loud demonstrations of friendship. In an animated conversation that Donovan couldn't manage to overhear—except to gather, somehow, that it was conducted in French—Lucca and Lemovin gave the impression of being two old friends, reunited after years, who were exchanging fond reminiscences about moments shared over campfires during long winter nights in the Pamir Mountains.

The façade they presented was one of simple camaraderie. Donovan knew better. A little-known subplot to the story of the Silk

Road exhibition was the opposition by a certain Pamiristani special interest group angrily opposed to having the emerging republic's priceless heritage trucked off to the U.S.A. The Muslim fundamentalists were eager to build an Islamic state out in the shadow of the Pamirs, and they wanted the Silk Road treasures destroyed. Taking their cue from the Egyptian fundamentalists who wanted to tear down the pyramids because they attracted Western tourists, the Pamiristani extremists hoped to return the Silk Road discoveries to the ancestral dust from whence they came.

Perhaps they would even destroy Kublai Khan's dagger, which according to the brochure would be the centerpiece of the exhibition. The thousand-year-old dagger was a secret gift from the Byzantine Emperor Michael to the great khan—an attempt to curry favor and encourage trade between Constantinople and China. The jewel-encrusted gilt-bronze cutlass was said to have been stolen by one of the many robber barons who preyed on Silk Road caravans, kept at the oasis city of Chandar, and buried there when the city was sacked by rival Mongol raiders and lost in time.

Rumor held that the dagger was priceless. No doubt it was what the VIPs were going backstage to see. As the thought formed in Donovan's head, Lucca led his select group of men behind the increasingly magical red curtain for their early glimpse of the treasures the explorer had brought back from the long-hidden Central Asian plateau.

Lucca's beautiful wife was left behind to smile, more or less alone, into the television lights and chat with the few functionaries who loitered about. The minutes slipped by: five, ten, then twenty or more. Donovan lost count. In time Katy grew bored and, looking around for more interesting company, spotted Donovan and smiled. Opportunities like that come but once in a mortal man's lifetime; Donovan moved quickly.

"I'm jealous," he said, stepping up to her.

"Of what could you possibly be jealous?" she asked, fixing him again with those eyes. "You have my phone number in your pocket."

Donovan's heart skipped three or four beats. Okay, he thought. *Got to play this game right.*

He smiled. "I'm sure that your flattery is the consolation prize for not being invited behind the curtain."

"Be my guest," she said, gesturing toward it. "All you'll see is my husband and his associates inspecting his little bits of junk."

"Is that how you see the treasures of the Silk Road? A few *tchotchkes* that Hubby brought home from the tundra?"

"Funny, Lieutenant, you don't look Jewish."

"Half Irish, half English. My ex is Jewish. Actually, she's also half black."

"Oh God, a real New York story! Let me guess: Her father is a jazz musician and her mother is a social worker. And I bet you watch Woody Allen movies but work out at Gleason's Gym."

Donovan was amused. "Nope. I watch foreign films and work out at home. But hey...I'm American: Every so often I toss a basketball around or catch a Chuck Norris flick. Occasionally I sit and think. So forget the exhibit. I'll stay out here with you."

"Smart man."

Donovan was smitten. The woman had Cindy Crawford's hot body but Lauren Bacall's smart mouth. He prayed, with every fiber of his being: *Please, God, make this moment complete. Have her pull out a cigarette in an ebony holder and wait for me to light it.* But that wasn't to be. She just stood there, steamily beautiful, penetrating him with those eyes, waiting for him to make a move.

He pulled out the matchbook that she'd given him earlier and glanced at the number on it. "Who do I get if I call?" he asked. "Your husband or you?"

"You dial the phone and you take your chances."

"Life is a crap shoot?"

"It sure is."

"How's your luck running these days?"

She thought for a moment, lifting her eyes briefly heavenward before returning them to meet his gaze. She rested the fingertips of one hand on his arm and her smile broadened as she got her answer.

"Dial the number and we'll see."

Donovan's breath caught in his throat and, despite all his wishes, he was certain she saw it. "I will," he said, and was about to say more when the curtain burst open. There was a hush from the crowd around them and then a scream as Morty Berman stumbled out into the glare of the klieg lights, his right hand holding a thousand-year-old bronze dagger, Kublai Khan's dagger. Blood dripped down the uplifted blade and onto the stretched white flesh of Berman's hand. The man's face was ghostly white, scared pale.

Katy sucked in her breath hard and Donovan swore he heard a soft, plaintive sound, like the mewling of a frightened lamb. He stepped in front of her, shielding her from the sight.

"Lucca's dead," Berman gasped, stunned, his eyes wide open.

The dagger twitched upward and seemed, for a second, to threaten Katy. Donovan caught the man's wrist, immobilizing it, holding the weapon up in the air as the TV cameras rolled and the flashes from the still cameras were fireflies in the night.

There was another cry from the girl, a louder and more desperate one. Donovan whipped his head toward her in time to see her face go pale and her eyes roll as she fainted. He swept her up, curling his arm around her back and holding her up as she went limp and her body draped over his bicep.

Donovan held Berman's arm and the dagger in one hand, and Katy Lucca—who had become, in an instant, the world's wealthiest and most beautiful widow—in the other. And that was the photo that the commissioner would see on the front pages of all four New York City daily newspapers the following morning.

SEVEN

TREASURE OF THE SILK ROAD

THERE WERE SCREAMS anew from the crowd, and the shouts of startled reporters; bodyguards began to bully their way across the Rotunda, overturning chairs and brushing aside patrons of the arts. Donovan lowered Katy into the arms of two of them, saying, "She fainted. Take care of her."

"Who are you?" growled a square-jawed man in a cheap tuxedo.

"Lieutenant Donovan, New York police. Somebody call the West Side Major Crimes Unit and tell whoever answers to get some cops over here."

"You got it."

Donovan turned his attention to Berman. The man was snapping out of it, sort of, remembering who he was and where he was and, Donovan sensed, getting his shambles of a story together.

I can't wait to hear this one, Donovan caught himself thinking.

"I found him...Lucca...back there. The dagger was in his belly. I pulled it out. I—"

"Smart thinking, Morty. No wonder my dad locked that gate on you in 1959. He was trying to save your neck. Show me where you found the body."

After ordering the bodyguards to keep everyone out until more cops arrived, Donovan swept the curtain aside and stepped past it, dragging Berman reluctantly back to the scene of the crime. Lucca was stretched out a few yards inside the exhibit, his head resting on the cold marble floor just inches from the base of a gigantic display—the Oasis Diorama—that depicted him and the team that accompanied him on the expedition looking two-fisted and stoic in front of a patch of lush oasis greenery. Donovan's eyes flashed across an amazing scene: A wax Lucca, complete with khaki jodhpurs, dust-caked brown leather boots, rust-colored felt shirt rolled up at the sleeves, battered fedora graced with the wing feather of a raven, and, of course, ammo belt and pistol, looked down on a stone block atop which a wax Pamiristani bearer unfolded what looked like a treasure map. Above their heads loomed a triumphal arch made of crossed palm trees, a cleverly executed bit of stage dressing intended, Donovan felt, to symbolize the entirety of the expedition. (The crossed-palms-and-oasis logo also appeared on the official brochure, on the tickets, and on the souvenir tote bags and T-shirts.) Despite the dramatic setting, the wax Lucca seemed, at that moment, to be looking down from the wall-sized diorama onto the lifeless body of the real thing.

As for that: Blood spilled from a massive stab wound just below the rib cage. There was lots of blood but no respiration and, Donovan discovered after a brief and vain search, no pulse. The man was dead as it was humanly possible to be, but his body remained at its normal, living temperature. Donovan pulled the man's shirt out of his pants and cummerbund and rolled him part way over to check for accumulation of blood in the tissues of the back. There was none—no bruising at all. He let Lucca's body fall back down. Berman still gripped the dagger as if to release it would be to lose a part of himself. He held it like an icepick, his knuckles white. Donovan asked, "Did you change your grip on that thing?"

"I...no, I didn't," Berman said, suddenly painfully aware he was holding the murder weapon. He let it drop to the floor. "Bill, I swear—I saw the body lying there and knelt next to him. You can see the blood on my knees. I didn't kill Lucca. You got to help me out."

"Let's see if I can. I'll need your cameraman and his services, but I get to keep the tape. Okay?"

"Sure. I'll call Phil in here."

"Have him shoot everything with blood on it."

"It's yours," Berman said, and a few minutes later it was done and Donovan held the tape in his hand.

"Morty, are you sure you didn't change your grip before I saw you?"

"Yes. Is it important?"

"Can you figure out an easy way to take a knife and backhand some one in the chest?"

"Oh God, you're right. Thanks, Bill. How can I ever repay you?"

Donovan shrugged. "Calm down and talk to me. Did you see anyone else? Where are the rest of the VIPs?"

Berman looked around and Donovan did too, but they saw nobody. Apart from a gentle swaying of the curtain caused by the press of humanity outside, there was no motion.

"After Lucca let us in here, he sent us through the exhibit by ourselves."

"Alone? He didn't go with you?"

"No. He apologized and said he had to stay behind to meet someone important, but would catch up with us. We went down the Silk Road and began to spread out. Not all those guys got along with one another so well, I think. Anyway, I was in the Persian section of the exhibit."

"You're interested in Iran?"

"I'm interested in the origins of Muslim fundamentalism. Study the enemy, I always say. Anyway, I heard a shout, and I ran back and found Lucca dead."

"Did you see anyone?"

"Just Jameson. He was in the Babylonian part of the show."

"Say again?" Donovan asked.

"Wally Jameson. Mrs. Lucca's first husband. The one from New Jersey."

"What the hell is *he* doing here?" Donovan asked. "She left him for Clark four or five years ago. I'll have to check this out. What happened next?"

"I nearly knocked him over running toward the sound."

"What kind of sound was it?"

"Sort of a yell and a moan together."

"Where were the rest of the VIPs? Ahead of you?"

"Yeah, all except for Jameson and Clark. I can't tell you where Clark is. He split twenty minutes ago, before we started through the exhibit."

"Clark split? Split where?"

"Went outside for a smoke. That's why he came back here, so he could sneak outside and light up. It wasn't to see the exhibit."

"I'm shocked," Donovan said.

There was a rustling sound and the curtain opened. Two uniformed policemen stuck their noses cautiously inside. Donovan showed them his badge. "Your men are on the way over from the West Side MCU, Lieutenant," one of them said. "Can we do anything in the meantime?"

"Yeah, keep everyone away from the curtain. Don't let anyone through but cops. Tell Lucca's bodyguards they won't be needed anymore. And see how Mrs. Lucca is."

"Katy Lucca's here? No shit!"

"This is her husband," Donovan said, indicating the body.

"Holy Christ! How'd it happen?"

"Somebody stabbed him."

"This guy?"

They looked with understandable suspicion at the blood-soaked Morty Berman.

"Nah. The only thing he ever killed was a couple hundred reputations. All the victims were politicians, so it's okay with me. Go check on Katy, would you? Find her for me."

"I heard something about a lady being taken back to a room upstairs. I'll check it out."

Berman was beginning to look half dead himself. Donovan took the opportunity to inspect Berman's hand. He twisted it gently, turning it to let the best light fall on the palm. After a moment that was agonizingly long from Berman's point of view, Donovan said, "You're no killer. You do things before you think about them, but you're not a murderer."

Berman let out a sigh that was audible halfway down the hall. He stood up straight and rubbed his shoulder, the muscles of which had begun to cramp from the tension.

Of course, I've been wrong before, Donovan thought.

The lieutenant stooped to get as close as he could to the dagger without touching the thing. The gilt-bronze dagger was about ten inches long, sparkling with pearls, red rubies, and blue lapis lazuli ornaments set in the gleaming gold. A ruby scarab beetle was the centerpiece decoration on the hilt, but set around the bug were scenes of hunting, drinking, and meditation.

"Where was this thing before the killer picked it up? Wasn't it in a display case somewhere?" Donovan asked.

Berman said, "I have no idea. Can I go, Bill? To tell the truth, I feel sick and need to sit down."

"Sorry, but you have to stick around for a while. Wait and I'll get you a chair or find a room you can sit in or something. But now I have to get the evidence team in here while the scene is intact. This is the best-kept crime scene I've ever stumbled over. The body landed on a clean floor and we have tape of the murder weapon while it was still hot. When I think of all the bodies I've hauled out of tenements, plucked out of woods, scraped off subway tracks, and dug out of shallow graves by the edge of the West Side Highway, let me tell you that this is a murder scene any cop would kill for."

Berman nodded and stepped away from Lucca's body, nearly colliding with Detective Sergeant Moskowitz. The man burst through the curtain, emerging from the black-tied throng wearing faded jeans worn through at the knees and what looked like the same Stanley's Canarsie Gym T-shirt he'd sported the day before. His gold detective's shield hung from the same gold neck chain as a fourteen-karat gold *chai,* the Hebrew letter symbolizing life.

"You've taken a shower since yesterday, haven't you?" Donovan grumbled.

"Who wants to know?" Moskowitz replied.

EIGHT

IN DEFENSE OF THE DEVIL

THE LIEUTENANT SAID, "This is what I know so far: The victim is Paolo Lucca."

"The guy you came to meet."

"It looks like he was killed with that dagger on the floor, which Morty Berman—you know him from Wolf News, right?"

"Sorry...it's on opposite *Seinfeld*."

"...which Morty pulled from the victim's chest."

Donovan gave the tape to his partner, who dropped it into the ubiquitous canvas shoulder bag that carried his evidence kit, note-book computer, and other gear considered essential by a not-quite-twenty-first-century detective in the city of New York.

"So this guy is clean?" He nodded in Berman's direction.

"Yeah, I'm sure of it. Either that or he's a smarter murderer than I am a cop, which is far from out of the question."

"Can I sit down?" Berman asked.

"Who's stopping you?" Moskowitz replied.

"Without a chair?"

"Something is wrong with the floor?"

Shaking his head, Berman moved a yard or two down the hall, where he slumped to the floor, and leaned against the façade of the diorama. He didn't notice that his head was resting against the glass right near a reconstructed stone table atop which sat a slender amphora that was decorated with the distinctive bull-and-dancer motif of ancient Minos. How a 2,500-year-old Cretan wine jug had traveled nearly two thousand miles by foot and camel to be buried in the sands of Pamiristan was giving archaeologists fits, Donovan knew.

"I'll get you something to sit on as soon as the rest of my men get here," Donovan said.

"They'll be right along," Moskowitz said. "Bonaci was in the car behind me and we got a forensic team coming up from One Police Plaza.''

There was a soft commotion down the hall in the direction away from the curtain. Donovan and Mosko swiveled their heads about to catch sight of more VIPs walking slowly toward the gruesome scene that marked the entrance to the Treasure of the Silk Road exhibit. The German led the jittery procession. A few paces behind him was Lemovin, the Pamiristani envoy. The others followed. All of them were gawking and none were talking. They walked like bomb squad officers approaching a suspicious-looking package.

"Who are they?" Mosko asked when they were still fifty feet away.

"Suspects, almost enough for a baseball team."

"The resemblance to the Mets is uncanny. Are there any others?"

"Yeah. Steven Clark."

"You got to be kidding? Clark? The Boss himself?"

"That's the guy."

"Oh, so it's gonna be one of *those* cases. If I knew I was gonna be on the television I would have dressed up."

"No, you wouldn't," Donovan said. "But starting tomorrow, you will. I want to see a suit on you, pal."

"Okay, fine. Where's Clark?"

"Out for a smoke. Which, if I recall correctly, takes seven minutes. To smoke the average cigarette, I mean."

"Maybe he's into cigars."

"Morty, how long has Clark been gone?"

Berman checked his watch. "Got to be half an hour by now."

"And Lucca has been dead how long, you think?" Moskowitz asked.

Donovan shrugged. "Twenty minutes is a pretty fair guess, but half an hour ain't out of the question."

"In defense of the devil, Clark split before Lucca got killed," Berman said.

"In defense of the detective, murder gets *very* complicated."

By that time, the German, Lemovin, and another man had formed up into a trio, recognized the police badges, and, apparently, decided that their curiosity would not be lethal that evening. They approached at a faster pace. The Pamiristani, blunt by nature, spoke first.

"Mr. Lucca...he is..."

"Dead," Donovan said.

A murmur passed quickly through the group.

"How was he killed?"

"Stabbed with Kublai Khan's dagger."

"That's not possible. The dagger is still in its display case. We all saw it."

"Check that out," Donovan said to Mosko, who ran off to do so.

Lemovin directed his next question to Berman. "Do you know these policemen?"

"Lieutenant Donovan is an old friend and the best detective in New York."

Donovan addressed the rest of the group. "Gentlemen, please wait over there by the wall. We'll need to speak to all of you in turn. If nobody tries to leave and everyone cooperates, we'll all get to go home soon."

He turned back to the Pamiristani, who was staring at the body. "You: Let's get to know each other."

Lemovin had seen more corpses, perhaps, than most of the other spectators, considering the numerous bloody struggles between his newly formed republican government and the Muslim fundamentalist independence movement that fought it at every turn. He broke off his stare, let out a huge sigh, and said, "Well...that's something."

He stuck out his hand. "Lieutenant Donovan?"

"That's me."

"Aleksandr Lemovin."

They shook. Donovan took the opportunity to inspect the man's hand. "Do you mind?" he asked as he turned Lemovin's hands—both of them—over in his own, looking at them from different angles.

"Are you looking for bloodstains?"

"Yeah. Nothing personal."

"I understand. But there is no blood on my hands, except perhaps in the metaphorical sense."

"What do you mean?"

"I must apologize to you, and to the American people. I could have averted this tragedy."

"How so?"

"The killers of Paolo Lucca are my countrymen."

"Who?"

"Isn't it obvious? The Thirteenth of September Movement."

"The Muslim separatist movement in Pamiristan?"

"The same."

At that point, Berman said, "What's September thirteenth mean—other than being today's date?"

"Out of the mouths of babes," Donovan said. "That *is* today's date, and today is the first anniversary of the victory of Muslim separatist troops over Pamiristani government soldiers in the battle of Murgab Pass."

"Do not distinguish them by calling them troops. They are terrorists, pure and simple."

"Whatever you call them, they won."

"A minor public relations victory, I assure you."

"If losing 517 men in one afternoon is a minor public relations loss for you, *mazel tov,* as my associate would say. Your troops should conquer all of Central Asia."

Lemovin looked around uncomfortably. "We may as well. To be honest with you, there are far richer lands than Pamiristan."

"What makes you think the Muslims killed Lucca? As I look around me, I come up short on Muslim terrorists."

"That's not quite true."

"Really? Tell me."

"I'm a diplomat, Lieutenant. I'd prefer that you find out on your own."

"Mmmf," Donovan exclaimed, eyeballing the rest of the VIPs. "How could you have averted this tragedy? Fingered the bum ahead of time instead of playing coy about him when it's too late?"

"I might have pressed harder for more security. I did warn your State Department that today is the anniversary of the Murgab Pass incident. I'm afraid there will be repercussions."

"If you mean that federal bureaucrats will be getting in my way, it's happened before. Let's hope they don't show up for a while. Thanks for the warning."

"My pleasure."

Lemovin straightened his jacket and, feeling the lump inside, reached into his pocket and withdrew a pack of Marlboros, the regular-sized ones in the red box. He flipped open the box and stuck a cigarette in his mouth. Instinctively, Donovan got the matchbook from his pocket and was about to light the ambassador's cigarette when he remembered several things. Mrs. Lucca was off someplace, and he still didn't know where. Clark was still missing. And there was no smoking in the museum.

"Where the hell is Clark?" Donovan asked.

"Yes, where is he?" Lemovin echoed.

The curtain opened again then and there appeared Howard Bonaci and a passel of cops and technicians. Bonaci was Donovan's stalwart crime-scene busybody, adept at accumulating the masses of data that the lieutenant would sift later, at his leisure. Donovan said to him, "Mosko will brief you on the details of who the corpse is and how he got to be that way, as much as we know of it at the moment. Find rooms for these gentlemen to sit in, and take statements from them. Get a doctor to look at Mr. Berman."

"Hey! The guy from the TV! I loved what you did to that guy from the Saudi embassy who molested the little girl."

"What happened?" Lemovin asked.

"He was recalled by his government and beheaded," Berman said, getting up slowly from the floor.

"You look like you did it yourself," Bonaci said, eyeballing the blood on the newsman's hand.

"Yeah, yeah. Can I please wash this off?"

"Sure. Bonaci here will get some scrapings and other stuff and clean you up. I've got to talk to these other guys, but I'll be back and—"

At that point Mosko ran back up, his badge bouncing off his well-muscled chest. "The guy was telling the truth, Lieutenant. The dagger is still in its case halfway down the exhibit."

"Then what the hell was Lucca stabbed with?"

At that moment the halls of the museum were filled by the sound of an alarm bell ringing. It came down the corridor, down the middle of the Silk Road exhibit, and appeared to originate in the bowels of the building.

"What's that?" Mosko asked.

"Maybe Murph the Surf is back," Donovan said.

"Who?"

"Before your time."

Jack "Murph the Surf" Murphy made headlines worldwide exactly thirty years earlier, when in 1964 he and two companions broke into the American Museum of Natural History. A professional beach boy and stunt man, he entered through an unguarded window and stole, among other baubles, the Star of India sapphire (563.35 carats), the Midnight Star sapphire (116.75 carats) and the DeLong Star ruby (100.32 carats) from the Morgan Hall of Gems. He was eventually caught, and the incredible notoriety (including books and a motion picture), prompted the museum to install better alarms in its windows and bulletproof glass in its more important displays. One of the alarms had just gone off.

"Bonaci, take over," Donovan ordered.

With Mosko trailing behind he ran down the hall, through the mazelike exhibits that told of rich and ancient treasures from the East, until he found a plain door set flush with the wall next to the Buzghashi Diorama, which showed a game of buzghashi, a sort of early Gobi Desert polo played not with a ball but with the decapitated carcass of a sheep.

The door was painted the same off-white as the walls and was well disguised. A careless observer would miss it entirely. That was no doubt the idea. There was no sign, although a tiny marker set near the handle read "Buzghashi Studio."

Mosko drew alongside with one hand on the handle and the other on his nine-millimeter Penzler automatic.

"I don't think we'll need that," Donovan said, nodding at the gun.

"Prove me wrong."

The alarm bell was ringing from within the Buzghashi Studio. Donovan could feel the piercingly loud bell vibrate the thin sheet metal of the hollow door.

Donovan flashed back on his father, who had died after failing to observe precautions before opening a door. Donovan drew his old-fashioned .38 Smith & Wesson revolver, then yanked the door open. The two detectives burst into the room, their weapons in front of them.

The room was filled with light and antiquity. All four walls were lined with assembly tables and work benches. There were four doors—to the hall, to the Buzghashi Diorama, to another room, and to the courtyard. Another workbench occupied the center of the room. Paint cans were everywhere, as were sculptor's tools and small woodworking implements. The air smelled of cleaning fluid, sawdust, and acrylic paints. On the center bench a Macintosh computer sat in darkened silence next to a handful of boxes announcing the presence of computer-assisted-design software. In varying stages of readiness were rejected parts of the Silk Road exhibit. These were things, Donovan assumed, that for one reason or another didn't make it into the dioramas and display cases. He would have to look at them later.

The door in the far wall looked out onto the immense courtyard that filled the center of the fortresslike museum. The door was industrial brown with a small central window, double-paned and wired with metal alarm tape. A red bell—curiously old-fashioned and, no doubt, of some antiquity itself—rang above the door. A cutoff switch was next to the light switch. Donovan killed the bell.

The glass in the door was broken clear through in one spot and spidered elsewhere. Someone had smashed it from the outside, setting off the bell, but had not gotten into the room.

"What's out there?" Mosko asked.

"Fire escape?"

"Hell of a time to try to break into the building. I would have picked another day."

"Me, too."

Donovan put away his revolver and walked to the door. A rush of cool September air came through the broken glass. Donovan could smell typical New York City courtyard smells: dank water, blue and green algae, rotting leaves, rust, and heating oil. There was a sound, too: groaning. Mosko yanked open the door and stuck his automatic in the startled, pallid face of Steven Clark.

"Clark!" Donovan said.

"The Boss," Mosko said.

"Thank God it's you, Lieutenant. I thought I'd be out here all night."

Mosko put away his gun. Clark clutched at his right wrist, which, like Berman's, was red with blood.

"Steven Clark with blood on his hands," Mosko said.

"I came out here for a smoke and got locked out."

He stood on the landing of the old wrought-iron fire escape, which zigzagged down from the fifth floor to the basement level of the courtyard. It was dark as sin out there at night, the black and gloom punctuated only by a few security lights that lit up this or that rough-hewn granite protuberance. Clark's perch was six feet deep by ten feet wide, although the stairs up at one end and the stairs down on the other took up fully half the width. At that time of night, there seemed nowhere safe to go and no clear path to get there, either up or down. All was dark immediately below.

A black, cast-iron pot of some kind sat by Clark's feet.

"I was hoping someone would come. When no one did, I broke the window and tried to reach in and unlock the door. I cut my arm."

"Let me see. Come into the light."

Donovan brought the man into the room and held up his hand to look at it. The wound was substantial. In his attempt to reach through the window Clark had gashed open a vein. Blood flowed strongly, soaking the fingers of the other hand that he wrapped around it in an attempt to stem the flow.

"You made some mess but I think you'll live," Donovan said, whipping off his silk bow tie and making a crude tourniquet. As he did so, Clark took advantage of the other hand's freedom to check his watch.

"Dammit. I've been out here over half an hour. Is the reception over? Where's Paolo?"

Donovan looked up and caught Clark's eye, staring deeply into the man's wide blue irises. "I'm sorry, Mr. Clark. I'm afraid he's dead."

"What!"

"He was found a while ago. Stabbed with Kublai Khan's dagger, I think."

"Who did it?"

"I don't know. Do you?"

"No. How could I? Paolo, dead! Oh, my God."

Clark's knees seemed to weaken then, and for a second Donovan thought he, too, was going to faint. Donovan helped the man to a chair and eased him into it. Clark looked down at the floor while Donovan finished making his impromptu bandage. When he was done, Donovan said to Mosko, "Call Bonaci and have him bring some men in here, too. And order an ambulance for Mr. Clark."

"You want the men to look at everything?"

"The whole kit and caboodle. Door. Glass. Pot. Fire escape. Cigarettes. What brand do you smoke, Mr. Clark?"

"Uh...Sherman's. You want one?"

"Yeah, come to think of it, I do."

"You do?" Mosko asked.

"A man's entitled to a vice," Donovan said, sharply enough to silence the younger man. Mosko reached into his shoulder bag and pulled out his walkie-talkie. Walking away from the scene, he brought the instrument to his lips to call Bonaci.

"In my inside pocket," Clark said.

Donovan pulled the pack and opened it, removing one cigarette and counting the others. Of the original twenty cigarettes, eleven remained. *Let's see how many butts there are at the base of the fire escape,* Donovan thought, though he wasn't quite sure what that would prove. He replaced the one he had taken and returned the pack to Clark's pocket.

"Did you go down the fire escape ladder to the ground or just hang out on top?"

"I stood up top. I wanted to smoke, not break my neck. It's dark down there. You can try it, if *your* vice is risking your life."

"Not anymore. These days I stick to women."

Clark nodded knowingly, then was struck by a thought. "Katy. Poor Katy. How is she?"

"She fainted, but she should be okay. Do you want to go to her before the ambulance gets here?"

"No. It would only make things worse. The woman hates my guts. Please don't tell that to the press. They think we had an amicable parting. You know—one of those modern, civilized ones."

"Ain't no such thing," Donovan said. "The last day my ex and I spent quality time together she was throwing plates at me. She broke eight place settings, and they were from Bloomingdale's, too. I thought that only happened in Cary Grant movies."

"Welcome to the club, Lieutenant."

"Thanks."

"Jesus, I think this makes Katy my partner. Paolo dead! Lieutenant, I think I'm going to have to lie down."

Donovan thought, *So maybe we're not as tough as our nickname suggests.* Clark hadn't lost that much blood. Perhaps the flab around his belly was indicative of a certain mental softness. Donovan wondered what Katy had seen in the man. Just money, he supposed, although he preferred to think she wasn't that shallow.

"Where the hell is she?" he wondered out loud.

Perhaps sensing that the question wasn't meant for him, Clark had bent over and was resting his head on one of the workbenches. His forehead touched the thick wooden surface, scarred by decades of woodworking blades and colored by a thousand stray drops of acrylics and oils, not far from a half-finished pastel miniature of the Gobi Desert dunes near Dunhuang.

As was so often the case, Mosko had the answer to Donovan's barely stated question. "Bonaci found the lady for you, Lieutenant. She's in an office on the fifth floor."

Clark looked up. Donovan said, "I have to go see Mrs. Lucca."

"Good luck," Clark said.

"I'll send someone to the hospital to pick up your bloody clothes, and we'll need to talk at length," Donovan said. "Can I see you tomorrow?"

Clark thought for a moment, then said, "Four o'clock at my office in Clark Tower. Is that okay?"

NINE

LAUGHTER AND THE LOVE OF FRIENDS

THE GOLD-LEAF SIGN on the door read "Department of Asian Antiquities: Arthur C. Kent, Ph.D., Curator," but the office looked more like something from Buckingham Palace. The nine-foot golden oak door opened into a showroom of an office with pecky cypress walls with built-in bookshelves that ran from the floor to the twelve-foot ceilings. A crystal chandelier hung above an eighteenth-century admiral's desk, the centerpiece of which was a globe that showed the world as it was known during the century before that. On the wall behind the desk were two artifacts of Commodore Matthew Perry's 1853 trip that opened up trade relations between the United States and Japan: a nautical ensign presented to Perry by Emperor Kōmei hung alongside a Japanese woodcut of the commodore. The old sailor seemed to gaze across the room at a Chinese woodcut showing an imagined meeting between Confucius, Lao-tzu, and Buddha.

A quill pen reposed in an early American holder adjacent to an equally old gentleman's pipe rack and humidor. A collection of meerschaums and hand-carved hardwood pipes filled all available positions in the holder. An eighteenth-century Persian rug dominated the parquet floor, setting off the bookshelves, which were laden with volumes covering every aspect of Asian archaeology. Across the room from the desk, a plush black leather couch was decorated with Katy Lucca. Next to it was a portable lady's valet—a coat and dress stand holding, most prominently, a black sable jacket.

She had been lying alone, her small black dress covered by a Shaker quilt, but jumped up when Donovan entered the room. It was he who had caught her when she fainted and it was into his arms she ran, burying her face against his chest. An elderly doctor halfheartedly pursued her, brandishing a hypodermic needle. Donovan backed him off with a raised hand that also held the detective's shield, then folded the badge into his pocket and patted her reassuringly on the back of the shoulders.

"I'm so sorry," he said, several times, while she sobbed too uncontrollably to talk.

"I'm going to give her a sedative," the doctor said, keeping his distance nonetheless.

"What kind?"

"Valium, ten milligrams."

"In a moment, Doctor."

The man tossed up his hands and walked away, rejoining two Lucca aides who hovered near the couch—waiting, perhaps, to see if they still had jobs. Donovan had seen both of them at her side during the reception.

"Who is this man?" Donovan heard one of them say, in a voice that sounded exasperated and effeminate. He ignored the provocation, preferring to hold Katy until the sobs went away. A handkerchief unfolded from Donovan's pocket dried her tears. When she had composed herself somewhat, he asked softly, "Can you talk for a few minutes? I have to ask some questions."

"I...I'll try."

He turned to the others and said, "Wait outside, please. I only need five minutes."

The doctor sputtered: "Officer, I can't let you—"

"Outside," Donovan snapped, giving the man a glance that sent him blustering out the door, the Lucca aides behind him.

"Sit back down," Donovan told Katy, urging her again to the couch. "Try to rest and in a minute I'll let that doctor give you a shot."

"I can't calm down. I feel like I've been run over by a truck. My heart is pounding."

"Sit down."

They sat, side by side, and Donovan arranged the quilt over her legs. He held her hand, which was soft and warm against the hard skin of his palms.

"Have you ever lost anyone you loved?" she asked.

"My father. It's hard, and I wish I could make it easier for you."

"Talk to me. Tell me there was a reason for Paolo to die. Tell me it makes sense."

"There are always reasons. Sense is harder to find. If it's any help, I promise I'll get the man who did it."

"Who could it be? The man from the TV station? The one who was supposed to introduce my husband?"

"No, I don't think it was him."

"But he had the knife."

"He was trying to help your husband. He did the wrong thing, but it was too late anyway."

"Who, then?"

"I'll find out. Now, tell me: Your husband sent the VIPs into the exhibit and then stayed behind to meet someone. Do you know who that was?"

She shook her head. "I kept out of his business."

"He never mentioned one man in particular that he had to talk to?"

"I'm sorry. Maybe if you give me a few days..."

"Sure. Can you think of anyone from that crowd who wanted to kill your husband? Any of those guys behind the gold rope?"

"Behind the rope? Lieutenant..."

"Call me Bill."

"Bill...God, I hate... What a time to think of this: I hate nicknames in men."

She laughed nervously and pushed her hair away from her eyes. She seemed to Donovan a frail thing in need of protection, hardly the tall and impossibly glamorous model and actress whose affairs had sold newspapers and supermarket tabloids for the past few years. He felt his protective instincts emerging.

"Call me...I don't know, call me anything: 'Hey, you.' 'Hey, flatfoot.'"

"William." She dabbed at her eyes with his handkerchief, then offered it back to him.

"Keep it. I got a deal on them at K Mart."

She smiled. "William, I can't think of anyone in particular from that crowd. My husband was a very accomplished mediator. He had enemies but, typically for him, he invited them all to the party and intended to win them over."

"There was no one he was especially worried about?"

"Oh, the Arab I suppose, if you force me to pick one of them."

"What Arab?" Donovan asked.

"The *Muslim,* rather. Not an Arab. The foppish man who always wears white gloves. Help me out—I don't know much about that part of the world. The one whose group is fighting with the government in Pamiristan."

"There's someone here from the Thirteenth of September Movement?" Donovan asked.

"Yes, that's them."

"So that's what Lemovin was getting at. He told me I should look into that gang, but not that one of them was on the premises. I guess he really did want me to find out for myself."

"Perhaps he was being diplomatic."

She dabbed nervously at her eyes with the handkerchief before changing the subject.

"I'm glad you came after me for another reason. What I said to you...what we said to each other...before all this happened. I want you to know—"

Donovan was way ahead of her. "That you didn't mean it. I understand."

She squeezed his arm at the same spot as earlier. "I did and I didn't. I was playing around."

"You don't really care about the Treasure of the Silk Road. You were bored stiff and looking for a way to amuse yourself."

Katy brushed yet another strand of honey-golden hair away from her face and looked again into his eyes. "I...I was attracted to you. I don't know if anything would have come of it. Probably not. Do you understand what I'm saying?"

"Sure. We're grownups, and we acknowledge liking to toy with dreams we never expect to come true."

"I was madly in love with my husband, but I guess I'm an incorrigible flirt. God, what a time to pick to do it. Maybe what the papers say about me is true."

"No truer than what they say about me."

"Will you forgive me?"

"It's all forgiven and forgotten."

She leaned back on the couch, then closed her eyes and let out a big sigh. She curled her legs under her and pulled the quilt up until it covered all but her head and her toes. "I'll take that Valium now."

"I'll get the doctor and, if you like and think it would help, I can get Steven for you."

"Oh, God no! Please, William, you will call me, won't you?"

"I have to."

"Yes, of course you do." She laughed again, incongruously, and said, "I guess I'm getting lucky after all. It will be me answering the phone."

Donovan sort of chuckled. He never could resist black humor. Laughing through tragedy always worked in his cop's world. At his father's wake, after he shed the very first tear, an old friend Donovan hadn't seen since high school—a born comic, once the class clown—came up and kept him, to the extent that it was possible, in stitches for most of the day. Then they went out and got stinking drunk and laughed some more and Donovan didn't sob until he was home in his own bed that night. *Well,* he thought, *that's what really defeats evil: laughter and the love of friends.*

"I'll give you my home phone in case you need someone to talk to," Donovan said. He inscribed it on the back of one of his business cards, adding, on a whim, his address, and handed it to the girl. She looked at it for a moment before casting about for a pocket or a purse and, none being available, folded the card in half and tucked it into her bra.

"Thank you, William," she said as he opened the door and called in the doctor.

TEN

"HAVE ONE SHOT AND BROUGHT TO MY TENT"

BY THE TIME Donovan returned to the Silk Road exhibit, an hour had passed. He had gone quickly through the displays, spending just enough time to see what Lemovin had asserted and Mosko had confirmed: Kublai Khan's dagger remained in its hallowed spot in a diorama depicting the excavation of Chandar.

The crowd had been sent home and the red curtain finally pulled aside to let in air from the Rotunda to clear out the oppressive smell of death that lingered.

For the first time, the exhibit's layout was clear. Donovan imagined a passenger train stuck on a horseshoe curve. Each country along the Silk Road was like a railroad car, linked but separate. Donovan counted them off on his fingers, their names now and their historical names. From the entrance to the exhibit, he listed:

1. Lebanon (Levant)
2. Syria (Assyria)
3. Iraq (Mesopotamia)
4. Iran (Persia)
5. Turkmenistan (Mongol Empire)
6. Pamiristan (Mongol Empire)
7. Uzbekistan (Mongol Empire)
8. Kazakhstan (Mongol Empire)
9. China

Within each country, the dioramas and smaller display cases—each one representing a specific city, shrine, or oasis on the west-to-east route—were arranged in geometric shapes, making it hard for a visitor to see outside his or her particular area. That was intentional, Donovan thought. Of the actual Silk Road, it was said that a merchant at an oasis in Pamiristan had no idea that the silk he sold came from China or that the buyer who wanted it hailed from the Levant. The Silk Road, like the museum exhibit that commemorated it, was truly a riddle wrapped in an enigma.

Now a top-notch forensics team from downtown was poring over the murder scene. Every conceivable aspect of the late Paolo Lucca and the spot in which he had died was being photographed, measured, vacuumed, scraped, dusted, and inspected. The murder weapon was put in an evidence bag. The army of evidence collectors was truly amazing.

"I shudder to think of the overtime," Donovan said to Bonaci, whose meager West Side Major Crimes Unit forensics budget allowed for less than one-tenth the investigation.

"The rich even die expensively, Lieutenant. You and me, we kick the bucket and we're lucky if a janitor shows up with a mop."

"Paolo Lucca gets stabbed in the Museum of Natural History and the Third Army lands." Donovan wondered if work would always be like this should he accept promotion to captain. He suspected that it would, in high-profile cases anyway. The power was already seductive.

"You said it. Look, there's a guy around here someplace who can help us identify the other dagger. I was talking to him before. Anything else?"

"I'll let you know when I think of something. Did you do the room where I found Clark?"

"It got the same treatment as this."

"Send a couple of guys down into the courtyard and count the cigarette butts. Clark smokes Sherman's. You know, the specialty brand you get in a store on Fifth Avenue?"

"I gave up Camels ten years ago. But I've seen Sherman's cigarettes around. They're perfumed, right?"

"I think Sherman's makes a perfumed brand."

"They're smoked by faggots and British actresses. And Steven Clark, the Boss? He smokes them?"

"Yeah, I wondered about that. If I wanted to put forth a tough-guy image to counter the bad press I got from the golden bathroom fittings episode, I would smoke unfiltered Camels and drink Jack Daniel's out of a galvanized-iron shot glass."

"I'll see how many Sherman's he left below that fire escape," Bonaci said, and scurried off to do it.

He was replaced by Morty Berman, who, having contributed his blood-soaked tuxedo to the pile of evidence, wore a blue NYPD jumpsuit with huge letters spelling out CRIME SCENE on the back. He held a microphone and dragged along Phil, his cameraman. Berman was shooting exclusive footage granted him in exchange for, literally, the shirt off his back, and had regained his composure. Donovan noticed that, apart from the blood scraped off by technicians, Berman had failed to wash his hand. Still splattered with blood, it now held a Wolf Television News microphone instead of a priceless antique dagger.

There's no business like show business, Donovan mused. As the light affixed to Phil's camera flicked on again, Berman stuck the mike in Donovan's face.

"A quick word if you will, Lieutenant Bill Donovan of the New York Police Department."

"Are you okay?" Donovan asked. "You feel better?"

"Much better, thanks. Tell the viewers how you're coming in your investigation."

"Well, it's too early to say anything except that we are going forward with the investigation and won't rest until the killer of Paolo Lucca has been caught and convicted. I personally promised his widow that."

"How is Katy Lucca?"

"She's devastated, as you can imagine, and has been put under sedation."

"Do you have any suspects?"

"None that I can discuss at this time."

Berman's face turned wry. Donovan saw the next comment coming and was ready for it.

"I'd like to get you on tape saying that I'm not one of them. I already told our viewers how I found the victim and, in a vain attempt to save Lucca's life, pulled the knife out of his body."

Berman twisted his hand so that the blood showed better. "You're in the clear, Morty. Nonetheless"—Donovan offered his own wry smile—"don't leave town."

Addressing the camera, Berman said, "He smiled. You saw Lieutenant Donovan smile when he said 'Don't leave town.' Back to you in the studio, Don."

The light flicked off.

"Thanks, Bill. I needed something to save the evening. Can I go now? I'm headed back to the studio, if it's okay."

"Sure, Morty. Take off. Get washed up, unless you plan to scrape all that blood off your hands and sell souvenirs."

"Maybe I'll send it to the lab and have it analyzed. Who knows what will turn up in Lucca's DNA?"

"Who knows. Maybe you can have him cloned."

"I left all my phone numbers with Detective Sergeant Moskowitz. Call me anytime."

"I will. I'll need to talk again once the forensics data are in."

"Anything."

Donovan saw the man and his assistant in the Rotunda, watching as they trudged slowly past the towering dinosaur scene, two tiny figures amidst the hugeness of natural history.

Donovan walked around the body, which awaited his attention before being wrapped for transport to the morgue. He bent over it for fifteen or twenty minutes, inspecting the hands, the face, and the posture, and thinking. Did Lucca fall where he was stabbed? Was he perhaps stabbed elsewhere—a few yards away, or more? If so, did he walk or run to the spot where he died, or was he carried there? Of course, the lab guys would know better once they took their usual long looks.

And what was Lucca doing by the crossed-palms diorama? Looking at his own wax image? Or did he see something else in that three-dimensional representation of himself standing astride the Silk Road? Nothing terribly suspicious caught Donovan's eye, but he knew he would have to take a much longer and more detailed look.

Donovan looked down at the body, then up at the wax figure of Lucca. It was weird: In death the man was watching himself. In fact, the half-dozen people whose tiny figures adorned the background painting of an oasis, making a Greek chorus watching Lucca the explorer, seemed to be gazing out of the diorama and onto the corpse of its creator. There was something about those figures...

Then Donovan felt a grumble rise up from his neglected stomach, and thoughts of the diorama fled him.

"Is there anything to eat?" he asked Moskowitz, who appeared from down the hall in the direction of the elevators.

"Whaddya want? I can order in."

"Mosko, this was to be a catered affair. Right now about a thousand very expensive platters of rubber chicken are going unclaimed somewhere in this building."

"You got a point. I'll send out a scout. In the meantime, are you ready for an update?"

"Let's hear it."

A technician interrupted, asking, "Can we wrap the body now?"

"I'm done with it if you are. Look, I think the menu included chicken Kiev, which I like despite the fact that it's salty. Some very clever caterer was trying to make a statement about the Silk Road's running through parts of the old Soviet Union, I suspect, when he put chicken Kiev on the menu. Kiev is a stone's throw away from Chernobyl."

"Maybe that's how the chicken got salty."

"Get me a plate. Some boiled potatoes, too. And broccoli."

"Do you want a beverage?"

"Water."

"I'll take care of it."

"Give me the update."

"I got Clark's statement and let him go. He was starting to make noises about how important he is. He made it clear he normally speaks only to God. But he gave me times and everything. I've got to say that the man appears to have his story together. No wonder he made a billion dollars and had a fling with Katy Lucca."

"Go on."

"The ambulance took him to Doctors Hospital a while ago to have his wrist sewn up. He gave himself a pretty good gashing when he popped the window with that pot."

"So it was the black pot he used?"

"Yeah. It has glass fragments in the paint. I marked it for evidence."

"Convenient it was just sitting there on the fire escape," Donovan said.

"I thought of that. He says he took it from a workbench and used it to prop the door open so he could get back in. But he knocked into it with his foot and the door closed on him. So after hollering for help for twenty minutes or so he bashed the window in."

"That's what I would have done."

"Then he tried to reach through the hole and that's when he cut himself."

Donovan said, "Bonaci is sending men down into the courtyard to count the cigarette butts. I'm curious to see how much Clark smoked while he was out there."

"Do you think he killed Lucca?"

"I don't see how. I also don't see what he'd have to gain by it, but the investigation's just begun."

"Getting the girl back?"

"He says she hates his guts."

"Does she?"

"I get that impression."

"Maybe money is at issue here. Clark was rumored to be out of bread a few years ago after the stock market collapsed."

"My friend, his 'out of money' and yours and my 'out of money' are very different things. Maybe he had to cut down his living allowance from two million a month to one. I don't see money as being a powerful motive for murder in this case and, anyway, it looks like the son of a bitch was out on the fire escape the whole time. I don't like Clark either, but let's move on to better suspects."

"Like who?"

"Where did you stash the rest of them?"

Mosko pulled out his notebook computer and pressed some buttons. A list flashed on the shimmering blue screen.

"Here we go:

"Number one: Steven Clark. At the hospital, surrounded by aides and lawyers. Number two: Morty Berman. En route to the TV station. Number three: Aleksandr Lemovin. He has diplomatic immunity and not being ready to bring charges, I had to let him go. He screamed and hollered. But I know where to reach him and he expects it. The rest I have on ice in various rooms down by the cafeteria. They ain't happy about it, I can tell you."

"Let them sue us," Donovan said.

"I told them that they had to have at least a preliminary talk with Lieutenant Donovan before they went home."

"Who else have we got?"

"Number four: Peter Vischer from Hamburg. A corporate big shot. Number five: Arthur C. Kent."

"Curator of Asian archaeology. I was in his office. Nice digs."

"Number six: Wally Jameson, Mrs. Lucca's ex-husband. According to *People,* Jameson misses her and would take her back in a heartbeat. Why was he invited? I guess Lucca really intended to clear up a lot of old problems."

"It looks more like the problems cleared him up. So much for conciliation. Interesting she chose not to mention the presence of her ex. I managed to get *mine* into the conversation."

"Oh, so you let her know you're single. Good work, Bill. I knew I could count on you."

"Who are suspects seven and eight?"

"Number seven is Georgi Mdivani, Pamiristani cultural attaché to the U.N."

"Strange that Lemovin never mentioned him. Didn't he holler diplomatic immunity too?"

"Nope. He seems to want to talk. Him and number eight. Check this out, babe: Mohammed Akbar, of the Pamiristani militant group known as the Thirteenth of September, currently at the U.N. on observer status."

"*He's* the one I want to see next," Donovan said.

"Yeah, he's lookin' forward to meeting you, too. The first thing he said when he heard Lucca was dead is 'I insist on speaking to the policeman in charge.'"

"What's your impression of him?"

"He looks like a sneaky little bastard. You know, the kind who talks too much and you can't trust a word he says."

Donovan nodded. "You know, between Mrs. Lucca not mentioning her ex-husband and Lemovin not bringing up either of these dudes, we got a real conspiracy of silence going. With her, I guess you could chalk it up to shock. But what about Lemovin insisting that 'the killers of Paolo Lucca are my countrymen' but failing to point out that one of their leaders was among us?"

"What about Lemovin not mentioning his own deputy?"

"Or taking him home to the embassy."

"Yeah, that too."

"The good ambassador said that members of the Thirteenth of September Movement are devious," Donovan said. "He seems pretty shifty himself. In fact, I'm not so sure I would turn my back on any of these people."

"Except Mrs. Lucca, of course," Mosko said.

"She looks okay to me, but my record with picking women ain't exactly gonna get me into the Hall of Fame," Donovan said. "I'm going down to talk to Akbar now. When your scout spots chicken, have one shot and brought to my tent."

ELEVEN

THE ADOLF HITLER OF ANCIENT HISTORY

As IT HAPPENED, no scout was required.

Moskowitz had taken over a series of small seminar rooms that were part of the reception center on the basement level of the museum, just down the hall from the Garden Café where Donovan had lunched the day before. Apart from the growing police presence in the noble old building, the normally bustling restaurant area was occupied only by a few security guards and several dozen distraught caterers. They were loading tray after tray of chafing dishes back into a succession of vans that had pulled off West Seventy-seventh Street and into the semicircular driveway that functioned as a pickup and delivery area. The smell of food—even increasingly cold food—was a welcome change from upstairs. As Donovan walked down the wide corridor leading from the Garden Café to the reception area, a uniformed policeman ran up and handed him a shopping bag on which was printed the logo of Lucca's exhibit—the crossed palm trees covering an oasis scene and a lone camel rider heading into a mammoth setting sun.

"What's this?"

"Your dinner, Lieutenant. I got you enough of everything to feed a small army."

"Thanks," Donovan said, fishing about inside the bag before finding a rolled chicken breast stuffed with butter and chives. Donovan held the piece of chicken as if it were a drumstick; when he bit into it, some butter squished out. Hardly a healthy meal, he knew, but very good. Donovan opened the door of Seminar Room 10 and stepped inside. Mohammed Akbar leaped to his feet, knocking over one of the dozen padded aluminum and vinyl chairs that circled the round conference table. He went to pick it up, then strangely jerked his hands back, clasping them behind him. Akbar was an unusually slender man for a guerrilla fighter, Donovan thought. He had thin limbs and a bony, dark yellow face dominated by deep-set eyes. A sparse mustache that curled down at the ends didn't quite hook up with a sparser goatee that looked as if it were shaved off and regrown with some regularity.

Akbar's getup was remarkable, however. He dressed in the manner of an Edwardian diplomat, with a spotless and perfectly tailored morning coat, a satin cummerbund, trousers that were pressed to a knife's edge, and expensive black shoes. All that was needed to complete the effect, Donovan thought, was a pince-nez.

Mosko was right, Donovan thought. This guy looked as trustworthy as a weasel.

"Lieutenant Donovan, I presume," Akbar said, in heavily accented English. Donovan stuck out his right hand, the chicken remaining in his left. After an awkward hesitation, Akbar reached out with bony fingers and they shook hands.

"Want some chicken?" Donovan asked, catching a fleeting glimpse of a tattoo: a winged skull wearing a beret had a lightning bolt passing through it. Odd, Donovan thought. For some reason, he doubted that Muslims wore tattoos. (Weasels, perhaps, did.)

"No. I am too nervous to eat. But thank you."

"Do you mind if I do? I'm starved."

"Not at all. Go ahead." Akbar set his chair back up and plunked himself down in it. Donovan sensed that the man was glad to see him; clearly he had something to say.

Donovan took a chair one place removed and deposited the shopping bag atop the table. He removed a bottle of mineral water and poured some into a plastic cup while he spoke.

"I was told you wanted to talk to me."

"Yes. The second I heard what happened to Lucca, I knew that we must speak. You see, I'm sure that his death will be blamed on me sooner or later."

"It already has been."

"Lemovin," Akbar spat.

"He didn't mention you by name. But he assured me that the Thirteenth of September Movement was behind the murder."

"I knew he would say that. It is, of course, preposterous."

"Why?"

"Because I didn't kill Lucca. Not that I'm mourning his death, you understand. I must be honest with you, Lieutenant: I hated the man. We all did. I know this may seem odd to you, but we are patriots in a sense, and we resent any Western incursion into our country."

"The Silk Road expedition."

"That, and more: the inevitable tourists that it will bring. You see, nothing personal, but we don't want you in our country."

"I know the argument," Donovan said. "It's the same one made by associates of the guys who tried to blow up the World Trade Center. Their comrades in Egypt would like to destroy the Pyramids and the Sphinx because they attract Western tourists—"

"—who bring with them Western vices."

"Including sex, drugs, and rock and roll. On two of those accounts, I'm inclined to agree. Personally, I have wanted to blow up MTV for about ten years. But Pamiristan has no comparable tourist attractions. I just don't see Mr. and Mrs. America packing up the Winnebago and driving to Pamiristan to gawk at the hole in the ground where Paolo Lucca dug up Kublai Khan's dagger."

Akbar's thin lips curled into a smile, and he raised a crooked finger. "Ah, but you are wrong. There already have been plans to rebuild Chandar and put in Western amenities, including hotel, casino, spa, and theme park."

Donovan shrugged off the notion. "Your country just has to get used to professional planners. More than likely the government, to show how progressive and forward-thinking it is, paid a couple of Washington lawyers a few hundred thousand dollars to come up with fancy plans that nobody ever intends to act upon. It's all smoke and mirrors. We have it in America all the time. Politicians commission studies of tax cuts they don't have the slightest intention of enacting. They look good to the voters."

"You are a cynic, but I see your point."

"On the other hand, I never would have predicted that Americans would fly to an alligator-infested swamp in Florida and pay thousands of bucks to stare at guys dressed up as mice."

"Mice?"

"Disney World."

"Oh. I will confess to having stopped at Euro Disney on the way here."

"You're not serious."

"I wanted to get an idea what America is like."

"My God."

"Ask Lemovin about the plans. He will tell you."

"I will. So tell me, Akbar...is that your real name?"

"Yes. I mean, it is my legal name. Not the one I was born with."

"Which is?"

"Mohammed Baku."

"So your taking the name Akbar is significant. You're suggesting that your ancestor—your spiritual one, anyway—was the Emperor Akbar."

Akbar's eyes lit up. "You're very well informed for a New York City police detective."

"When I heard that the Silk Road exhibit was coming to town, I read up on the history of Central Asia."

"The great Akbar was descended both from Mohammed and Genghis Khan. When Akbar died in 1605, his empire extended all the way from Persia to Calcutta. His grandson built the Taj Mahal, you know."

"Speaking of Disney World," Donovan said.

Akbar ignored the quip. "The leaders of the Thirteenth of September Movement, following the example of our leader, all use names that honor great men from our history."

"And your top man is...?"

"Timur the Second," Akbar said proudly.

Donovan wasn't sure if he should be aghast or amused. "Timur? After Timur Lenk, known as Tamerlane? The Adolf Hitler of ancient history? That's your leader's role model?"

"Timur Lenk was the greatest conqueror in history, more accomplished even than Alexander the Great. He ruled an empire that stretched, by his death in 1405, from the Bosporus to the Ganges."

"He had two thousand Afghans cemented together into a totem pole," Donovan said. "He had four thousand Albanians buried alive just so he could keep his sunny little promise that no blood would be shed if they surrendered. In Persia, he had a pyramid constructed out of the skulls of seventy thousand persons. In India, he slaughtered all his prisoners—as many as a hundred thousand, by some accounts."

"All of which will be recounted in the theme park that Lemovin and his corrupt government have planned," Akbar said.

"I retract my earlier cynicism," Donovan said, sighing deeply. "Americans flock to Transylvania to see where Dracula lived, and he was a fictional character. They will indeed go to Central Asia to see the home of the Mongol hordes that conquered most of the known world. And, yes, they will bring with them sex, drugs, and rock and roll. Perhaps even MTV. My apologies. If you make the bomb, I'll light the fuse."

"Part of our leader's reason for selecting the name Timur was to frighten Westerners into staying away. Timur was a brilliant leader, but admittedly a fiendish killer."

"However, the caravans ran on time," Donovan said.

"You are an interesting man yourself. I can't tell when you are being serious."

"About murder I'm deadly serious. Everything else is negotiable. You see, my lifelong belief is that good people should live forever. I get angry when that doesn't happen."

"I am a good man, Lieutenant."

"You will have to convince me."

"The truth of my words will convince you.... And let me assure you that Paolo Lucca was *not* a good man."

"I would like to have discovered that on my own. I was planning to do it, but someone stuck a dagger between his ribs. Whoever did it knew just where to strike, too. This was no amateur act."

"It wasn't?" Akbar said.

"Would you be able to kill a man with one or two swift strokes of a dagger?"

Akbar held his hands up. "I am merely my people's representative at the United Nations, an observer. If you would like to flatter me, you might call me a diplomat. But a murderer? Never. I'm afraid I wouldn't know how."

"But Timur would," Donovan said.

"Most assuredly."

"Where is he now?"

"Our leader is a very private man. He does not appear in public. No one but a close circle of advisers even knows what he looks like. I regret that I am not among them. I have heard that he is in Samarkand, but I cannot tell you if that is true."

"Where were you when Lucca was stabbed?" Donovan asked.

"At what time did it happen?"

"I'll know better tomorrow after an exact time of death is established, but a good guess would be nine-fifteen."

"Fifteen minutes after the private showing began," Akbar said. "We were inside the exhibit. Well on our way down the Silk Road."

Donovan raised an eyebrow.

"Have you not seen the exhibit, Lieutenant?"

"I was planning to, but something came up," Donovan said. "You grew up along the Silk Road and should be a good guide. Tell me about it."

"It's fascinating, really, laid out like the actual thing."

"I ran down a stretch of it and noticed that it twisted and turned a lot."

"Apart from the diorama containing that silly little oasis scene, which Lucca told us was created specifically so the TV cameras could shoot it during tonight's opening, the exhibit follows the west-to-east route of the Silk Road itself. The exhibits are grouped according to the country of origin. If I recall correctly, there are major dioramas about Tyre in Lebanon."

"Which is to say, ancient Phoenicia."

"Damascus in Syria, and also Palmyra."

"The biblical Tadmor, said to have been built by Solomon."

"Baghdad in Iraq."

"Conquered by Timur the First in 1401. I wonder what the body count was from that little excursion."

"Hamadān and Neyshābūr in Iran."

"If I remember correctly, the latter was the birth and burial place of Omar Khayyám. Earthquakes flattened it twice and the Mongols did it once. Your people sure got around."

"We will again, Lieutenant. We will again. From Persia the Silk Road exhibit goes on to Merv in Turkmenistan, of course Chandar in my country, then Samarkand—"

"Timur's ancient capital."

"—and Bukhara and Tashkent in Uzbekistan. Alma-Ata in Kazakhstan. From there the trail leads into China: I-ning, Urumchi, Turfan, Ha-mi, An-hsi, Lan-chou and, finally, Sian."

"Where the Han Dynasty ruled for centuries and where Marco Polo wound up. Your memory is impressive, Mohammed Akbar."

"Thank you."

"So which city were you visiting at nine-fifteen when Lucca was killed?"

"At that moment I was two-thirds of the way down the Silk Road—and pondering all the treasures that Lucca stole from Samarkand."

"Was anyone with you?"

"No. I was quite alone. Did you think I would walk with Lemovin, my enemy, or Mdivani, his lackey?"

"I was just wondering. May I look at your hands?"

The man looked startled and held back for a second. A bit of fear flashed across his eyes. Donovan saw that fear, and Akbar quickly realized he was caught. He held out his palms. Smiling faintly, Donovan scrutinized first one, then the other. There was no evidence of blood or anything else suspicious.

"That's a nice tattoo," Donovan said. "Is it a symbol of your movement?"

Akbar laughed nervously. "No. I'm afraid it was a whim.... I indulged myself while in Paris."

"I've heard that's a good place to do it."

"I'm a bit embarrassed. You noticed that."

"I noticed something," Donovan said. "If you say it was embarrassment—well, that's fine with me. I never got a tattoo myself, but an old girlfriend of mine had a rose on her... Well, she had a rose." Donovan did look embarrassed, and that put Akbar more at ease.

"You asked if I went through the exhibit with anyone. I walk alone, Lieutenant. But listen to this: The road may have many twists and turns but there were only two dimensions. You went forward or you went back. There was no sideways. In order to go either way I would have stumbled over others. I cannot say which of my fellow VIPs were in front of me and which were behind. Come to think of it, Lemovin and Mdivani may have been behind me, but I'm not certain."

"In either case, to get to where Lucca was found you would have stumbled over witnesses," Donovan said.

"Most assuredly."

"I'll have to talk to the others."

"Of course."

"But if what you say is true, you have nothing to worry about."

"Allah blesses the forthright," Akbar said.

"Is that from the Koran?"

"No. From Timur."

Donovan finished his chicken and wiped his hands on a napkin before plucking a bunch of white grapes from the bag and offering some to Akbar. Again he was refused.

"Tell me, why are you here?" Donovan asked.

"Because I needed to speak with you. I cannot let Lemovin blame me for a murder I did not commit."

"No. I mean, if you hated Lucca why did you come to his opening?"

"To study the enemy. It is a basic rule of warfare."

"There was a lot of that going on tonight," Donovan said.

"In this case, I had two enemies to study: Lucca and Lemovin. Besides, Lucca invited me."

"Why do you think he did that?"

"I imagine he thought he could buy me off. Buy us off. Do you know the Persian word *baksheesh?*"

"I've heard it in a couple of taxis. It means 'tip' or 'bribe.'"

"Exactly. Well, Lucca left a trail of *baksheesh* the entire length of the Silk Road. He handed out hundred-dollar bills left and right as he made his imperial way across the ancient trade route from the Mediterranean to China. I am told that he spent several million dollars in bribes alone."

"That's a lot of money to give to border guards."

"The border guards and innkeepers got the hundred-dollar bills. The politicians got the heftier stipends. How much do you imagine—how much *can* you imagine—it cost Lucca to buy the co-operation of Saddam Hussein? Of the mullahs in Iran? Of the Chinese Politburo? Of the Russian apparatchiks, such as Lemovin and Mdivani, who are still clinging to power in former Soviet republics such as mine?"

"A lot, I guess."

"And he thought he could buy the Thirteenth of September Movement as well."

"But he was wrong?" Donovan asked.

"Dead wrong."

Donovan raised his eyebrows again and, seeing it, Akbar quickly added: "That is a figure of speech."

"If you didn't kill Lucca, who did?"

Akbar tossed up his hands. "I have no idea."

"Who do you *think* did it?"

"Who are the suspects? Only those in the VIP group?"

"Yes, if, as you say, they were the only ones with access to Lucca at the crucial time. My men will be checking that tonight, and I'll form my own opinion in the morning after I see what they found."

"Of those in the VIP group..." Akbar thought for a moment, running a scrawny fingertip across his mustache. "It's tempting to blame Lemovin, but I can't imagine why he would kill his own patron. Besides, Lemovin is a soft Russian bureaucrat, a Yeltsin supporter, full of chocolate cake and vodka. I doubt he's any more capable of violent action than I am."

"What about the other one? Mdivani?"

"An old-line Communist thug. A Brezhnev appointee from the bad old days. He's capable of murder, but dim-witted and totally lacking in imagination."

"The cultural attaché is dim-witted?"

Akbar laughed. "What a joke! The man was commissar of a tractor factory that was moved east of the Urals during World War II to get it away from Nazi bombers. Then he was a district manager...the apparatchik responsible for suppressing dissent in the Chandar region. Don't ask me how he got into the Foreign Service of my country. But it's good for him that he did, for Timur would certainly have assassinated him by now had he remained in Chandar Oblast...the province in which the lost city was found."

"Both Lemovin and Mdivani are ethnic Russians, right?"

"Lemovin is Russian," Akbar said. "His lackey is from the Caucusus. Can't you tell from the absence of manners?"

"They and most of the government in Pamiristan are from Moscow or other parts of the Western Soviet Union. You and your Thirteenth of September Movement are Mongols."

"Are you asking whether ethnicity has something to do with my animosity for them? Of course it does. They make up twelve percent of the population of my country but they run everything, especially the repressive regime."

"Which is how an old Commie thug, as you call him, gets to be cultural attaché," Donovan said.

"That is exactly how: a payoff for his long service persecuting my people. Enough, Lieutenant. I've run out of opinions on the man. In fact, I'm out of opinions generally. I am sick of the whole business. I didn't come to New York to see the Treasure of the Silk Road. Let the American Museum of Natural History *keep* Kublai Khan's dagger and the rest of the treasures that Lucca stole from my country. As long as they are here, the tourists just might stay away. May I go back to my hotel now?''

"Sure. Just don't leave town without notifying me."

"Where would I go? I came to New York to attend the opening of the General Assembly of the United Nations. There I will lobby for Security Council intervention to prevent the repressive colonial regime in Pamiristan from continuing to slaughter my people. But that's not for another week. I'll be here in the meantime."

"You've been very cooperative," Donovan assured the man before letting him out of the room and getting a detective to escort him back to the hotel.

TWELVE

SOCCER PLAYERS GET RUN AROUND LESS

"MDIVANI IS NEXT," Donovan said to Moskowitz, who had come running down the stairs from the Silk Road exhibit upon getting the word that the lieutenant was done with Akbar.

"He's in Seminar Room Nine. How did it go with Akbar?"

"It went well. He stood his ground, never blinked, and half convinced me that he's innocent."

"Only half?"

"If the layout of the exhibit and the positions of the suspects were as he described them, he can't have done it," Donovan said. "On the other hand, you were right. He *is* an oily little prick who talks too much."

"Bill...the guy is a diplomat. That's what they do."

"And there's this tattoo he says he got in Paris. Do you know anything about Muslims and tattoos?"

Moskowitz gave the lieutenant a withering glance. "Oh, my favorite subject—Arabs and their habits."

"Never mind," Donovan said.

"I may be able to shed some light on the physical layout of the exhibit, however," Mosko said. "I went through it myself with some men and opened doors. And I hope to have a blueprint by morning. I also found this guy who knows the whole setup."

"Is his name José?"

"No, it's Bernie. I know that you have this theory that every time an official in a suit tells you that nobody can get in or out of such-and-such a building, there's always a janitor named José who lives in the basement and can prove him a liar."

"I've taught you well, my son."

"This time José is named Bernie. He's a diorama artist who works for the museum."

"Where is he?"

"Trying to track down the blueprint of the exhibit. I'll keep after him."

"Do that. So tell me, after walking through the 'Treasure of the Silk Road'—is there any way in or out other than the entrance and the exit?"

"Not that I could find in half an hour. Unless, of course, you jump out a window or run down Clark's fire escape. But then you couldn't get back in. If you're asking if one of our suspects could slip away from the exhibit and murder Lucca without anyone noticing...forget about it."

"But we'll still wait until we see the blueprint," Donovan said.

"Absolutely."

"I'm going to talk to Mdivani now, partly because he's the biggest big shot of our remaining suspects and partly because Akbar singled him out."

"Akbar thinks he killed Lucca?"

"He said Mdivani was an old Cold Warrior who's capable of murder. You mentioned that he wants to talk."

"He insisted on it."

"No doubt he means to finger Akbar, whose organization would have killed Mdivani had he not split Chandar for the cultural attaché's job in New York."

"It's kind of refreshing to hear about someone coming to New York to *avoid* being killed," Mosko said.

"Yeah, isn't it? I may submit this yarn to the mayor's reelection campaign as being another reason to love the Big Apple."

"While you're on the phone with the mayor, you might get him on your side now that the politics has started," Mosko said, his tone of voice heavy with meaning.

"What politics?"

"It just arrived upstairs and is momentarily absorbed watching the corpse being removed."

"Who arrived?"

"Deputy Chief Inspector Pilcrow."

Donovan rolled his eyes. Pilcrow was an old nemesis, the man responsible for wresting the John Lennon murder investigation away from Donovan nearly a decade and a half earlier. It was Pilcrow's long-standing goal to become commissioner of police. It was his equally long-standing fear that Donovan would, somehow or another, stand in the way.

In the old days, Pilcrow had worried that the lieutenant would be a mammoth embarrassment—would get drunk and lose the body of a murdered politician, or something. Now Pilcrow must have gotten wind of the commissioner's offer of a captain's shield, Donovan thought. Drunk and a lieutenant in a fairly small precinct, Donovan was little more than an embarrassment; but sober, promoted, and ensconced at One Police Plaza with power in his pocket and money in his budget, Donovan could be a real threat. He could actually make the commissioner look good and, therefore, more likely to keep his job in case the mayor failed in his reelection bid.

Give me back the good old days when all I had to worry about was remembering to inform a suspect of his rights, Donovan thought.

"Pilcrow found out that this was a celebrity case and on my turf," Donovan said. "He's come to take it away from me, the way he did with John Lennon."

"What are you gonna do?"

"I'll call the commissioner if I have to. In the meantime, can you keep the son of a bitch busy while I talk to Mdivani?"

"I'll hold him off as long as I can."

"I sense that the old Commie thug is going to say something important. I want to hear his story before he gets the chance to think about it and confer with the folks back home."

Donovan found the man sitting at the seminar table, enveloped in a cloud of gray-white smoke, a coffee cup half full of cigarette butts in front of him. A second cup was also half filled, but with black coffee. Seven or eight packets of cane sugar had been torn open. The paper littered the tabletop alongside two matchbooks and an empty, crunched-up pack of Kools. The air smelled of mentholated cigarettes, coffee, and alcohol.

"I haven't been to one of these parties in years," Donovan said with a smile as he strode into the room and grasped the man's beefy hand.

"What party?"

"Nobody in New York smokes and drinks anymore. I guess you weren't told."

"In my country we do it all," Mdivani said with a shrug. "And in your Brighton Beach, where I am living these days, we smoke and drink too."

"Brighton Beach is in Brooklyn. I guess I should have said, that in Manhattan nobody smokes. In Brooklyn, no holds are barred. I've been to Brighton Beach, and it's like walking into a time warp to the 1950s. Back to the age—"

"—when men and women knew how to live. You must be Donovan. Your associate told me all about you. I am Georgi Mdivani."

"*Bill* Donovan. What do I call you? Minister Mdivani? My diplomatic protocol is a bit rusty."

Mdivani frowned. "Call me Georgi. Lemovin is a minister. I am just a man. A simple working man who is perhaps out of his element."

"Maybe I should call you *Tovarich*," Donovan said, using the Russian word for "Comrade."

"God forbid. You will get me shot. In Manhattan they don't smoke, you say; in my country nobody is 'Comrade' anymore. I burned my Communist party card four years ago, when Gorbachev gave the Soviet Union away to the bankers. Nowadays being a Communist brings nothing but trouble. Trust me, Lieutenant: It's safer to be a Communist in America these days."

"It must be easier than being a Democrat," Donovan said with a smile; he liked few things better than irony. He was beginning to feel that, despite Akbar's warnings, he would like Mdivani. The man was like a dozen men Donovan had known in bars over the years: sixtyish, hardworking, with thick, callused hands, a beer gut the size of a bowling ball, and wide, muscled shoulders. If Mdivani used to be an oppressor of the people and a thug, he must have had a good time doing it.

"I'm sorry to have kept you waiting," Donovan said, helping himself to a chair.

"Don't worry. If I weren't having a drink here, I would be having a drink at the Gemini."

"On Brighton Beach Avenue? I know the place. My favorite is the National, across the street."

Mdivani dismissed the thought with a contemptuous wave of the hand. "Too many Russians over there. Next time you are in the neighborhood, come to the Gemini. That is where the Georgians drink."

"You're Georgian?"

"Yes, exiled to Pamiristan years ago by duty to the ancien régime."

"You ran a tractor factory, I'm told."

"Aha! Akbar read you my résumé. No doubt he told you I am the reincarnation of Ivan the Terrible."

"He mentioned something about oppressing the native population."

Mdivani took a half-pint flask from his inside pocket and spilled some into his coffee. "Did I do that? Yes, I sure did. Why in hell do you think I was sent to Pamiristan? Not because of my good manners or good looks, I can tell you. I oppressed them, all right. I hired only the ones who were loyal to the party and I paid them only what I was told to pay them. Did I kill anyone? Not that I'm aware of. I may have worked one or two of my employees to death, but that is how the Japanese are rebuilding their empire. Did I kill Lucca? I surely did not."

"Let me see your hands."

Mdivani shrugged and extended them. Donovan gave them a good look, finding nothing of interest.

"Where were you at nine-fifteen?"

"Is that when it happened? I have no idea. I am not a clock watcher. If I was with someone at nine-fifteen, then I guess I have an alibi. If I was not, I have no alibi."

"Were you with anyone?"

"I was with Lemovin most of the time. Sure, we wandered here and there and sometimes I was around the corner from the man for a few minutes. Was that long enough for me to run back and kill Lucca? I doubt it. Why don't you try it and see how long it takes?''

"I will. What did you see?"

"In the exhibit?" Mdivani asked, shrugging. "Rocks. Sand. Stuffed goats. Mongol tents. Bows and arrows. Buddhist shrines and more Buddhist shrines."

"You weren't paying attention," Donovan said.

"Of that I plead guilty." Mdivani took a new pack of Kools from his inside pocket and lit one. He offered another to Donovan, who declined.

"Akbar thinks that you may have been walking behind him."

"That is perhaps true. I certainly wouldn't have let a terrorist walk behind *me*."

"He was in Samarkand, in the Uzbek exhibit. That puts you in the Pamiristan exhibit. Back in the old oblast."

"It is quite possible. I can tell you that I saw enough to remind me of what it was like living in Chandar Oblast. Give me Brighton Beach any day, even with all the Russians."

"You mentioned Akbar. Did you know him when you were in Pamiristan?"

"No. I never set eyes on the man until tonight."

"How did you find him?"

"He seems bright enough. You understand that we simply said hello, and not where the TV cameras could record us doing it. We're at war with his group back in Chandar, but that doesn't mean I can't say hello to the fellow when he comes to the United Nations."

"He found it odd that you were named cultural attaché."

"Because I know nothing of culture, apart from an ability to hum a few Puccini arias? But then I knew nothing about tractors when the ancien régime assigned me to run a tractor factory on the far side of the moon. I am what you Americans call a middle manager. I run things."

"And what are you running now?"

Mdivani smiled conspiratorially and squeezed Donovan's arm. "A pretty fair sports book on Brighton Beach Avenue. Do you want some action on the European soccer finals?"

"I know less about soccer than you know about culture," Donovan said. However, he was aware of the fact that some soccer players were given less of a runaround than he was getting that night. "What are you *really* doing in New York?"

"I am a cultural attaché." Mdivani elevated his hands in a gesture that said, "Isn't it obvious?"

"I think one reason you're here is to alibi Lemovin."

"What do you mean?" The Georgian seemed suddenly aware that the lieutenant was serious in his questioning.

"Maybe Lemovin killed Lucca and you're his alibi. That's why you graciously offered to stay behind and give me the runaround."

"I am telling you the truth. Lemovin and I weren't together the whole time. We strayed apart for a few minutes here and there. But you are right: I am his assistant, and blunter than him. To allow him to be the diplomat, I sit here and point the finger at Akbar."

"I suppose I'll find that the 'few minutes' Lemovin and you were apart isn't enough time to run back through the exhibit and commit murder."

"I can't say what you will find."

"If Lemovin didn't kill Lucca, then maybe you did," Donovan said. "Akbar felt you were capable of it."

"What does he know of me other than terrorist propaganda?"

"He seems pretty smart, you said. But there is another possibility as well, an explanation for your presence in New York that satisfies me more than your suddenly being named cultural attaché."

"And what is that?"

"It is that you really are, as Akbar asserts, an old Commie thug and were sent here not to hum Puccini, not to run a sports book on Brighton Beach Avenue, not even to alibi Lemovin on the odd chance he killed Lucca, but to find out as much as you can about the Thirteenth of September Movement. You told me a moment ago that you do Lemovin's dirty work."

Mdivani tried, without luck, to suppress a smile.

"I'm right, aren't I?" Donovan said.

Mdivani shrugged. "It pays to know the enemy."

"Funny. That's the same thing Akbar said about *his* being in New York."

"Ah, but what enemy was he referring to?"

"Lucca and Lemovin. He included you and Lemovin in the same package."

"How could he do that? Lemovin is a Russian. I am a Georgian. The difference is night and day."

"You are both in Pamiristan as colonial governors—in a sense, and speaking from his point of view. His group wants all foreign influences out—including Russians, Georgians, and future American tourists."

"Which Lucca was threatening to bring. Yes, I have seen that argument printed on flyers and posted up all over Pamiristan. Westerners will bring drugs and prostitution."

"And blue jeans and rock and roll," Donovan said.

"That too. Look, Lieutenant, do you want Pamiristan turned into another Iran? That is the entire question. They do. We don't. That is the kernel of our conflict."

"Frankly, Georgi, I don't give a damn."

"You don't live there and probably never will go. For better or worse, Pamiristan is my home. I don't want to go back to find that Allah has decreed that my wife must cover herself in veils and walk six paces behind me, as is the case in Iran. Not that it doesn't have its advantages, you understand. It's easy for Americans to dismiss the importance of Pamiristan. Apart from the curiosity value of the lost city of Chandar, there's nothing in my country that Americans want. You have enough cotton, and that is our main crop. Forget tractors; yours are, frankly, better—and in that case I know what I'm talking about: We copied them for years. Now, if Pamiristan were bristling with gold mines or oil wells it would be another matter, but it isn't. America went to war over Kuwait, which has oil wells, but stayed away from Bosnia, which has nothing Americans want. So it's easy for you to say, 'Let the Muslim fanatics have it.' Only those of us who live there think Pamiristan worth fighting for."

"What do you know of plans to turn Chandar into a tourist attraction?" Donovan asked.

"That is another charge you see plastered on telephone poles all over my country: "The Americans will build a Disneyland.'"

"Well?"

"If there is a huge interest in tourism as a result of the Treasure of the Silk Road exhibit, no doubt some of my countrymen will rent out rooms and sell trinkets. What of it? The natives of Eka-terinburg in Russia rent rooms, cook dinner, and sell trinkets all around the house where the czar and his family were butchered.

Same thing. You cannot listen too much to the Thirteenth of September people. They will say anything to advance their cause—the most outrageous things. There is not even an atom of truth to most of them.''

"And the others?''

"One or two atoms of truth at most. When we get our hands on Timur—and we will—the world will see that his whole movement is based on lies.''

"That *is* why you're here, isn't it?'' Donovan said. "To learn more about the Thirteenth of September movement.''

"I would like to know who Timur is,'' Mdivani said. "My suspicion is that his given name is Fatah Fasi and that he was once in a Soviet prison. I have heard that he was convicted of murdering a Russian black-marketeer with a knife. I have heard that Timur managed to get out of prison after Gorbachev gave the country to the bankers and everything fell into a shambles. Yes, I would like to know if Timur is Fasi and where I can get my hands on him. I would enjoy showing the world that the great leader of the Thirteenth of September Movement is a common murderer.''

"And you think you can find out from Akbar.''

"I am sure that he knows.''

"He says that he doesn't.''

"He lies.''

"Maybe you came to New York to kill Akbar and haven't had the time to do it yet,'' Donovan said.

"That is nonsense. Akbar is a cog in the revolutionist's wheel. He is not worth killing. But if he gives away who Timur is, then he will have been a valuable cog and I will return to Pamiristan a happy man. Is that fair enough?''

"I suppose so. One more thing: Why did you think Lucca invited all of you to be his guests for a private showing of the exhibit?''

"What does Akbar think? I'm certain you asked him.''

"Akbar thinks that Lucca meant to buy you all off.''

"It is possible,'' Mdivani said, expelling a mighty cloud of mentholated smoke and watching as it billowed toward the ceiling. "But I think not. I believe that Lucca was a conciliator, like your American president. I believe he wanted to get all the combatants in one room and convince them that what he had done was really a good thing.''

"And if some money changed hands..."

"So much the better."

"I hear that Lucca's Silk Road exhibition was, in fact, one long gravy train. He spread money across two continents."

"I have heard that also," Mdivani said. Donovan noticed a trace of bitterness in his voice.

"But you didn't get any."

"Not a penny. Not a ruble, which I think is worth less than a penny these days."

"And you're bitter about that."

Mdivani shrugged. "Perhaps a little. But not enough to kill over."

"Did Lemovin take money from Lucca?" Donovan asked.

"Why don't you ask him? I am not his baby-sitter—no matter what you think."

Donovan was tired of getting the runaround. The anger showed on his face and in his voice. "If you don't start giving me answers, I'll haul him into my office in leg irons," he snapped.

Mdivani was obviously surprised by the sudden shift in mood. Apparently he had thought he had the lieutenant wrapped around his finger. The Georgian shifted uncomfortably in his chair.

"If not Lemovin or you, who do you think killed Lucca?" Donovan asked, his voice calming a little.

"Is the list limited to the VIPs?" Mdivani asked.

"At the moment, yes."

"Akbar looks like a physical weakling to me. He looks like a scrawny graduate student or accountant. But he is a terrorist, and you never know. Do not be fooled by the ridiculous clothes he wears. The absurd formality of his dress is only to make you think he is...what is the popular American word for weakling?"

"Uh...wimp."

"That is it. I doubt very much that Akbar is a wimp. Well now, who else was there? The old man, the scientist or whatever?"

"Kent."

"Much too old."

"I think so, too."

"I don't really know the rest. Nobody said much. I talked to Lemovin. Akbar kept to himself; he even refused to shake hands with us. The rest...the only one who stood out was the man who was so upset-looking."

"Which one is that?"

"I'm trying to remember his name. An American, about thirty years old. He looks like a kid. You know, Katy Lucca's ex-husband."

"Wally Jameson. He looked upset?"

"He looked angry and upset. Wouldn't you be, in the company of two men who have slept with your wife?"

"True," Donovan agreed. "Both Clark and Lucca replaced him in Katy's heart."

"More to the point, they replaced him in her *bed*."

"I guess that could be unnerving."

"Are we agreed that Mrs. Lucca is a beautiful woman?"

"Oh yes, I think we see eye-to-eye on that."

"Well then, Lieutenant, there you have your motive for murder. Forget about the internal politics of Pamiristan: A woman like that is something to kill for."

"And you think that Jameson might have killed Lucca hoping to get her back?" Donovan asked. He was starting to like the Georgian again.

"She is not only beautiful...but absurdly rich. And maybe she needs someone to turn to right about now."

"I suspect that she might," Donovan said.

"Either Jameson killed Lucca in an attempt to get her back, or he killed Lucca out of simple revenge. So much the better if Clark is implicated in the killing. In one stroke, both adversaries are out of the picture. How do you like my theory?"

"I like it," Donovan said. "I like the way you think. You could be a policeman."

"I *was*," Mdivani said proudly, stubbing out his cigarette and lighting another. "Back in Chandar Oblast, when I was oppressing the native population, I was in charge of the police force. I even had a title."

"Which was?"

"They called me Captain."

"It's a good title," Donovan replied.

"You and I, we have a lot in common. You come have a drink with me at the Gemini. I am there every night, till one or two in the morning. Come, I will show you how men were meant to live."

THIRTEEN

THE DEPUTY CHIEF INSPECTOR
OFFERS COMPLETE SUPPORT

DEPUTY CHIEF INSPECTOR Paul Pilcrow was the highest-ranking black detective in the NYPD. With that distinction came many honors, among them being considered a spokesman for the New Order of multiculturalism in the department. Pilcrow often turned up on local television's equivalent of *Meet the Press,* expounding on affirmative action, "minority empowerment," gender-blind promotion practices, and other trappings of what was considered progress in the heavily Democratic and nearly always liberal politics of New York City. When a race riot struck, as one did between blacks and Jews in the Crown Heights section of Brooklyn a few years earlier, Pilcrow was among those public figures called upon to wave the flag of reason and tolerance.

But being the highest-ranking black detective had its rough side. As much as Donovan admired the man on some counts, Pilcrow was, in the lieutenant's half-Irish opinion, "a control freak and a scrotum-tightened neatness nut who makes Al Gore look like the bum who used to sweep out the dugout for the old Brooklyn Dodgers." Pilcrow despised the untidy and hated the unconventional. He especially loathed Donovan for being at once untidy and unconventional yet brilliant and, since he'd stopped drinking, upwardly mobile.

Donovan's longtime partner until their parting of the ways a few months earlier, black Sergeant T. L. Jefferson, had another take on Pilcrow. Typically for Jefferson, the opinion was strongly spoken but only half right. "He hates your white ass because you're sleeping with a black woman," Jefferson had said on more than one occasion. That opinion came from a man who had long verbally abused the lady in question, then Detective Sergeant Marcia Barnes, for being half Jewish. And so it came to pass that attacks on Donovan and his former love interest came from both sides of the political spectrum in New York City.

"As if it isn't tough enough being an Irish cop with progressive political opinions in New York City in the 1990s," Donovan once complained to Moskowitz, "I had to get in between the blacks and the Jews."

Donovan expected Pilcrow, as the waver of the flag of reason and tolerance, to be supportive and understanding. Of course, he was not; Donovan's newfound favor in the eyes of the commissioner tipped the scales.

"With some people I'm screwed no matter what I do," Donovan lamented to Jefferson one time.

"Now you have an idea what it's like to be black," Jefferson said.

"Or Jewish," Mosko added when he, too, heard the same lament.

Shortly thereafter, for a wholly unrelated reason that they were bound—almost but not quite on pain of death—not to discuss with anyone, Donovan and Jefferson agreed not to work together anymore.

Pilcrow was waiting outside the seminar room when Donovan finished with Mdivani and opened the door to release the tobacco smoke. Thus liberated, the smoke followed the opening door into the hallway, startling a museum security guard who had been posted nearby to assure that smoking and other offenses did not occur.

"Hey," the man said, starting forward but halting when Pilcrow fixed him with a murderously cold stare. The guard retreated to his position by the elevators.

"Minister Mdivani," Pilcrow gushed, sticking his hand out to be grasped by the Georgian, who did so with a bit of surprise and clear reluctance. "I am Deputy Chief Inspector Pilcrow, and I would like to apologize for my men keeping you here and interrogating you at such a tragic moment. I hope you see the necessity."

"Sure," Mdivani replied, straightening his jacket and patting the pockets to make sure he had taken with him the vodka and the cigarettes.

Donovan coughed some of the smoke out of his lungs.

"Lieutenant," Pilcrow said.

"Chief."

"Minister Mdivani, can I get you a ride back to the embassy?"

"I don't live at the consulate. I live in Brighton Beach. And my car is in the lot. Thank you for your kind offer. I need only to retrieve my overcoat from the VIP cloakroom and then I will be on my way."

"I hope that Lieutenant Donovan hasn't inconvenienced you."

"Not at all. I was only doing what I'd be doing in any case."

"What men do who know how to live," Donovan said.

"I enjoyed talking to you, Lieutenant. Take me up on my offer. Bring the colonel with you if you like." He tilted his head in Pilcrow's direction.

"That's 'Deputy Chief.'"

"Yeah. Fine. So long, Lieutenant. Colonel."

Mdivani walked into the elevator with the security guard eye-balling him suspiciously, noting his smoke-smelling tuxedo and vodka breath.

"What were you talking about?" Pilcrow asked when the Georgian was done. "'What men do who know how to live'?"

"Smoke and drink. He's a big fan of both."

"Is that what I smelled? What were you doing in there, running a tavern?"

"He brought his own in a flask. What was I supposed to do, arrest him and risk an international incident?"

"God, no. I was just asking. Was it difficult for you being in the room with him?"

I knew you would bring that up, Donovan thought. He said: "You mean about the booze? It's been a long time. I'm immune. The smoke was killing me, though. How are you, Paul? It's been a while."

"I'm fine, thanks. Look, Bill..."

Here it comes, Donovan thought.

"This is a *very important matter,* and—"

"Murder usually is."

"—and one that must be handled perfectly. Do you understand me? Perfectly."

"That's the only way I know."

Pilcrow shifted his weight nervously. Donovan had provoked him twice, and he had said nothing. He was biting his tongue. But why? The man had never been reluctant to criticize the lieutenant before, even in front of others, breaking the rules. Pilcrow's relative silence now was significant.

"This case must also be wrapped up *fast*."

"What's the hurry? Lucca isn't going anywhere. I've talked to my top suspects and we've got statements from the rest. I was going to interview all of them tonight, but I need to see a blueprint of the exhibit and check some other stuff first. I think I'll let them go for tonight. Of course, I'll have them all under surveillance."

"I'm sure they'd like to go home. I know the museum would like to get its exhibit open. The media will be all over you, and it's started already. Did you happen to see the ten o'clock news on Channels Five, Nine, and Eleven?"

"I was talking to Mdivani."

"Well, they went *crazy* with this story. Between Lucca being killed, Morty Berman pulling the dagger out of him, and Mrs. Lucca swooning in your arms—"

"Oh, they showed that?"

"All three stations. There are now a couple of hundred reporters camped outside Clark Tower looking for a glimpse of Mrs. Lucca. They're all over the West Side Major Crimes Unit too, waiting for you to come back. They might even be at your apartment building."

"Nobody knows where I live except my friends," Donovan said.

"I hope you can trust them. Bill, I have to tell you, there's heavy money involved in this. Mrs. Lucca is now worth a billion. She has more money than the Queen of England. Do you know what that makes her?"

"A widow. I'm sure that's all she's thinking about right now."

"Maybe. But her late husband was a VIP and, God knows, his partner, Steven Clark, is a major factor in the city's economy. Please...*please* don't tell me he's a suspect."

"No. At the moment I don't think so. The returns aren't in from all precincts, but Clark has a pretty good alibi."

"Thank God. That's all we need: Paolo Lucca murdered by Steven Clark while his widow faints in the arms of one of our detectives."

"Look, Paul, I didn't ask for this. I was here at the invitation of the commissioner, who gave me the ticket for my birthday."

"I didn't know it was your birthday. Congratulations."

"Thanks. Let me celebrate it by finding Lucca's murderer."

"Oh, don't get me wrong. I didn't come here to take the case away from you."

Donovan was silent, and crossed his arms stoically.

"I know you've been tight with the commissioner lately."

So he's heard about the offer of a captain's shield.

"I want you to know that I consider you absolutely the right man to replace John O'Donnell."

Sure you do.

"And I told the commissioner how proud I am that you came up on my watch."

Sure you are.

"I simply came here to give you my complete support as well as to express my confidence that you will wrap this thing up soon."

"Thank you."

Pilcrow extended his hand, and Donovan took it.

"Let me know if you need anything—money, men, equipment, facilities."

"I might need a thing or two. An investigation of this size will kind of stretch my budget."

"All you have to do is call. Who's helping you on this?"

"The usual suspects: Moskowitz, Bonaci, and the rest."

"What about Jefferson? Your old partner."

"He's on vacation," Donovan said.

"I heard that the two of you got a divorce."

"We thought it best to work apart for a while."

"This wasn't a black-white problem, was it?" Pilcrow asked.

"You can't be serious. My taste in friends has always been pretty ecumenical."

"Oh, yes—how *is* Marcy?"

"Good."

"How does she like being a civilian?"

"So far she seems to be prospering," Donovan said.

"Give her my best."

"I will."

"For a while, though, you'll have to look after Mrs. Lucca. Take special care of her."

"I'll try to do that."

"I hope *she's* not a suspect."

"As you know, she was with me when it happened," Donovan said.

"So she was. Lucky you." Pilcrow winked at the lieutenant as if to say, "Hey, hey, hey!" "Well, thank God for small favors. Now you have only the politicians to look out for."

"Which politicians do you mean?" Donovan asked.

"The Democrats, of course. Clark was a *big* contributor. And Mrs. Lucca is one of Clinton's Hollywood buddies. No doubt the mayor will insist that you do all you can to wrap this case up quickly."

Donovan forced a smile. *I hate black conservatives,* he thought, as it suddenly occurred to him how much Deputy Chief Inspector Pilcrow looked like Clarence Thomas. They both had square, squat bodies, with rounded, bumpy facial features, short fat mustaches, and small eyes. Both smiled too quickly and looked like they didn't mean a bit of it.

Donovan thought: *How badly will I mess up my life if I look you straight in the eye and say, "You're just dying for me to fuck this up, aren't you?"* A lot, he concluded, and held his tongue.

"Thanks a lot, Paul," Donovan said, forcing his own smile and grasping the man's hand. "I knew I could count on you."

"And if you do decide to join us at One Police Plaza, let's be sure to do lunch."

"You got it," Donovan said.

"I'll be on my way now," Pilcrow said, turning and walking into the same elevator that, a while earlier, took Mdivani away.

"What's this about One Police Plaza?" Moskowitz asked, slipping up from behind. He had heard the tail end of the conversation. Donovan had hoped to keep the offer a secret for a while longer. Well, the Lucca murder changed everything.

"What this is, is one very big secret that I will kill you if you tell anyone."

"Hey. Do I look like a yenta to you? Let's hear it."

"I've been offered a captain's shield."

"No shit! That's great!"

"John O'Donnell is retiring and the commissioner wants me in his job."

"Fantastic. You said yes, of course."

"Not yet. I'm thinking it over."

"What's to think over? It's a big promotion. A lot of prestige. A lot of money."

"A lot of headaches. A truckload of *tsuris*."

"You pronounced that pretty good for a goy, Bill. You'll be a big hit at One Police Plaza. Take the job."

"It's easy for you to say. You only joined my unit two years ago. I'd be leaving guys I worked with for fifteen years."

"So you go and see them on weekends. Are you out of your mind? Take the job. Better yet, take the job and take me with you. You'll need a right-hand man you can trust."

"You'd like that. One Police Plaza is an easy commute from Canarsie."

"But it's a real schlep through downtown traffic. Jesus, Bill, what great news."

"Keep it to yourself until I make up my mind."

"You have my word."

"Let's get through this case and I'll see what I want to do. In the meantime, Pilcrow is dying for me to screw up."

"Yeah, he did kind of have that look about him. The smile was too broad."

"If you help me avoid mistakes, maybe I'll take you with me. In the meantime, Pilcrow promised me anything I need in terms of men, money, and equipment. If you have a Hanukkah list I'd like to see it. Now, where the hell are Bernie and the blueprint?"

"Upstairs, in the same office where you talked to Mrs. Lucca. He's got it with him."

"Let the rest of the suspects go for tonight. Give them the usual warnings about sudden departures and tell them I may want to talk with them tomorrow."

"You don't want to see them now?"

"Akbar and Mdivani talked both my ears off and I've had it for the night," Donovan said. "I'll say this for these VIP types—they're more fun to talk to than your average murderer. You know, the uptown janitor who stabbed his mother-in-law with a steak knife? Anyway, I'll have better questions after I see the blueprint and take a quick look at the exhibit. In the course of talking to Akbar and Mdivani, I realized that I need a better perspective on the physical layout, the locations of all the suspects, and the timing of everything."

"That we can get from the statements they gave us. Then you can ask them more pointed questions after that."

"Thank you, Sergeant Moskowitz."

"Do I get to be a lieutenant when you become a captain?"

"You would have to wear a clean shirt."

"Forget it, then. Before you go up to meet Bernie, Bonaci wants a moment of your time."

"He found the cigarette butts," Donovan said.

FOURTEEN

A GUY SMOKING ALONE

CLARK'S FIRE ESCAPE dropped down three flights from where he had been standing to the basement. The portable lights that Bonaci had set up revealed the base of rickety cast-iron emergency stairs that looked as if they had been idle for years.

Fire escapes were rare in a building of the museum's age and imposing dimensions. This one looked as if it had been added forty or fifty years before, perhaps to mollify one of the reform-minded governments that New Yorkers now and then elected.

Its bottom terminus was an iron ladder that dropped straight down from the ground floor to the basement level. That ladder was made to remain in the up position and descend only in emergencies, after a lever was pulled. The idea was to keep it retracted so as to discourage burglars from climbing up the fire escape.

But since all doors to the central courtyards of the museum were routinely locked, and basement-level and ground-floor windows were protected by iron gates, burglars weren't anticipated, and the ladder remained permanently down. At the base of it, Bonaci found the expected cigarette butts.

"We got them, Lieutenant," he announced proudly when Donovan arrived on the scene.

The lieutenant got there through a basement-level door, one reached only after an excursion through the immense commercial kitchen serving the Diner Saurus cafeteria.

From his fifty years in New York City, Donovan knew that the sealed-off courtyards of buildings were used for more than ventilation for the tenants and flyways for the pigeons; they could be havens for lovers, chutes for garbage, and storage for janitors. In keeping with that tradition, this particular corner of the museum's central court served as a repository for rock salt. Bags and bags of it were piled against the brick wall, making what looked for all the world like a World War II vintage sandbag bunker on both sides of the plain dark-gray door.

The bags ran forty or fifty feet along the wall, awaiting the snowy December day when their contents would be cast upon the West Seventy-seventh Street cobblestone driveway to melt ice. They were two deep against the wall and not quite high enough to obscure the bottom sills of several iron-gated windows. There was a thin sprinkling of rock salt on the ground. It crunched beneath Donovan's feet.

"How many butts were there?"

"Nine," Bonaci answered.

"Let's see them."

He dangled a plastic zip-top evidence bag in front of the lieutenant's eyes.

"So Clark smoked nine of his twenty Sherman's, and it looks like he smoked 'em all down to the filters," Donovan said.

"Did you ever smoke?"

"Now and then in bars, just to be sociable. I haven't in years, though."

"I gave it up a while ago. When you smoke 'em down to the filters you wind up with a lot of burnt filter in your mouth. The guy must have had a real bad nicotine fit."

"I guess so."

Donovan peered up the fire escape into the dark, shielding his eyes against the powerful crime-scene light. Then he looked down at the concrete pavement.

"Show me exactly where you found the butts."

"Right at your feet. I got a picture of them before I picked them up. You'll have a copy tomorrow."

"How spread out were they?"

Bonaci shrugged. "Not very. Two or three feet. Is there a problem?"

"I guess not. So what if Clark smoked 'em and dropped 'em straight down."

"Where else would he drop them?"

"I would have flicked one off this side of the fire escape, one off the other, tried to knock down a moth with a third. A guy smoking alone in the night can get pretty bored and desperate for small ways in which to amuse himself. Do you see what I mean? It's almost as if Clark meant for us to find them, and put them all in one spot to make sure that we did."

"I think you're looking for a reason to nail the guy," Bonaci said.

"Maybe, but that's what I get paid to do, isn't it? Do you know anything about Galileo, who disproved Aristotle's view of gravity by dropping things off the Tower of Pisa?"

"Not too much, boss."

"I plan to redo that experiment, this time dropping cigarettes off that fire escape. I want to see if they fall as neatly as Clark's did."

"Maybe Clark knew about Galileo, too, and was trying to do the same thing."

"He doesn't strike me as being the scientific type," Donovan said."

"Whatever," Bonaci said. "Let's do this experiment in the daytime. We can't see evidence-grade detail even with the lights."

"Absolutely. I'm tired too, and I'm looking forward to going home to bed. It's been a long night."

"Answer me one thing, Lieutenant," Bonaci said, sweeping his arm along the wall to point out the barred-up windows. "Are you suggesting that Clark could have faked going for a smoke, run down the fire escape, planted the cigarettes, gotten through one of these windows, run up to the exhibit, gotten in without anyone noticing, killed Lucca, and gotten back here, without anyone seeing him?"

With a faint smile, Donovan said, "Tell me if it's possible and I'll give you a yes or no answer."

"Well, he could have faked the smoking and run down the fire escape and planted the cigarettes. Now, could he have gotten through one of these windows…?"

Bonaci paused, scratching his chin, and after a moment Donovan said, "Well, could he?"

"I don't know. They look good and locked to me, but I'll check tomorrow."

"Do that. And also see if there's any other way to get into the building from out here."

"I'll seal off this place for the night," Bonaci said.

Donovan bobbed his head up and down in agreement. "If you have to, treat this entire wing of the museum like a crime scene. Seal off every place that a guy could use to get in or out and kill Paolo Lucca."

Donovan stretched his arms and expelled a mighty yawn into the September air. The rain had stopped for the evening at last, but its crisp chill hung in the air and a fine mist hovered like a ghost and flowed around the massive, rough-hewn stones that made the interior wall of the courtyard look like the mountains of the moon. A crescent moon peeked over the roof, haloed by the fine clouds that trailed behind the storm front that had just passed through.

Bonaci saw his boss looking up at the sky, and said, "It's a beautiful night."

"It is that," Donovan said, and went back into the building.

THE OFFICE on the fifth floor was getting quite a workout that night. When Donovan left it a while back, the cypress- and book-lined room had been a sort of infirmary, with Katy Lucca decorating the couch and a solicitous doctor hovering about brandishing a hypo of Valium.

Now it resembled nothing so much as a college dorm on graduation day. The teak-and-glass cocktail table had been stripped of its decorations. The brass hookah picked up in the souk in Marrakesh was sticking out of a brown cardboard shipping carton alongside the old globe that showed the ancient world. The pipe rack filled with meerschaums and hickories had been stuffed into another box. It looked sad; its place on the admiral's desk showed a ring where the pipe rack had stood for years.

A young man sat on the couch between the two packing crates and pored over a gigantic blueprint that he had spread across the cocktail table. His attention was unbroken, despite the constant muttering of Arthur C. Kent, who stood precariously on a chair while removing the nautical ensign that had been presented to Commodore Perry by the emperor of Japan.

Moskowitz stood, arms folded, at the door, watching in quiet bemusement. When Donovan walked up, Mosko said, in a quiet voice for him, "Mrs. Lucca was taken home and, I think, put to bed."

"At Clark Tower?"

"Yeah. She left asking for you."

"What's happening here?"

"The old guy has to move out. He's not happy about it."

"I understand. If I could get my office to look like this I'd never leave. How is the blueprint?"

"Outstanding. It has every inch of the Treasure of the Silk Road exhibit."

"Including ways in or out for a murderer?"

"Maybe, man. We have to go over it at length. Do you want to meet the guy who found it?"

Donovan nodded, and entered the room with his right hand extended. "I'm Lieutenant Donovan."

"Bernie Metz."

The man was thirty at most, but a good deal of his reddish-brown hair was already missing. A few wisps blew across the top of his skull and down over the forehead, failing to cover the freckles that seemed to be replacing strands of hair as they marched relentlessly across his skull and toward the back of his head. Metz had red hair on his chest too, and wore a gold Star of David at the end of a gold chain. Matching wire-framed reading glasses perched at the end of a thin nose. The clothing was what Donovan called scientific/academic: jeans and red lumberjack shirt worn with cross-training sneakers.

"How you doing, Mr. Metz?"

"Call me Bernie. My father is Mr. Metz."

"Whatever you say. Thanks for finding the blueprint for us. Where was it?"

"Oh, Arthur forgot he had it in his office. I suspected that's what happened."

"You mean Dr. Kent."

"The doddering old fool standing atop the chair," Kent said, revealing keen hearing. The office was large, and Donovan hadn't been talking loud.

"Good to meet you, Dr. Kent."

"The pleasure is mine, Lieutenant. Here...take this for me, would you?"

He slipped the oak-framed ensign off its nail and extended it in the direction of the lieutenant, who took several strides across the room to accept it. While he admired the century-and-a-half-old flag, Kent hopped down from the chair. He was amazingly spry for a man who appeared to be at least seventy, with a face tanned a light olive—from, Donovan preferred to think, recent months on an expedition, although long weekends in East Hampton were also a possibility. Kent was on the short side and compactly built, with no trace of age in his walk and only the lines on his hands and neck and around his eyes, and the flowing shock of white hair, to betray his years.

He took back the ensign and held it up for Donovan's closer inspection.

"Beautiful workmanship, isn't it? Look at the stitching in the wing feathers of the eagle. Can you see the distinct lines of Japanese painting?"

Donovan said that he could; he was being polite, for Asian art was hardly one of his specialties.

"Matthew Perry led an American naval squadron to the shores of Japan in 1853 on a mission intended to open up trade. He demanded supplies and the opening of diplomatic relations between Japan and America. The Japanese were deeply suspicious of all foreigners. Like my British ancestors and island-dwellers everywhere, they were intensely xenophobic and afraid of invasion."

"Kublai Khan tried, didn't he?"

"In 1274 he attacked Japan with thirty thousand men, but was beaten back by violent storms. Shades of England and the Spanish Armada. Seven years later Kublai tried again and succeeded in landing in Kyūshū. But the resistance was well organized, and once more the weather was foul. The attack failed. Kublai Khan died before he could launch a third assault."

"Six centuries later the Japanese were still afraid of foreigners."

"Indeed, and not without reason. The emperor opened relations with America in 1854, and within ten years shots were being fired. The Japanese were copying Western-style warships and cannons and, well, here we are today."

"Detroit is copying Japanese-style cars."

"And not doing especially well, either. At least we got this flag." Kent put the ensign into the packing crate alongside the pipe rack and the humidor.

"Where are you going?" Donovan asked.

"Away. Home. Back to England, I suppose."

"Why?"

"You mean you haven't heard? I've been sacked."

"Fired? When?"

"Several months ago I was given until my seventieth birthday to clear out. My birthday is Sunday."

"Mazel tov," Mosko said, and Donovan tossed in his congratulations.

"What happened?"

"I made the grievous error of opposing the Treasure of the Silk Road exhibit."

"Why?"

"Because it's bad science, Lieutenant. Good showmanship, unquestionably. But very bad archaeology."

"You're referring to the manner of collection."

"You know about the bribes?"

"I was recently told."

"The late unlamented—unlamented by *me*, anyway—Mr. Lucca moved into the tragic rubble left by the collapse of the Soviet Union and *bought* cooperation left and right. He *bought* excavation rights. He *bought* politicians. He exploited the fact that the emerging independent nations of Central Asia are absolutely starved for hard currency. He exploited the fact that the apparatchiks still in charge of things in Pamiristan and other places had an absolute need to fatten their Swiss bank accounts in preparation for the inevitable day when popular insurrections put them on the lam. After all, there's nothing of value in those countries—just a lot of sheep and goats."

"By 'popular insurrections' you mean the thirteenth of September Movement," Donovan said.

"They're Muslim fanatics and I'm not too keen on that bunch but, yes, they qualify as a popular insurrection. Probably would be better for their country than the leftover Soviet hacks still clutching at power."

"So you support the Muslims?"

"Lord, no. I don't like any of the alternatives currently being offered as management for those poor people. But I'm a scientist, Lieutenant, not a politician. This is my crime: I seek to know. I simply have old-fashioned standards about how knowledge should and shouldn't be acquired."

"And you feel that Lucca—"

"—should never have been rewarded for his act of thievery.

My God, it was like the bad old days of imperial curiosity. You want to know about the Aborigines of Australia? By all means, kidnap one and bring him back and put him in a circus. That was done. You want to know about Kublai Khan's dagger? By all means, steal it after paying the caretakers to look the other way. What Lucca did to Pamiristan was no different from what Schliemann did to Turkey.''

"Carry off the artifacts of Troy and put them in a Western museum,'' Donovan said.

"Precisely. The government of Turkey is to this day trying to get them back. The government of Pamiristan will be trying to regain that dagger in the year 3000. I guarantee it.''

"But don't you think it's at least interesting to know that it exists? To see it?''

"Absolutely. It's fascinating to learn that the Emperor Michael not only had contact with Marco Polo but gave him that carving knife to carry to the great khan in an attempt to encourage trade between Constantinople and China. Nobody previously knew that Polo went anywhere *near* Michael. But the dagger should be sent back afterward.''

"And you're saying that it won't be.''

"Perhaps in the year 3000. Believe me, Lieutenant, the British Museum will return the Elgin Marbles to their rightful place in the Temple of Athena Nike in Athens first.''

Donovan said, "So your opinions got you fired?''

"It was just as I said. I felt that Lucca was practicing bad science. The powers that be in these hallowed halls wanted the money that the exhibit will bring in. Have you seen it?''

"Not yet. I had intended to be among the first, but it looks as if I may be among the last.''

"Apart from the dagger, there really isn't anything new. Oh sure, Lucca picked up a trinket here and a trinket there, most of them seen before. To Asia experts or to anyone faintly well read about the Silk Road, little in this exhibit will prove startling.''

"Oh,'' Donovan said, the disappointment showing.

"Did I burst your bubble? I *am* sorry.''

"So Hubby brought home a few *trinkets* from the tundra after all,'' Donovan said.

"Beg pardon?''

"I was echoing Katy Lucca's opinion of the Treasure of the Silk Road."

"Did she say that?"

"Yes. Before her husband was killed."

"Well, my respect for the poor woman just went up a thousand percent. However, I must confess it wasn't high to begin with. Look, the 'trinkets' *will* be popular. They're a great draw. As Barnum said, 'There's a sucker born every minute.' Present company excepted, of course."

"Thank you, Arthur," Metz said, using a singsong voice.

"*He* likes the exhibit," Kent said.

"Do you two get along?"

"Fabulously," Kent said, "despite the fact he thinks the Silk Road exhibit is just grand. Well, everyone's entitled to his delusions. I like my young colleague despite his absence of taste."

"Professor Kent, if you hate Lucca and his exhibition, why are you here tonight?" Donovan asked.

"Isn't it obvious? I'm clearing out my office."

"You could do that more comfortably during the week. Why did you come to the opening?"

"I was invited. Isn't it wonderful?"

Kent fished a pipe from the rack. It was intricately carved: a bust of a nineteenth-century gentleman with wild, swept-back curly hair and tiny, oval, wire-framed glasses that rode high on his nose. Kent waved the pipe proudly in front of Donovan after filling the bowl with tobacco.

"Am I supposed to recognize that man?"

"Franz Schubert. My idol and muse."

"Because he wrote great melodies or because he lived in poverty and died unappreciated?"

"Both," Kent said proudly as he lit up. The air began to fill with the scent of black walnut.

"You can't smoke in here, Arthur," Metz said, looking up and smiling.

"What are they going to do, fire me? Lieutenant, you asked why I'm here. Let me be honest with you. I came for the same reason we *all* came—to get my piece of the pie."

Moskowitz was astonished. He walked from the periphery of the room to the center, waggling a finger in the air and looking like a man divining water. "You mean... Are you telling us that all the members of the VIP group came here to get paid off?"

"Of *course*," Kent said gleefully.

"Every single one?"

"Without exception."

FIFTEEN

"FRANZ AND I NEED PASSAGE HOME TO ENGLAND"

"Even Steven Clark?"

"Especially him."

"And you, Professor? What about you?" Donovan asked.

"I more than Clark even. Franz and I need passage home to England." Once again he waggled the pipe in front of Donovan.

The lieutenant waved a veil of smoke from in front of his eyes. His scowl was then more obvious to the old man.

"Oh, come *on*, Lieutenant. I'm entitled. Lucca paid off every toll-booth clerk from Tyre to Sian, some of them quite handsomely. Furthermore, most of them kept their jobs afterwards. I got nothing from the whole thing except the old heave-ho. It is my considered opinion that Lucca owed a special debt to those of us who lost our jobs on account of him."

"Those of us? Did I hear a plural raise its ugly head?"

"You did, Lieutenant. Very good."

"Who among the VIPs lost his job other than you?"

"Mdivani, of course."

"Mdivani? My sense of him is that he's here to keep an eye on the Thirteenth of September Movement, perhaps to find out who Timur, their leader, is."

"He may be in New York for that reason. But he surely was here tonight to get in on the loot. You see, the real treasure of the Silk Road was coming from Lucca's pocket. The man would pay anything to keep his name in the papers."

"He'll be on every front page tomorrow," Mosko said.

Donovan asked, "Wouldn't Mdivani have gotten money from Lucca in Pamiristan?"

"He should have. But you see, he didn't. Poor Mdivani made the same mistake that poor Dr. Kent did: he opposed Lucca."

"That wasn't the impression I got."

"Ah, but he did. That's why he's no longer running the show in Chandar Oblast."

"He wasn't made cultural attaché to reward him?"

"Lord, no. He was made cultural attaché to get him out of Chandar, where he was standing in the way of Lucca's archaeological dig."

"Why would he have done that? Some hidden sympathy for the Thirteenth of September Movement?"

"Not a chance. More like some hidden sympathy for cash. I don't know all the details. He held up the permits for *some* reason. I assume it was to jack up the cost of the payoff. Anyway, Lucca made an end run to Lemovin. The project is approved, the ancient city of Chandar rises again from the dust, and Lemovin takes Mdivani to New York, where he can keep an eye on him."

"And when it came time for the opening, the pair of them decided to go back to the well, to hit up Lucca for more cash—who knows, perhaps even in payment for their silence."

"There you have it," Kent said, finishing off the tobacco in his pipe.

"Just what kind of money are we discussing here?" Donovan asked.

"I have no idea how much they wanted. When Lucca phoned me—"

"He did this personally?"

"Yes. All his negotiations were face to face. He never used intermediaries. When he called me two weeks ago he said that he was sorry about my losing my job, wished we could be friends, and wanted to make it up to me. Would I be interested in joining his Asian explorations? He said there would be money in it for me, a lot of money. I should come to the opening of the exhibit and meet the other members."

"The others in the VIP group."

"Oh yes, we all were there for the loot. Every man behind that gold rope had the nervous look of the hustler about him. Did you not notice it?"

"My attention was elsewhere," Donovan said. "Look, Professor, I've seen a lot of strange stuff in my time but I'm having trouble finding a reason for Paolo Lucca to have a fit of conscience over you losing your job. You were his enemy, and all of a sudden he wants to give you money? Not only you, but his other enemies?"

"I have no idea what was behind this supposed largesse," Kent said. He broke into a laugh then, and said, "We really were a hungry-looking lot. I'm quite ashamed of myself. Well, I suppose now I will get nothing for my trouble. May I finish packing?"

"Yes and no. You may finish packing but you can't take anything out of here before my men go through it."

Kent tossed up his hands. "I knew it. I knew that nothing but trouble would come from an association with Lucca. His 'Asian explorations,' indeed."

Kent went to the couch and slumped down alongside Metz, who was leaning back with his eyes closed. It was nearing midnight and everyone had suffered a very long day.

"One question, Dr. Kent, and then you can go."

"Where was I when the murder took place?" Kent said wearily.

"Exactly. Where were you at nine-fifteen?"

"Do you know the rough organization of the exhibit?"

"It goes according to country, right?"

"Correct. I was in Pamiristan attempting to fathom the rationale behind the Chandar exhibit."

"You're sure that's where you were at nine-fifteen?"

"I'm very good about time of day. Besides, all my interest lies in Chandar. I recall that the Pamiristani contingent was ahead of me."

"That would be Lemovin and Mdivani. Who was behind you?"

"The German chap. Vischer, I think his name is."

"Do you know anything about him?"

"I'm a Briton of a certain age, Lieutenant. The man is German. That tells me all I need to know. See here, I stayed near the Chandar diorama because I was keen to see a display of the spot from which Lucca stole Kublai Khan's dagger."

"Which brings me to my next question? Are you sure the dagger in the exhibit is Kublai Khan's?"

"Of course it is," Kent said. "Why do you doubt it?" Donovan gestured to Moskowitz, who reached into his shoulder bag and withdrew a large plastic evidence bag containing the murder weapon. The blood-encrusted, bejeweled dagger looked satanic and angry even through the plastic. Donovan held it toward Kent and Metz, who had opened his eyes and sat up straight. Donovan warned them not to touch.

"That's it," Metz said, leaning forward. "I put it in the display case myself. How did you get it?"

"I don't understand," Kent said.

"You're sure this is the real thing?" Donovan asked.

Metz said, "I can't be absolutely sure without examining it, but I think so. What's that on it, blood? My God! You don't mean..."

Donovan said to Moskowitz, "How did you tell them Lucca died?"

"I said he was stabbed. I didn't say with what."

Kent said, "No, no. That can't be. I saw this dagger in the display case at the precise moment you tell me that Lucca was killed. I assure you that it's Kublai Khan's."

Donovan scowled and said, "Okay, guys, how many of these things are there?"

"One," Kent said.

But nearly at the same instant, Metz said "Two. I mean, there's only one *real* Kublai Khan's dagger. One real dagger and one copy. I made the copy myself, with the guys in the metal shop, so I know. The real one has three tiny hash marks beneath the ruby scarab beetle."

"Which one did you put in the display case?"

Metz lowered his eyes for a moment, sighed, and said, "The copy."

Mosko was outraged by the false advertising. "You mean, all the people who came here tonight for the party would have seen a phony?"

"The replica was only to be on display until the security cameras are online."

"I didn't notice any security cameras," Donovan said.

"Exactly my point. There are a few, but they don't have complete coverage of the exhibit and none of them is pointed at the Chandar diorama. They're to go online by the end of the week. Then I'll take the real dagger out of the safe and destroy the replica. But...I'm confused."

"Join the club," Mosko said.

"The replica is in the diorama. We saw it. Kublai Khan's real dagger is in the safe."

"Safe?" Donovan asked.

"Over there, behind the Chinese philosophers." Metz gestured over his head to the woodcut of Confucius, Lao-tzu, and Buddha.

"You kept Kublai Khan's dagger in my wall safe and never told me?" Kent exclaimed.

"You had been fired and were sitting out in the Hamptons sulking," Metz said defensively. "Besides, who would think to look for it in the office of the man who so vehemently opposed the exhibition?"

"Please open the safe, Professor," Donovan said.

Metz was going to say something but Donovan shushed him and urged him off the couch and out of the way. He obliged, rolling up the blueprint and tucking it under his arm.

Kent stepped onto the couch, balancing on the soft cushions with remarkable agility as he lowered the woodcut and handed it to Moskowitz. "I was about to pack this when you burst into the room," Kent said.

As before, he muttered while twirling the nob on the brown-faced wall safe that rested comfortably in its nook in the plaster wall. Two tries at opening the safe failed, as did a third. At last Kent hopped down from the couch, his palms up to indicate emptiness.

"You changed the combination."

"I was about to say so," Metz replied.

"Open it, please," Donovan said.

Metz handed the lieutenant the blueprint, then replaced Kent atop the couch. A moment later the safe was open and—Donovan could see from halfway across the office—empty.

Metz was aghast. "Where's the dagger?"

"Here," Donovan said, waving the evidence bag.

"But how?"

"How did it get out of the safe? When did you last lock it in there?"

"Yesterday morning, about ten."

"And you didn't open the safe—"

"Until just now," Metz replied, sinking back into his old sitting position on the couch.

"How many people have the combination?"

"Two. Lucca and me."

"That's interesting. Where were you at nine-fifteen?"

Metz looked sharply at Donovan for an instant, then closed his eyes. "Downstairs in my studio."

"Where's that?"

"On the same floor as the Treasure of the Silk Road—but nowhere near the murder scene."

"I'll be the judge of that," Donovan said. "But I'll be it tomorrow—after I've had the chance to take this blueprint home with me and study it. And after I've come back tomorrow morning and walked through the exhibition. You'll be here to take me through it, right?"

Metz nodded. He didn't seem happy, but he was compliant. He muttered, "I had no reason to kill Mr. Lucca."

"I'm sure you'll have no trouble convincing me of that," Donovan said.

"How could this have happened? I'm the only one with the combination other than Lucca, and he was vehement about it staying in the safe until the security cameras were working."

Donovan said, "You're a talented man, Mr. Metz. You made a convincing replica of Kublai Khan's dagger and, if Lucca hadn't been murdered with the real thing, no one might have known."

"Thank you."

"But tell me this—is locksmithing one of your talents?"

Metz looked up, the color returning to his face. "No. Of course not. Hold on." He fumbled his wallet out of his jeans pocket and took from it a wad of business cards. After a few seconds he pressed one into Donovan's palm.

He read out loud: "'Columbus Avenue Locksmiths, Anthony Di Bello, proprietor. Established 1983.' God, I love people with a sense of history."

"He's bonded," Metz said. "He's a real wizard with locks."

"I'm sure he is," Donovan said. "Murph the Surf was a pretty fair surfer, too, in addition to being an outstanding thief. We'll drop in on Mr. Di Bello tomorrow."

Later on, after Metz and Kent were let go for the night and that entire wing of the Museum of Natural History was sealed tighter than King Tut's tomb had been before it fell open, after centuries, at the hands of Howard Carter, Donovan walked out of the building with Moskowitz and Bonaci. The sky had entirely cleared. The crescent moon had moved higher in the sky, approaching the zenith. Its rays glinted off the mammoth, rain-misted sculpture, which showed Theodore Roosevelt astride a magnificent steed, flanked by a partly robed Indian and a nearly naked African.

Midnight had come and gone. Central Park West was again deserted (not counting the array of police vehicles that lined the broad boulevard separating the Upper West Side of Manhattan from Central Park). A light breeze rustled the leaves in the park. Far beneath the concrete, a lonely A train rumbled down the tracks leading from Harlem to midtown. The red carpet had long since been rolled up, and the bare pavement quivered beneath Donovan's feet.

He said, "I'm going to Marcy's for a drink. Anybody want to come? I'm buying."

"Not me, boss," Mosko said. "It's a long drive home and I'm beat."

"Howard?"

"Not tonight, Bill. My regards to the little lady."

"See you tomorrow," Donovan said, and got into the commissioner's limousine for the ride back to Broadway.

WHEN DONOVAN KNOCKED on the door of Marcy's Home Cooking it was nearly one in the morning. Despite the hour, the lights burned brightly inside the storefront restaurant. The ten round tables that were set up in the front room had been rearranged yet again as the new owner searched for a layout that satisfied both aesthetics and waitress traffic. The exposed brick on the south wall had a solitary decoration, a framed print. Hanging alone was a reproduction of Eastman Johnson's *Old Stage Coach.* The bar had been moved to the back of the front room and was shrunk to six seats—large enough for a few regulars, yet small enough to discourage long-term residency.

Four figures sat at it. Marcy was behind the bar, hunched over it studying her menu. Jake Nakima, Richard Marlowe, and George Kohler occupied stools. Marlowe was a white-bearded Columbia professor of English, a walking encyclopedia of a man who seemed to spend half his life doing crossword puzzles. Kohler was Riley's old bartender who stayed on under Marcy's ownership after demonstrating—to everyone's great surprise—a talent for cooking. Donovan knocked louder to be heard over the radio, which was tuned to a classical music station.

George had gotten a haircut and begun tucking in his shirt in honor of his new respectability, but still looked like a mountain man. He lumbered to the door and opened it.

"Hey," Donovan said, stepping inside and locking the door behind him.

"Lemme smell your arm," George growled, grabbing Donovan's left and hoisting it up to his nose.

"Is there a point to this?" Donovan asked as his friend sniffed his forearm about halfway between his wrist and his elbow.

"I wanna see if any trace of her lingers."

"Of who?"

"Of Katy Lucca. How many women have fainted in your arms lately?" Not finding any scent, he released the arm.

"Sorry. She must have forgotten to perfume her spine. The next time we get together I'll bawl her out for that."

"Make it so," George said, and began trudging back to the bar with Donovan following.

As he approached, Jake stood and hoisted a bottle of light beer in a toast.

"To my friend, Errol Flynn. Or is it Clark Gable?"

"I thought you weren't drinking these days," Donovan said.

"I started again after watching the eleven o'clock news and seeing the most gorgeous woman in the world—"

Marcy looked up.

"—present company excluded—in your arms."

Marcy looked back down at her fledgling menu.

"I'm glad I could bring some light to your life," Donovan said. "Evening, Richard."

"Bill," Marlowe said, barely taking his eyes off the *New York Magazine* crossword.

"You want a drink, Bill?" George asked.

"Yeah. Kaliber, thanks."

George reached over the bar, produced a bottle of the nonalcoholic brew, and handed it to Donovan, who twisted off the top and took a sip.

"Good evening, Marcy," he said, with exaggerated formality.

She didn't look up, but said: "Donovan. You always loved the grand gesture. You outdid yourself this time."

"The woman fainted on me. What was I supposed to do, drop her on the floor?"

"It might have been nice. Did you come here to gloat about your achievement?"

"I came for a drink. It's been a long day."

"You know, most men who turn fifty fantasize getting themselves a mermaid or a red sports car. You couldn't be like most men."

"Hey, don't blame me. Blame whoever killed Lucca. What's that slogan they paint on the side of police cars in L.A.? 'To serve and to protect'? That's what I do for a living. Can we change the subject?"

"Gladly. —Look, you have pretty good taste in food. What do you think of this? It's my tentative lunch menu."

"Go ahead."

"Appetizers: Kentucky nachos."

"*Kentucky* nachos? What makes them Kentucky?"

"Never mind. Buffalo chicken wings."

"That's expected."

"And: Texas egg rolls."

"Uh..."

"Fried chili peppers stuffed with beef or chicken. You'd love them. Also: Fried mozzarella sticks. Chicken fingers. Barbecued baby back ribs. Fried potato skins. Cheese or chili fries. Guacamole and chips."

Donovan said, "I see that the age of health food is over. And not a moment too soon, too. I was getting sick to death of having a total cholesterol count of 180."

"Donovan."

"Make sure you put loads of salt on all that fat. It'll be a smash hit."

"You're on thin ice with me after that performance on the news. Shut up."

"The appetizers sound great. What about the entrées?"

"Tex-Mex burger."

"Let me guess: chili, sour cream, and fried onions."

"*Grilled* onions. Kentucky barbecue burger."

"Kentucky again. Is there a connection between the nachos and the burger?"

"Chili," George said.

"Also on the entrée list is Kentucky beef and vegetarian chili."

"As an entrée?"

"The platter is big. Continuing: Chicken club sandwich. Rib eye steak. Barbecued chicken. Roast beef on French bread. Texas cheese steak. Grilled swordfish. Salmon filet. Broccoli quiche. Marcy's Broadway Chicken."

"What's that?"

"Grilled chicken with melted Monterey jack cheese, bacon bits, onions, and chili."

"What makes it Broadway?"

"My saying so," Marcy said, closing the menu and yawning. "So what do you think?"

"It's good but needs work."

"Like what?"

"Like you missed the obvious: Kentucky fried chicken."

"The name was taken."

"How about a salad?"

"I'm working on one."

"A pasta dish."

"That too."

"Whose pasta recipe are you using?" Donovan asked.

"Mine," both Marcy and George said simultaneously.

"Use his," Donovan said, taking another sip of beer and putting the bottle down on the bar.

"Dono*van*," she growled, twisting the last syllable of his name as if it were a wet rag in need of wringing out.

Donovan yawned, following her earlier example, and looked around the restaurant. The place didn't look at all like the bar it used to be. There were no video games or pinball machines; there was no smell of beer and tobacco; no football pools were posted on the walls; no brightly colored signs announced drink specials. There was just a handful of small, round tables, overlooked by a brick wall and a painting of a stagecoach. Donovan experienced a sudden burst of nostalgia for the old barroom.

"I know what this place needs," Donovan said.

"What?" Marcy asked suspiciously.

"A tree," he said, a look of gleeful recollection in his eyes.

SIXTEEN

A FRIGHTENED LITTLE GIRL IN THE NIGHT

"YES," JAKE SAID HAPPILY, giving Donovan a high five.

"I'll go get my chain saw," said George.

"Am I missing something?" Marcy asked.

"It happened in this place eight or ten years ago, during one of those episodes when the owners were looking for something that would raise it above the level of neighborhood bar. There were several such phases. They tried new gimmicks all the time and never lost their reputation as being a corner bar."

"Maybe because you guys were the only ones who would go in here and you scared away the upscale crowd," Marcy said.

"We were proud of that," Jake said.

"Well, George was under pressure to come up with a gimmick. He was sitting here drinking one day trying to imagine what would give the place a lift. He had recently refurbished the ceiling." Donovan pointed up at the twenty-four-foot stamped-copper ceiling. "And he'd put in ceiling fans, but that did no good. No one ever looked up from their beers."

"So I was looking out the window one day and admiring the new trees that the city had planted in the middle of Broadway," George said.

Broadway ran the length of Manhattan, and on the Upper West Side it was a four-lane road the uptown and downtown stretches of which were separated by a mall containing trees, shrubs, and "islands" of stone benches occupied, mainly, by hoboes and old ladies.

"My eyes fell upon a stripling maple that was twenty-four feet high—perfect for the new copper ceiling."

Donovan continued: "The chain saw came out of the trunk of his car and ten minutes later the tree was propped up inside the bar, the topmost branches just touching the ceiling."

"You just walked out into the middle of Broadway with a chain saw, took down a tree, and brought it into the bar, and nobody stopped you?''

''Would you stop a six-foot, four-inch drunk carrying a chain saw?'' Donovan asked.

She nodded in mute acceptance of the logic.

''I might ask what you were doing with a chain saw in Manhattan, but I suppose that would be missing the point.''

''Hey, we used to get some pretty rough customers in here. That's why I invited the cops to drink free. The rest, as they say, is history.''

Donovan said, ''So George wired the tree in place against the wall between the kitchen door and the pool table. This was a tree in the full bloom of spring with a full complement of leaves. George's plan was to wait for the leaves to fall down, then make the tree permanent by affixing new, never-to-die plastic leaves. He went out and bought a hundred bucks' worth of them.''

''They were having a sale on plastic leaves over at Meyer the Buyer on Amsterdam,'' George said.

''In an admirable display of interior decorating and bravado, George climbed on a ladder and wired up six plastic leaves, first pulling off six real ones. Then he got tired and went back to his beer, leaving the box of plastic leaves on the floor next to the tree, where it remained.''

''For about a year and a half,'' Jake added.

''The original plans called for an autumn tree-decorating party where everyone would wire up plastic leaves after the real ones fell.''

''We saw this as being, you know, a thing to do at halftime of a Jets or Giants game.''

''At the same time, the Broadway Tree Conservancy was running around trying to find out what happened to its maple. No one there had the sense or the courage to wander into Riley's to look for it. So the tree stood where it was wired. The leaves never fell. Spring turned to summer. Autumn turned to winter. Another spring happened. Every other leaf north of the Mason-Dixon line did the expected thing and fell; not the leaves of this tree. A barfull of drunks sat there watching and waiting for the leaves to fall. They never did. Occasionally someone would get especially drunk and offer to wire up another plastic leaf, but by then George had lost interest, so he discouraged it. I think, also, that it had become a mighty struggle between the tree and him."

"I wasn't gonna give that fucking tree new leaves until it gave up the old ones," George said defiantly.

"After a while, George began acting as though he had no idea how the tree got there. Or he pretended he didn't see it. Remember that this thing took up fully one quarter of the room."

"A guy would come in for a drink and ask, 'Where'd you get the tree?'" Jake related. "And George would say, 'What tree?'"

"What happened in the end?"

"I got sick of it after a year and a half, two years, and took the chain saw back out of the trunk of my car and vaporized it."

"When he hauled the pieces out on the sidewalk the leaves were still on the branches," Donovan said.

"I returned the thing to the Broadway mall. The Tree Conservancy never figured out who did it."

Marcy laughed. "All this used to go on in the place I bought and am planning to turn into a respectable restaurant? My God, no one will ever come in here. Donovan, how come you never told me how bad it got in Riley's?"

He finished his Kaliber and shrugged. "In those days I was trying to impress you."

"What happened?"

"I have to go home," he said, turning to go.

"Are you planning to pay for the beer?" Marcy asked.

"Oh, you expect me to *pay?* Times have changed more than I thought." He took three dollars out of his pocket and left it on the bar.

"See you guys tomorrow."

Jake said, amicably, "Good luck with catching Lucca's murderer."

"Thanks."

"Any suspects?" George asked.

Donovan shrugged; then an idea popped into his head and he tapped a finger atop Marlowe's long-labored-over crossword. The man looked up, scratched his white beard, and asked, "What's a nine-letter word for 'Roman catch basin?'"

"Impluvium," Donovan said, after counting it out on his fingers.

"Thank you," the man said brightly, and inked it in.

"Richard, a quick question."

"Anything for you."

"Do Muslims have tattoos?" Donovan asked.

"Absolutely not," Marlowe said emphatically.

"Not ever?"

"Not religious Muslims."

"What about a highly placed official of a Muslim fundamentalist group?"

"Out of the question," Marlowe said. "It would be as unthinkable as wearing gold."

"No gold either? I've seen Arabs with wedding rings."

"*Silver* ones. I've seen secular Egyptians wearing gold chains; these are the same guys who also drink. But religious Muslims consider nearly all adornments to be sacrilegious. Is this important?"

"Yeah, actually, I think so," Donovan said, patting his friend on the shoulder. As a prominent member of a Muslim fundamentalist group, Akbar should hardly be wearing a tattoo. Moreover, he wouldn't have *gone out of his way* to get the tattoo while en route to speak for his cause at the U.N. No, there had to be more to the tattoo story. Donovan recalled reading something about tattoos and the old Soviet Union a year, perhaps a year and a half earlier.

Unable to recall what it was, Donovan started to the door. But Marcy came out from behind the bar and chased him down.

"What?" he asked, when she caught him by the shoulder and spun him around. She was tired from working all day and half the night, but the old fire remained in her eyes. She had a look about her at certain times when there was weariness or anger inside her. At those moments she could go either way—start a fight or make love—often one followed by the other. Marcy had that look that night. If she and Donovan hadn't broken up on such an angry note, they would probably have followed this fiery attitude of hers into the nearest bed.

"What perfume does she wear?" she asked.

"Does who wear?"

"*Katy Lucca.* Am I the only one here?"

"I thought you didn't want to talk about her."

"I don't. I'm just asking."

"Opium."

"Opium? That's what you used to buy for me."

"That's what she wears," Donovan said.

"I hate you," Marcy snapped. "Get the hell out of my place."

DONOVAN LET the hot shower thunder over him, washing away the evening's frustrations. He toweled off while listening to a samba interpretation of "New York State of Mind" on the jazz station. Then he slipped on his cutoff jeans shorts and made a cup of tea and took it into the study, where the blueprint of the Silk Road exhibition was spread out over his desk.

What a maze it was, he thought. Although it looked as if you started at point A and emerged at point B, the actual exhibit was far from simple. For one thing, behind each country's section, in back of every bay window shaped exhibition case, was a separate studio/storeroom. Donovan was far from expert at reading blueprints, but it looked as if some of the studios were interconnected. So what appeared to be an arguably one-way path through the Treasure of the Silk Road might, in reality, be a whole lot more complicated. He would have to return the next day, when he was fresh, and have Bernie Metz walk him through every inch.

Donovan had had enough for one day. He rolled the blueprint back up, secured it with a large rubber band, and leaned the resultant paper tube against the old oak bookcase beside which he kept his desk. The tube began to roll to one side, so he moved it near the oversized books and propped it in between *The Times Atlas of the World* and *Dorland's Illustrated Medical Dictionary*. Then he switched off his desk lamp and left the study.

With the clearing weather had come a cold front, and the brisk, end-of-summer air puffed out the curtain alongside Donovan's bed. He turned down the covers and pulled off his shorts, then climbed under the sheet and pulled the comforter up to his chest.

He picked up the remote and tried television. It was nearly two in the morning by now, and nothing much was on that early on a Monday. Donovan wasn't interested in *Star Search, Comedy Showcase, Travel Update,* or *Superstars of Wrestling.* Neither was he up for the overseas headlines on CNN, or the "World Seniors Golf Challenge." One cable channel was showing the colorized version of *The Maltese Falcon,* but Donovan nixed that too; he knew the black-and-white original by heart.

He switched off the television and turned off the bedside lamp. The crescent moon was by then low enough in the western sky to shine in the window. Filtered through the curtains, it cast a shimmering pattern of lace roses on the comforter and across the hardwood floor to the door. Donovan closed his eyes and gave himself to a succession of images from the day: the feel of Katy's hand on his arm, the look of her husband's body, the glint of the jewel-encrusted dagger, the smell of Mdivani's cigarettes, the crunch of rock salt beneath the feet in the museum courtyard.

As the pictures melted into one slowly moving impression of the day's events, Donovan drifted off to sleep and suddenly was jarred by the ringing of a bell. Where was that bell coming from? Donovan opened his eyes and realized that the sound was his own doorbell.

He lowered his feet to the floor and pulled his shorts back on, then checked the time on the clock radio. It was 2:11 a.m. "If this is Moskowitz, I'll kill him," he muttered to himself.

Donovan went to the door and, expecting his partner and preparing to kill him, hurled it open. "This better be good, or—"

"—or you'll kill me?" Katy Lucca said, looking up at Donovan with big, doe eyes that were stained red from crying.

The world's wealthiest and most beautiful widow looked, in that instant, like the most vulnerable. Her hair was mussed from having been tucked under a wig and her makeup was lined with tear marks. She wore a plain gray sweatsuit tucked into cowboy boots and partly hidden beneath a short, teal-colored jacket that Donovan recognized from the L. L. Bean catalogue. A brunette wig was jammed into a large, soft leather shoulder bag atop a lot of other stuff.

Donovan was astonished. "Mrs. Lucca! What are you doing here?"

"I can't be alone tonight. Please."

And with that she stepped into Donovan's open arms and snuggled her face against his neck. As his arms wrapped around her, Katy began to cry. "Don't you have family?"

Her words came between sobs: "My parents died when I was a baby. They left me alone. I can't stand to be alone. I get scared in the night. Now it's happened again."

"Friends?" Donovan asked.

"Not in New York."

"Servants?"

"Only one here, and it's not the same thing. May I come in?"

She pulled back from him then, and Donovan's hands moved from her back to her shoulders. She dabbed at her eyes with a handkerchief, which she then handed to him.

"I brought this back."

"Thank you."

"You tried to make me smile before."

"Laughter can help. I know. When my father died I was starved for it."

"Please let me come in."

"It's not a good idea."

"Why not?"

"Because it isn't. We're here alone. You're in shock from the death of your husband and I'm investigating his murder. Trust me, it just doesn't look good."

"Why did you give me your home address, then?"

She brushed her hair away from her face and tried to compose herself. She wasn't doing an especially good job.

"I don't know," he replied in embarrassment. "I guess I thought it would help. Knowing there was somebody out there on your side."

"It helped. Please, William. No one saw me leave the apartment. No one will know I'm here. Let me stay here tonight."

She looked into his eyes with her hurt-doe look and he melted. He took her hands and pulled her into the apartment, closing and locking the door after looking in both directions down the hall.

There goes the captain's badge, he thought. *If Pilcrow gets wind of this, there goes my whole career. I guess I'll always be a loose cannon, like they say.*

"There's a daybed in my study," he said.

"I can't be alone tonight, I knew you'd understand. You had a feeling about me, didn't you? That's why you gave me your address."

"A feeling?"

"That despite all you've heard I'm just a scared little girl."

He put his arm around her and steered her down the hall to his study. She felt tiny and timid beneath his strong right arm as he led her into the study and flicked on the desk lamp. It cast long, angular shadows onto the day bed, which was covered with a Santa

Fe Indian blanket and sat between two more bookcases. Above it, with blues and yellows that matched the blanket, hung a print of Magritte's *On the Threshold of Liberty*.

Donovan sat her on the bed and fluffed up two throw pillows. "When I get tired from reading I sometimes fall asleep here. It's more comfortable than it looks."

Katy looked around the room, scanning the four bookcases, the computer, and the rack of software and compact-disk databases. "You read a lot," she said.

"It's kind of a hobby."

"Your apartment is big and warm, like your heart." She yawned, covering her mouth with the back of her hand.

"I'm going to get a shirt. Can I make you some tea?"

"No. You've done enough. I'm really tired."

"I'll be right back."

"Wait. Forget the shirt."

She reached into her shoulder bag and plucked from it a large white T-shirt that bore the logo of the Silk Road exhibition. "I brought this for you," she said, handing it to him. "Paolo had a boxful of them to give out. I got you an extra-large."

"Thanks," he said, admiring the camel and rider before slipping the T-shirt over his head. "I always wanted to ride a camel into the sunset."

"You did?"

"No, not really."

She curled her legs onto the bed and propped herself up on the pillows. Donovan took her bag and put it on the floor, next to his desk. As he did so the wig fell out. He held it for a moment, looking at the curly black hair. It reminded him of Marcy's hair, and that struck him as funny.

"I like it," he said.

"It's my best one. I go everywhere in it."

"You really can walk around the city unrecognized?"

"Funny, isn't it? To test myself, I once walked in to the offices of *People* magazine and bought a back issue with a photo of Steven and me on the cover. Nobody had the slightest clue it was me, and I've been on half a dozen covers. They've had photographers following me around the Mediterranean, but once I'm in the black wig and sweatpants I could be anyone. God, I'm tired."

She put her head down on the pillows and closed her eyes.

"I heard there was a horde of reporters outside your building tonight."

"There's a basement exit no one knows about."

"I'll get you a comforter."

"No, really, I'm warm and you've done enough. And I swear I'll make it so you don't get in trouble for being good to me."

"Don't worry. A certain amount of weirdness is in my job description. I always land on my feet."

"That's a talent I wish I had."

"I think you do."

She laughed bitterly. "Maybe. I have money now, and money makes everything possible, doesn't it?"

"I've heard that."

"William, if anyone tries to make trouble for you because you took pity on a poor widow, I'll pay them to stop. I learned how to do that from my husband. He said, 'If you have enough money you can make any problem go away.' Steven told me that once, too."

"Maybe they're right," Donovan said.

He got up and went to switch off the light.

"Leave it on," she said. "When I was a little girl and afraid of the dark I slept with the lights on."

"The nearest bathroom is through that door," he said, pointing to the one on the street side of the room. "I'm just down the hall to the left if you need anything. I make a mean breakfast, but you can sleep late if you like."

"Tomorrow *I* make breakfast for *you*."

"Okay. Good night."

"Come here," she said, reaching up to him.

Donovan leaned over and accepted a kiss on the cheek.

"Thank you so much," she said.

He left her then, closing the door halfway.

He returned to his bedroom and got back under the covers. Sleep would be hard to come by, so he switched on the table radio to the classical music station and turned the volume low. The announcer promised Fauré's *Ballade for Piano and Orchestra*. Donovan closed his eyes and watched a whole new succession of images, beginning with the sensation of her kiss on his cheek.

Imagine being able to buy anything you want, even your future, he thought. The rich do live differently. Ten or fifteen minutes passed. The Fauré had given way to Debussy's *En Bateau*. Donovan heard a rustling in the hall. He opened his eyes as the comforter moved down and Katy slipped under it and nestled next to him, absorbing his warmth.

"Just hold me," she said.

Katy was curled into a ball, her back to him. Donovan rolled towards her and slipped an arm over her and pulled her to him.

"I get so frightened when I'm alone in the night," she said.

After a short while, they both fell asleep.

SEVENTEEN

WHOEVER DIES FIRST

"WE SHARED SOMETHING last night," Katy said, stirring her coffee. Just-showered and wrapped in Donovan's white terry-cloth robe, her hair wet and straight and parted down the middle, she looked even more anonymous than she had at his door. The sparkle, the allure, the smile—these things were still far from her. She had changed from the night before, though; she was more controlled. Donovan ate the western omelet that she made for him while he was shaving and dressing. He watched as she stirred her coffee carefully, holding the spoon by its very tip and swirling the coffee first clockwise, then counterclockwise.

She continued: "What I mean is, when we first met and flirted with each other, we meant one thing to each other. We were attracted to one another and were having fun. Harmless fun, like men and women do. Nothing would have come of it, probably."

"No," Donovan agreed. "Nothing would have come of it."

"Then that awful thing happened: Paolo was killed and you were there with me when I heard the news. That man Berman came at me with a knife—or seemed to—and you stopped him. You saved me. Then I collapsed and you saved me again."

"Morty was as much in shock as you were. He wasn't attacking you."

"That was what it seemed like."

"And I only caught you when you fell. It wasn't like—"

"You saved me," she said firmly.

"Whatever."

"Then you sensed my fear and gave me your address. You offered yourself to me as my protector."

"It's what policemen do."

"Please stop diminishing what you have come to mean to me. You reached out to me and I owe you a lot."

"You gave me a shirt and made me breakfast. Consider the debt paid."

Katy looked up from her coffee cup and caught a glimpse of herself reflected in the toaster.

"God, I look a mess," she said, pushing her wet hair off her cheek.

"Now who's diminishing herself? I'm glad to help and flattered that you turned to me."

"Is there someone in your life who my being here will upset?" Katy asked.

"No. Not a soul."

"Your ex?"

"Nope. That's over."

"And I certainly am alone...again." She forced a smile, then shook her head and sipped fitfully at the coffee. "What's your schedule today?"

"I should get to my office soon. If I don't, the phone will start ringing off the hook. And you?"

"Paolo and I had an agreement. When he learned that... Well, whoever dies has the other cremated within twenty-four hours and the ashes scattered in the nearest sea. Paolo was a great sailor. Did you know that he financed the Italian entry in the last Whitbread Race?"

Donovan knew.

"When he died he wanted to be returned to the sea before the mourners began to gather."

"I understand. I want a Viking funeral myself. Put me in a rowboat, set me on fire, and push me out in the Hudson. What mourners do you mean?"

"The CEOs of his corporations. The lawyers representing his many interests. His brother."

"There's a brother?"

"Tommaso. I called him with the news. He's coming in from Paris on the Concorde to represent the Lucca family at the service."

"You have a service arranged already?"

"No, but it's the first thing I'll do. Surely some funeral parlor can arrange such a thing on short notice. We'll have it at seven or eight tonight."

"I'll see if I can get the body released."

The word *body* seemed to make her flinch. She said, "Oh. You mean..."

"There will be an autopsy. It may even have been done already. A necessary formality."

Katy looked down into her cup for a while, then back at him. She shrugged. "I guess, if you have to. Look, William...you *will* be there?"

"At the service? If you want me to."

"I insist on it. You were there when he died. You must help me bury him."

"If you like."

"The service will be very small and very private. I'll make sure the press doesn't find out."

"Isn't it going to be hard on you, doing all this?"

"I won't do it personally. Those men you threw out of the museum office last night? They're Paolo's personal assistants. I guess now they're mine. They can arrange anything. I just have to say the word."

"I knew a man like that once," Donovan said. "He fixed things up. You told him, 'Get me a camel,' and the only question he had was 'One hump or two?'"

Katy smiled, reached across the table, and squeezed Donovan's hand. "You're a very special man," she said. "Thanks for trying to cheer me up."

He got up and put his plate in the sink. Then he poured himself another cup of coffee. He said, "While you're drying your hair and getting dressed I'll do some work in my study. There are some things I want to check. When you're ready I'll drive you home— or to wherever is the secret entrance to Clark Tower."

"I'll show it to you."

"That information may come in handy someday. Look, use the

bath that's through my bedroom. It's more private there, and I need to get to my desk.''

"How big *is* this apartment? I didn't get the chance to look around."

"Three bedrooms, three baths. Living room, dining room, kitchen. Just your basic, old, West Side, rent-controlled monster. I'd invite you to use the gym, but we have to get going."

"I remember you said you work out at home. Do you still watch Woody Allen movies?"

"Uh, yeah. I still do that too. Sometimes I watch his movies back-to-back with Roman Polanski's. If you want to get a real hot glimpse of what L.A. is like, watch *Chinatown* together with *Annie Hall*."

Katy smiled. He reached over and lifted her chin so she looked straight into his eyes. And he said, "You have to do that more often."

"I'll try. You'll help me."

"I don't have a blow dryer, so I don't know what you're going to do about your hair."

"I brought my own," she said, hefting her bag as she rose from the chair.

Donovan went into the study and a few minutes later heard the distantly familiar sound of a blow dryer coming from his bathroom. He hadn't heard it since Marcy stormed out six months ago. It was a sound he'd never thought he would come to miss.

Katy had put the throw pillows back neatly in their places and smoothed the Indian blanket. He sat down at his desk and reached for the blueprint, which was still leaning against the bookcase. Donovan was about to pick it up when he noticed the difference: It was propped up between the *Times Atlas* and the 1993–1994 edition of *Jane's Infantry Weapons*. But Donovan clearly recalled propping the rolled blueprint up on the other side of the atlas, between it and *Dorland's Illustrated Medical Dictionary*. He had always been proud of his peripheral vision—both the actual, visual sense and the ability to recognize tiny discrepancies. Donovan distinctly recalled having left the blueprint standing between his two biggest books, the atlas and *Dorland's*.

Donovan looked in the direction of the blow-dryer noise. *She's been snooping around,* he thought. He recalled the fifteen-or twenty-minute period when she was alone in the study with the light on. In that time she could have opened the blueprint and looked at it, maybe even changed it somehow. *How could I be so stupid?* he thought. *I'm taking her home and that's the end of it.*

He snatched up the silver Mark Cross pen given him at the party celebrating his thirtieth anniversary on the force, and secured it partly up his sleeve, well hidden. Whistling, he made his way back into the bedroom.

The blow dryer was still on. He lingered outside the partly open bathroom door and called out, "Mrs. Lucca, are you decent?"

The dryer went off.

"What?"

"Are you dressed?"

"Yes."

He stepped inside to find her combing out her hair, the ledge behind his sink suddenly filled, once again, with small colored bottles.

"The stuff that a woman carries around with her," he said, bending over her bag, which sat on the floor next to the toilet.

"What's the matter?"

"I think we had an accident."

He plunged his arm into her bag and began taking items out and depositing them atop the toilet seat. Out came the wig, a beige Victoria's Secret bra and panties, a folded pair of Calvin Klein jeans, a striped rugby shirt, a Filofax, a bottle of Opium, a bottle of Prozac, and a tube of Ultra Concentrated Emergencee Polymeric Hair Reinforcer.

"Hey, I was looking for that," she said, snatching the hair stuff away from him.

The last item he took out was her scallop-shaped diaphragm case. "You forgot your compact too," he said, with a sly grin.

She blushed. "I haven't used this bag in a while and forgot that was in there. What are you looking for?"

"Found it," Donovan said triumphantly, holding up his Mark Cross pen.

"How did that get there?"

"It must have rolled off my desk and fallen into your bag last night," he said, standing and shoveling her possessions back into it.

"You're a good detective," she said, turning back to the mirror and her hair.

Back in his study, Donovan felt perplexed. He had found nothing in Katy's bag to suggest that she'd messed with the blueprint. Maybe it fell down on its own and she put it back up, but in the wrong place. Maybe she only looked to see what it was. But maybe she didn't touch it at all. It might be his memory that was at fault, though he considered that unlikely. At any rate, he felt like an idiot.

"What am I getting myself into with this woman?" he muttered to himself as he spread out the blueprint. His momentary resolve to have no more to do with her was gone. It had been replaced by intense curiosity. Donovan considered going along with her, just long enough to find out what was on her mind. Coming to his apartment the night before was unusual. Snooping around his study—if that was what she had been doing—was extraordinary. Maybe it was just that Donovan, by most counts a pretty regular guy, found it hard to believe that Katy Lucca would be curling up in his bed without one whopper of an ulterior motive.

It's been six months since I've been with a woman, and look who shows up in my bed, Donovan thought. I have to see where this road is taking me.

THE SECRET ENTRANCE to Clark Tower turned out to be in a small commercial building next door, on the side away from Fifth Avenue. A Szechuan Chinese restaurant shared a six-story brick building with an office-supply wholesaler. A maintenance tunnel connected the lobby with the first basement of the tower. Donovan pondered out loud the frequency of links between prominent Manhattan towers and Chinese restaurants. A decade or two back he had been taken through the dank and twisting tunnel that linked the *New York Times* Building with the Sun Luck West Chinese restaurant on Forty-fourth Street.

"There is an inevitable connection between the richness of Manhattan life and egg rolls," he said before dropping Katy off, getting one final smile out of her before saying good-bye for the day.

Donovan drove up Madison Avenue for a few blocks, stopping near Fifty-sixth Street to run into a high-priced tobacconist's and purchase a pack of Sherman's cigarettes. When he came out, a yellow cab with a crumpled right front fender was double-parked alongside him, the driver also off in the tobacco shop. Donovan might have hassled the man, but was tickled to find a young white cabdriver who was thoughtful enough to wave his newly purchased cigar and yell that he was sorry. The cab pulled away, stopping down the block to pick up a fare.

Donovan drove the two or three miles between midtown and the Upper West Side in twenty minutes, taking the Seventy-second Street transverse past the RollerBladers, hansom cab ride takers, and street musicians who frequented that part of Central Park, near Bethesda Fountain. He turned north on Central Park West and cruised past the museum, noting with satisfaction the continued presence of NYPD roper-offers and evidence-pickers and with chagrin the arrival of new TV crews. Morty Berman was among the newscasters on hand. Cleaned up and looking as busy as a ferret, he was taping a report while holding a copy of the *Daily News*. He showed the camera the front page, which carried the fateful picture of Donovan, Katy, and him, along with the banner headline MURDER AT THE MUSE.

Donovan slowed down, honked the horn long enough to get Berman's attention, then waved and sped off. He got as far as the corner of Eighty-first when something that had been nagging at his subconscious all night came roaring to the forefront. Donovan jammed on the brakes and, after nearly getting rear-ended by a yellow cab with a crumpled right front fender, made a hard left onto the side street. Donovan whipped down the block and soon was pulling into the museum parking lot.

A few minutes later he was standing in the same courtyard where he'd stood, thinking of Steven Clark, cigarettes, and Galileo, the night before. This time, though, what was on Donovan's mind was rock salt—bags and bags of it. There was a connection, he realized, between the rock salt in the museum courtyard and the blueprint in his apartment. A man with good peripheral vision sees when something is out of place.

Bonaci was tired and bleary-eyed from having pulled an all-nighter. So when Donovan showed up unexpected and unannounced, the crime-scene boss was at once upset at having nothing new to report and grateful that his double shift was over.

"We found nothing here, Lieutenant," he said. "There are twenty windows that a guy could use to gain access to the exhibit and kill Lucca, but none of the ones we've looked at so far have been opened recently. Sorry."

"How closely did you look?" Donovan asked. "Let me show you something."

Bonaci led the way to one of the windows and, requisitioning an immense flashlight from a crime-scene technician, lit up detail on various parts of the black wrought-iron gate. It was sturdy, although hardly strong enough to serve at Fort Knox. Two horizontal bars an inch wide by half an inch thick supported five vertical struts of equivalent dimensions but with decorative arrowheads on top and bottom. The entire apparatus was hinged on the left and locked on the right with a padlock.

Donovan peered over Bonaci's shoulder as he ran the flashlight over the gate.

"It doesn't look like it's been opened," Donovan said.

"This gate hasn't been open in a year," Bonaci said.

"Did you check the hinges to see if the rust has been moved around?" Donovan asked.

"Yeah," Bonaci said wearily.

"Did you check the lock to see if a key has disturbed the soot, dust, and other grime that things tend to accumulate in New York City airshafts?"

"There's so much soot in that keyhole a boll weevil couldn't get his dick in it," Bonaci said, dissolving into a yawn.

"Has the window been opened even if the gate wasn't?" Donovan asked.

"We didn't check."

"Why not?"

"Who cares? If the gate stayed closed, no one went in or out of the window."

Donovan said, "*I* care, because if the window has been opened recently it tells us that someone has been using it for ventilation, which means that someone sits on the inside of it."

"And?"

"And he or she might have seen something of value to this investigation," Donovan said. "Have you been getting enough sleep lately?"

"Not last night," Bonaci said.

"I want you to check inside every window that might be opened on this courtyard to see what's on the other side and who might be using it. Then I want you to talk to them. Okay, Howard?"

"Sure, boss," Bonaci said, yawning again.

"Go lie down for an hour or two and I'll catch you later in the day. Before you go, how many windows did you say there are?"

"Twenty. We've taken close looks at five. Maybe if you can think of some way to narrow them down..."

"That's why I dropped in on you," Donovan said. "I was thinking of rock salt."

"There's lots here," Bonaci said, sweeping his arm along the rows of sixteen-pound bags that were stacked two deep against the wall. The stacks went up to the windowsills and down the wall for between forty and fifty feet.

Donovan stood back and surveyed them, and right away saw clearly what had stuck in his peripheral vision the night before. One man—or a group of men acting on one man's specific instructions—had stacked the bags so that the fat ends alternated. The bottom bag had the flat end against the wall. The one atop it had the narrow end against the wall. The pattern continued to the top of the pile. In that way, the pile was even and could reach the window sills without toppling. Seen from the side, the rows of bags was symmetrical—with an exception.

Halfway down the wall, just below the eleventh window, there was a break in the symmetry. In that spot and in that spot only, the bags were stacked haphazardly. They looked as if they had been pulled from their neat perches and, some time later, replaced in a hurry and without regard to their original order. The pile was wobbly-looking at that point. Donovan walked to it, crouching a few paces away to inspect the ground. Bonaci followed.

"See where the salt and dirt on the ground were displaced?" Donovan asked.

Bonaci crouched and looked at the ground, his eyes widening. "It looks like someone dragged these bottom two bags away from the wall," he said.

"And pulled off the other ones, too," Donovan said.

"And put them back in a different order," Bonaci said. "Like a guy would do if he was in a hurry."

Bonaci trained his flashlight on the gate. It was old, like all the gates nearby, but the cylinder in the lock gleamed as if recently installed. "See that?" Donovan asked.

"I see it," Bonaci replied. He aimed the beam of light on the window itself. The frame was painted industrial brown. The two simple panes were glass sandwiches enclosing quarter-inch mesh wire. A layer of dirt on the sill had scrape marks in it, as if something—a pants leg, perhaps—had been dragged over it. The dirt was vintage New York and ran right up to the bottom rail. A layer of fine silt—the gray-brown of a million unscrubbed city window surfaces—looked as if it hadn't been touched in years. Except where something had been dragged through it. And *that* inadvertently cleaned spot was very new.

"Someone was in this window last night," Donovan said. "I wonder what's on the other side."

"A storeroom, probably."

"We can ask Bernie Metz," Donovan said.

"The guy that Mosko was talking to? Did he find the blueprint?"

"He found it. Maybe he also knows ways in and out of this building. Maybe I really won't have to coax Murph the Surf out of retirement to show me how to do it."

"Hey, is he still alive?"

"So I'm not the only one old enough to remember him? I'm relieved."

"Sure, I remember that guy. I read the book and saw the movie. When I was a kid I wanted to be a jewel thief like him. You know, a real second-story man like the suave cat burglars that were supposed to have worked the Riviera."

"That's a tough fantasy to maintain living in a walkup on Carmine Street," Donovan said.

"No shit. And I was afraid of heights anyway, so I became a cop, figuring that if I walked a beat it would be hard to fall down and break my neck."

"You always were a sensible man," Donovan said.

Bonaci stood and sighed. "I'm sorry about not finding this window myself, Lieutenant," he said. "I promise I'll get the whole story on it for you."

THE WEST SIDE Major Crimes Unit occupied the second floor of an old two-story building on the west side of Broadway between Eighty-seventh and Eighty-eighth streets. Sharing the second floor was a gym that Donovan had used until it went upscale and color-coordinated outfits and soft rock chased out the serious exercisers. Sharing the block were a sporting-goods shop, a Chinese restaurant, a candy store that fronted for a numbers parlor, an army surplus store, and Marcy's Home Cooking. Donovan parked in the alley out back and walked up the flight of stairs, the blueprint tucked under his arm.

The unit's squad room was square and jammed with gray metal desks decorated with computers and potted plants. The walls had the usual assortment of bulletin boards, posters, and blackboards upon which were kept often-used phone numbers. The only live decoration, however, was the goldfish atop Michelle Paglia's reception desk. She was giving her pet a pinch of fish flakes when Donovan walked in and every man and woman in the unit rose in a standing ovation.

"Lieutenant!" she exclaimed. "You're in every paper. You're a celebrity."

"And this time I didn't shoot myself in the foot," he said, waving to the assembled.

"Every reporter in town wants to talk to you."

"Tell them I'm out. Tell them politely, of course."

"Yes, sir."

When the men and women settled back down, Detective Sergeant Corrigan came up and asked, "So what's it like to have your arm around the most beautiful woman in the world?"

"It straightened my arthritis right out," Donovan replied, playing at rubbing his arm where Katy had fallen on it.

"I'll bet it limbered up *all* your joints," Corrigan replied.

"Enough of that. The poor woman is a widow. Find Moskowitz and send him into my office."

"I think he's in the can, spiffing up."

"Say what?"

"You're gonna love this."

Donovan got a cup of decaf from the coffee station and carried it into his office. The pile of phone messages was indeed formidable. He pushed it to one side and removed his calendar and pencil holder to clear the desktop enough to spread the blueprints out. That he did, anchoring the paper with the telephone, the pencil holder, the calendar, and his gun. When Moskowitz arrived ten minutes later, Donovan had been over the layout of the exhibit once.

"Yo, Lieutenant, check this out."

Donovan looked up to see his aide sporting a navy blue wool suit that fit as well as could be expected taking into account the man's narrow waist and oversized chest and shoulders. A red-and-blue striped tie and handkerchief completed the ensemble.

"Outrageous," Donovan said. "I didn't know Herman's World of Sporting Goods carried a line of men's suits."

"Is this cool, or what?"

"You look spiffy."

"Spiffy schmiffy. I look *great*."

"What news from the front?"

Mosko pressed some buttons on his notebook computer. "The autopsy was done early this morning."

"Who did it?"

"Dr. Lifshitz handled it personally. The preliminary results are this: Lucca died of a single stab wound that penetrated the heart."

"A *single* stab?"

"Yes, sir. One and only one."

"Our killer was sure of himself."

"Well, yes and no. You see, after embedding the knife in the victim's right ventricle, he must have taken off. The cause of death was penetrating trauma to the heart setting off massive hemorrhage. Death came from cardiac tamponade: blood filled the pericardium and the resultant pressure stopped the pump, so to speak. Lucca lived thirty seconds, maybe a minute."

"Even if there was a doctor in the house, he couldn't have done anything," Donovan said.

"Not even a whole surgical team could have done much."

"Anything else?"

"Yeah, Lucca showed torn capillaries in his right shoulder, indicating that the killer may have grabbed hold of him."

"With the left hand."

"While stabbing him with the right."

"We have a right-handed killer," Donovan said. "What about time of death?"

"Considering that we knew the approximate time range and taking into account what you reported—normal temperature and no lividity—Lucca died about when you thought. The doctor says between nine-ten and nine-twenty."

"Nine-fifteen it is."

"Further refinement of the time of death awaits the results of the"—Mosko studied his notepad more closely—"of the examination of the vitreous humor. Now, Lieutenant, you know the old saying? You go to an Irishman to find a bartender. You go to a Jew to find a doctor.''

"Mmf," Donovan grunted.

"Well, you're pushing the limits of my medical knowledge on this one. I know that the vitreous humor is in the eye."

"The ratio of potassium to sodium in it changes gradually after death," Donovan said.

"Is that so? You'll have the results ASAP."

"It won't change anything, but it's nice to know when science backs up an old detective's observations." He switched on the TV and VCR that sat on a shelf across the room from his desk, plugged in a tape, then went to his chair and leaned back in it, picking up his coffee. Phil's tape rolled silently. The first part of it had been shot outside the museum, as celebrities (including Donovan) were walking up the red carpet. Donovan watched as the TV lights glistened off his widening forehead, and smiled to see Akbar dressed in full formal evening regalia, including white gloves and walking stick. Later in the tape, the close-ups of Lucca's body and the blood that soaked his shirt and the floor were real enough for Donovan to imagine he smelled the death.

"Has there been a sighting of my bow tie?" Donovan asked after a moment.

"Definitely. The blood on it is O positive."

"And Lucca's blood is...?"

"B negative."

"And the blood on the dagger is..."

"Likewise."

"And the blood on Morty's clothes?"

"Ditto."

"Am I to assume that the only O-positive blood that turned up last night was in and around Steven Clark?"

"Yeah. And furthermore, no B-negative blood was found anywhere near Clark. Of course, we only have your bow tie and a few splatters around the fire escape and on the floor of that studio to go by. Too bad his lawyers wouldn't let us take the tux. All in all, though, I would say that the hematological evidence lets Clark off the hook."

"Just the same, run DNA profiles of his blood and keep them on file. Do the same for Lucca's blood."

"It's already being taken care of."

"How long before I get it?"

"Uh, tomorrow maybe."

"There's something else, too," Donovan said, and proceeded to fill in Moskowitz on what he had found at the museum.

"It's too bad we don't have Clark's pants so we can look for dirt stains that match the dirt on that windowsill," Mosko said.

"Call Clark's office and ask again for the clothes the man wore last night," Donovan said. "Tell him to think what happened to Nixon after *he* withheld evidence. We can pick the tux up when we talk to him this afternoon."

"We should have gotten his clothes last night the way we did Berman's. But Clark cut himself and had more lawyers than doctors at the hospital."

"Yeah, so he did," Donovan said. "Convenient, wasn't it?"

Donovan switched off the videotape just at the point where the cameraman finished panning around the whole scene—the Oasis Diorama, the body, and the hallway disappearing into the Treasure of the Silk Road exhibit.

"Berman didn't kill Lucca. The pattern of blood on his hands is all wrong. He has no possible motive, either. And, you know, I don't see how *anybody* could have killed Lucca without being seen." Donovan took out a yellow legal pad and drew a large horseshoe on it. Then he drew a stick figure next to the horseshoe's left foot.

"Whazzat?" Mosko asked, bending over.

"Lucca's body as it lay near the entrance to the exhibit. After taking a quick look at the blueprint, I fail to see how anybody but the guys nearest him could have done it."

"And they are?"

"Morty Berman and whoever was bringing up the rear in that parade of VIPs. What you and I have to do is sit down now and figure out where everyone was—or says he was—at nine-fifteen last night."

"Let's do it. So you looked at the blueprint last night?"

"That's one of the things I did," Donovan replied.

EIGHTEEN

LOITERING IN BABYLON

"HOW DID IT GO at Marcy's?" Mosko asked, pulling up a chair.

"Good."

"Are you guys getting along these days?"

"She didn't try to punch me out."

"That sounds like an improvement. How's her menu coming?"

"Like gangbusters. It's full of salt and fat. You'll love it."

"Dynamite. I tell you, you've got to come with me to Roll-N-Roaster someday for cheese fries."

"I don't need to drive all the way to Brooklyn to make myself sick. The mere thought of the borough does that for me."

"That's not fair. Look, you said that with the money Pilcrow promised you I can get some toys."

"What do you have in mind?"

Mosko reached into his shoulder bag and produced a cellular phone. "I can carry this in my bag along with my notebook computer. I can run the modem through the cellular line to upload and download files. That way we can be in the field and still be hooked up to the office. We can get info anywhere—even at Roll-N-Roaster when we go for cheese fries."

"You bought the phone already?"

"Nah. This one's a loaner from my uncle Stanley."

"Your uncle sells gym supplies *and* cellular phones?"

"The man can get anything. So if you give me the go-ahead, he'll put the purchase order through."

"I assume he's giving you a good price."

"Hey, this is me you're talking to. Only schmucks pay retail."

"Remember that we're still a city agency. You have to get three bids and document them."

"Yeah, yeah, yeah. I got it covered."

"Well, fine. Only promise me one thing. I have a deep suspicion of people who flaunt their cellular phones. If you ever see me sitting in a restaurant or on a bus or walking down the street talking on the phone I want you to drag me into an alley and shoot me.''

''Same as if I catch you wearing spandex at your age, huh? Okay, it's a deal,'' Mosko said. ''Let's look at the blueprint.''

Donovan switched the coffee mug to his left hand, then plucked a pencil from the holder and used it as a pointer. ''Here's where Lucca's body was found,'' he said, tapping the pencil near the left foot of the horseshoe. ''If you step inside the exhibit the first thing you see is the display on the Levant.''

''Do they have stuff from Israel?''

''A few things, yes. The exhibition brochure mentions the Tel Dan Fragment.''

''The what?''

''A stone tablet from the ninth century B.C. with Aramaic writing that includes a mention of the House of David. It's the first mention of him found outside the Bible. So maybe King David was a real person.''

''Cool.''

''I'm glad you're into this,'' Donovan said. ''Anyway, the brochure says the exhibition starts out with a display on Tyre, near where Polo set out on his journey. That's just a tablet's throw from Galilee. I doubt that any of our suspects remained in that area of the exhibit, though, because it's right at the beginning.''

''Anyone who did might have been waiting there to ambush Lucca. Lebanon is a good place for that sort of thing.''

''Did anyone own up to it?'' Donovan asked.

''Not a soul.''

''Okay. Moving halfway up the left leg of the horseshoe, we pass through Syria/Assyria and then Iraq/Mesopotamia. That's easy killing distance from where Lucca was found. Anyone say they were peering at the Babylonian Diorama at nine-fifteen?''

''Yeah...Jameson.''

Donovan was surprised. He hadn't expected anyone to say that. ''Mrs. Lucca's first husband? That's as far as he got down the Silk Road? In twenty minutes or so he only walked fifty feet?''

''That was it. When I asked him what was so fascinating about Babylon, he didn't have an answer for me. The guy is a little flaky, boss. Nervous, like. Jittery. My gut reaction is that he was hanging out there hoping Mrs. Lucca would walk by.''

"What, he can't reach her by ordinary means so he has to ambush her at her husband's exhibit? He doesn't have her address?"

Donovan felt the testosterone coursing through his veins, making him hot under the collar.

"You let your subscription to *People* lapse," Mosko said. "Her full-time address is in the Aegean Sea, on a Greek island called Rodi. And I don't think she needs the alimony."

"Rhodes," Donovan said, a flood of romantic fantasy replacing the anger. "Fought over by Athens, Sparta, and Rome going back to the fourth century B.C. Held briefly by Alexander the Great. Home during the Crusades of the Knights Hospitalers of St. John of Jerusalem. Is that where the Lucca palace is?"

"Palace? Who said anything about a palace?"

"Well, why not? If I had a billion, I'd sure as hell have a palace. A nice cozy one, with a big dog and a roaring fire and lots of history."

"No moat?"

"Nah. I like people these days."

"I thought you didn't like people with *money.* I remember all the abuse you used to heap on Republicans and golfers. You hated 'the fancy people.'"

"That was my parents talking. I turned fifty, son. When that happens a man likes to think of things like comfort. Comfort and friends."

Mosko looked around to assure himself that no one was listening, then leaned into the lieutenant and said, in a loud stage whisper: "Take the captain's badge. You can save up and buy a palace in a few years."

"I just might do that," Donovan said, smiling.

"She doesn't have a palace," Mosko concluded. "According to *People,* it's a designer villa overlooking the harbor."

"Is that *all? I am* disappointed."

"The point being that when your ex-wife is living on a Greek isle, it makes it kind of hard to bump into her. Especially when you don't exactly have a job."

"Let's talk to Jameson and find out what the hell he was doing loitering in Babylon for twenty minutes. Where does he live?"

"In Joisey."

"Where in New Jersey?"

"West Ridge. It's fifteen minutes from the George Washington Bridge. You want me to make an appointment?"

"Yeah, for this morning. Will he be home?"

"If I ask him to be. Like I said, Jameson doesn't have a full-time job."

"What is he, on welfare?"

"He said he climbs trees and does other stuff for a landscaping company, but work is hard to get."

"Interesting. Guys who do that sort of thing have pretty good upper-body strength, I would think."

"Now that you mentioned it, Jameson does look in shape. I'll put a star next to his name on the suspect list."

"Put three stars," Donovan said. "He's strong, he's broke, and he misses his ex-wife, who has a billion in her bank account. Add to that the fact that he looked nervous at the exhibition. Both Mdivani and you noticed it. Put *four* stars next to his name. The guy is now highly ranked in the *Michelin Guide to Murder Suspects.*"

Donovan returned his attention to the blueprint. "Moving farther up the left leg of the horseshoe, we pass through Iran/Persia. Persia is where Berman was when Lucca was killed. On to Turkmenistan, land of sheep, goats, and a thousand oases much like the one in the exhibition's snazzy logo. Was anyone looking at it at nine-fifteen?"

"Yeah. Peter Vischer, the guy from Germany," Mosko said.

"Who is he, anyway?" Donovan asked.

"He told me he had his own company: Vischer Exploration, Hamburg."

"And what is that?" Donovan asked.

Mosko shrugged. "Something to do with archaeology?"

"Let's try to find out. I'll do a computer search and see what we get."

While Mosko went into the squad room to answer a phone call, Donovan powered up the Gateway 2000 P5-60 that sat by his desk. He logged on to the information superhighway, finding the computer database that bragged of an ability to locate and make available anything that had been recently published in the English language about a given subject. Donovan began a search for Vischer and the company that bore his name.

Donovan remembered Akbar's tattoo and how hard he was trying to cover it up. Surely he had read something about the old Soviet Union and tattoos. It could be important. So Donovan began a key-word search in which he asked the computer to search for all newspaper or magazine articles that contained the words "Soviet Union" and "tattoo."

"I hope Pilcrow's largesse extends to paying for my online charges," Donovan grumbled as Mosko ambled back into the room.

"Bernie Metz is meeting us at the museum around noon," he said. "Bonaci is there too, with something he wants us to see. Clark, however, is being a bad boy."

"In what way?" Donovan asked.

"I called him before to ask again for his clothes…?"

"He sent them to the cleaners."

"He had them *burned*. According to his secretary, there was blood all over them from the cut on his hand."

"Oh *man*, we should have just ripped them off his back last night," Donovan said.

"Pilcrow would have had your ass," Mosko said.

"I should have taken the chance."

"Furthermore, Clark is *not* going to meet you at four. He's 'much too upset by Paolo Lucca's tragic death and needs time to recover.'"

Donovan said, "Clark is stonewalling. You're not old enough to remember Watergate, are you?"

"I was just a little kid," Mosko protested.

"The White House tapes that incriminated Nixon? There was all this wrangling over whether or not Nixon would have to turn them over to investigators? Well, William F. Buckley wrote later on that, if he were Nixon, he would have taken those tapes and made a bonfire on the White House lawn before turning them over."

"I guess Clark reads William F. Buckley," Mosko said.

"No doubt he does," Donovan said. Returning his attention to the blueprint, he traced his pencil from Turkmenistan to where the body had been found, and back. "Clark will never talk to us, so let's deal with the rest of the suspects. Vischer, for example, about whom we know too little. He probably could have run back through the exhibit, killed Lucca, and gotten back to Turkmenistan in time, but not without tripping over Berman and Jameson. You see, after we go down the Silk Road past Jameson, all these guys are like pearls on a chain—they alibi each other.''

Mosko nodded.

Donovan continued: "Let's track them all anyway. Moving east into Pamiristan, we encounter next Professor Kent, who was eye-balling the lost city of Chandar which, it occurs to me, I probably will never get to see.''

"Maybe you can sneak a peek today.''

"Now, the Pamiristan section is by far the biggest in the exhibition. Look at the size of it on the blueprint. It takes up the whole top part of the horseshoe. Lemovin and Mdivani were there too, I understand, and Kent was behind them.''

Donovan moved the pencil halfway down the right leg of the horseshoe until he reached the section marked for the Uzbekistan display. "This is where Akbar said he was at nine-fifteen—staring at the display on Samarkand, a principal city.''

"Akbar was the first in line?''

"Yeah. Everyone else was behind him.''

"It occurs to me...''

"I see it, too. Jameson was a stone's throw up the left leg from the entrance. Akbar was the same distance up the right leg from the exit. The entrance and exit are pretty close to each other, so...''

"Akbar could have gotten to Lucca without any of the others seeing him,'' Mosko said.

"We think that Lucca stayed pretty close to the entrance,'' Donovan said. "He sent the VIPs down the Silk Road by themselves, saying he had to wait for someone. Now, who could that be?''

Mosko shrugged.

"Clark split off from the rest and went for a smoke. The VIPs walked through the exhibit and, as they did so, they spread out. At the moment of Lucca's murder, it looks as if Clark was on the fire escape and both Jameson and Akbar would have been able to get at Lucca undetected—Jameson, by trotting back from Babylon; Akbar, by scooting through the China display and out the exit and a couple of yards down the main hall to the entrance and the oasis diorama.''

"Both Akbar and Jameson have solid motives,'' Mosko said.

"But who the hell was Lucca going to meet?''

"Whoever it was, the man killed him. Maybe Mrs. Lucca knows.''

"I asked her," Donovan said. "She doesn't."

"Are you going to see her again?" Mosko asked, waggling his eyebrows much as Groucho Marx had when pondering a hot babe.

"It may happen. I also wouldn't mind seeing Clark again. It's unknown how much power I have over him, but we know exactly where he was, don't we?"

"Let's see if Bonaci found anything to change our opinions."

Donovan set down his coffee cup and bent over the blueprint, tracing a finger up and down the line of the Silk Road. The Buzghashi Studio, through which Clark had passed in search of a place to smoke, was on the right leg of the exhibition, rather toward the exit. Its door opened into the exhibition space right next to the Buzghashi Diorama, which displayed the bloody game.

"Look at these studios," Donovan said. "Each one services a particular country—sometimes a single diorama. You get into the Buzghashi Diorama by way of a door from the studio. These fancy display cases are like department-store windows."

Moskowitz bent over the blueprint until his tie fell on it. Tossing the end of the tie over his shoulder, he said: "A lot of these studios are interconnected, too. Look, you can go from that studio into this little area here...what's that thing with the crossed lines?"

"A service elevator. That's what 'svce. el.' means."

"And from that area into a studio behind the China part of the exhibit, including the Buzghashi diorama."

"They're all connected," Donovan said. "You can go from one to the other, moving behind all the dioramas without anyone on the outside being the wiser."

"I know what you're thinking. One of the suspects could have snuck up on Lucca from behind. Look, there's a door right near where Berman found the body. It leads behind the Oasis Diorama. But I checked last night—all of those doors leading from the studios to the exhibit were locked."

"With the exception of the one where we found Clark," Donovan noted.

"Yeah, that one was open. But Clark was locked out on the fire escape, so what difference does it make?"

"The fire escape leads down to the basement, which is where the service elevator goes. And look..." Donovan pointed out two more service elevators, one in the center of the horseshoe and another in the left leg. "Both these service elevators emerge in studios behind the Phoenician and Lebanese dioramas."

"Close enough to Lucca to reach out and touch him."

"With a dagger," Donovan said triumphantly. "It's a possibility—Clark could have faked smoking, gone down that fire escape, in through a window, and up the service elevator that comes out near the studio servicing the Oasis Diorama."

Mosko added, with equal glee: "Then he could've jumped out that door, surprised Lucca where he was waiting for his mystery meeting, stabbed him, and retraced his steps."

"There's a problem," Donovan said.

"Only one?"

"How did the murderer—whoever he is—get the dagger out of the safe in Kent's office on the fifth floor?"

"Oh," Mosko said, his considerable shoulders slumping.

"You see, Akbar or Jameson had easy access to Lucca. But Clark, with his proximity to the service elevators, was better able to get to the dagger."

"But Clark didn't have the combination to the safe," Mosko protested.

"See if you can find out how honest that locksmith really is."

"I'll run a computer check on his name," Mosko said, getting up and heading back into the squad room.

Prompted on the subject of computer searches, Donovan returned his attention to his Gateway. The computer searches had borne fruit: Vischer had indeed been a man in the news. Moreover, the computer had found a newspaper article that contained the words "Soviet Union" and "tattoo." Two computer files—a thick one on Vischer and a slender one on tattoos—were ready to be downloaded. Donovan did so without looking at the material, loading the documents onto a floppy disk that he then slipped into his pocket.

When Mosko returned to announce that a search for a criminal record on the locksmith would be delayed due to down time at One Police Plaza, Donovan switched off the VCR and stretched. "I just have to figure out who could have gotten to Lucca when," he said, picking up his Smith & Wesson and stuffing it back in its holster.

NINETEEN

TO TOUCH HER LIFE AGAIN

WEST RIDGE was a small, tree-lined town in northern New Jersey, less than a forty-minute drive from the West Side of Manhattan. It had a three-block-long main street filled with gift and candy shops, boutiques, small restaurants, takeout chicken and Chinese places, and a bagel shop. A red-brick train station sat alongside the rail line that took commuters to Hoboken, there to transfer to the PATH subway for the ride to Manhattan. A town green was centered around a gazebo bandshell in which were held Sunday-afternoon concerts.

"I thought all of Jersey was oil refineries and chemical plants," Mosko said.

"Come on. They don't call it the Garden State for no reason."

"I thought that was kind of a joke. I like this town, Lieutenant. It reminds me of Canarsie."

"Nothing in Brooklyn is as nice as this," Donovan said.

"Brooklyn Heights is as nice as this," Mosko argued.

"You know what Brooklyn Heights is? San Francisco without the hills. It's cute and brownstony and hygienic and filled with gays. I'll take West Ridge, New Jersey, any day. It reminds me of the town on Long Island where my aunt and mother live. I think I'll retire here. I talked to this guy last year who had been on one of these small-town PDs for three years and was pulling down sixty grand."

"You're a Big Apple lifer."

"I thought I'd never leave the West Side for a captain's badge, either," Donovan said, turning his car into the driveway of a red-brick and white-shingled house on a small, carefully landscaped plot near the end of a dead-end street within walking distance of town. "If we get time today I want to run into Brooks Brothers and order some suits."

Mosko was aghast. "Moe Ginsburg," he said.

"Who?"

"You don't buy suits anywhere but at Moe Ginsburg on Fifth Avenue down by the Flatiron Building. Lieutenant, you can't help being a goy but you don't have to be a schmuck."

"I yield to you on this matter," Donovan said.

There was a mulberry tree in front and a willow in back. Donovan pulled to the end of the driveway and stopped just before a two-car garage the doors of which were open, revealing a small, aluminum boat on a makeshift trailer in one bay and a decrepit Oldsmobile up on cinder blocks in the other. The car listed slightly to one side and was pockmarked all around with spots where dents had left the metal bare to rust out. The left front turning signal was patched up with tape.

"This guy could use an infusion of cash," Donovan said as he spotted Jameson. The young man was pushing a lawn mower, wearing old jeans worn through at the knees, well-seasoned sneakers, and a T-shirt that bore the name of the Pascack Valley Tree Service. His sandy hair was long and unwashed. Between the roar of the motor and whatever was playing on his Walkman, Jameson failed to notice the arrival of guests.

"I think I know where this guy is coming from," Donovan said. "On Long Island where my family lives these days, the main industry is digging clams and scallops."

"I think I ate a couple once. The fried clams are incredible at Randazzo's."

"Surprise me. This place is in Brooklyn, right?"

"Yeah. Down the block from Roll-N-Roaster. How'd you know?"

"A wild guess. Anyway, when the clamming and scalloping is bad—I think at the moment there's a red or a brown tide or something killing all the shellfish—the local hippie clamdiggers go on welfare and spend all their time getting high, listening to rock and roll, and getting into fights over pool games at the corner bar."

"There *was* a bar on the corner, now that you mention it."

"Half of them lost their driver's licenses for operating a vehicle under the influence, so they walk to the bar and otherwise hang out picking up odd jobs here and there. It's funny: there are no cars in the lot, but fifty guys in the bar. And they all look like this one—a stoner who stays in shape."

"There aren't any clams in the Pascack Valley," Mosko said.

"No, but there are lots of nice houses with landscaped yards. I'll bet that working for landscaping companies is what the Bergen County hippies do in lieu of digging clams. When times are bad in the tree trade they listen to their Walkmans and smoke dope."

"I'll run Jameson's license plate to see if you're right," Mosko said, taking his computer out of his bag and pressing some keys. "This way I can also see if I can access the unit's computer through my cellular modem."

"O brave new world, that has such gizmos in it," Donovan said.

It was late in the season for lawn mowing. Jameson was taking advantage of the first sunlight in the New York area in three days. The grass hadn't dried thoroughly, though, and when the mower scattered the blades many stuck to Jameson's ankles.

"I have trouble connecting this guy with the woman I met last night," Donovan said.

"Lots of people have humble roots, boss," Mosko said. "Marilyn Monroe married some local schlub when she was a kid. But which of her husbands do people remember? Arthur Miller and Joe DiMaggio."

"Let's go say hello." Donovan got out of the car, slamming the door loud enough to be heard despite the music and the lawn mower.

Jameson turned around to see Donovan's gold badge flashing from his palm as the lieutenant and his aide walked across the lawn. The young man cut the engine and slipped the earphones down around his neck.

"What are you listening to?" Donovan asked.

"Uh...the Lemonheads. Do you know them?" Donovan detected on his breath the faint perfume of marijuana.

"Who are they?"

"They're sort of a punky sixties rock band."

"Sorry, I like jazz and classical. I'm Lieutenant Donovan. I think you met Sergeant Moskowitz last night."

"Hi. Yeah, good morning, Sergeant. I dig the suit."

"Thanks. I dig the T-shirt. Is that the landscaping company you work for?"

"Right, when they need me. I may get a call to come in Wednesday."

"Does that give you enough money to pay for this place?" Donovan asked, looking at the small but well-maintained house.

"I only rent the ground floor, Lieutenant. All I need to work is two days a week to cover the rent. Do you want to come in?"

"Sure."

Jameson led the way in the back door and into the family room, wood-paneled with a high ceiling and a small, well-worn couch facing a nineteen-inch black-and-white television that stood atop two plastic milk crates. The rest of the room was dedicated to exercise equipment: a weight bench, a rack of free weights, a stationary bike, and a treadmill. The room also smelled of marijuana.

"Have a seat."

Donovan plunked himself down on the couch, but Mosko inspected the weights, especially the bar that was set up atop the chest-press bench.

"You press two hundred?" he asked.

"Yeah. That's about it for me. And you?"

"Three twenty."

"Did you always work out?" Donovan asked.

"Yeah. I started in high school and kept it up. Being in shape helps me get jobs."

"Did your wife work out, too?"

"Nah. Not her. She was naturally in shape." Jameson smiled sheepishly and looked down at the ratty red carpet on the floor. "What can I do for you officers?"

"Did you kill Lucca?" Donovan asked, his eyes bearing down on the young man.

"Did I...wow...Jesus, no. I mean, *no*. How could you ask me that?"

Stoned and grooving along with the Lemonheads when Donovan walked into his life, Jameson was now as nervous as he'd seemed the night before. Donovan would have sworn that the guy was yearning to light up.

"I opened my mouth and out it came. Where were you at nine-fifteen last night?"

"Is that when it happened?"

Donovan nodded.

"I...I guess I was looking at that same exhibit. I kind of got fixated on it."

"What exhibit?"

"On Babylon. On Lilith, that is."

"A biblical figure?" Mosko asked.

"A Babylonian deity who survived in Jewish lore," Donovan said. "According to the program, the Treasure of the Silk Road includes a clay relief of her discovered two summers ago and, I presume, bribed away from Saddam Hussein by the late Mr. Lucca."

"Yeah," Jameson concurred. "She was mentioned in 'The Epic of Gilgamesh.' It's an awesome document, Lieutenant. Did you know that it backs up the biblical story of the flood?"

"I didn't know that," Donovan said. Jameson's stoned delivery of the fact made the lieutenant embarrassed at having had the same thought when he was a youngster. "Look here, the ancient importance of Lilith is that she was the goddess who measured the length of a man's life. Did you go to the museum last night to take the measure of Lucca's?"

"Huh? Do you mean, did I go there to kill him? Hell no, I went there to get the money."

"What money?" Donovan asked.

"He told me he wanted to make things right with me. I assumed he intended to give me money. You see that I can use it."

Again Donovan was hearing about Lucca's planning on giving away money. There was something wrong with this picture.

Moskowitz's computer beeped; he glanced at the screen before showing it to Donovan. He turned back to Jameson and said, "Your license has been suspended three times for driving under the influence of drugs."

"Yeah, well, you got me on that. You wanna bust me for smoking marijuana? I had a joint before you drove up."

"No, it's not in my portfolio these days, and anyway I believe that smoking marijuana doesn't rank very high on the galactic scale of crime."

"In that case, do you want a few hits?" Jameson asked.

Mosko smiled. "No," Donovan said sharply. "Tell me when Lucca offered you money."

"Two weeks ago, maybe three."

"Exactly what did he say?"

Jameson summoned up a thought, then said, mimicking Lucca's Italian accent: "'Mr. Jameson. We have never met, but you know who I am. I want to say that Katy also wishes you well.' So at this point, I say, 'Yeah, sure. I wish the two of you well, too.'

He goes on, 'She tells me that you may need money. Well, don't ask me to explain more than to say that I am at that point in my life where I want to set things right with some people I may have hurt in the past.'"

Jameson paused, prompting Donovan to ask, "And you said what?"

"I told him, 'You never did anything to me.' And he said, 'Then Katy hurt you. Katy and me: same thing. So, here is what I would ask you to do. Come to the opening of my exhibition at the American Museum of Natural History in New York City on Sunday, September thirteenth. You will receive an invitation in the mail, and I will send a car to pick you up. I understand there is a problem with your driver's license.'"

"How did he know that?" Mosko asked. "From Katy?"

"No way. I was a straight arrow when we were together, and we haven't talked since the divorce. You figure it out. Anyway, Lucca said, 'You and the others will have a tour of the exhibit, have dinner, then we will all go back to my apartment and talk. It will be well worth your while. Believe me, Mr. Jameson, it is important to me: I want to wipe the slate clean.' That's it, Lieutenant. That's all he said."

"Wow," Mosko replied. "He wanted to *wipe the slate clean?* What the hell does that mean?"

"Make up for old wrongs, I guess, but like I told him, I don't hold it against him about Katy."

"Do you hold it against *her?*" Donovan asked.

"No, not really. I mean, I was pretty pissed off at her for leaving me, but that was four years ago and I got over it."

"Did you?"

"Yeah...not at first, though. Think about it. She left me for a better meal ticket. When Clark ran low on cash she left him for Lucca. You might say, 'Is there no end to this woman's ambition?' And it was pretty rough, being Katy Jameson's...Katy Lucca's...ex old man. I took a lot of kidding."

"I can imagine," Donovan said.

"You were lucky you don't live in Brooklyn," Mosko added.

"So are lots of people," Donovan quipped.

"I could hear them thinking, 'See that guy in the dirty clothes working on the rich people's yards? He used to be married to Katy Lucca, but she left him and now she owns half the world.' I can't imagine what's next for her now that she's got all his bread. Move to Hollywood and go after Robert Redford, I guess.''

"I think he's taken.''

"As if that would stop her. Hell, maybe she'll come back to me. Now that she's seen the top of society maybe she'll go back to her roots at the bottom.''

"Maybe,'' Donovan said.

"She needs a guy, you know. Some women just need a man around the house, someone to lean on, and she's one. Katy won't stay by herself for long. There will be someone else. I guarantee it.''

"So after she left you turned on and tuned out, so to speak.''

"Exactly. I'm glad somebody understands.''

"I understand more than you could possibly imagine,'' Donovan said, thinking of his father's funeral and of Scotch.

"To finish the story, I'm in the head where now I don't mind so much. I kind of like it, in fact—I like the attention. It's not so bad; hell, how many men have done what I have—been with Katy?''

"Not too many.''

"You know, we were a hot item at West Ridge High. Wally and Katy, the cutest couple in town. Everyone said we were going places. She wanted to be a model, so I worked two jobs to help her get her career started. We said, She makes it and we move to New York and jump into the fast-lane. Well, she made it to the fast lane and here I am, not even able to drive.''

"I wouldn't have killed Lucca; I would have killed her,'' Mosko said.

"Not my style. Maybe it was for the best. I'm just a plain guy from a small town. A regular Joe, you might say. Katy was always too rich for my blood. But, you know, I miss her. When I accepted that invitation, sure, it was for the money. But I also wanted to see her. Hell, it's been years since I've even heard her voice.''

"Did you think you might get her back?'' Donovan asked.

Jameson laughed. "Are you asking did I dream about it, or are you asking if I really expected it to happen?''

"You dreamed about it but never thought it would happen.''

"Exactly. She's a very special person, Lieutenant. Got a magnetic quality you wouldn't believe. When you're with her you forget about everything else.''

"I can see that."

"You probably saw more of her last night than I did. Hell, I was happy just to hear her voice."

"How did it sound?" Donovan asked.

"Pretty much like Katy. Not as, I don't know, *alive,* maybe. She was preoccupied about something and didn't look *really* happy to see me. There wasn't time, either. What can you say in a receiving line? I got upset about her being cool to me—sure I did. So when I walked into the exhibit I didn't get very far."

"You stared at the clay relief of Lilith."

"She has nice boobs too," Jameson said, forcing a laugh.

"Did anyone else see you looking at Lilith at nine-fifteen?"

"The TV guy nearly knocked me over running toward the entrance. Other than him, nobody."

"Why did you think he was running?"

"There was a sound. Somebody cried out. *'Oh,'* you know, like that. Deeper, maybe. Then there was the sound of a man running away and then some moaning. That's all I heard."

"This running. It was definitely coming from the direction of the entrance?"

Jameson nodded. "I'm sure it was the...what's that word cops use? The perp?"

"I try not to use that one myself, but I hear it a lot. How long did this running last?"

"Two or three seconds. Then it disappeared...like the guy turned a corner. And then the TV reporter started toward the sounds."

"Why didn't you run after him?"

"If it was a woman screaming I would have figured Katy was in trouble and I would have run like hell. But it was a man's voice and I thought, 'Jesus, am I out of my element in this crowd!'"

"I know that feeling, too," Donovan said. "Was there anyone else behind you? I mean, between you and the entrance?"

"Nope. Just me, and then Berman ran past. I froze. I'm sorry, Lieutenant. Could I have done something to help?"

"Not a thing."

"That's something to be thankful for, I guess."

"So you have no idea how much Lucca planned to give you?"

"Not a clue. He only said he would make it worth my while. I assumed he was talking about money. Wait a second: I want to show you something."

Jameson went into another room and returned a few minutes later carrying a handful of papers. He shuffled through them and handed one to Donovan. It was a photocopy of a clipping from *USA Today*. The headline read: ITALIAN BILLIONAIRE TURNS PHILANTHROPIST.

Donovan read a fragment of text: "'Dashing Veronese billionaire Paolo Lucca, owner of a global manufacturing, shipping, and media empire, surprised the philanthropic world when he announced the formation of a $500 million charitable foundation designed to ease poverty in the Middle East and parts of Asia and the former Soviet Union.' When did this story appear?"

"Last week."

"When I was spending every spare minute reading up on the Silk Road." Donovan sighed. "No wonder I didn't know."

Mosko looked over his shoulder and, reading on, said, "Here's also why you don't know: 'Initial reaction to the story was to dismiss it as a publicity stunt connected with the upcoming opening of Lucca's Treasure of the Silk Road archaeological exhibit in New York City.'"

"So the story probably never made it into the *Times* and I never read it. I must reevaluate my reading habits. Do you think it's true?"

"How should I know?" Jameson asked. "But after getting that call from Lucca, I figured it was worth my time to find out. Besides, I was getting a free limo ride and the chance to see Katy again. Would those reasons have been enough for you?"

"Yes," Donovan said. Again he had the feeling that there was something wrong with Lucca suddenly making this Scrooge-like transformation into a philanthropist. Jameson quoted him as saying "I am at that point in my life where I want to set things right." What point was that? Donovan wondered. The *USA Today* reporter had apparently shared the skepticism.

Jameson sat on the seat of his exercise bicycle. "I guess I'm a pretty good suspect," he said.

Donovan thought for a moment, then said, "You were a better one an hour ago. While you're not entirely off the hook, let me say that I'm intrigued by this clean-slate business and want to look into it further."

Jameson let out a loud sigh and his shoulders slumped in relief. Looking down at the ratty red carpet, he said, "It's kind of a horror story: Katy Lucca's ex—the dope-smoking ne'er-do-well from New Jersey—gets blamed for the murder of her celebrity husband. Do you see how easy that could happen?" Donovan nodded.

"In the real world, Lucca would never give me money and she would never come back to me. So I'm not too upset: The best I could hope for is what I got last night." He looked up again and Donovan could see the mist in his eyes.

"And what was that?"

"I got to touch her life again for a moment," Jameson said.

Once Mosko and he were on their way back to the city, the sergeant asked, "What clean-slate business were you talking about back there?"

"Lucca suddenly turning into Mr. Generosity."

"Yeah, now that you mention it."

"Call Dr. Lifshitz and ask him to answer one question for me."

"What's that?" Mosko asked.

"At the opening Lucca looked thinner and paler than I imagined him," Donovan said. "When I first caught a glimpse of the guy I dissed him for looking like a fashion model. Now I want the pathologist to tell me if Lucca was dying of anything at the time of his murder."

TWENTY

SMOKING AS A DYING ART

THE LATE-MORNING AIR was notable for a strong breeze that swept in off Central Park and swirled around the heavy stone gothic courtyard of the museum. The wind riffled through Donovan's hair, blowing strands down and tickling his ears. It also made it nearly impossible for him to light a cigarette.

"I thought I would be pretty good at this, living as I do on Riverside Drive, the wind capital of Manhattan, but I guess I'm not." Donovan said those words as he pitched his sixth match in a row over the edge of the cast-iron fire escape on which Clark stood the night before.

"Turning your back on the wind does no good," Mosko said. "It only whips around you and puts the flame out. You got to face straight into the wind, strike the match, touch it to the head of the cigarette, and inhale fast before the tip of the match burns down."

Donovan tried it. He struck a match and raced it to the head of the cigarette, the wind smacking him straight in the face. He inhaled a mouthful of acrid chemical smoke.

"Ack," he swore.

"Of course, that way you got to deal with a mouthful of sulfur."

"You do it," Donovan said, pushing the pack of Sherman's at his assistant.

"No fuckin' way. I care more about my body than to put smoke in it."

"Oh, but cheese fries are great." Donovan tried again and, three attempts later, successfully lit his fourth cigarette in the twenty minutes they had been standing there. He smoked it down, taking care not to inhale the smoke, and when he had finally gotten it to about the point where Clark smoked his, pitched it over the side.

Mosko and he bent over the rail to watch where it went.

"Where'd it land?" Mosko asked.

"In Nebraska, I think. I can't see it anywhere."

"Maybe we should try this when there's less wind."

"Maybe we should admit once and for all that smoking is a dying art. What we have to do is find a cop who smokes…"

"You only got yourself to blame. You hocked everyone in the unit and all of your friends until they got healthy. Now you're pissed off that you can't find a cop who smokes. Listen to me: Maybe if you didn't smoke them so far down they wouldn't always land in Nebraska."

"Can't do it. For one thing, Clark smoked them down. I have to be faithful to the scientific principles involved here. For another thing, the more cigarette the more windage. It would blow even farther from the target than my four did."

Donovan slipped the pack back in his pocket.

"Maybe Clark used a butane lighter," Mosko said helpfully.

"Damn. I forgot about lighters. That would make the cigarette easier to light, I think. Do lighters blow out in the wind?"

"I should know?"

"But that still wouldn't get the butts any nearer the target. No, I'm afraid this experiment is a bust. Galileo's reputation is in no danger from me. I don't see how Clark managed to drop them all in a three-foot circle from this height, but in the absence of contradictory information I must assume it was possible. Did you call Dr. Lifshiftz and ask him to check out that hunch for me?"

"Yeah. He said he's nearly done with round two of the autopsy and will call us back." Mosko patted his cellular phone, which was fast becoming the envy of the West Side Major Crimes Unit. "I love this thing," he said.

They went back through the Buzghashi studio and out into the hall. The Silk Road exhibit was as empty as it had been the night before, having been cleared of anyone and everyone so Donovan could conduct yet another experiment. Now, in the China display, he hung a right and began walking slowly counterclockwise along the Silk Road—moving, as it were, from East to West.

"Is Bonaci in place?" he asked.

"Yeah. Just give the word."

"Tell me when we get to where each of our suspects was standing at nine-fifteen."

"None of 'em were in China. Akbar was in Uzbekistan. We'll be there in a minute."

"When this case is over and before the public is let in I plan to come back here and go through it, nice and slow."

"By yourself?"

"I was thinking of bringing a girl."

"Anyone in particular?"

"Maybe. I met someone. I'll let you know if anything comes of it."

"Well, *this* is interesting. Keep me informed. So listen, I get the impression you think that Jameson is innocent."

"He spun a pretty good yarn, more convincing even than Mdivani."

"I've noticed that you like those down-home, plain-folks types, the ones with blue collars and dirt under their nails, and tend to believe them before you'd believe someone like Steven Clark."

"Am I that shallow?"

"Transparent."

"So because I like Jameson, I think he's telling the truth. He's the odd man out in our group of suspects. All the rest are relatively high-powered people, truly VIPs: a corporate president, a couple of diplomats, a distinguished professor, a visitor from Germany with a two-hundred-dollar haircut, and a TV journalist.''

"And a terrorist.''

"I was lumping Akbar in with the diplomats. We have no evidence he's other than that.''

"Mdivani told you he's a terrorist.''

"Didn't Menachim Begin have a death sentence on his head from the British at one point and then go on to become prime minister of Israel? Success breeds respectability. When your side wins, the first thing you do is shred the wanted posters. The second thing is fill out the form that comes in the mail from *Who's Who.*''

They reached the Uzbekistan exhibit. Mosko halted his boss by tapping the back of his hand against Donovan's chest and then pointing up at a spanking-new closed-circuit security camera mounted at the juncture of wall and ceiling. It pointed "west" along the Silk Road, picking up, first of all, an Uzbek diorama that included a thousand-year-old, primitive cannon used by Mongol troops against those of the Chinese Sung dynasty emperor shortly after the first millennium.

"That's one of the two cameras that were online by last night,'' Mosko said. "This one near the exit faces 'west' down the Silk Road. Another closer to the entrance faces 'east.' Bonaci played back the tapes, which are time-stamped.''

"What did he find?''

"Akbar was where he said he was, looking at Samarkand in Uzbekistan, starting at nine-ten. But he wandered out of the frame at nine-thirteen, heading toward Kazakhstan.''

"A man's watch can be off by two minutes,'' Donovan said. "Is there any indication where he went?''

"Nope.''

"So he could have run out the exit, stabbed Lucca, and run back.''

"It's possible.''

"Where's the other camera, exactly?''

"In the Iranian display, pointing toward Turkmenistan.''

"Is anyone on it?''

"Yep: Berman. He's right there in the foreground, obsessing on the ayatollah or whatever, until nine-seventeen, when he hears the sound and runs toward it.''

"Unless I'm wrong, these tapes alibi everyone but Jameson and Akbar. And Clark, of course. But he was trapped out on the fire escape."

Mosko agreed. "The rest of them are links in a chain that's stretched between the two cameras. This case is like murder on a railroad train, Lieutenant. If you know what the guys at the ends are doing you know about the rest of the suspects."

"Akbar or Jameson could have run to Lucca, stabbed him, and run back," Donovan said.

"In Jameson's case it would have been more like a stroll. He was that close. I wouldn't be so quick to write him off as a suspect. If you must eliminate someone, eliminate Clark."

Donovan asked, "Has Bonaci found any way Clark could have entered through a courtyard window and gotten to Lucca by way of a service elevator?"

"He's still looking." Mosko consulted his watch, looked around in annoyance, and asked, "Where the hell is Metz?"

"What time were we supposed to meet him?"

"Noon. It's quarter after."

Mosko led the way a bit farther into the Uzbek display, stopping finally before a diorama that depicted the ancient city of Samarkand. "This is where Akbar was standing at approximately nine-fifteen," Mosko said.

"Call Bonaci and have him give a shout," Donovan said.

Mosko got Bonaci on the other end of a walkie-talkie link and said, "Make like you've been stabbed."

A tinny "oh" came over the walkie-talkie.

"With the transmit button off," Mosko said, irritated.

"Louder," Donovan said, cocking his head in the direction of the exit.

"Again. Louder," Mosko transmitted.

Still there was no sound.

"Have him holler as loud as he can."

Mosko repeated the message, but still there was nothing.

"I can't hear a damn thing," Donovan said. "Lucca could have been trampled by a herd of wild boars and Akbar wouldn't have been aware of it."

"So it seems." Mosko got back on the radio and said, "That was great, Howard. We couldn't hear a thing. Are you sure you were yelling."

"Like a wild boar," Bonaci radioed back.

"We're moving on to where Lemovin and Mdivani were standing and we'll try it again."

"I'll be here. But I think you guys ought to see what I found."

"My ideas first," Donovan said. "Then his."

There was a clicking off to one side then, and Donovan whirled around to see a door pop open next to the Samarkand Diorama. Funny; he hadn't been aware there was a door. It was discreetly labeled "Samarkand Studio."

"What are you doing?" Bernie Metz asked, stepping out of yet another studio filled with artists' supplies and easels. The red-haired diorama artist had traded his lumberjack shirt for a School of Visual Arts T-shirt.

"Glad you could make it, Bernie. We're trying to establish if any of our suspects could hear Lucca cry out. What's in that room?"

"Stuff that didn't make it into the Samarkand diorama. There's more than enough for *two* exhibits, Lieutenant. You know the story: The Uzbek khans who took Samarkand as their capital got fabulously wealthy through the caravan trade. They built golden palaces and mosques and gardens and kept their wealth for centuries, until the British, French, Dutch, and Spanish started shipping things by sea."

"At which point Chandar was sacked by pirates and buried by nature, and it and the rest of Central Asia slipped back into being a good place to herd goats. It looks like Lucca brought back a lot of hidden treasures," Donovan said, glancing at several gleaming golden relics from the Secret Shrine of Bukhari.

"The man was a wonder," Metz agreed, closing and locking the door behind him. "I'm sorry I'm late. I'm working on a new background painting for the Samarkand Diorama. Lucca felt that it was too impersonal. He adhered to the old museum-artist tradition of painting your friends into the backgrounds of dioramas—making them natives, you know—as a way of personalizing the displays."

"Did he?" Donovan said.

"So—what can I do for you?"

"Are all these doors locked?"

"Yeah, like I said last night. Every single one of them. I saw to it myself."

"But not the door to the Buzghashi Studio."

"Where Clark went for his smoke? No, not that one."

"Why wasn't it locked?"

Metz laughed, and said, "Because Lucca asked me to keep it open."

"Why?"

"So Clark could go outside for a smoke, of course."

"Of course."

"The man was going to be cooped up in here for a few hours, Lieutenant. You know how smokers are. And Lucca said there was another man who might be smoking—one of the envoys from Pamiristan."

"Mdivani. But he's not too particular about obeying the anti-smoking laws. He has diplomatic immunity."

"Lucca was trying to be accommodating. He wanted everyone to be happy."

"So the Buzghashi Studio was the boys' smoking lounge," Donovan said.

"It's been done before. It's the only room in this wing with access to a fire escape, to a terrace of sorts where you can light up. Kent used to slip out there from time to time, when he couldn't get away with smoking in his office."

"Were there any other special rooms that I don't know about?"

"Other than the cloakroom and Kent's office, you mean?"

"What cloakroom?" Donovan asked.

"Down the hall from Kent's office. Where the VIPs left their outer garments."

"Why didn't you think of that?" Donovan asked Mosko.

The man shrugged, but made a note on the screen of his notebook computer.

"What was special about Kent's office—other than that he was trying to clean out his desk?"

"That was the Luccas' dressing room," Metz said. "It's where Mrs. Lucca prettied herself up before the reception. She carries a ton of cosmetics and other stuff around with her."

"Does she? I hadn't noticed. So that's why the bodyguards carried her back there after she fainted. Well, I was wondering about that. It makes sense. Kent's office was Mission Control, sort of."

"And Lucca felt better knowing that Kublai Khan's dagger was in the safe, too. He liked being near it."

"He got as close as it's possible to be last night," Donovan said.

The three men walked "west" along the Silk Road until they entered the Pamiristan section. At the spot where Lemovin and Mdivani had estimated they were at nine-fifteen, Mosko and Bonaci repeated their earlier experiment. Not a sound was audible there either, so the trio continued west through the exhibit. At the spot that had been occupied by Kent, farther west in the mammoth Pamiristan exhibit, Bonaci's voice couldn't be heard at all. Where Vischer stood in the Turkmenistan exhibit, Bonaci was audible only when he was shouting as loudly as he could. And even then he was barely audible; certainly, Donovan felt, Lucca's dying voice would never have been heard over the low background rumbling caused by the huge crowd in the Rotunda.

But where Berman stood in the Iranian exhibit, Bonaci's emulation of a man's dying shout was clearly heard. At Jameson's reported spot, the cry was actually alarming, resonating as it did off the crystalline structure of the exhibition cases.

"Jameson told me he heard Lucca cry out," Donovan noted. "But Jameson also heard the sound of someone running away. Let's try that. Is Bonaci up to a couple of wind sprints?"

"After all that pasta? You got to be kidding. I'll ask him, though."

Moskowitz was right about Bonaci's physical condition; a young detective did the footwork. As Donovan, Moskowitz, and Metz listened, the young man started near where the body was found and sprinted off in all the directions that Donovan thought likely.

Right away there was a problem. Anyone running *away from* the spot where Lucca was found couldn't be heard at all by Donovan or the others. And Jameson had definitely said "running away from."

"Jameson said the killer ran away for two or three seconds and then turned a corner," Donovan noted, looking west down the Silk Road through the Phoenician-Syrian exhibit and toward the entrance. "I see only one way that could have happened."

"How?" Metz asked, elevating his uplifted palms.

"Like this," Donovan said, leading the way through the Syrian space to the lip of the Lebanese. He stopped alongside the Phoenician Diorama, which offered a stunning tribute to the glories of the ancient capital—especially the fabulous garments made there from silk carried by caravan from the East. "Lucca is stabbed here. The killer knows that there are people farther into the exhibit— 'east' down the Silk Road—so he runs out the entrance and hangs a left. The entrance looks like a two- or three-second sprint from here."

"Why a left?" Mosko asked.

"There's nothing to the right but a dead end, and straight ahead is the curtain separating the exhibit from the Rotunda and a thousand witnesses. To the left is the Oasis Diorama and the exit from the exhibit."

"And Akbar," Mosko said.

"Yes. And Akbar. Get Bonaci and his leg man in here and have them run some trials from this spot. Let's check out all the possibilities that arise once we assume Lucca was stabbed in front of the Phoenician Diorama and not the Oasis Diorama."

Donovan went back to the spot where Jameson reported hearing the sounds. Ten minutes and a variety of sprints later, he returned to the group—Bonaci and the young detective had joined Moskowitz and Metz—clustered about the Phoenician Diorama.

"This is the place where it happened," Donovan announced.

"But Lieutenant," Metz asked, "Is it possible for a man to get stabbed in the heart and stagger a hundred feet or more before dying?"

"Suffering from cardiac tamponade, which Lucca was, and with the knife partly closing the wound, sure. I've heard of it happening."

"Without getting blood on the floor?" Mosko asked.

"Did we look this far from the body?" Donovan asked Bonaci, who shuffled his feet.

"We didn't, did we?" Mosko asked.

"Come on, guys... The body was *out there!* I was about to start looking for blood farther from it when you drafted me for your experiment in shouting and running. We'll look for blood here, now that we think maybe Lucca was stabbed here and not outside the entrance."

"It's not too late," Donovan said, glancing down at the floor. "There may be a drop or two, and after all, we know the genotype.

If there's a molecule of Lucca's blood on this floor, we can magnify it using PCR and identify it. But I could be wrong; Lucca could have been stabbed where we found him, and Jameson was mistaken or lying.''

"Jameson was telling the truth," Bonaci said. "Lucca was stabbed here.''

"I appreciate your confidence in my hunches," Donovan said.

"That was a damn good one, Lieutenant. You remember there was something I said I wanted to show you?''

"What is it?''

"The reason the only fingerprints on the murder weapon belong to Berman.''

Bonaci beckoned to a technician, who produced a clear plastic evidence bag. It held a pair of men's white, formal evening gloves. The right-hand one was soaked with blood; its companion was less so.

"Where'd you find these?''

"Inside that room," Bonaci said, pointing at a door marked, discreetly like all such doors, "Phoenician Studio.''

"Was that door locked last night?" Donovan asked Metz.

"Absolutely.''

"There was no special use for it?''

"Not one.''

"It wasn't the ladies' smoking lounge or anything.''

"No, Lieutenant.''

"Who has keys?''

"I do.''

"Who else?''

"There's a master down in the security room. The night watchman who makes rounds up here can fetch it if he hears anything funny within a studio.''

"Bonaci, check on the status of that master, would you?" Donovan asked. "See if anyone had it out last night.''

"If it's any help, I checked the locks on all these studio doors and came to the conclusion that they're not pickable. I mean, they *are* to a pro, I suppose.''

"But not to a corporate executive or a museum vice-president?" said Donovan.

"The locks aren't the type you can pop using a credit card,''

Bonaci said. "This isn't like the back door to Riley's, where you used to pop the lock using your Visa card."

"What's Riley's?" Metz asked.

"A part of my past that we needn't belabor here," Donovan said. "Bernie, just for the hell of it, tell me who services the locks on the studio doors."

"You mean the locksmith. Oh, it's the same guy who did the safe in Kent's office."

Donovan beamed. "Columbus Avenue Locksmiths, Anthony Di Bello, proprietor. What an incredible coincidence. Mosko, we have got to meet this remarkable man."

A bit unnerved by Donovan's sarcasm, Metz said, "He's bonded. I told you."

"So is a lot of Scotch, but it can still kill you. Mosko, I want to know bell, book, and candle on Mr. Di Bello. I mean his *entire* client list."

Metz said, "I don't think he'd jeopardize his contract with the museum—"

"Unless his contract with the Clark real estate empire is a whole lot more lucrative," Donovan said. "Like the man said, 'If you have enough money, you can make any problem go away.'"

"Who said that?"

"Lucca did."

"Where'd you get that bit of info?"

"I have my sources. Are we scheduled to see Di Bello today? Is he in?"

"Nope. His shop is closed on Mondays. It will have to wait until tomorrow, unless you want to go with me to see him tonight. He lives in Mill Basin."

"Which is next to Canarsie. Doesn't John Gotti have a place in Mill Basin? Never mind, I know that I'm unfairly tarring the good people of Brooklyn by making such a scandalous association."

"Not to mention knocking Italian-Americans," Bonaci said.

Donovan bristled. "Political correctness went out of my life when Marcy did," he snapped. "We'll see Mr. Di Bello tomorrow at his store on Columbus Avenue. And if he thinks I'm stereotyping him because he's Italian—well, what the hell, I'll buy the son of a bitch a pizza."

Bonaci shook his head, but smiled just the same. "Come into this room and see where I found the gloves," he said.

TWENTY-ONE

"WEE GOT HIM," MOSKO SAID.

"What makes you think that Di Bello works for the Clark empire?" Mosko asked as they stepped inside the Phoenician Studio.

"I don't know if he does. I was making a point. He might, though. Any man who owns as many office buildings and apartment towers as Clark does must need a lot of locksmithing."

"I'll see if you're right."

Bonaci waved through the open door to Metz, saying, "I'd appreciate it if you'd step down the hall a bit and leave this space clear. We're going to go over the floor looking for bloodstains."

"Okay," Metz said, stepping away.

"Lieutenant, Moskowitz, please try to make as few footprints as possible while you're in here."

"Right," Donovan said, scanning the room and finding what he expected. A big workspace with benches around the wall, a central bench, and two internal doors that led to other studios. As was the case with the Buzghashi Studio, the air smelled of cleaning fluid, sawdust, and acrylic paints.

"You ever been to an exhibit at the Javits Convention Center?" Donovan asked.

Neither of his aides had.

"They take this big, empty space, and fill it with movable walls. The result is something like this: an artificial environment built basically to show off stuff but also for the convenience of the designers. To make it easier to move things from the service elevators to the display cases they made all these rooms interconnecting. If Jameson hadn't heard the killer running away, I would swear he escaped by ducking from one studio to another."

"Don't complicate my life," Bonaci said. "Focus on the gloves. We found them in the trash barrel by the door."

He pointed out a large, round, brown-painted metal pail. Donovan peered into it, finding nothing.

"The last garbage pickup was Saturday morning. No one worked in this room on Saturday or yesterday. So anything dropped in the barrel was most likely deposited during the party last night."

"By the killer," Mosko said.

"I don't know anything about formal gloves, but these ones are expensive and are covered with blood."

"If you don't know anything about gloves, how do you know they're expensive?" Donovan asked.

"I know fabrics," Mosko said, reaching for the evidence bag. "My Uncle Stanley—"

"Don't start with me," Donovan said, snatching it away from Bonaci and holding it up to the light.

Bonaci said, "I know because there's a label. It's from a shop in Paris."

"Curiouser and curiouser. When was the last time I heard about Paris?"

"Akbar said he stopped off there on the way to the States," Mosko said.

"Right...to visit Mickey and Goofy and buy white gloves," Donovan said. "This guy cuts a *strange* figure for a terrorist...or a diplomat, whichever he is."

"Oh, so now we're admitting the possibility that Akbar is the bad guy that Mdivani makes him out to be?" Mosko said.

"Weight is added to that opinion by virtue of the fact that Jameson heard someone running away," Donovan replied. "The only place to run *from*—given the constraints we have—is this room; the only place to run *to* is about where Akbar admits he was. Let's also not forget that Akbar *did* wander out of the frame of the security camera. Furthermore, when I looked at the reel of videotape that Berman's cameraman shot..."

"Yeah?"

"...I saw Akbar walking into the museum wearing white gloves like these."

"We got him," Mosko said triumphantly.

"I want you guys to trace these gloves and do it fast," Donovan said. "I also want you to see if anyone saw Akbar walk out of here with whites gloves on. Call Morty Berman, and tell him we need to see any tape that may have been shot as the VIPs were on their way *out* of the museum last night."

"You got it," Mosko replied, not even slightly distracted by the beeping of his cellular phone.

Turning to Bonaci, Donovan said, "And I want this room gone over—every millimeter of it. This evidence seems to show that Akbar was the man Lucca had the secret meeting with. He stabbed Lucca and tossed the gloves into the trash can before running back to the other side of the exhibit."

"It ain't very smart, stabbing someone to death while you're wearing the formal white gloves that you bought in Paris," Mosko said.

"I have a problem with that too, but not enough of one to stop me from arresting the bum. Where is he, by the way? Surveillance hasn't lost him, has it?"

"At last report Akbar was in his room at the U.N. Plaza Hotel," Mosko said, taking the phone from his bag and shutting off the buzzer.

"I'll have a preliminary report for you by this evening if you get the hell out of here and let me work," Bonaci said, stooping to give brief scrutiny to some specks on the floor that had suddenly taken on new significance.

Moskowitz put the phone to his ear and walked out of the Phoenician Studio. Donovan followed, tossing over in his head the reasons that Mohammed Akbar might have had for killing Lucca. The most obvious was revenge for having ripped off and carried away Pamiristan's priceless cultural heritage (even though the official revolutionary line was happiness that the stuff was gone). A second possible motive was dissatisfaction with the level of bribes. Perhaps there were more.

One thing was for sure: Akbar was hardly one of the candidates for Katy's hand, so possession of a beautiful woman was easy to rule out as a motive in his case. Lucca met Akbar and died for his trouble, but what was the fight about? No matter how eloquently Mdivani described the battle for his homeland, Donovan couldn't bring himself to think Pamiristan worth fighting over. *Well,* he thought, *I don't have to live there.*

Donovan's musing was interrupted by Mosko's hand on his arm. The squeeze he gave was urgent and meaningful. Donovan looked over to see an expression of shocked amazement on his friend's round face. Mosko's eyes were wild with speculation. He said, "Dr. Lifshitz has finished the autopsy and can release the body to the widow for burial. That hunch you asked Dr. Lifshitz to check out?"

"I was right, wasn't I?" Donovan said, his adrenaline level skyrocketing. "There was a reason that Lucca seemed to be giving away large chunks of his fortune."

Moskowitz nodded. "Lucca was suffering from inoperable, small-cell carcinoma of the lungs. Very nasty, very hard to detect. It had metastasized to the brain. At the moment that Akbar stabbed him, Lucca only had six months to a year to live."

IT WAS one of those brilliantly clear and crisp nights that New Yorkers love to brag about, telling visitors, "This is how it is all the time." The sky was cloudless and the previous day's rain had washed all the pollutants out of the air and into the gutters. It was a snappy fifty degrees at ten in the evening and Mars was suspended like a ruby over the Statue of Liberty.

The New York City fireboat had picked up its passengers on the public dock near the Thirty-fourth Street Heliport and chugged busily down the East River, below the brightly lit Williamsburg, Manhattan, and Brooklyn bridges and out into the Upper Bay. It passed two Staten Island ferries laden with late commuters before turning south toward the Verrazano-Narrows Bridge, which linked the boroughs of Staten Island and Brooklyn and served as an east west interstate link for cars and trucks eager to bypass Manhattan to the south. It had been Donovan's suggestion to cast Lucca's ashes beneath the bridge named after Giovanni da Verrazano, the Italian navigator who discovered New York Bay in 1524.

Dressed in black and with a black veil pulled over her eyes, Katy Lucca had spent the entire hour aboard the fireboat sitting on a hatch cover near the bow, holding the urn that bore her husband's ashes and communicating either with him or with her own private demons. She wanted to be alone; Donovan stayed aft with the small funeral party, which included the two Lucca aides he remembered from Kent's office as well as the funeral director and Tommaso Lucca.

He was a man of Donovan's age, fifty or so, but with close-cropped, graying hair. Tommaso Lucca was better fed than his late brother. This Lucca's white skin and plump face testified more to a life indoors than to the days of an adventurer.

As the engines stirred up salt foam that blew lightly over them in the following breeze, Tommaso said, "My brother told me of the carcinoma a year ago. It was a difficult thing for him at first, to accept that he was dying and that the best doctors in the world could do nothing to prevent that. There he was, in the prime of his life, with a new young wife, and it was all being taken from him."

"But he accepted it in time."

"Yes, and made a good adjustment. Frankly, I don't think I would be quite so noble in the face of death. But Paolo was an outdoorsman. He knew his limitations. I suppose his death was the ultimate one."

"It sure would put a crimp in *my* style," Donovan said.

"Mine, too. But Paolo was not like you and me. After the initial shock, death failed to bother him. He set out to accomplish certain things in the time left him."

"Such as giving away his fortune."

"Well, yes and no. He couldn't possibly give it *all* away, although he was trying to do nearly that. You see, our father left us each fifty million dollars. I was happy with my portion. Paolo was not, and increased his fifty million twenty times over. When he learned he was dying, he vowed to give away all but the original amount. That's how much Katy would get to keep."

"I'm told Paolo was the wealthiest man in the world."

"Oh no, I doubt that. I believe there is an Arab or two who has more. Once you're at his level of wealth, adding it all up gets very complicated. But Paolo was worth over a billion, if that answers your question. He had much more than me."

"Are you happy with that?"

"Very much so. I have my houses, my library. Do you know anything about me, Lieutenant?"

"Not a thing. I hope you don't take that personally."

"I don't. I hate the limelight. I like books, Lieutenant, I like them a great deal."

"Me too," Donovan said.

"So I bought myself a great many. I established the Institute for the Humanities in Verona, the Lucca family home. We commission works of scholarship, especially of the Enlightenment. I sit on the board and administer the library collection. We have quite a remarkable one."

"I would like to see it someday."

"You are welcome always. So you see, my brother and I are similar, but different. We both were fascinated with antiquity; he merely liked *older* things and was prepared to run with a rough crowd to get them. Does that help you?"

"How did he increase his inheritance so much?"

"His business dealings are beyond me. If you need to know about them, you will have to ask someone else. I am not a very good capitalist. I am a fair scholar of the Enlightenment."

"I see that you, too, know your limitations."

"I try."

"Did Katy take the news of the carcinoma as well as Paolo did?"

"Katy? No, poor thing. She was devastated. But in time she came around. My brother's strength was infectious, you see. The trust between them was amazing. Their arrangement was remarkable."

"Arrangement?"

"About disbursing the bulk of the estate. About his death."

"She told me that whoever died first would be cremated within twenty-four hours and the ashes strewn at sea."

"True, true. Paolo loved the sea. He so wanted to have his ashes strewn over the Golfo di Venezia. She could have flown there with the ashes, but chose to remain in New York for some reason. No matter; New York Bay will do. All the world's seas are connected, and at least Katy is keeping her promise." Tommaso leaned momentarily over the starboard rail, the better to catch sight of his sister-in-law on her perch in the bow. "I wonder if she will keep the other ones."

"What other promises?" Donovan asked.

"Paolo made her swear she would do two things. Give away all but the original fifty million. And remarry right away and have children, a whole houseful of them. They wanted children, but couldn't have any. It had something to do with radiation treatments and sperm counts."

"She strikes me as a woman who needs a man," Donovan said.

"Yes—well, good luck to her. I like Katy, Lieutenant. Of course, I don't really know her that well. Again, it is a matter of differing styles. She likes life in the fast lane, to go to dinner and to go to clubs and to sail the Aegean on her yacht."

"Would she have had to cut back her lifestyle had Paolo lived longer?"

"Oh, my, I see what you're asking. Heavens, no, I don't think so. One can live fairly well even on fifty million."

"I think I could get by on it," Donovan said.

"As for me..." Tommaso looked as if he were searching for words, so Donovan offered a few: "You would rather curl up with a book about Voltaire."

"Perhaps Rousseau, but in essence you are right. Well, what the hell, my brother is gone, but now I can buy more books."

"He gave you a chunk of money."

"Indeed."

"He gave you a lot?"

"No. He left *me* nothing. But he gave the institute $50 million dollars. You see, now I have doubled my original inheritance and I am a happy man. As happy as a man can be who has lost his brother. What do you think, Lieutenant? Is this all very strange to you, a family having made such an extraordinary adjustment to the death of a loved one?"

"It sounds better than the one I made, actually. I'm very jealous."

"Why is that? Do tell me a story unrelated to my illustrious family."

"I guess, looking back on it all, I partly blamed myself for the death of my father."

"What happened?" Tommaso asked.

"He was a policeman, too, killed in the line of duty."

"Was that supposed to have been your fault?"

"I should have been walking the beat with him, which he wanted but I didn't. I wanted to get out from under his shadow, and the department wouldn't allow a father and son to work together anyway. Also, he and I didn't get along politically, and it was the late 1960s, a very political time."

"You were young and more progressive."

"To put it mildly. He was very Irish and more than a little bigoted. I had Italian, black, and Jewish friends."

"Oh. I see. You were enlightened."

"Yes. And I requested an assignment in Morningside Heights."

"I don't know that part of town."

"Columbia University. I liked to be around people who think.

Well, I was up in Morningside Heights arguing how best to bring American troops home from Vietnam on the day that my father was shot to death elsewhere on the West Side.''

Tommaso shook his head. "That is not your fault."

"I never was able to convince myself. Until..." Donovan thought of the commissioner's advice to stop walking his father's beat. "Well, until recently. So now I'm going to stop getting shot at, and...let's just say that maybe I'll expand my horizons a little. I'm no longer afraid. So you see, I completely agree with the arrangement that Paolo made before he died. When I go, I want the funeral pyre lighted quickly amidst a terrific party.''

Tommaso brightened and said, "Like they do in New Orleans, right? A jazz funeral?''

"Yes. With music by Ellington."

"I will rejoice when there is born another Paolo. Katy promised to name her firstborn son after my brother."

"That's nice," Donovan said. He had given quite a bit of himself to Tommaso, had revealed enough to justify asking the big question. "So tell me, who benefits most from Paolo's death?''

"In terms of money? Why, Katy, of course. She gets all that's left which, I guess, is in the order of a billion dollars."

"Could Katy have been involved in her husband's death?''

"That is absolutely out of the question. She adored him. Besides, I thought she was with you when it happened.''

"That's true. Still...well, never mind. It was just a thought. So she's now worth a billion dollars?''

"Temporarily, of course, and depending on how far Paolo got on his new Asian adventure."

"What *was* that?''

"I honestly don't know. I assumed it was the foundation he was setting up to improve conditions in the Middle East and parts of Asia and the former Soviet Union. I was wholeheartedly behind that and was, in fact, putting him in touch with some economists who were figuring out a kind of Marshall Plan for the former Soviet Union. You know, like the plan America began to restore Europe after World War II.''

"You both were good men."

"On the other hand, I recently got wind of some other endeavour, a venture of some sort involving Pamiristan. This was very new. He called it his Asian exploration. I think he was going to talk to someone important about it on the night he was killed. Last night.''

"Do you know who that was?''

"It was a man. That's all I know. Since Paolo used the word 'exploration,' I assumed the venture was another archaeological dig, although he had precious little time left in which to conduct one. Maybe I was wrong. His Asian exploration could have been a business venture.''

"A business? Wasn't there too little time for that, too?''

"Indeed. However, Paolo liked to make money. It was truly in his blood. If he smelled a killing, he was unable to resist. There was a certain edge to his voice when he smelled a profit. Is this important?''

"It could be very important. Tell me also: Other than Katy, who do you think benefits most from your brother's death?''

Tommaso searched his memory for a moment, then tossed up his hands. "My specialty is Rousseau, not Machiavelli. I honestly don't know. But you told me you have a suspect, that man Akbar. You found his gloves and they had Paolo's blood on them.''

"Well, you're partly right. We found gloves that have *some-body's* blood on them. The rest is being checked out.''

Tommaso Lucca shrugged. "What bothers me most is not the fact that my brother died. As I said, we were all prepared for that. What does bother me is the possibility that maybe he did something new to bring it on.''

"Something *new?*''

"I talked to him for years about the smoking. Small-cell carcinoma of the lung? That's what you get for abusing your body like that. It was Katy who got him to stop. She's violently allergic to smoke and can't stand to even be in a room formerly occupied by a smoker. Paolo had to give it up to marry her. But, alas, it was too late.''

The fireboat's engines began to slow. A moment later, an officer brought Katy back into the aft compartment as the boat turned into the wind. The Verrazano-Narrows Bridge stretched overhead, outlined by the strings of electric pearls draped over its steel webbing. The breeze had kicked up a bit of chop, which was added to by the fast current in the Narrows, where the waters of the Upper Bay squeeze through a slender channel on their way to join the Atlantic.

Katy pushed the veil off her face, tucking its loose ends beneath the collar of her sable jacket. Her eyes were red from crying through the final moments with her husband's ashes. She turned first to Tommaso, then to Donovan, and said, "Help me." Each took a shoulder and steadied her as she stepped to the transom and poured her husband's ashes into the roiling water of New York Harbor.

"Good-bye, my darling," she said. Then she turned and handed the empty urn to the representative of the funeral home. She hugged her brother-in-law while the fireboat headed for home, the engines powering up and making a chesty roar.

"I can't believe he's gone," she said when she had pulled away from the men, and took off the veil entirely.

"He didn't want you to mourn," Tommaso said. "He wanted you to get on with your life. He made you promise. Listen, Katy, maybe it's better this way. There was no wasting away, no agonizing months spent in hospital rooms waiting for the end."

She nodded. "You're right. It's better. Paolo suffered less."

"Not that it matters, but the Lieutenant has a suspect."

"Yes, he told me. That terrorist Akbar. I want to promise you that none of Paolo's money will be going to Akbar, his terrorist organization, or to anyone in that awful part of the world. Lieutenant…"

"Yes?"

"Would you take me home, please?"

TWENTY-TWO

"PICK THE SON OF A BITCH UP AND CUFF HIM TO THE RADIATOR IN MY OFFICE," DONOVAN SAID.

IT WAS THE stuffed toucan that put Donovan over the top.

For the first five minutes he spent in Katy's triplex penthouse high atop Clark Tower, the residence struck him as being relatively tasteful, as tasteful as it was humanly possible to be when you spend several million dollars designing and decorating an apartment.

He liked the basic layout of the triplex, which was designed so that most vantage points offered views of the other two floors. A mammoth living room housed an immense marble fireplace next to which was a computer-controlled grand player piano that, with nobody touching the keys, dispensed Fauré and Debussy. ("I guessed that you would like Fauré," Katy told her guest as she plugged in the microdisk that programmed the music.)

The piano sat to one side of the marble floor, opposite the roaring fire and across from the bar, the three-steps-down media nook with the giant-screen television, and the adjacent landing with steps leading up to the bedrooms or down to the pool. Katy turned up the lights in the pool, which was kidney-shaped and ringed with a neon strand that shimmered, just below the surface, in pastel red. The pool house was redwood and surrounded on three sides by a marble terrace that offered magnificent views of Central Park to the north and midtown Manhattan and the Empire State Building to the south. The pool was surrounded by eighteen-foot-high palms interspersed with round lawn tables and cushioned chairs. At the far end of the pool, fresh water bubbled and gurgled down a ten-foot rock waterfall. Atop this was perched the stuffed toucan. The bird seemed, to Donovan, to glance down on the proceedings with a beaky, ironic smile.

"The parrot was Steven's idea," Katy said, brushing a strand of honey-colored hair from in front of her eyes.

"Is this where Steven and you lived together?" Donovan asked.

"This is the place. When I left him, he locked it up and hasn't set foot in it since. It's been two years or more. In lending it to Paolo and me, I suspect, he wanted to remind me of times we had together."

"He did it to needle you?"

"I think so, and also to make sure we knew he didn't need the money he could get by selling the apartment."

"How much is that?"

"Three, maybe four million. Who knows? The market is terrible. The point is that Steven hates me. He didn't even call to express his condolences. He only lives a few stories away."

"Maybe he lost the phone number," Donovan offered helpfully.

"Anyway, who needs a measly three or four million?"

She smiled, and he explained, "I'm trying to get into the spirit of all this."

"You're doing very well. I'm going to get myself a drink. Can I offer you anything?"

"Diet Coke, if you have it."

"I have everything. And what I don't have I can send out for."

"How many servants do you have in this place?"

"Normally only one, a maid and cook who has her own room downstairs. But I gave her the night off. There's a cleaning service that comes in weekly. They were here Saturday. I don't need more than that for this place. The kitchens are really well stocked."

"Kitchens? Two of them?"

"Well, one kitchen. Two bars. A soda fountain."

"Where's that?"

"Downstairs, next to the gym."

"Oh. The gym."

"Hey, even you have one. There's nothing so special about that. Would you like to see it?"

"Sure. Lead the way."

"You can hang out there while I make drinks and change."

She led him downstairs, away from the sound of the player piano and into another realm in which classical music gave way to the occasional pinging of video games. Katy had neglected to mention the video arcade—a nook in which sat two pinball machines, three video games, and a vintage Wurlitzer jukebox. The arcade was between the soda fountain and the gym, which had a Universal machine like Donovan's, a treadmill, a stationary bicycle, and a weight bench.

"Amazing," Donovan said, eyeballing the setup. "This whole area is full of boy toys."

She nodded. "Steven never quite grew up. He *idolized* Arnold Schwarzenegger."

"I liked the man too, until I found out he was a Republican."

"Paolo also liked the toys. He was a very good pinball player."

"Me too, at one point."

She sighed, and said, "I guess I'm just attracted to men who never grow up. Make yourself comfortable, William. I'll be back in ten minutes."

"Do you mind if I use the phone?" he asked, having spotted one atop the soda fountain.

"Use whatever you like. My home is your home."

She disappeared, and after he watched her go Donovan looked around the room. The equipment was gleaming and expensive, but had seen considerable use. The weight bar, for one thing, was well oiled with palm sweat. It sat in its cradle, ready for someone to start doing chest presses. Assuming, of course, that the someone was prepared to press 280 pounds. That was how much iron was left on the bar.

The room smelled odd, too, not like any gym Donovan recalled. It smelled of smoke, of cigarettes. There was the distinct odor of smoke in the carpet and in the wallpaper. If Katy was violently allergic to smoke, you couldn't tell by her lack of reaction to the atmosphere in the gym. Donovan poked around until he found what he suspected was there; flakes of tobacco ash in the carpet here and there and, in a dishwasher that was built into the soda fountain, an ashtray stamped with the logo of Clark Casino International in Atlantic City. Someone had recently ground out several cigarettes. Donovan slipped the ashtray into an evidence bag and put that in his briefcase.

Then he sat down at the counter and dialed the number of Moskowitz's cellular phone.

"You," was the answer.

"Hey. It's me."

"Lieutenant! How was the wake?"

Donovan heard laughter in the background. "Oh, I get it. Burial at sea...ashes...boat...wake. That's very good, Brian. I'm impressed. The wake was fine. I'm at her apartment now. You ought to catch this place. Anyway, what news from the front?"

"Good news. We got him, Lieutenant, we really got him. The gloves were bought in Paris, all right. They look just like the ones Akbar wore going into the museum last night."

"But not going out?"

"Nope. He went out bare-handed. We got another tape from Berman and compared it with the one that showed the VIPs earlier in the evening."

"What about the blood on the gloves?" Donovan asked.

"It's Lucca's, all right. There's a positive I.D."

"Awesome, as you might say."

"Furthermore, Bonaci found traces of Lucca's blood on the floor of the Phoenician studio and on the floor of the exhibit hall heading toward the entrance. Your reconstruction of events has been right on the mark."

"Do one thing for me—"

"I'm not done. Bonaci got back the analysis of scrapings from the soles of Lucca's shoes. There was blood mixed with acrylic dust."

"Let me guess. Acrylic dust coats the floor of the Phoenician studio."

"You got it."

"So Lucca met his killer in the Phoenician studio, was stabbed, and ran or staggered down the hall to the entrance, where he collapsed in front of the oasis diorama, perhaps while taking a last look at the wax figure that showed himself at the height of his career."

"That's it. Should we pick up Akbar?"

"Where is he?"

"He went out to eat an hour ago. He's at an Indian restaurant on Forty-seventh Street."

"Is he meeting anyone?"

"Not that we can see."

"Okay, pick the son of a bitch up and cuff him to the radiator in my office."

"You'll come in to question him?"

"I have my hands full here."

"I'll bet."

"That's beneath you. I want you to handle the questioning. Find out exactly what he was doing at every minute last night. Show him the security tape and ask what he did when he stepped out of the frame at nine-thirteen."

"I'll take care of it."

"Akbar's Edwardian-diplomat getup was just too crazy to be real," Donovan said. "I think he's a wolf in tailored silks. My suspicion is that he ain't the only one." He looked around and saw, to his relief, that he was still alone.

"In that case, take care of yourself, Bill. Where will you be?"

"I'm keeping Mrs. Lucca company for a while. You can phone me at home later. Beep me if you hear from Moscow."

"Great. 'Bye."

Donovan hung up just as she returned, having changed into a pair of jeans and a T-shirt. That was plain white except for a small depiction of a rock rising out of the Aegean and the word "Rodi." It was a souvenir of her home island, Rhodes. She carried two glasses and put them both on the bar, extending her arms to him for a hug.

"I need to be held," she said.

Donovan drew her to him and wrapped his arms around her. The red was still in her eyes, but she had put on Opium and touched up her makeup and looked magnificent. Everyone should look so good while mourning, Donovan thought. There must be something to these pre-death arrangements.

When she pulled back, she picked up the glasses and handed one to him.

"Thanks. What are you drinking?"

"Stoli on the rocks. Want some?"

"It disagrees with me. Look, there's news. I don't know if you want to hear it."

"I don't know *anything* about this whole mess, either Paolo's murder or his business dealings or, least of all, the Treasure of the Silk Road. I'm just a dizzy broad who married a guy with a lot of different interests. But, what the hell, tell me." She said this fatalistically, tinkling the ice in her glass. But at least there was a light tone to her voice for the first time in twenty-four hours.

"We have enough evidence to pick up Akbar. The white gloves I told you about are his, and they have Paolo's blood on them."

She nodded. "Does he have an alibi?"

"Not much of one. He could have done it. In short, he had motive and opportunity."

"And his motive was...?"

"Revenge for your husband's digging up and hauling off the treasures of the Silk Road, I suppose. Akbar's group, the Thirteenth of September Movement, is the spiritual cousin of the Muslim fundamentalists who are trying to keep foreign influences out of Egypt by killing tourists. Killing the first major archaeologist to dig there since the Soviet Union collapsed surely will have that effect."

"I see. So this was a terrorist act. Well, these things are common enough in Italy, and now they are becoming commonplace in America. A terrorist. Paolo was killed by a terrorist." She shook her head.

"The other suspects just aren't cutting the mustard," Donovan said.

"Just for the hell of it, tell me who they are," she said, helping herself to a stool alongside the soda fountain. She reached over to a stainless-steel console and pressed some buttons. The far-off sound of the piano disappeared, and the Wurlitzer came to life. Accompanied by a trio, Jimmy Scott began to sing Cole Porter.

"Well, the only two with both motive and opportunity are your two exes—Jameson and Clark."

"You must be kidding." She laughed. "Why would *they* want to kill Paolo?"

"I'm *looking* at the motive," Donovan said dryly. "Your hand—especially if it's holding a check for a billion dollars—is a powerful motive for murder."

"My hand? You don't think I would *go back* to either of them, do you?"

"Would you?"

"Of course not. How could you think such a thing?"

"Is there any way either of them could have the impression you might?"

"I can't imagine how. I haven't spoken to Wally in years, and Steven and I can't stand to be in the same room with one another. If you're thinking of revenge as a motive, that's crazy too. I mean, Wally is a dear, but let's face it, the man is stuck in the seventies. And Steven—he's a pussycat. Besides, didn't he lock himself out on the fire escape?"

"He sure did."

"So how could he have killed my husband?"

"You're right," Donovan said. "Clark has a world-class alibi. He is, in fact, the only one of the VIP group who bothered to line up a world-class alibi."

"What do you mean, 'bothered to line up'?"

"Hell, were I running the risk of being accused of murdering someone, I sure would manage to get locked out on the fire escape, too, cutting my hand and howling like the devil and setting off alarms to get back in."

Katy gave Donovan a funny look, then said, "You're putting me on. You're trying to cheer me up again. I mean, the mere idea of Steven being capable of murder is laughable."

"So laugh," Donovan said.

"Okay," she said, a bit irritably.

"No, it looks like Akbar murdered Paolo, the reason being revenge for his having brought home quite so many trinkets from the tundra."

"Case closed?" she asked.

"Case closed. I'm gonna take some time off from detecting and dedicate myself to the mayor's reelection campaign. I hear he needs help. How do you like my newfound sense of civic responsibility?"

"It's stunning."

"You have a great place," Donovan said, looking around.

"Thank you. I mean, it's not *mine,* you know. It's Steven's."

"Is that his weight room?"

"It sure is. I don't lift weights, and Paolo was too weak recently to do any lifting. He never came down to this level of the apartment. Besides, Steven doesn't like people touching his stuff. He really hates it. It makes him furious."

"I guess that means that Steven can press two hundred and eighty pounds," Donovan said. "That's the weight he left on the bar."

"Oh, he did? Wow, I never looked at it. I guess maybe he could have lifted that much years ago, although I can't say I ever saw him do it. But certainly not now. Did you see him last night? He must have put on twenty pounds since we broke up."

"I was just wondering," Donovan said, in a tone of voice that suggested he was dismissing the thought. To further that illusion, he rubbed his forefinger along the surface of the counter, as though looking for dust.

"Who does the cleaning here, your maid?"

"Narnia Cleaners on East Fifty-sixth. Steven and I used to use them. Why do you ask?"

"I could use someone to come in every few weeks."

"They're good. Give them a call."

She sipped her drink quietly for a moment. Then she said, "Would you like to go someplace for a drink? You know, hear some live music or something. Get *out?*"

"How would that look?"

"I really don't care what people think of me. Besides, you heard about the arrangement between Paolo and me."

"Reporters are waiting outside. We'd have to use the secret entrance again, and my car."

"I'll put on the wig. The same one as the last time. You like it, don't you?"

"It's stunning. I always had a weakness for brunettes."

"Did you have other plans for tonight? I seem to have taken over your life."

"My job is to protect you."

"Is that the only reason you're here? It's your *job?*"

She touched him again on the arm, just the way she did the night before, and fixed him with those cover-girl eyes. Once again, she electrified him. He smiled, a bit dopily perhaps. But at the same time he thought, *What this situation calls for is a dopey smile.*

"Let's go," he said. "You like vodka. I know a place where the Stoli is ice cold and the music is red hot."

TWENTY-THREE

LET'S FACE THE MUSIC AND DANCE

BRIGHTON BEACH AVENUE was in the middle of its nightly transition from fruit and vegetable and imported-rug market to seedy, under-the-elevated boulevard of broken Russian dreams. Half a dozen nightclubs were strewn along a four-block stretch of the avenue that was Main Street to the largest expatriate Russian community in the United States. By day fruit stands and import stores spilled out onto the sidewalk. By night the D train rumbled overhead on the start of its hour-long journey through Brooklyn and over the bridge into Manhattan. The vibrations shook the windows, which were plastered with cheap glossy photographs of sundry Russian entertainers posing with guitars and microphones and leering down on barrel-chested men and beehive-hairdoed women out for a night of straight-up *wodka,* unfiltered cigarettes, and Russian Jerry Vales pouring their hearts out to the accompaniment of Casio electric keyboards and automatic drummers.

"You haven't lived until you've heard 'Raindrops Keep Falling on My Head' in Russian," Donovan said as he led Katy across the sidewalk from his car and toward the entrance to the Gemini. As he did so, he saw in the corner of his eye a yellow cab with a crumpled right front fender. He made a mental note of the license-plate number.

"Is this place safe?" she asked, looking with vague alarm at the four large and dangerous-looking men by the door. Two of them wore what passed for a uniform on Brighton Beach Avenue: tight jeans and black leather jackets over military-style brown sweaters that had leather shoulder pads. Looking down on them was the Gemini logo—the familiar constellation with the twins, Castor and Pollux, depicted in neon.

"Of course it's safe. This is a Russian Mafia joint. There's no place safer to park your car and wear expensive things than a mob joint. The last thing they want is street crime. Not while, inside, the big boys are cooking up a new way—"

"To rob trucks, right?"

"Well, in the case of the Russian Mafia it's a new way to screw the tax authorities on huge shipments of gasoline."

"That's an unusual racket, isn't it?"

"Not really, but they do it especially well. Nobody knows more about screwing bureaucrats than the Russians," Donovan said. "Frankly, I wish them nothing but blue skies."

On Donovan's instructions, Katy was wearing her sable jacket over the T-shirt and jeans. "To impress the maître d'," he'd told her earlier, and it worked. When they stepped in, the tuxedo-wearing man rushed up, his look of admiration at the sight of the stunning brunette in the very expensive fur alternating with a look of consternation that said, *Is this guy a cop?*

"Can I help you, sir?"

"Georgi Mdivani," Donovan said tersely.

The man brightened. "Oh, you're friends of Georgi. Come, come...this way."

He led them through the small vestibule, a plain entranceway holding a cloakroom, a cigarette machine, and several straight-backed chairs. An eight-by-ten glossy taped to the cloakroom door betrayed the name of the night's entertainer: "Straight from Tbilisi, Alex Onegin."

There were four steps down to the ballroom, a gargantuan

square room with cafeteria-style tables for families and more intimate settings for romance or, more commonly, the making of deals. The tables surrounded a round dance floor, at one side of which was a raised bandstand. Just as they lorded over the sidewalk, Castor and Pollux cast their neon glow over Alex Onegin, a Georgian one-man band who played keyboards and sang while a computerized drummer ticked away behind him.

Onegin was pure Sinatra, circa 1947, with the pomaded black hair and the tendency to sing to each of the women in the room as if he were courting her personally. He spotted Katy as she traversed the dance floor on Donovan's arm and directed his rendition of "Do You Know the Way to San Jose?"—sung half in English and half in Russian—at her.

"I think you're a hit," Donovan shouted in her ear, just barely managing to make himself heard.

"You sure know how to show a lady a good time," she shouted back, rolling her eyes but smiling nonetheless.

"You wanted live music. I just hope you won't be recognized."

"Don't worry about it, William. I've done this a million times. They don't look at my face."

To augment the point, she wiggled her ass. That earned her a war whoop from the entertainer, who assumed she was reacting to him.

As the song ended and Onegin began a five-minute break with a shouted welcome to the brunette in the fur coat, the maître d' brought Donovan and Katy to a table for four on the far edge of the dance floor. The spotlights were turned down there, the better to talk in privacy, but a candle flickered in a plastic-webbed teardrop.

Mdivani's barrel chest fairly burst through the strained buttons of a white silk shirt open nearly to the navel, showing off a black forest of body hair as well as a thick strand of gold chain. He held a glass—like a shot glass, but twice the size and untapered—in one hand and a Kool in the other, while lecturing two companions in Russian. A beige Princess telephone was plugged into a socket in the center of the table. It sat near a liter carafe of Stolichnaya, a pot of black coffee, and two bottles of Georgian mineral water.

The maître d' was about to say something when Mdivani looked up and recognized Donovan. He was startled, but only for a second. He rose from his chair and Donovan saw his lips curling to mouth the word "lieutenant." But the Georgian caught himself and said, "Bill...you accepted my invitation, and the very next night. Sit down, sit down."

A few words of Russian sent his friends scurrying. Donovan pumped Mdivani's hand, then held a chair for Katy to sit. "I brought a friend," Donovan said.

Mdivani's vodka-soaked eyes, red from the immense amount of cigarette smoke that filled the room like a London fog, focused on Katy's face. He squinted, then said, "My God!"

Donovan put a finger over his lips.

"Oh, not a word from me. I guarantee it. What a shame! I wish I could tell the world. I would be a big hero around here."

"I thought you were already."

"Maybe a small hero," he said, making a pinch with the thumb and forefinger of his right hand. Mdivani lowered his voice conspiratorially and leaned toward Katy, saying, "Mrs. Lucca. I don't know what to say. I am glad you are here, of course. But I am so sorry about your husband."

"Thank you."

"I don't know what to say."

"Never mind, Georgi. I *know* how you feel. Without boring you with the details, Paolo and I had an agreement. If one of us should die, the other would immediately go on with life. I needed to get away from that gilded cage on Fifth Avenue and be around some life. William brought me here."

"This is the spot. I told you, Bill...it is better that I call you that, no?"

"Yes."

"I told you that here at the Gemini we know how to live. What will you have?"

"Some of the mineral water will do fine."

"Okay," Mdivani replied, handing Donovan a bottle of it and a glass.

"And you, Katy? Will you drink with me?"

"Is that Stoli?" she asked, pointing at the carafe.

"What else would it be? I find myself saddled with Russian produce. But at least they do *something* well." He filled a glass to the top with ice-cold vodka and handed it to her.

Donovan, Mdivani, and Katy clinked glasses together. "Naz drobvaya," Mdivani toasted.

"Now *that's* vodka," Katy said, whistling softly as the silky liquor burned the back of her throat.

"My friends, surely you did not come here to listen to Alex Onegin from Tbilisi."

"Why not?" Donovan said. "You invited us."

"Do you want to eat?"

"Not me, thanks."

Katy also shook her head.

"Then it must be to trap me into saying something unfortunate."

"Volunteer the information and save me the trouble," Donovan said.

"I have none to give. I know why you're here: to place a bet on the soccer matches."

Donovan smiled broadly and said, "Twenty bucks on Ireland."

Mdivani laughed. "You are a fool, but I will take your money."

Donovan fished a twenty from his pocket and put it on the table. When Mdivani had folded the bill into his shirt pocket and made a notation on a small slip of yellow paper, Donovan said, "I thought you were kidding about running a sports book."

"The life of a diplomat is too boring for an old oppressor of the masses. I need something to keep the blood flowing. This doesn't make me more than pocket change, but it gives me a reason to live."

"I offer you another one: It is my opinion that you did not kill Paolo Lucca."

"I told you as much," Mdivani said, tossing up his hands in a gesture that said "So what?"

"Yes, but it's *my* opinion that counts."

"So it is. Is Lemovin also off the hook?"

"Yes."

"May I ask what convinced you of our innocence?"

"You were on the security camera entering the exhibit and you didn't leave it until after Katy's husband was dead."

"I didn't notice cameras. Well, I am a happy man. Now if you will only tell me who is *on* the hook."

"Your old friend, Akbar."

"I told you that too," Mdivani said gleefully. "The man is a nefarious terrorist, not a diplomat with a taste for Edwardian clothes."

"I seems that you are right. We found Akbar's fancy white gloves with Paolo's blood on them. We also found the spot where the stabbing took place. It was nowhere near you. It was, however, within striking distance of Akbar."

"Case closed, eh?"

"Yeah. Approximately."

Katy perked up at that. She had been staring dreamily across the room and had seemed to be thinking of nothing. But she turned to Donovan and said, "What do you mean, 'approximately'?"

"I still have your two exes to think about."

"I said that too," Mdivani gloated. "A man could kill over a woman like this. I could. Couldn't you?"

"Absolutely," Donovan said, reaching across the table and squeezing her arm, a gesture that Mdivani noted with clear interest.

"Wally couldn't do anything to hurt me, and Steven was locked outside. That's nonsense. We had this discussion before and you said you were only being so ridiculous to cheer me up."

"I'm still waiting for the laugh," Donovan said.

She forced a chuckle, then shook her head. "You can be maddening," she said.

"If you'd rather be bored I can take you back to the gilded cage."

Katy sighed, chuckled more genuinely this time, and reached over to Donovan and looped her arm through his. Mdivani's eyes followed her arm every centimeter of the way. She noticed that he noticed and said, with a loud and sexy exhalation, "Who cares who knows?"

Donovan attended to his beeper, which had gone off.

"Well, well, well," Mdivani said, bolting down his Stoli and pouring another. "And I was told that life in America would be boring."

The music came back on and, as soon as it did so, Mdivani snapped his fingers at a passing waiter and whispered to the man. Then he turned to Katy and asked, "What's your name?"

"Who do you want me to be tonight?" she asked Donovan. "Give me a good Irish name."

"I'm only half Irish."

"So give me half an Irish name," she said, a bit exasperated.

He thought for a moment, then grinned and said, "Brigid."

A minute later Alex Onegin announced that he was dedicating his rendition of "Witchcraft" to Brigid.

"I look about as Irish as you do Georgian," she said to Donovan as the music began.

"May I have this dance?" Mdivani asked, standing and requesting her hand.

"William? Do you mind?"

"Go ahead. I have to make a call."

"Do you *never* stop working?"

"Not while the bad guys out there are getting away on me," Donovan said as Katy and Mdivani stepped onto the dance floor.

Donovan used the Princess phone at the table to call Moskowitz. When the man answered, Donovan said: "Tell me what happened."

"We picked up Akbar in the middle of dessert and brought him in. He ain't too happy about it, but I don't think he's very surprised either."

"What has he said?"

"Not much. He's cool as ice, boss. He'll only talk to you."

"Did he say anything about what he did after nine-thirteen?"

"He wandered around that little area but didn't go far. He said that much and then got stuck on the word 'Donovan.' He wants you, boss."

"I seem to be in demand tonight," Donovan said.

"The press has already gotten wind of Akbar's arrest. They want to see the killer of Paolo Lucca and are gathering in force outside the unit, the museum, and Clark Tower. I don't think Mrs. Lucca will get a lot of peace and quiet there." Moskowitz listened to the rendition of "Witchcraft" raging in the background, and said, "You don't seem to be getting much peace and quiet yourself. Where the hell are you?"

"Brighton Beach."

"No shit. I thought I recognized the drummer. Which joint are you at? Brighton Beach is on my way home. I'll meet you for a beer."

"Forgot it. I'm delivering a message and then I'm outta here. I'm going home and I don't want to be disturbed unless the sky falls."

"What if it does?"

"Disturb me, but call first. Don't just show up. One other thing before you get off the line. Run a plate for me. A yellow cab, could be a '92 Chevy, New York license ACM-3929."

"What's the deal?"

"It's crossed my path three times in the past day or so and I'm getting a creepy feeling."

"You got it," Mosko said.

Donovan hung up the phone as the song ended and Mdivani and Katy drifted back to the table, all the eyes in the room on them. Beaming, Mdivani said, "She dances beautifully, as I knew she would."

"You're not so bad yourself," Katy said, picking up Donovan's glass of mineral water and sipping it. The room was hot and smoky and she took off her sable and hung it on the back of her chair. "I hope this is safe here."

"Leave it to me," Mdivani said, sitting back down and reclaiming his vodka. "I tell you, this is a night to tell the grandchildren about."

Donovan said, "More good news, Georgi. We picked up Akbar."

"Good! Did he say anything?"

"Just that he wants to speak to me. I'll do that tomorrow."

"You mean you're not going to run back to your office?" Katy asked, expectantly.

"Not a chance. I want the next dance."

"All *right*," she replied, reaching to draw him to his feet.

"Georgi, I'm now off duty for the night. Ring up 'One for My Baby' on the jukebox for me, would you?"

Mdivani snapped his fingers for a waiter and a moment later Alex Onegin was warbling the opening bars of the 1943 Arlen-Mercer song.

"Come on, Brigid," Donovan said, sweeping Katy out onto the floor. He wrapped his arms around her and pulled her against him until he could feel her warm breasts through the soft fabric of the T-shirt.

The smell of vodka was beginning to seep from her pores along with the scent of Opium. After two drinks, she was getting a little woozy. It liberated her Lauren Bacall mouth.

She brought her lips to Donovan's ear and said, "So who's Brigid, your old maiden aunt?"

"That's not exactly how I think of you."

"What's her last name, whoever she is?"

"O'Shaughnessy."

"That sounds like a whore. Or a nun. Maybe a whore who *used* to be a nun."

"It's someone from an old movie."

"Woody Allen, I suppose."

"Older than that. So, how do you like the Gemini?"

"It's fabulous, William. I adore it. Mdivani is a nice man, you know, despite the gruff exterior. He's a big Russian teddy bear."

"Georgian," Donovan corrected. "The distinction is important to him."

"Everything on that continent is so mixed up," Katy said, tracing lines up and down Donovan's spine with a fingertip. "Paolo and his damn explorations got in the middle of it and nothing will ever be perfectly clear again."

TWENTY-FOUR

THE NOBLEST DONOVAN OF THEM ALL

"YOU'RE GOOD TO LET ME stay here," Katy said, plopping a canvas L. L. Bean carryall bag down on the floor of Donovan's study. Then she sat on the studio couch and reached into the bag, pulling out a hairbrush and her blow dryer. Donovan leaned against his desk, watching her.

"I'm making myself a cup of tea. Want one?"

"No. It would wake me up. I want to stay drunk. God, I'm starting out on the rest of my life and I'm drunk and back sleeping on a studio couch."

"It's been a while?"

"Wally and I began our lives together sleeping on a daybed. He had to pull it out every night. The hinges creaked like a rusty old garden gate. You can't imagine how that killed the spontaneity."

"Marcy and I were attached to shady glens and assorted floors," Donovan said.

"No good. Pine needles and splinters. I'm allergic to *everything*. I used to drive Wally nuts, the poor man."

"Was that why he got into drugs?"

"He didn't start until after we broke up. I wouldn't have stood for it."

"Doesn't having an ex-husband who's a druggie put a crimp in your being Clinton's anti-drug spokeswoman?" Donovan asked.

"Bill has Roger," she replied offhandedly.

Katy held the brush and dryer up for a moment, trying to decide what to do with them, then tossed them back into the bag. "I'll deal with the details of life in the morning. I'm *tired.*"

The high-pitched whistling of a tea kettle came from the kitchen. Donovan cocked his head in that direction and said, "Try to get some sleep. We have Akbar in custody and you're safe here. Stay as long as you like."

She kicked off her shoes and stretched out on the bed, nestling her head into the pillow. Donovan pulled the comforter up to her waist, covering her jeans. She looked up at him and puckered her lips to be kissed. He bent over and gave her a peck.

"You're a good dancer and a wonderful man. You succeeded in taking my mind off everything that happened. Now I can get on with my life, the way Paolo wanted."

"You'll do fine."

"I promise I'll behave from here on. I'm a big girl and can deal with living alone."

"Good night, Katy," Donovan said, and slipped out of the room.

Ten minutes later he set his cup of tea on the night table and took off his clothes. His briefcase, which normally would have stayed in the study, went into the closet along with his overcoat. Donovan emptied his suit pockets and found the computer disk that contained the downloaded results of the computer search on Peter Vischer. There had been no time to look at it and, with Katy sleeping in the study, the job wouldn't get done that night. Donovan put the disk in the old pewter dish that held his change and keys.

He sat on the edge of the bed and was about to climb under the covers wearing the same T-shirt and shorts that he had on all day, but he felt that something was amiss. Switching on the radio and hearing Sinatra start to sing "Taking a Chance on Love" told

Donovan what it was. He took off his underwear and tossed it in the hamper, pulling on instead his cutoff jeans. Then he went into the bathroom, brushed his teeth, and washed the smell of Gemini smoke off his face. *Allergic to everything, eh?* he thought, splashing on a bit of aftershave.

Then he got back into bed and began to drift off, listening to jazz and watching the glow from the light left on in the hall. There was a sound then, bare feet on hardwood, and a shadow as Katy came down the hall. She paused in the doorway. For dramatic effect? Donovan wondered. She seemed even taller with the light coming from behind. What was she wearing? Her Rhodes T-shirt and panties? That must be it.

In three long strides she was across the room. He flipped down the comforter and stretched out his right arm; she slid alongside him, facing him this time, and his arm curled around her. She smelled of Opium, smoke, and vodka, and said to him in a sulky voice: "You must think I'm awful."

He said nothing, but rolled toward her and stroked her hair with his other hand. She had taken off her bra. The T-shirt had twisted and pulled tight until it coated her voluptuous body like the paint that had adorned it on the *Vanity Fair* cover. Her long legs curled down to the end of the bed.

"I'm incorrigible. I'm either a tease or I'm too needy. I'm not half as smart as I make myself out to be. I'm really a mess. Please tell me what you think of me."

"I think you're drunk," he said at last.

"You must hate me."

"What I have come to hate, in my newly discovered, fifty-year-old wisdom, is long talks about feelings. Let's go to sleep."

"You don't want to make love to me?"

"You're drunk, you just buried your husband, and I think that if I live to be a hundred I will never get another chance to be this noble. Close your eyes and go to sleep."

She sighed, long and loud, and then leaned into him and kissed him below the ear, nipping at his skin with the fine, sharp points of her teeth and whispering, "I love you, William."

Sure you do, he thought, rolling onto his back and holding her until the softness of her breathing told him that she was asleep at last.

When he was sure that she was out for the night, he carefully pulled his arm from under her neck and got out of bed. Walking softly and avoiding the floorboards that creaked, Donovan made his way to his study, the computer disk in his hand.

He powered up the Gateway 2000 P5-60, the twin of the one he kept at the West Side Major Crimes Unit, and selected Word-Perfect from the menu. He slipped the disk into the slot and called up the file named "download.doc."

The thick file was heavy with import; it seemed to weigh a ton. What it revealed was that the only reason Peter Vischer's name had escaped Donovan's attention in the past was his lack of interest in European economics. His eyes wide with discovery, Donovan read that Vischer Explorations was hardly an archaeological firm. It was, in fact, deeply involved in *oil* exploration and exploitation, especially in emerging nations.

Vischer had made his fortune by using space-age technology to uncover long-hidden petroleum reserves and then applying his considerable skill as a negotiator to pry them loose from the Third World nations where they were found. Donovan noted with special interest Vischer's use of the SIR-C space shuttle imaging system to discover vast oil fields on the Kamchatka Peninsula in Siberia.

"And Lucca said the system was designed specifically for him to use in finding lost cities," Donovan swore. "Dad was right: You can't trust the fancy people."

The most recent entry for Vischer was a small item in the *International Herald Tribune*. It mentioned his formation of a new firm, Asian Explorations, Ltd., with Paolo Lucca "and unnamed other partners."

Donovan recalled Mdivani's words from the night before: "Apart from the curiosity value of the lost city of Chandar, there's nothing in my country that Americans want." Akbar also downplayed the value of Pamiristan. "There's nothing there that Americans would think worth fighting for," everyone was saying.

Donovan stored that computer file and called up the other, the results of his key-word search of several years' worth of newspaper and magazine articles. What Donovan read startled him nearly as much as had the revelation about Vischer. Akbar too was more than the diplomatic flunky he made himself out to be.

Donovan's talent for remembering bits and pieces of arcane information proved its worth again. A year-and-a-half-old article in the *Times* described how prisoners in the old Soviet system displayed their status—and warned off potential big-house aggressors: by having symbols of their crimes tattooed on their bodies. Murderers commonly decorated their limbs with skulls, Donovan read anew on the screen of his Gateway.

He had gotten a lot of useful information from his little PC. Vischer was an oil explorer. And the tattoo that Akbar was so desperate to hide showed that he must have served time in a Soviet prison for murder. He was a very cool and extremely dangerous customer.

A plague on both their houses, Donovan thought. He made backup copies of the files and printed out the *Times* story on the LaserJet. He folded the printout and secured it to the floppy disk with a rubber band.

Donovan shut off the light in his study, went into the kitchen, made himself another cup of tea, and drank it while staring out the window at the early morning blackness of the Hudson River.

TWENTY-FIVE

PRIDE AND PRESCIENCE

THE SHERRY Netherland Hotel is an understated pearl on Fifth Avenue just north of the touristy strip of expensive shops that includes Tiffany, Bergdorf Goodman, and F.A.O. Schwartz. Its Old World elegant suites overlook the southeast corner of Central Park, where horse-drawn carriages line up across from the Plaza and everyone takes pictures standing in front of the pond with the buildings of Central Park South in the background.

Donovan watched the scene from the eighteenth floor of the Sherry Netherland, a demitasse balanced in his palm. The aroma of the coffee curled around his nose as he watched the long shadows grow just past dawn. Apart from the tinkle of coffee being poured, silence ruled the room until the waiter left.

Then Peter Vischer laughed and said, "What kept you, Lieutenant? I expected you long before this. Be that as it may, congratulations—you figured it all out and it only took you thirty-six hours.''

"I could have done it in twenty-four, but I was entertaining and put off reading the file on you. Why did you expect me earlier?''

"I pride myself on my prescience. You nailed us dead to rights—not for murder, I assure you, although you seem to have Akbar on that score—but for the crime of greed. I don't mind telling you the story now because it's signed, sealed, and delivered: We were only in it for the money.''

"Kent said that the Silk Road expedition was largely a matter of loot," Donovan said.

"He was right, the good Dr. Kent was, and he should know. He's the one who first made the connection between Paolo, me, and the peculiar geology of Pamiristan. He threatened to scuttle the museum exhibit unless we cut him in. We were using them the way we used Chandar, as a convenient way to cover up what I assure you will be immense profits. As for Kent, the museum was preparing to ease him out because of his age, and he decided to blackmail us into augmenting his pension.''

Vischer walked across the room and joined Donovan by the window. They stood shoulder to shoulder, watching as the line of hansom cabs standing across from the Plaza in wait for tourists grew from one to three to ten. If the German had been nervous and stiffly aloof at the exhibit opening, he was aggressively in his element in the opulent hotel suite. His darting gray eyes, which had earlier seemed uneasy, now appeared to be those of an eager carnivore. Vischer was a hunter showing off a trophy buck.

"So both the expedition and the exhibit were only a coverup for oil exploration?" Donovan asked.

"For me they were. Paolo, I think, actually *liked* archaeology and felt he was doing something valuable for science and mankind. Perhaps he was trying to write his name large in the history books. Instead of Paolo Lucca, industrialist, we get Paolo Lucca, philanthropist and man of science. Does that seem odd to you?''

"No. In the 1992 presidential campaign, Ross Perot dropped out of the race and then got back into it. Some commentators felt that he was resuming the campaign in order to rewrite the first paragraph of his obituary. From Ross Perot, quitter, he went to Ross Perot, scrappy fighter. What did your other partners think of the Treasure of the Silk Road?''

"As you know, Kent thought the exhibit was rubbish. Akbar seemed happy to get the so-called treasures out of his country. His group is trying to discourage Western tourists. (They are not, I assure you, trying to discourage the oil industry's venture capital.) Lemovin and his deputy, Mdivani, couldn't care less about the treasures. They want the money to assure their continued solvency during their inevitable retirement on the French Riviera."

"After the Thirteenth of September runs them out of town."

"Precisely. They know it's coming."

Donovan thought for a moment, then added, "It's almost as if Paolo and you have been negotiating the peaceful transition from an apparatchik government to one run by the Muslims."

Vischer smiled broadly and said, "You have a wonderful mind. Paolo would indeed have liked you. Yes, it's possible that one day the people of Pamiristan will wake up to find that their old rulers are off in Nice working on their tans."

"What about Jameson and Clark? How do they figure into it?"

"Understand that there are two groups of players, Lieutenant: the major partners and the minor partners."

"The majors are you, Akbar, and Lemovin/Mdivani," Donovan said.

"And Lucca. Well, Katy Lucca now. The minor players are Kent, Jameson, and Clark."

"How is Jameson involved?"

"He's blackmailing Katy. Or so Paolo told me. She has for years successfully covered up a drug problem that cropped up during her first marriage. Should her onetime addiction become known, that would be the end of her presidential spokesperson-ship."

"It could jeopardize several things she has in mind," Donovan said. "And Clark? What hold does he have?"

"He was included at Katy's request. Paolo said she felt guilty about having ditched Clark for him. And Paolo felt guilty for taking her. She is quite a prize...very beautiful. I presume you noticed."

Donovan said that he had.

"Plus Clark needs the money. And Paolo *was* dying and *did* want to balance the books a bit, so to speak. Needless to say, I feel no such compassion for Clark who, to me, is something of a clod."

"I read in *Paris Match* that you're a very perceptive man," Donovan said.

"Besides, the relatively small amount that he will get as a junior partner in Asian Explorations Limited will not cure his financial woes as I understand them."

"Which are?"

"I believe that, due to his gross overbuilding in a depressed real estate market, Clark needs upwards of five hundred million dollars in order to rescue his faltering empire."

"And as a junior partner...?"

"He gets an initial payment of five million. With a one percent share in the profits, maybe if he lives to be one hundred he will get five hundred million dollars. But not a day earlier. He, of course, thought he should be a *major* partner and was furious to learn otherwise. All this for giving up a woman! Not even Cleopatra fetched such a price. But then, Paolo told me that Clark goes crazy when someone touches his playthings. Anyway, Paolo was unwilling to go so far as to make Clark a major partner, and I agreed. So, he gets a few dollars and maybe can pay the fuel bill on his yacht. I hear that he's been using his association with Paolo to try to talk some gullible bankers into extending him further credit. I doubt that they're quite so stupid. Anyway, if Katy's conscience is still bothering her she can give Clark money out of her share. Now that she's a billionaire she can afford it. He's certainly not getting an extra cent from me."

"Tell me...who do you think killed Lucca?"

"Didn't Akbar?"

"He says he's innocent."

"But you found his gloves with Paolo's blood on them. And he does have a motive, doesn't he? Avenging what Paolo did to his country."

"As you said, Akbar doesn't seem to care about losing the Silk Road treasure as long as other Westerners stay away. It's hard to make a case for revenge against those who have stolen artifacts when Akbar's group is philosophically aligned with the Egyptians who would blow up the Pyramids to keep tourists away. I suppose that preventative terrorism is a motive. Although... Let me ask, is the Thirteenth of September Movement still a major partner? I mean, even if Akbar is in jail for Lucca's murder?"

"Absolutely. They can stop the whole project. So can Lemovin and Mdivani. The cooperation of the two combatants in Pamiristan is imperative. And they *are* combatants, Lieutenant. How many people died in the fighting last year?"

"Several thousand, I think."

"The whole point of the Treasure of the Silk Road exhibit—at least from my point of view—was to give the combatants the excuse to get together in New York and sign the papers."

"When will that happen?"

"It already did—on Sunday afternoon, before the opening, in this very room."

"Lemovin, Mdivani, and Akbar were here?"

"Yes, all the majors. Except Paolo, of course. I already had his signature and he was busy at the museum taking care of some detail." Vischer chuckled, and said, "Akbar wore those silly gloves even while he signed the contract. What was that about, do you know?"

"Since you're his partner now, I think I'll let him tell you. Does the deal go on even if Akbar is convicted of Lucca's murder?"

"Absolutely."

"Katy told me that not a penny of Paolo's money would go to Akbar and his group."

"Not Lucca money, perhaps. But the Muslims remain major partners in Asian Explorations. I have signed contracts."

Donovan shrugged. "Then Akbar can rot in jail for murder. It's not as if he hasn't done it before."

Vischer pricked up his ears at that remark but said nothing.

Donovan continued: "My life is made easier. I'll file charges this morning and take the rest of the week off. As I said, I've been entertaining."

"A lady, I assume."

"Well, a woman."

Vischer laughed. "I like you, Lieutenant. You're very thorough. So thorough that I am compelled to ask why I am not a suspect. At Paolo's death I became the principal partner in Asian Explorations."

"Maybe if you were a locksmith and a sprinter, and capable of making yourself invisible, you could have killed Lucca."

"Then I must be innocent. I have zero technical ability and no interest in athletics. Well, I suppose that using the excavation of ancient cities as a cover for oil exploration is enough of a crime for one man. I should do what Paolo did, renovate a wing of a museum and write *my* name large in the history books. Is there anything else?''

"There is one more thing," Donovan said.

Vischer set his cup down on the windowsill and faced Donovan, his hands folded.

"After Lucca sent all the VIPs off to look at the exhibit he stayed near the entrance. He told several people he was planning to meet someone. A man. Do you know who that was?''

"Of course. It was Akbar.''

"Are you sure?'' Donovan asked, surprised.

"Absolutely. Paolo told me of the planned meeting earlier that day. My understanding was that money would change hands. A little something for Akbar the man, himself, beyond what the Thirteenth of September Movement would get. Paolo was the facilitator, after all, the one who prided himself on an ability to bring people together. He would grease the man's palm a little. You see, the Muslims are suspicious by nature, wary of Western capitalists, and in arms against the government of Pamiristan. They don't feel there's a soul in New York who's on their side.''

"Apart from a few thousand cab drivers,'' Donovan said.

"Be that as it may, Akbar wanted more than his name on a slip of paper. He wanted something for himself: a gratuity. Paolo dispensed a lot of gratuities during the Silk Road expedition—especially to customs agents who suspected that our high-tech archaeological gear looked suspiciously like petroleum exploration equipment.''

"I'm shocked. Shocked.''

"Akbar gave us the impression that he had something of an unsavory past—I mean, beyond his position as the spokesman for a terrorist group. He seemed like a man who knew the value of money. So Paolo was going to give him some, or promise him some, or whatever.''

"How much?''

Vischer shrugged. "I don't know. Did you search Akbar?''

"No. The man is the representative of his people at the U.N., after all. We looked for blood, not money. Not finding any, we sent him back to his hotel.''

"Well, as I said, he wanted a one-on-one with Lucca and he got it. Now Lucca's dead and Akbar is in custody. So what? The deal goes on. If we learned anything from the 1980s, it's that being in jail hardly disqualifies one from being a player on the field of international finance.''

Vischer checked his watch and picked up his empty cup from the windowsill. ''Anything else, Lieutenant?'' he asked. ''I have several more players to deal with before this day is done.''

''More players? Are any of *them* in jail?''

''Not yet, but we are, as you Americans say, in the early innings.''

''Does this deal also involve the Silk Road?''

''No, that is old business. I have something new, in Sumatra as it turns out. I would appreciate your keeping that fact to yourself. Unless, of course''—Vischer curled his lips into a sarcastic sneer—''you want to blackmail me and become a player yourself.''

''Not a chance,'' Donovan replied.

''I HAVE SOME THINGS for you to do,'' Donovan said the moment Moskowitz came into his office.

''Before or after you talk to Akbar?''

''Before.'' Donovan leaned back in his chair and put his feet up on the edge of his desk. ''Take notes,'' he said.

Mosko sat and balanced his notebook computer on his lap.

''Go.''

''Get a search warrant and run over to Akbar's hotel room. We're looking for any money that he may have received as a bribe from Lucca. Akbar turns out to be the man Lucca was going to meet that night. If cash changed hands and the bills have Lucca's fingerprints, we can place Akbar in the room with him when he was killed.''

''Got it.''

''Do you remember the last name of Evgeny Something-or-Other, the Moscow cop we met last year at that convention?''

''The Russian homicide cop. Evgeny Goncharov. What about him?''

''Fax Akbar's photo and fingerprints to him.''

''Akbar is a Pamiristani, boss, not a Russian.''

''Pamiristan was a Soviet province until four years ago,'' Donovan said. ''Akbar has on his hand the tattoo of a winged skull, wearing a beret, with a lightning bolt passing through it.''

"Maybe he belongs to the Chandar Oblast chapter of the Hell's Angels," Mosko suggested.

"If you read the *Times* and not the *National Enquirer* you would have seen, about a year and a half ago, an op-ed piece that describes the tattoos that hard-case inmates in the Soviet prison system used to identify themselves. Murderers use the tattoo I just mentioned."

"No kidding? Okay, it's afternoon in Moscow now. We should get pretty good turnaround on this request. So you think this guy Akbar has already been up once for killing someone? How does a murderer get out of a Russian prison?"

"The whole continent has been in chaos for five years," Donovan said. "Stranger things have happened."

"Got it. Maybe they couldn't afford to pay the guards and had to let everyone go. You want to know about your yellow cab?"

"Sure," Donovan said.

"The plates are phony," Mosko said. "They were stolen off a Honda in Orange County two days ago."

"What a surprise," Donovan said.

"You want to tell me what's going on?" Mosko asked.

"I think someone's been following me around."

"Do you want some protection? We can take care of this problem for you."

"No, I'm curious to see where this is leading."

"That curiosity of yours is gonna get you killed some day," Mosko warned.

"Go and send that fax now," Donovan said. "Tell Evgeny that I need results ASAP."

Moskowitz did as he was told. When he returned it was with a smile. "We lucked out," he said. "The man was in his office and promised to put Akbar's prints on his computer right away. He said if you wanted a rush on some fingerprints from a Pamiristani it must be a big deal."

"I'm flattered," Donovan said. "Where does surveillance put Clark?"

"He's in Atlantic City."

"How long has he been there?"

"When he left the museum Sunday night he went straight back to Clark Tower. The following morning—right after I called to ask for the clothes he wore the night before—Clark went by limo to the East Thirty-fourth Street Heliport, where he caught his private chopper to Atlantic City. He's been at his hotel there ever since.''

Donovan handed his assistant a slip of paper with two numbers written on it. Moskowitz read them and his brow furrowed.

"Call our friends at the phone company and get hold of all long-distance calls made for the past two weeks from the first number and the past two days from the second."

"Who belongs to the first number?" Moskowitz asked, clearly perplexed.

"Katy Lucca. It's the private line in the apartment that Clark loaned to them."

"Okay. You want to tell me why you're checking up on her, boss?"

"Not now."

"This second number is your home phone."

"And so it is."

"I don't suppose..."

"...I want to discuss it. No, I don't. Just get the records."

"O-*kay*," Mosko replied, drawing out that syllable as if it were saltwater taffy.

"And keep the search to yourself."

"Fine. Anything else?"

"Yeah. I want a deep background check on Katy: everything she did while living with Jameson in New Jersey. The key word is 'drugs.'''

"Really?" Mosko said in obvious surprise.

"Yeah. Jameson is blackmailing her, Vischer says. Jameson claims to have information that could scuttle her image as the Clinton administration's clean-living 'Inner Strength' anti-drug spokeswoman. I think that Clinton has had it with skeletons in the closet, no matter what Katy says about Roger."

"Roger who?"

"Roger Maris. Roger Rabbit. What difference does it make?"

"I was wondering what hold Jameson could have on the Luccas."

"That appears to be it."

"I'm relieved. This thing about giving away piles of money just for the sheer joy of it was making me sick."

"Me too."

Moskowitz made several entries on his computer, ran out of the room to check on the status of the Moscow request, then came back bearing coffee and doughnuts. He reclaimed his notebook computer, scrolled up a few pages, and peered intently at the screen. "Everything else is going smoothly with surveillance," he said. "Clark is in Jersey. Jameson is in West Ridge; he has a darts tournament this afternoon at the corner bar. Kent is in the Hamptons."

"We're sending cops all over the map today, aren't we?" Donovan remarked.

"Yeah. I'm glad that One Police Plaza is picking up the tab for this investigation. To continue: Lemovin remains at the consulate. Mdivani left Brighton Beach half an hour ago and, as we speak, is stuck in three miles of bumper-to-bumper traffic on the BQE."

"With luck I can live a good, long life, and never have to get on the Brooklyn-Queens Expressway."

"Amen to that. So much for the surveillance report. While we're on the subject, though, the guys on Mdivani would like to know when you got back together with Marcy."

"I wasn't aware that I had."

"They said you went into the Gemini with a babe on your arm last night. It was dark beneath the el, but she was tall and brunette."

"Tall and brunette, huh? Jesus, it must have been Marcy. Sometimes I surprise even myself. Compliment surveillance on their eyesight for me, would you?"

"Sure thing," Mosko said, completely missing the sarcasm.

Donovan plucked his briefcase from alongside his desk and held it on his lap while opening it. He removed the evidence bag that contained the ashtray he'd stolen from Lucca's apartment the night before, and handed it to Moskowitz.

"What's this?"

"I swiped it from Lucca's soda fountain last night after the wake."

"Soda fountain? Oh yeah, you were gonna tell me about the apartment. Something about a stuffed toucan on top of the waterfall? There was a soda fountain too?"

"Doesn't everybody have one? I'm gonna have one put in my place right next to the gym equipment you bought me. Have Bonaci check the ashes on that tray to see what brand of cigarette was ground out in it. Also have him look for prints.''

"Whose are we looking for? Lucca's? *Mrs.* Lucca's? You want to see if they were closet smokers?''

"I already know that story. He used to be. It would have killed him if Kublai Khan's dagger hadn't gotten there first. Katy is *not*, despite all accounts to the contrary, violently allergic to smoke.''

"Is that important? Sorry, you thought of it so it must be important.''

"There's one more thing: Check out Narnia Cleaners on East Fifty-sixth Street.''

"What happened, you spilled borscht on your Brooks Brothers suit last night? I told you that you should go to Moe Ginsburg and get some new threads.''

"Narnia Cleaners handles Lucca's apartment. I want to know the last time they cleaned it and how thorough a job was done. Specifically, could they have missed that ashtray? I found it in the dishwasher in the soda fountain.''

"I've noticed that you get a lot of mileage out of your nights on the town," Mosko said. "Do you mind telling me what all this jazz is about?''

"When I'm done with Akbar I want to visit the locksmith, Di Bello. Where's Akbar now?''

"I guess that means you're not answering my question. Akbar is in the holding pen. Are you ready for him?''

"Check Moscow first," Donovan said.

While Moskowitz was out of the room, Donovan helped himself to half of the man's butternut doughnut. The sergeant was gone for quite a while. When he returned, he was happily waving a sheet of fax paper.

"We just got the results back," he said.

"What did Goncharov say?''

"Akbar's prints set off bells throughout what remains of the old Soviet police system.''

"I knew it," Donovan said.

"Our friend isn't really Mohammed Akbar. He also ain't Mohammed Baku. His real name is Fatah Fasi—''

"Who is better known as Timur, leader of the Thirteenth of September Movement," Donovan said.

"That's it. You got it. Timur got out of the Soviet prison at

Krasnoyarsk in 1990, just as the U.S.S.R. was falling apart. He made his way home, where he hid out in the Pamir Mountains, reinvented himself as a revolutionary, and raised an army.''

''His subsequent terrorist acts made him famous,'' Donovan said. ''When he defeated Lemovin's Pamiristani forces on September 13, 1993, at the battle of Murgab Pass, he became a legend—''

''—and moved beyond the reach of conventional law enforcement,'' Moskowitz interjected. ''Now comes the bad news: Timur is a diplomat. He may have killed Lucca at the Museum of Natural History, but...''

''He can claim that his was a revolutionary act, justifiable revenge for the plundering of his country's heritage. The fact that he killed Lucca with the very priceless dagger that all the fuss was about makes this case less of a simple New York homicide and more of an international incident. Of course, I can still charge the murdering little bastard if he doesn't tell me what I want to hear. Bring him in.''

''When you're done, Bonaci wants to see you at the museum.''

''What's it about?''

''I don't know. He's being mysterious, but it's something about Bernie Metz and the cafeteria.''

''Maybe he's cooking up some brontosaurus burgers. Okay, we'll run over after we do everything else.''

TWENTY-SIX

HE LOOKED AT IT, SMILED STRANGELY, AND COLLAPSED

''HITLER ADMIRED Barbarossa,'' Donovan said when Akbar was seated across the desk.

Akbar looked confused, so Donovan simplified matters for him by reaching over, grabbing the hand with the tattoo, and exposing the ornament to plain view. Akbar resisted for a second, then relaxed his muscles and, after a moment, broke into an ironic smile.

''Barbarossa was a pirate. I admire Timur Lenk, so I, too, am a pirate? Is that what you're saying? Or are you comparing me to Hitler? My grasp of logic is limited. They didn't have many courses in it at Krasnoyarsk. That's how you traced me, correct?"

"Devout Muslims don't wear tattoos, but prisoners in the Soviet system get them as a matter of course. Murderers often get death's-heads. I sent your fingerprints to a colleague in Moscow," Donovan said, letting go of the hand.

Akbar sighed. "Another day or two and I would have had it removed. I have an appointment with a Park Avenue doctor, an expert in the laser removal of tattoos—the only specialist with the requisite skills between Chandar and here. There is a man who works at Euro Disney who removes tattoos as a sideline, but he was sick and unable to help me."

"I'm glad you didn't go there to see Mickey Mouse," Donovan said.

"I couldn't tell if you believed that. So, Lieutenant, what are you going to do with me? Turn me over to Mdivani or simply put me in jail forever?"

"Did you kill Lucca?"

"No."

"Then how come we found your gloves, with his blood on them, in the room where the murder took place?"

"I don't know. The last I saw them was in the cloakroom. I had intended to wear them all night, but I took them off to tie my shoes and left them behind. Doesn't that seem a little like a setup to you? Someone stole my gloves and used them to frame me."

"Let me get this straight: All the VIPs except for Paolo and Katy Lucca left their outer garments in the cloakroom?"

"Correct. The Luccas had their own dressing room—Dr. Kent's office."

"Why is that?"

"I heard that Mrs. Lucca couldn't stand to breathe the same air as Steven Clark, and so requested a private place in which to leave her mink."

"It's a sable," Donovan said.

"Whatever. She hates the man."

"I keep hearing that. In one way or another, that message has been repeated to me about five thousand times. So you left your gloves—"

"Along with my overcoat, hat, and walking stick."

"—in the cloakroom. Tell me: Why do you dress so fancily? Is this just a matter of personal preference?"

"No," Akbar said emphatically. "I find that when people gape at your coat and pants they're less likely to remember your face."

"Or the tattoo you made the mistake of getting while cooling your heels in the gulag."

"That was no mistake. You can get killed by the other inmates unless you wear something telling them how dangerous you are. The tattoo was an absolute necessity while I was in prison. Once I got out I should have had it removed right away but, as I said, the best man for the job is in New York and this is the first time I've had the chance to come here."

Donovan turned on the TV monitor and the VCR and showed Akbar the security tape that detailed his movements at the approximate time that Lucca was killed.

Donovan said, "As you can see, the museum camera shows that you were where you said you were, looking at the Samarkand Diorama, starting at nine-ten. You walked off in the direction of the Kazakhstan exhibit at nine-thirteen."

"I did not lie to you, Lieutenant."

"You didn't tell the whole truth, either," Donovan said. "I know the details of the financial arrangement." He took a moment to outline what Vischer had told him. All the while, Akbar looked down at his tattoo, then covered the decoration up by scratching it with his other hand. At last he returned his gaze to meet Donovan's.

"*You* were the man with whom Lucca planned to have a special meeting while the others were previewing the exhibit. You were there to get a bribe—a little baksheesh above and beyond the Thirteenth of September Movement's cut. Come on, Akbar—Allah blesses the forthright."

The man smiled—a bit sheepishly, perhaps.

"Was that when the meeting was supposed to take place? Around nine-fifteen?"

Akbar nodded. "Lucca was to go there at nine-fifteen and wait for me. I was to tell no one, for fear of having others demand extra as well. I was only asking for a little something to cover my expenses."

"How much?"

"Fifty thousand dollars. I know that sounds like a lot."

"Not by the standards of *this* crowd it doesn't," Donovan said.

Looking a bit relieved, Akbar said, "It's also an act of faith for a man to offer something in advance. Lucca was promising my organization a very great deal, a lot of money..."

"And the implicit agreement of Lemovin and Mdivani to leave town peacefully."

"There are some in my group who believe that Lucca was, in effect, buying Pamiristan for us."

"Frankly, I think he was buying it for himself and didn't give a damn if you and your enemy wiped each other out. That probably would have made things easier for him."

"Not really, though I must admit that killing Mdivani would give me great joy," Akbar said. "As you have discovered, I am capable of it—I killed a black marketeer who was cheating my people. The man was intercepting medical supplies that the Red Cross was sending by truck to rural areas of my country. So I executed him."

"With a knife to the chest?"

"No, with a bullet in the back of the head. That knife story is more Russian disinformation. Have they requested my extradition?"

"My inquiry to Moscow didn't go through official channels," Donovan said. "But it *could* if you lie to me again. I have a feeling you'd rather do a life sentence in America than in Russia. If we put you away for killing Lucca you'd be a celebrity prisoner able to give lessons in the Koran to grateful American prison audiences. That is, if you *know* anything about the Koran."

"Enough to impress an American prison audience," Akbar said.

Donovan continued, "Books will be written about you, and William Kunstler will handle your appeal." Despite himself, Akbar smiled.

"Whereas in a Russian jail..."

"Never mind. I know the situation better than you. I won't lie to you again, and you have my sincere apologies for having underestimated you. But I am innocent of killing Lucca."

"So what happened at nine-fifteen? It would only take a few minutes for you to run to the Phoenician Studio, stab Lucca, and run back. You got the dagger and killed him. But how *did* you get the dagger?"

"Exactly my point? How could I have gotten it? It was in the exhibit the last I saw it. I walked by it one moment while it's in its glass case and a very short while later it's embedded in Lucca's chest. Later on, it's still in the diorama. If you can explain how I did that, I will gladly confess to the crime."

Donovan fell silent, and his silence triggered a reaction.

"You see? You cannot explain that, can you?"

"Maybe Lucca got the dagger himself. Maybe he was planning on giving it to you as a bribe."

"But I don't *want* the dagger. I don't ever want to see it again. My Egyptian brothers and I have made it clear that we *don't want* the ancient junk that American archaeologists dig up in our countries. We just want to be left alone. Don't you understand? So what if Kublai Khan's dagger is worth money? I would have to sell it, and that act would diminish the moral validity of the Thirteenth of September. No, I wanted *money*. Lucca promised me a Swiss bank account. I simply wanted to meet him to tell him how much to put in it."

"There are two daggers," Donovan said finally. "The one in the display case is a fake. The real one was in a safe in Kent's office."

Akbar waggled an I-told-you-so finger at Donovan. "See? A fake dagger! The exact reason I asked for something in advance. You cannot trust these people. Find out who could get the real dagger out of that safe and you will have your murderer. I presume from what you said that Lucca had the combination. Who else had it? No, don't tell me. I don't care."

"What happened at nine-thirteen? You left the exhibit and hurried to meet Lucca."

"I was well ahead of the pack so I could slip out the exit and go down the hall, back in through the entrance to the exhibit, and meet Lucca in that room behind the Phoenician Diorama. I got as far as the exit, turned the corner into the hall, and saw Lucca with the dagger in his chest."

"Where was he?"

"He had just run out of the entrance. Half run, half staggered. He seemed to be headed for the curtain, as if to get you, as if to get help. Then he turned and staggered to the Oasis Diorama. He looked at it for a second, then smiled strangely and collapsed. I realized he was dead; I have seen men die, Lieutenant. I also knew that if I were found with him I would be the number one suspect. You know—Muslim fundamentalist terrorists. How fair a hearing might I have gotten in America so soon after the Muslims who arranged the World Trade Center bombing were convicted?''

"Point taken," Donovan said. "So you ran back to where you were in the exhibit."

"And waited until someone told me what had happened."

"Who was it?"

"Oh, Mdivani, actually." Akbar laughed. "I think the man was still trying to see if I looked as if I might be who I am—Timur the Second. Does he suspect me?"

"No, actually. He thinks you look like a graduate student."

"As I said, the man is a Brezhnev appointee and a thug. There is not a brain cell in his entire head. Lieutenant, the matter is as plain as day to me: Lucca was buying peace, quiet, and cooperation in Pamiristan for his oil company. Do you find that startling? It has happened often enough before. The United States bought the early retirements of the shah of Iran and Marcos of the Philippines. Popular governments took their places. The same thing is happening now in Pamiristan. The apparatchiks will leave quietly. We will take over. Since we don't care about the ancient city of Chandar or anything else that isn't mentioned in the Koran, Asian Explorations, Limited, can build oil wells wherever it likes so long as we get our cut. Is that clear?"

"Perfectly."

"Can I possibly be more honest than that?"

"I'll ask you one more time: Did you kill Lucca?"

"Absolutely not. And you can see that, once you get out of your head the ridiculous notion that we sought revenge for the 'plundering of our treasures,' I have no motive for killing Lucca. In fact, it was to my advantage to keep him alive—although we do have a contract, and I think that Vischer will honor it. He is, after all, the oil man and we do, after all, have the oil."

"Terrorism is a motive—to keep tourists away."

"Yes, and we will do that, if necessary...*after* the oil wells are producing. First we get Western capital, then we chase Westerners out."

"All of them except the petroleum engineers," Donovan said.

"Exactly. Look at Iran after the shah. That's what they did and it's what we will do. So you see—no motive for killing Lucca. You know that I am innocent. I can see it in your eyes. I leave it to you to prove me so."

"You know that I could just charge you with his murder and go fishing and not get an argument from any of my superiors."

"Yes, but you won't do that. Your reputation is that you are a little eccentric but scrupulously honest."

"Only a *little* eccentric?" Donovan said.

"Forgive me. I have not been in your city long enough to hear all the stories about Lieutenant Donovan."

The Lieutenant leaned back in his chair and thought for a while. Akbar mimicked him. In short order, both men had their hands behind their heads and were staring at one another, thought processes churning in their heads. After a while, Donovan asked, "Who knew that you were meeting Lucca at nine-fifteen?"

"Vischer and Lucca. Nobody else. Who had access to the safe?"

"Lucca. A museum employee, Bernie Metz. And the locksmith, of course."

"Interesting," Akbar said.

"Yes." Donovan fidgeted nervously with his suit jacket, trying to smooth the lump in his pocket that was pressing against his skin. He reached for it and found the packet of Sherman's cigarettes that he had used to conduct the Galilean experiment concerning Steven Clark. Donovan took them out and looked at the pack.

"Do you smoke?" he asked.

"God forbid."

"Me neither," Donovan said, putting the pack on his desk. "It's no good for you; takes away your wind. Did you say that you saw Lucca running out the entrance?"

"Yes. Not fast, but he *was* running. You can do that, you know, with a knife in your heart. I have seen it, in the fighting in the Pamir Mountains. You can't run for long, of course. Why do you ask?"

"Jameson heard a man running. I assumed it was the killer. Now I think it was Lucca."

Akbar smiled, and once again he waggled an I-told-you-so finger at Donovan. "You see that I tell the truth."

Donovan slapped his palms on his legs and stood. He sucked in a deep breath and said, "I have to run myself...over to the museum to check out some things. You'll have to wait for me in the holding cell for a few hours. Maybe I'll have good news for you.''

TWENTY-SEVEN

THE BOMBARDIER ON A B-17 RAID OVER GERMANY

DONOVAN LEANED OVER the fire-escape railing and looked down, holding the cigarette between thumb and forefinger and aiming it at the circle Bonaci had chalked in the concrete two stories below. The Sherman's was clipped halfway down—Donovan's solution to the problem of smoking.

"Ready when you are, Lieutenant," Moskowitz said.

Donovan replied, "You missed out on this growing up in a single-family home in Canarsie."

"Missed out on what?"

"When I was a kid I used to stand on the fire escape and drop pebbles and pretend I was the bombardier on a B-17 raid over Germany."

"Vischer will be glad to hear that. Kent, too."

"*Jawohl!* I got pretty good at it. Developed the ability to get seven out of ten pebbles into a tin can from three stories up."

He let go of the cigarette and watched as it fluttered down, landing a good seven feet off target.

"Of course, as rough as they are, pebbles are more aerodynamic than cigarettes." He straightened up, looked askance at the now empty pack, then crumpled the box and tossed it down too. It also missed the mark.

"Ten cigarettes dropped. Only two landed within the same circle that *all* of Clark's cigarettes landed in. There's no wind out today; the air is stiller than it is in Timur's tomb. I consider this strike one against Clark's airtight alibi. Obviously he came to the party with a Baggie full of cigarette butts and dumped them all at the base of the fire escape while on the way to murder Lucca."

"You couldn't just be happy with putting Akbar away for life, could you?"

"Am I supposed to do that simply because he's a Muslim, my Irish-Scottish-Jewish friend?"

"Yeah. Why not? Strike a blow for Judeo-Christian values."

"You don't really mean that."

"Or strike a blow for English-speaking cab drivers."

"There aren't any left," Donovan said, stepping off the fire escape and into the Buzghashi Studio.

"There'll be two more when Pilcrow hears that you're giving Akbar a pass and going after Clark: you and me."

"You know, I used to have a lot of fun playing on the fire escape. Then we moved to a fifteenth-floor apartment in a fireproof building on Riverside Drive. No more playing bombardier."

"No more playing cop after Pilcrow gets done with us."

"What's the big secret you wanted to tell me?" Donovan asked Bonaci, who was hovering nearby looking like the cat that ate the canary. With him was Bernie Metz, who also glowed.

"The floor on which we stand? The floor on which Steven Clark stood after you let him in off the fire escape Sunday night?"

"What about it?"

"Melt-Down. We found traces of it ground into the floor tiles."

"What's Melt-Down?"

"A proprietary chemical used to melt snow and ice. It's made up of calcium, sodium, potassium, strontium chloride, and water. Commonly but wrongly called rock salt."

"I'll continue to call it that," Donovan said. "Rock salt: the concrete pavement in the courtyard below is covered with it."

"The chance of a guy walking in the courtyard and getting rock salt on his feet and coming through the cafeteria, down a couple of halls, up an elevator or two flights of stairs, and through the exhibit and into this room and *still* having rock salt on the soles of his shoes is about next to nothing," Bonaci said.

"The stuff got here when Clark came back up the fire escape. We also found it on the fire escape itself."

"Strike two against Clark's airtight alibi," Donovan said, swelling a bit with pride himself. "What else did you find?"

"I got to admit that *I* didn't find it. Bernie did."

Donovan looked at the young scientist, who smiled.

"How you doing, Lieutenant?" he said. "Come this way."

The cafeteria kitchen was spotless. It barely even smelled of food or, worse yet, the twin olfactory evils of old cooking oil and roach spray. That was how most restaurant kitchens in New York City smelled, in Donovan's experience. The tables were stainless steel, as were the cabinets and stovetops. Several hanging racks of pots and utensils were recently polished. Donovan ran a finger along the rim of a sink and it came up clean. The only odor was, in fact, that of Ajax.

"Do you guys get awards for keeping the place this clean?" he asked.

"We get fines if we don't. There's a Health Department inspection tomorrow."

"Their trouble is our luck," Bonaci said. "Look what Bernie found while helping me snoop around."

He pointed out a metal folding chair beneath an old window cut into the cafeteria wall just next to a poster that showed how to perform the Heimlich maneuver.

"Is this the window you and I looked at from the outside?" Donovan asked.

"The same."

A foot away from the other side from the poster was the start of a bank of brand-new refrigerators. Metz walked to the first one and pulled it open. Inside was what looked like a year's supply of Dannon low-fat yogurt.

"My favorite flavor is cappuccino," Metz said, plucking out a container and displaying it. "I eat it with Cheerios."

"Yogurt and Cheerios?"

"Try it. It's low-fat and filling. I dump the yogurt into a bowl and add two handfuls of cereal and mix it up. I toss in a Sweet & Low. Two hundred calories and your tummy is full."

"You don't look like you need to diet," Donovan said, inspecting the man's slender frame.

"Every man needs to reduce his coronary risk. You too, Lieutenant. Sergeant."

"Forget about him. He lives on cheese fries."

Metz shook his head in disapproval. "To finish the story, I work nights because the museum is a madhouse during the day. You know, some days I think there must be ten thousand schoolkids in here. Most of them are at the dinosaur and Star Trek exhibits, but their voices carry. Do you have kids?"

"A glaring hole in my life. Someday maybe I'll meet the right woman.'' Donovan thought for a moment, then said, "On second thought, based on recent experience maybe I won't.''

"So to get work done when it's peaceful and quiet, I come in at night. I take my lunch down here, usually between one and two in the morning. I bring down my own Cheerios—they don't sell them in the cafeteria—and get a yogurt from the fridge. I have an arrangement with the cafeteria manager. I leave him a buck in a coffee can by the register.''

"And you eat sitting by the window,'' Donovan said.

"Yeah, where the radio reception is pretty good. I bring down a portable radio and listen to the news. The reception is no good upstairs—all the lights and steel in the building—but down here by the window to the courtyard, I can pick up the all-news station pretty well.''

"And Saturday night?''

"I tried to open that window and it wouldn't budge. I like fresh air, so last night when I came down here I tried it again and the window popped right open.''

"Someone opened it on Sunday,'' Donovan said.

"You got it,'' Bonaci replied. "It had been pried open with a screwdriver or a pocket knife or something. Whoever did the job took the trouble of replacing a bit of weather-stripping that he'd accidentally dislodged.''

"What about the iron gate outside?''

"It opens with a key. Close inspection reveals that a new cylinder was put in recently. There's almost no city grime in it—you know, diesel exhaust and soot, the stuff that coats all our windowsills. Moreover, my expert tells me that the hinges were used recently. Once again, the usual coating of grime was disturbed when the gate was unlocked and swung open.''

"Clark,'' Donovan said.

"Yeah. And on the floor inside the window...''

"Rock salt.''

"Exactly.''

"That's strike three against Clark's airtight alibi.''

Metz agreed. "There's no reason a museum employee would come in that window over the weekend.''

"And walking through the door to the courtyard—a hundred feet and several aisles away—you'd have no reason to walk to the inside of this window, plus you'd lose the rock salt from your shoes."

Donovan said, "I suppose it's too much to hope for that you found rock salt in the Phoenician Studio?"

"Where Lucca was stabbed? Not a chance. Too far away."

"Show me how far the Phoenician Studio is from Clark's fire escape and how long it takes to get there."

"We ran three timed runs and compared them with the statement Clark gave us," Bonaci said, leading the way down the aisle toward a connecting aisle that ran through a double swinging door to the service elevator area. "He told us he got the idea to go out for a smoke at nine o'clock. The little binger on his watch went off, so that's how he knows. Give him five minutes, maybe ten, walking casually and not arousing suspicion, to get out on the fire escape. Then he runs down to the courtyard. What I'll give you is an average of the times on our three runs. Thirty seconds to get down the fire escape. Ten seconds to take a plastic Baggie of cigarette butts out of his pocket and dump them on the ground. Ten seconds to get to the window."

Donovan interrupted as they waited for the service elevator to descend from the fourth floor. "How would he know which window to go to? Inside information?"

Metz shook his head. "Several of these windows are unlocked. Mine always was."

Bonaci added, "The feeling is that it's impossible for an intruder to get into the courtyard to begin with, so why worry too much about one breaking in a window? I mean, you have to break *out* of a window in the first place, or go down the fire escape, to get into the courtyard at all."

"Go on," Donovan said, as the elevator arrived.

"Thirty seconds to unlock the security gate. A minute to pry open the window and climb inside."

"The cafeteria was empty Sunday night?" Donovan asked.

"Yep. The caterer for the Silk Road party worked out of the Garden Café, where you told me you had lunch Saturday. How was the tarragon chicken salad, by the way?"

"Excellent."

"Thirty seconds to get to the service elevator."

"I count two minutes and fifty seconds so far."

"That's right. Now, if the elevator was on the top floor it would have taken two minutes to get here. We can't know where it was, so let's assume a minute waiting time."

"Almost four minutes have gone by."

"Yeah. Add another twenty seconds to get to the second floor, where the Silk Road exhibit is."

At this point the elevator stopped. Donovan and the others got out. "We're here," Bonaci said. "Now, this door..."

He indicated a double steel door that was mounted with roll guards so a man pushing a cart could push it through without causing damage.

"Leads into the studio next door to the Phoenician studio."

"Does it really?"

Bonaci nodded. "There's a lock."

"But it works off the same master key that opens all the studio doors," Metz interjected.

"So add twenty seconds to unlock the door and slip inside," Bonaci said. He fished a key out of his pocket and unlocked the door. Soon the small group of men was standing in the studio, which was brimming with artifacts from the Babylonian Diorama. A reconstructed stone hearth caught Donovan's eye, and he walked up to it.

"What's this?"

"A hearth from Tel Leilan, a prosperous third millennium B.C. town on the Euphrates, founded during the reign of Sargon of Akkad," Metz said.

"Why isn't it in the exhibit?"

"It's not finished. Archaeology is an ongoing thing, Lieutenant. The exhibit gets added to when new finds are incorporated."

"This is the Babylonian Studio," Bonaci said. "The door on the opposite wall leads into the Phoenician Studio. Add five seconds to walk to it and push it open."

"No key is needed," Metz added.

"And Clark is in the Phoenician Studio four minutes and fifteen seconds after first appearing on the fire escape."

"Beautiful," Donovan said, following Bonaci into the Phoenician Studio. The sergeant threw open that final door and announced, grandly, "The scene of the crime."

Donovan picked up the narrative. "That puts Clark at the murder scene by nine-fourteen or nine-fifteen, maybe a little later."

Donovan added, with a flourish rivaling Bonaci's, "Gentlemen, he could have done it."

Moskowitz added, "Akbar said that Lucca was to wait for him in this room at nine-fifteen."

"He was waiting, probably by the front door, when suddenly Clark bursts in the back door," Donovan said. "I don't think many words were exchanged. Clark was on a tight schedule. He stabbed Lucca and the man went down. Clark tossed Akbar's gloves into the trash and ran back out the way he came. Retracing his footsteps, Clark could get back on the fire escape and light up a cigarette for real by nine-twenty or so. Add a minute or two to tamp back down the weather-stripping that he knocked off when he pried open the window. He waits long enough for Lucca's body to be discovered, then smashes the window, setting off the alarm. Clark probably cut his hand on purpose, too. His blood would cover up any of Lucca's that might have gotten on him. Because he's a leading citizen of this city, we rushed him right to the hospital and didn't do a close inspection."

Donovan pushed open the door of the studio and stepped outside into the exhibit. The Treasure of the Silk Road show remained closed. The glass-encased artifacts sat unappreciated amidst empty corridors. "Clark thought Lucca was dead, but the man got back on his feet, opened the door, and let out the cry that Berman and Jameson heard so clearly. Then, with his last burst of strength, Lucca ran down the hall."

Donovan led the way to the spot where the body was found. The wax-figure Lucca gazed down on them with casual indifference. Donovan looked at the diorama, then at the still-closed curtain that sealed off the Treasure of the Silk Road. The normal din of museum visitors could be heard beyond it. Lucca might be dead and his famous exhibit still unseen by the public, but throngs of young and old filled the rest of the museum to capacity, viewing fish and fowl, Eskimo and Pacific Islander, kayak and Indian canoe, dinosaur and *Apollo* astronaut.

"If Lucca could have burst through the curtain somebody might have been able to save him," Donovan said.

"Not without a cardiac trauma unit," Moskowitz replied.

"But he turned and gazed at the Oasis Diorama. What in hell was so interesting that he would do that? Akbar said he smiled strangely. Lucca dropped dead looking at something that amused him. What did he *see?*''

"His own self, full of life?" Moskowitz wondered.

"There's something about this diorama," Donovan said, staring at the three-dimensional display. "I tried to see what it was before but couldn't. It's not the wax figures or the artifacts. But it *is*"— he squinted to see better—"in the background painting. Bernie, did you do this one?"

"Yes."

The painting showed a fictional oasis chockablock with fictional oasis figures: palm trees, camels, horses, some tumbledown sandstone-block buildings, and, of course, natives. These particular natives were Pamiristanis of Mongolian descent, to judge by their dress, although much poetic license had been taken. The figures were only two or three inches high; placed in the background of the six-foot-deep diorama, they were difficult to make out without trying hard.

Donovan tried harder, squinting some more, and then it hit him. The "natives" shown standing around the oasis well staring at the wax Lucca were his partners—both the major and the minor ones. There was a wild-eyed radical bearing an immense rifle, almost an elephant gun: Akbar. There was an older, white-haired man: Kent. An aging hippie type—Jameson—leaned against a rusting Jeep. A stylishly coiffed man in his thirties had Vischer's predaceous eyes. A stocky, muscled ethnic—Mdivani—guarded a suave-looking tribal elder: Lemovin. And prominently shown were a startling couple. A blond man with a gut that was overshadowed only by his puffed-up chest lorded his importance over a honeyhaired slave girl. Even in the far background of the diorama, the figure based on Katy Lucca had that *Story of O* look of subservience.

"A *slave girl!*" Donovan exclaimed.

"That's how Lucca wanted her painted," Metz said. "He said it was a little joke that no one would get. I figure, you know, sometimes men and women have weird relationships."

"Do they? Well, I think I got the joke. Lucca *wanted* you to paint her this way? The others, too?"

"He practically stood over me—chuckling the whole time— while I did it. He was here all day Sunday while I was putting the finishing touches on it. I told you the other day that Lucca believed in the old diorama-artist's dictum that you paint your friends into the background. Make them Eskimos or Maoris or something. This is how he told me he wanted Mrs. Lucca portrayed. It was his nickel, Lieutenant. It was his joke."

"Who else knew?"

"Just him, me, and now you. No one else. Hell, Mrs. Lucca wasn't even interested in the exhibit. She was home all day Sunday while he was busy here. And during the opening she didn't even go behind the curtain. She stayed outside bullshitting with you. Well, at least no one will ever accuse her of killing her husband. That's a hell of an alibi."

"Yeah. Almost as good as being locked on the fire escape."

"Do you notice a pattern emerging, boss?" Moskowitz asked.

Donovan shook his head, then changed direction and bobbed it up and down. "Yes. No."

"You're not sure."

"I'm sure I'm appalled. Look, I gotta get out of here. Bernie, thanks for your help."

"No problem, Lieutenant."

"Bonaci, you're a wonder worker as usual. See you later."

"*Ciao*, Lieutenant," he said as Donovan walked off with Moskowitz at his side.

"Where are you going?"

"To a darts tournament," Donovan said.

"What about the locksmith and the commissioner?"

"Put them off."

TWENTY-EIGHT

KATE SMITH SINGING "GOD BLESS AMERICA" AT FULL BLAST

"WITHOUT EVER setting foot inside this place I can tell you exactly what it's like," Donovan said, eyeballing the Shamrock Pub from the back of the surveillance car across the street.

"Tell me what it's like," Moskowitz said with mild interest, not looking up from the message that was coming in on his notebook.

"You see, whenever the sign outside has a shillelagh dancing with a martini glass, the insides are all the same. There's a law about it; they're like Wendy's...the joints have to be identical. There's a bar with twelve stools, four of them broken. The cigarette machine is in the front, alongside the pay phone. The wall behind the pay phone is pockmarked with holes where guys who run auto body shops or lawn maintenance companies have tacked up their business cards. Scribbled on the wall is an insulting reference to a girl named Tina, along with her phone number. The pool table is in the back of the room along with two old Formica tables where the owner and his wife sit. Both are in their seventies. Laid out on one table is a copy of the *Daily News* open to the sports page. The ice machine is next to the bathrooms. Only the men's room works; the ladies' room has been nailed shut for six months. That doesn't matter, because apart from the owner's wife the only woman who sets foot in the place is widely suspected of being a bull dyke. She's also the local pool and darts champion. The dart board is hung on the wall next to the men's room door. They still talk about the day Jimmy from the Mobil station got a dart in the ass while going in to take a leak. The TV set is over the bar. The remote is broken. The bartender has to climb on a chair to change channels. That doesn't matter, because the set is tuned mainly to the Sports Channel. The only time the set is touched is to change from baseball to hockey. No basketball is allowed in the Shamrock Pub."

"Why?" Moskowitz asked, looking up from his computer.

"Basketball attracts African-Americans."

"There's a bar on Flatbush Avenue where they play Kate Smith singing 'God Bless America' at full blast every time a black sits down in the place," Moskowitz said. "Local lore holds that the song drives them away."

"It would chase me the hell out of there, too," Donovan replied. "What just came in on the computer?"

"Like you suspected, there is indeed a story behind Mrs. Lucca. We got it from a friend in the Jersey state police."

Donovan leaned back in the seat and closed his eyes.

"She used to be a cokehead. She was busted for possession twice, but both times Wally took the rap for her. He adored her, boss, but they had a complicated relationship. He also slapped her around a little.''

Donovan opened his eyes wide.

"Our contact says that the talk among the local cops is that she liked it. They got called to that house to break up fights. They took her to the emergency room three times. But she never pressed charges against the guy. They say that when she divorced him, she cried all through the hearing.''

"All this got hushed up somehow," Donovan said.

"I think that in this crowd you've been hanging out with lately a lot of money gets tossed around to smooth over a lot of rough edges," Mosko said.

Donovan put his hand on the doorknob. "Dial the number of that bar and get Jameson on the phone. Tell him that Lieutenant Donovan would like a word with him alone, now. I want to meet him on that park bench over there." Donovan pointed out a bench near the gazebo where the good people of West Ridge heard concerts on Sunday afternoons.

"You don't want to go in the bar?"

"Why? The joint is a museum of my past and I've seen enough museum this week.''

A few minutes later Donovan was sitting on the bench, his legs stretched halfway across the concrete walkway that led across the green to the train station, his London Fog wrapped around him to keep out a September chill. When Jameson came out of the pub he wore a red down coat and a blue Giants cap. He had a cigarette in his lips and another perched behind his ear.

"Hey, Lieutenant," he said, sliding onto the bench next to Donovan, "How come you didn't come into the bar? You could get into the match. Do you play darts?"

"Not any more. I didn't want to come in because I didn't want to embarrass you in front of your friends.''

"Oh shit. That sounds like bad news.''

Donovan turned his head toward the man and said, "I need to know a few things about Katy.''

Maybe there was something in his voice, in the way it lowered and softened when he spoke her name. Maybe it was that he said "Katy" and not "Mrs. Lucca." Whatever Donovan did to give away the largely personal nature of his visit, Jameson, in his stoned and affable way, decided to call him on it. Jameson looked into the lieutenant's eyes, smiled, then shook his head and looked down.

"It's *you*, isn't it? You're the one."

Donovan offered a quizzical look even though he understood perfectly well.

"She got to you. I mean, *you* got to *her*. And I bet you didn't even try. You're her next number. I had that feeling, sort of, when you came to my house. Now I'm sure of it."

"Her next *number?*" Donovan asked, the sound of that word striking him as appealing as a rusty old can.

"You know what I mean. You're a *regular guy*. You work for a living. You have dirt under your nails, sort of. You work out, right?"

"A little, yeah."

"She likes that. Give me credit for knowing what my ex-wife likes. You have all the credentials. You carry a gun. You're tough. Lieutenant, I got to know... You mind if I ask you something really personal?"

"Go for it," Donovan said, intrigued.

Now it was Jameson's turn to lower his voice. "You ever hit a woman?"

Donovan felt all the blood drain out of his face. It soon came back though, and his temper rose.

"No. That I never did."

"But you wanted to."

"Hey, I have enough *assholes* out there on the streets that I can use as a punching bag if I fucking well feel like it," Donovan said angrily, twisting his body toward the man. "I never hit a woman." His anger turned his cheeks red in the chill air. Jameson saw it, got a little scared, and backed off.

"Hey, I know I'm an asshole. But I don't want to be one of the ones you slap around. You got a nice temper on you, Lieutenant, the same as me. Only you have a badge that makes you a hero and not some jerk from a small town in Jersey. She fell for you. I can see it a mile off. Maybe you fell for her, too."

Donovan frowned.

"Okay, deny it," Jameson said. "That's cool too. Look, I fell for her, even though I knew from day one that it was a mistake."

Donovan turned away and leaned back, his muscles relaxing. He managed a polite smile.

"And now you want to know what it will be like. All I can say is, hang the fuck on. It will be one hell of a ride."

"I know about the blackmail and I don't think you're gonna get the money," Donovan said.

Jameson tossed up his hands. "Well, what the fuck. The story of my life. Am I gonna go to jail for trying?"

"Not from anything I do."

"Thanks. Like I said, you're a regular guy."

"Okay, Wally, forget whether she's fallen for me. I don't care one way or the other, and anyway, all that stuff is too much for regular guys like you and me to figure out. You saw that picture of us in the newspaper? She fainted and I caught her?"

"Yeah. Cool."

"Could she have faked that?"

"Faked fainting?"

"Faked everything. Could she—and if you breathe a word of this I swear I *will* use you as a punching bag—could Katy still be in love with Steven Clark? Could she have worked with him to kill Lucca?"

"Not a chance in the world."

"Clark is a jerk. *He* probably slapped her around."

"I know he did. She told me. But she also told me that when she left him and married Lucca, she was cured. I know I said we never spoke, but we did on the phone from time to time. She'd call me in the middle of the night when she needed someone she could talk to about her problem. We made our peace, sort of, and I became something of a big brother to her. I guess I fucked that up when I tried to blackmail her. Story of my life."

"The problem you mention is that she's attracted to the wrong guys," Donovan said.

"Yeah. She did a lot of therapy over there in Europe and she's over it. Lucca was a new life for her. He was different. I always thought he was kind of a faggot, but what do I know? He liked to dress up like Indiana Jones, and I guess he loved her. Now she's turned on to you. Well, I can see why."

Donovan stood up. "I got to go back to the city and nail Clark's fancy little ass," he said.

"She *does* faint, Lieutenant. She did it a couple of times on me. She's an emotional girl and needs a strong man to protect her. Go get Clark. I'll be betting on you."

"I'm counting on you to keep quiet. If I find out that you sold this story to Maury Povich or someone, I'll come back here and have you for breakfast.''

Jameson mimed zipping his lips and then waved at Donovan as he headed back in the direction of his car. After a moment, Jameson too got up and loped quietly back to the bar.

Donovan crossed the park and stood on the curb across from his car, tossing over events in his head. He stepped into the street then, distracted further by lights and bells, a flashing red light and the clanging of a crossing-gate bell as a commuter train approached the small station. There was also the roar of a car engine, and a squealing of wheels, and the hint of yellow off to one side. It was the yellow cab with the bashed-in fender, and it was roaring straight at the lieutenant. The man behind the wheel, the same one Donovan had seen at the tobacco shop, grinned horribly while chewing on a thick brown cigar.

Off in the distance Donovan heard Moskowitz shout. Donovan froze for an instant, then dived backward onto the curb, falling into a heap of flailing arms and bunched-up trench coat. The right front wheel of the cab bounced off the curb, the fender scraping concrete as the driver whipped the wheel around to avoid a tree. Mosko came flying out of Donovan's car and across the street as the yellow cab flew across the railroad tracks, whipping around the front of the train as it pulled in to the small station. The tearing of wood told Donovan that part of the black-and-white-striped crossing gate had been turned into splinters.

Mosko helped him to his feet.

"Jesus, are you okay?"

"My life is getting very complicated," Donovan said as he brushed the leaves, grass, and dirt from his coat.

"That's the cab you told me about," Mosko said. He brought his cellular phone to his lips and called the local cops as Donovan walked—very cautiously, and with a bit of a limp from a strained muscle—to his car.

"I'm letting Akbar free and filing charges against Clark," Donovan told his assistant when the man rejoined him.

"That was a warning from Clark, wasn't it?" Mosko said.

"You bet."

"I told the West Ridge cops what happened. They have a car on the way over." Mosko gestured out the window at the far-off but approaching siren

"They'll find that cab abandoned a few miles away with no useful prints on it," Donovan said. "We'll never get that driver. Too bad, too. He might be the only young white cabdriver in the city of New York."

"On one hand I can see that Clark could have murdered Lucca and sent that guy to try to scare you off. On the other hand, we have Akbar dead to rights. It would be so easy to file charges and go back to bed."

"Do you want to spend your life doing things the easy way?" Donovan asked, all fired up.

"I wouldn't mind doing *something* the easy way. And it wouldn't hurt you, either, judging by what I just saw. Face it, Bill, you're not getting any younger."

Donovan bristled. "I feel like a kid. Clark has got me mad now. This testosterone surge in my veins has knocked ten years off my age."

"Let's get back to the city as fast as we can," Mosko said. "Pilcrow wants to see you, and the commissioner is lined up behind him."

"There's something I want you to do first. Call Clark. Call his secretary or his lawyer or whoever you have to deal with. Here's the message: Lieutenant Donovan insists on speaking with the man again. There are some aspects of his story that are giving the lieutenant a problem. Find out when I can see him."

"YOU'RE GOING to *what?* Let Akbar *go?* You're out of your mind, Lieutenant." Deputy Chief Inspector Pilcrow's face had reddened improbably and his eyes were bugging out as he stared across the desk at Donovan, who stood his ground.

"I'm going after Clark," he said.

"Oh my God," Pilcrow swore.

"Akbar was clearly set up. Clark stole his gloves from the cloakroom and wore them while stabbing Lucca. Clark got the dagger from the safe because it also links Akbar to the crime. Clark figures that, given the anti-Arab feelings rampant in this city following the World Trade Center bombing, we'll rush to judgment and throw the book at this scrawny little Pamiristani militant. The way this was set up to look, Akbar the Muslim terrorist used the ancient weapon stolen from his homeland to exact revenge on the thief. I don't buy a word of it."

"Akbar is a convicted murderer, I understand, escaped from a Russian prison."

"Actually he was let go in the confusion over there in 1990. But they haven't asked for him back. The hell with Russian justice anyway. Akbar says he killed a black marketeer who was ripping off and reselling medical supplies, and nobody has come forth to contradict him."

"Before your buddy the commissioner gets here, there's something I have to say: I had a feeling that you would screw up," Pilcrow said. "I just didn't know what form it would take."

"I'm sorry that you're disappointed in me, Chief," Donovan said, crossing his arms. "But I'm right on this one. Clark did Lucca and I mean to nail him for it."

"How did Clark get the dagger out of the safe?"

"I'm looking into the background of the locksmith who handled both the safe and the locks on the studios. My suspicion is that Clark paid him for the combination to the safe and a copy of the master key that ultimately let him into the studio where the crime was committed."

"Why would Steven Clark, one of the wealthiest men in the world, murder a business partner? Certainly not for money."

"Don't be too sure. Lucca was only giving Clark about one percent of what he needs to solve his cash-flow problems. Clark wanted more. He probably was pissed off. And there's the matter of Mrs. Lucca."

"What about her?"

"Clark is famous for flying into rages when someone plays with his toys," Donovan said.

"So you're saying that Clark was mad because he didn't get as big a share of Asian Explorations as he wanted, and furious because Lucca got the girl?"

"I believe that the true motive is grazing somewhere in that pasture, yes."

Pilcrow looked up at the ceiling and then down at the floor, his fingers playing nervously with the buttons on his double-breasted jacket. Donovan thought, *Here it comes: the next move in the poker game called "Will Donovan get the captain's shield?"*

Pilcrow said, "Okay, Lieutenant, here's what we're going to do. I—"

He was cut off in mid-sentence when Moskowitz blustered into the office, leading the commissioner. Mosko said, "Lieutenant, the big guy's here," then hurriedly left.

Pilcrow whipped around and said, "Commissioner! How good to see you."

"Hello, Paul. Bill. I like your new partner. What's his name? Bruce Moskowitz?"

"Brian."

"Oh, *Brian* Moskowitz? Therein hangs a tale, no doubt. With your friends, there's usually a pretty good story."

Pilcrow forced a smile and said: "The Lieutenant was just filling me in on the Lucca case."

"Can I hear it, too?"

Donovan repeated what he had told Pilcrow. When the tale was over, the commissioner whistled softly—a few notes from *West Side Story,* Donovan thought—and jammed his hands in his pants pockets to jiggle his change and car keys.

"If you had told me this morning that you were going after Steven Clark I would have called you an asshole or worse," the commissioner said at last.

"What's worse?" Donovan asked.

"Never mind. But an hour ago I got this call from the mayor."

A glimmer of malicious, I-told-you-so glee flashed across Pilcrow's face.

The commissioner said, "At three o'clock this afternoon Steven Clark, who despite his reputation as a civic biggie hasn't done a goddamn thing for this city in two years, phoned in a fifty-thousand-dollar contribution to the mayor's reelection campaign. On top of it he gave the mayor another fifty thousand to be donated to the Fund for the Families of Policemen Killed in the Line of Duty."

"A hundred thousand, just like that?" Pilcrow said.

"Yeah. You know what the mayor's exact words to me were?" Donovan shrugged.

"He said, 'Who the hell did he kill?'"

Donovan smiled and did his best to appear modest. He didn't do an especially good job. Donovan's demeanor was further altered by the next bit of information.

"Guess in whose name the donation to the Families' Fund was made?"

"Paolo Lucca's?" Donovan guessed.

"Wrong. It was in the name of William Michael Donovan, Sr., killed in the line of duty."

"My father? Clark gave that money to the Families' Fund in my father's name?" Donovan sat down behind his desk and stared blankly at the commissioner, who was nodding slightly. Pilcrow looked stunned.

"Does Clark know you're after him?"

"Uh, yes," Donovan said, shaking off his surprise. "A few hours ago I had Moskowitz try to make an appointment for me to go over some problems in Clark's alibi."

"Did you get an appointment?"

"No. I got brushed off by his lawyers: 'Mr. Clark is busy in Atlantic City and not coming back to New York in the immediate future. Mr. Clark will be glad to cooperate with the Lieutenant at a future date,' et cetera, et cetera."

"Freely translated, that means he's never going to talk to you if his lawyers can do anything about it. He wouldn't talk to you but he turned around and called the mayor and put on the pressure. The message was clear: Get Donovan to back off."

"The SOB tagged the message with my father's name," Donovan said. "This is getting even more personal than it got an hour ago when he tried to have me run down."

"I heard about that. I don't like the sound of it. Nobody can push this police department around, not even the Boss. Look, Captain—"

"There's that word again," Donovan said.

"Are you sure that Clark killed Lucca and is trying to pin it on the Muslims?"

"I'm sure."

"Prove it and you're a captain. Agreed, Paul?"

"Absolutely," Pilcrow said quickly. "But how are you going to get to Clark if he won't even talk to you?"

"I have a plan to make him come to me."

"How can you do that?"

Donovan smiled and said, "It's clear now that his legendary short fuse is no myth. He tried to have me killed this afternoon because I'm getting too close to him. Well, I've been offered the opportunity to play with one of his toys—an act that is known to make Clark furious. I'm going to make sure he hears about it."

WHEN AKBAR WAS brought back into Donovan's office from the holding cell, the lieutenant said right away, "I'm announcing to the press that I'm not charging you with the murder of Paolo Lucca. This decision is going to cause me a lot of grief. You can help by going back to your hotel room and staying there for a few days."

Akbar reached across the desk and grasped the lieutenant's hand. "You are a wise man. Is there anything I can do to help?"

"I'll have men watching you, of course. The men should be there now, in fact, looking for any bribe you may have gotten from Lucca."

Moskowitz came into the room, shut the door behind him, and whispered in Donovan's ear, "They were in and out already. If our friend here got a bribe we can't find it. We've been watching him for two days and he didn't go near a bank, either."

"The money wasn't to have changed hands that night, but I'm glad that you're looking," Akbar said. "I understand."

"Don't go out and make me look like an idiot—and cause me more grief—by trying to get past my men. Stay put until you hear from me."

"I will do as you wish," Akbar said. "I have heard a great many things about American cable television. Anything else?"

"Don't talk to anyone except me. I'll give you my home phone number. Call me anytime if there's a problem. And, most of all, don't forget that I can reel you in and charge you at any time. Besides...you could have done it."

"I could have," Akbar said. "But I did not."

"The sergeant here will arrange for you to be driven back to the hotel."

When Moskowitz had done that and returned, he carried with him a message taken down by Michelle Paglia at the front desk. "Who's Brigid?" he asked.

The lieutenant shook his head. "What does she want?" he asked, trying to pluck the message from his partner's fingers, but the man pulled it back and read it aloud.

"'I'm making dinner for you tonight, so don't eat anything and spoil your appetite.' That's so *cute*. An Irish girl and she's making you dinner. No doubt this is going to be an Irish seven-course meal."

"A six-pack and a potato. I was in the seventh grade the first time I heard that joke. Gimme the message."

He read on: "'Pick up a bottle of wine. Red.' So I guess it's gonna be hamburgers." Moskowitz handed over the message, which Donovan glanced at before stuffing in his shirt pocket.

"What's her last name?"

"O'Shaughnessy."

"Brigid O'Shaughnessy? That's the name of the girl that Bogie sent up the river at the end of *The Maltese Falcon*. She tried to double-cross him but he wasn't fooled for a second."

"Is it? I didn't know that. I don't watch old movies. Anyway, this girl is different. She says she only wants to make me happy, and who am I to argue? There—does that sound noble enough?"

"You're a prince, Lieutenant."

"'Cause that's as noble as I plan to be for a while."

"You don't need to stop for wine. Michelle and I never touched that bottle you were saving."

"I don't need it. Despite what Brigid has planned, I'm taking her out tonight."

Donovan got up from behind his desk, stretched, and checked his watch. "What time is it? Almost four. Okay, let's go see that locksmith and then I'm calling it quits for the day. When I'm safely gone you can take that statement I typed up about Akbar and read it to the press. Make sure that Morty Berman gets it first. I also want you to make sure the boys show up for the party. I want an army of cops in there."

"Will do."

"And while you're at it, remind him that he owes me a favor. I need him tonight about eight."

"What's tonight?"

"It's the grand opening of Marcy's Home Cooking—what party did you think I was talking about?"

"Right. Sorry."

"Tell Morty I want him there with a crew. Tell him to follow my lead on this one, don't ask me anything tough, to trust me. As we used to say in 1968, 'Go with the flow.' It's not such a big favor, considering I saved his neck."

"Let me get this straight. You want Morty Berman the investigative reporter to cover the opening of your girl's restaurant."

"*Ex*-girlfriend," Donovan said emphatically.

"Whatever. Will you be at the opening, too?"

"I wouldn't miss it for the world," Donovan said. "Moreover, I'm thinking of bringing Brigid."

Mosko grimaced. "That should start some fireworks."

"I sincerely hope so," Donovan replied.

TWENTY-NINE

THE WORLD'S WEALTHIEST AND MOST GENEROUS

COLUMBUS AVENUE Locksmiths was little more than a decade old, but in that time had amassed a lot of clients. Many of them were immortalized by having photos of their establishments framed on the walls of the medium-sized, very busy shop a few blocks from the museum. The store itself was unremarkable; it was a locksmith's shop, made unusual only by the fact that it existed side-by-side with some of New York City's trendiest boutiques. Before he entered, Donovan stood on the sidewalk scratching his chin and pondering real estate trends.

"I saw this interview on TV with Martin Scorsese a few weeks ago," he said. "The guy was talking about how he directed *Raging Bull*. He shot the interior scenes for Jake La Motta's apartment—I remember his exact words—'in a tenement on Columbus Avenue.'"

Moskowitz chuckled.

"Yeah, that was my reaction," Donovan said. "There hasn't been a *tenement* on this street since about 1975, which is about when, I guess, he shot the movie. In fact, last month Presage, the Paris clothier, closed its Columbus Avenue shop claiming it could no longer afford the fifteen-thousand-dollar-a-month rent. That was a block from here. So..."

"How does Columbus Avenue Locksmiths, Anthony Di Bello, proprietor, continue to pay the rent in this neighborhood? A very good question, Lieutenant, and I think I got the answer."

He punched some keys on his notebook computer. "It's a little-known fact that you got to list your other clients in order to get city contracts, and Di Bello did the work on the museum. This man's clients include—are you ready?—Clark Beach Village in Canarsie and Clark Tower in Manhattan.''

''As I thought. When was this work done?''

''Both jobs were within the past year. They were big jobs, too.''

''I'm dying to hear this guy's story,'' Donovan said. ''Let's see if he's as talkative as our VIP friends.''

Donovan pushed his way into the shop to find a showroom for various locks and keys. The place gleamed with brass and smelled of lubricant. A Plexiglas display case was filled with the latest in apartment-door security devices. One edge of a sample door nearby was lined, top to bottom, with locks. And every inch of wall space that didn't have locks or keys on it was covered with framed photos. Included in this gallery were neighborhood shops, restaurants, high-rise apartment buildings, several views of Yankee Stadium, the natural-history museum and several others, brownstones, and granite Riverside Drive monoliths. There was nothing, however, to suggest either Clark Beach Village or Clark Tower.

There were, however, two empty spaces where photos had just been removed. While Moskowitz called the proprietor out of the back room, Donovan inspected the spaces. There was no dust on them, in contrast with the layer of grime that coated everything else. One thing reliable about New York City, Donovan knew, is that soot will land on something within hours and that if an object is absolutely clean it only just got that way. He thought back to the recently moved bags of rock salt in the museum courtyard. Clearly, the photos had been removed from two spaces within the past few hours.

Nearby, however, hung a photo that had been up for years and bore a respectable layer of city soot. The picture was of Abbracciamento, a restaurant on the Canarsie Pier. The place was one of Donovan's favorite stops on the Belt Parkway, which looped around the coastline of Brooklyn en route to John F. Kennedy International Airport and, beyond, Long Island.

He was looking at the photo and reminiscing about old girlfriends and sunsets when Mosko brought Di Bello up. ''You did the locks in this place?'' Donovan asked, tapping the photo and then inspecting the soot that stuck to the tip of his finger.

''Yeah. That's my hangout, Lieutenant. I put in the security system and I service it regular. I live in Canarsie.''

"Me too," Mosko said.

"No shit. Whereabouts?"

"Near South Shore High School," Mosko said. "You know Stanley's Canarsie Gym?"

"I drive by it every day."

"My uncle's place."

"I used to take dates to Abbracciamento to watch the sunsets," Donovan said.

"The best in the world. I was there Saturday. You should have seen the sun go down that night. Beautiful, orange, you know?" The man seemed friendly and alive, as so many Brooklynites do when comparing notes on their favorite spots. But when Di Bello paused several long beats and asked, "So what can I do for you?" his voice turned nervous and irritable. Donovan sensed that he did not want to get down to police business. If he had been hooked up to a polygraph at that moment, Di Bello would have made spikes the size of Pike's Peak.

The man was short and heavyset, with a bald spot that covered the crown of his head and made the surrounding hair resemble that of a monk. His gut stuck out above a pair of light blue pants fastened with a custom belt buckle that featured his initials. His white polo shirt had "Columbus Avenue Locksmiths" stitched over the left breast. Di Bello mopped the sweat from his brow onto a handkerchief.

"You did some work for the museum?" Donovan asked.

"Which one?"

"Natural history. How many museums do you do?"

"I also did Jewish and Cooper Union. What about it?"

Donovan didn't like the way the man said, "What about it?" The voice was one step removed from "What's it to you?" "Who wants to know?" and even "You got a problem with that?"

"You did the safe in the office of Arthur C. Kent, curator of Asian archaeology?"

"The old English guy," Di Bello said, folding the handkerchief over and mopping a brow that sweated like a broken hose. "What of it?"

"Who knows the combination?"

"Me and him. No, not him, the young guy who works there, Metz. Oh, and the guy who got killed: Lucca."

"That's it? Nobody else?"

"Not another soul," Di Bello said, dabbing at the sweat in the corners of his eyes. "I swear to God."

"You didn't give the combination to anyone else? I hope you're not lying to me."

"Not another living soul. Are you accusing me of lying? Why should I lie?"

Donovan didn't answer the question. Instead he asked, "Did you do the locks to the studios in the Treasure of the Silk Road exhibit?"

"Yeah, I done them too. You wanna know who got copies?" Donovan nodded.

"The head of security. And Metz."

"Those keys are accounted for. Anyone else get copies?"

"No one, I swear on my mother's grave. Look, Lieutenant, I'm trying to be nice and you're accusing me. My lawyer said I don't have to talk to you. No way."

Di Bello tried his best to puff his chest up. He stepped back from Donovan, but the lieutenant moved forward on him to keep up the pressure.

"Your lawyer said that?" Donovan said, interested in this development.

"Yeah."

"You asked your lawyer about talking to me?"

"I talked to him this afternoon. You got a problem with that?"

"That's interesting. You know, Mr. Di Bello, I talk to lots of people in the course of investigation. Dozens."

"Hundreds sometimes," Moskowitz added. His anger also aroused, he too stepped in on the man.

"And not that many of them think to check with their lawyer before talking to me," Donovan said. "Fewer than one percent, if I had to put a number on it. You're a very well-prepared man. Tell me this: Did you ever do any work for Steven Clark?"

Di Bello's veins stuck out on the sides of his head and he blurted out, "No, I never did no work for Clark Towers and I never did no work for Clark Beach Village! Look, I think I'm gonna take my lawyer's advice. Here's his card." Di Bello fished it out of a pocket and handed it over. "You wanna talk to me any more you talk to him first."

"Thank you, Mr. Di Bello," Donovan said. Then he added, pointing out the bare spots on the walls, "You ought to get something to hang up there. I can get you some stunning pictures of Sing Sing and Attica. That's where they send you for complicity to murder.''

''Murder? I didn't have nothin' to do with killing Lucca.''

''Let me tell you this, Mr. Di Bello,'' Donovan said. ''I'm taking Clark down and I'm stealing his favorite toy on top of it. You can tell him that for me. Have a good one.''

When they were back out on the street, Donovan said, ''He lied to us, the little shit. We *know* that he works for Clark.''

''The way he said it was interesting, too. Did you catch that?''

''Yeah. I asked him if he worked for Clark and he blurted out 'I never worked for Clark *Towers* or Clark *Beach Village.*' This guy Di Bello may be a professional locksmith but he's an amateur liar. I guess I must have rattled him and he shot his mouth off.''

Donovan handed over the business card to Moskowitz. ''Check out this shyster. Ten to one he's on retainer with Clark.''

''Will do. Were those bare spots on the wall where Di Bello had pictures of the Clark places nailed up?''

''I'm sure of it. Clark called him this afternoon and told him to shut up. Di Bello probably just had time to get the pictures off the wall before we got there. Well, we know one thing for sure.''

''Clark scares easy.''

''Exactly. Now let's see how quickly I can drive him into a fury.''

''What do you expect to get out of this?'' Moskowitz asked. ''A confession?''

''No, but I might cause him to do something incredibly stupid. Let me push some more buttons and we'll see how it goes. In the meantime, tighten up the surveillance on him. If Clark even *thinks* of leaving Atlantic City I want to hear about it.''

They got back into their car and drove south on Columbus to Seventy-ninth Street, then made a right and drove the two blocks over to Broadway. They parked back outside the West Side Major Crimes Unit. Nearby, Jake Nakima and George Kohler were busy cleaning up the window of Marcy's Home Cooking for the grand opening. Marcy herself was on a stepladder putting up red, white, and blue bunting. If she saw her former lover drive up, she didn't show it.

Mosko finished a last check on the computer to see if anything new had come in. He still awaited a rundown on the phone numbers Donovan had requested as well as the ashtray in Lucca's apartment, among other things. Nothing new came in, so Donovan called it a day. It was dinnertime; the sun was dipping low over the Hudson River and the Jersey shoreline and casting long shadows up the narrow side streets west of Broadway. Mosko put the computer back in his shoulder bag.

"You ought to get a briefcase for that," Donovan said.

"Please, boss. I'm just getting used to wearing a suit. So look, have a good time tonight with your new girl."

"I'll try. Get outta here and let me go home to her."

"See you tomorrow."

Mosko got out of the car and walked across the pavement to the Unit. Marcy looked down from her perch atop the stepladder, saw him, and waved. But she never looked around to see if Donovan was there, and he nearly always was.

It really is *over,* Donovan thought as he put the engine in gear and made the turn down the side street toward Riverside Drive and home.

He parked in his spot in the garage and rode the elevator to the lobby floor to pick up the mail. The broad marble lobby was full of life as neighbors drifted home, got the mail, compared children, and argued over the Giants' chances to make the playoffs that year. The concierge handed packages, dropped off by deliverymen during the day, to tenants whose arms were already overloaded with bags from the supermarket. Donovan had shopped in a suburban supermarket once. He got halfway across the parking lot carrying eight bags when he realized everyone was staring. *Oh. You take the cart out of the store and push it to your car. What a concept.* In New York you schlepp everything by hand. It was, he was sure, the real reason he still had such good upper-body strength at age fifty.

Myron Glass the landlord stood by the concierge booth, arguing with an old man about the hot water in the building. Donovan normally avoided Glass, for their conversations were always the same:

"When are you going to buy your apartment so the whole building can go co-op?"

"When I win the fucking lottery, Myron. I'm a cop, not a banker."

If being a policeman kept Donovan among the honest poor, it

also kept him free from the harassment frequently accorded recalcitrant New York City tenants who held doggedly to their rent-controlled apartments. By virtue of having inherited the lease on his monster of an apartment from his parents, Donovan paid in rent only about one-sixth what the flat would have fetched on the open market. If he weren't a cop, Myron would long ago have used such landlord tricks as shutting off the hot water on Saturday night or stalling on fixing a broken radiator in January. All in all, it was best that the two men not speak to one another.

But not that day. For, the second he spotted Donovan walking past, Glass hurried up, extending a glad hand.

"Good to see you, Myron," Donovan said and kept walking.

Undaunted, the man called after him: "Lieutenant. I got the good news from your lawyer and will have the papers ready for your signature on Friday."

Donovan took a few steps farther, then stopped dead in his tracks and slowly turned around.

"What did you say?"

The landlord was actually gleeful, as if unable to believe Donovan's—and his—good luck. "Your lawyer called this afternoon and gave me the good news. I'm drawing up the papers now."

Donovan walked slowly up to the man. "What papers are those?"

"The purchase agreement for your apartment, of course."

"I'm buying my apartment?" Donovan asked, his mind racing.

"What did you think you were doing, planting a tree in Israel? I have no idea where you got the money for an outright purchase, but let me say that I'm delighted."

Donovan shut his eyes, then opened them slowly. When he did, he could see clearly.

"Let me ask one thing."

"Anything," Glass said.

"How much am I paying?"

"How much did I ask?" The man lowered his voice. "Half a million dollars, of course."

Donovan thought: *Damn, the rich really are another species. What did she say that first night? With enough money you can make anything possible? So this is how it's going to be—donations to the mayor's reelection campaign, contributions to the Families' Fund, buying apartments, and God knows what else.*

"Is something wrong, Lieutenant?"

"God, Myron, where can I possibly begin?" Donovan started to turn away again, but Glass stopped him with a hand on the arm.

"Is it the price? 'Cause if that's it, we can talk."

Donovan pulled his arm away, but smiled to soften the message. "I got to have a few words with my banker," he said. "Let me get back to you in a few days."

THIRTY

"YOU FORGOT THE GOLDEN RETRIEVER," HE SAID

DONOVAN'S APARTMENT smelled of roses and freshly brewed coffee. The radio in the living room was tuned to WBGO, the Newark jazz station that was Donovan's longtime favorite. And his armchair in the living room was prepared as if in a dream: his slippers, a cup of coffee, and neatly folded copies of *The New York Times* and the *International Herald Tribune*.

He stood in the middle of the room gazing in absent-minded wonder at the wish-list scene, which contained everything he could possibly want except, perhaps, for a glass of excellent brandy and a pipe, both of which he had forsworn for health reasons. It was then that she came in from the kitchen, very much a vision of her own. Her long, honey-colored hair flowed over bare shoulders that graced the top of a small black velvet dress, the décolletage of which was decorated with a diamond brooch. Katy wore about her neck a strand of pearls and about her right ankle a gold chain. She had on high heels, and her eyes blazed at the sight of him.

"Welcome *home*," she said, slipping his raincoat from his shoulders.

"You forgot the golden retriever," he said.

"What?"

"You know the old game? 'What's missing in this picture?'"

"Yes," she said as she hung up his coat in the hall closet and rejoined him.

"What's missing is the golden retriever curled up by the roaring fire. Actually, the roaring fire is also missing, but since the fireplace is badly in need of cleaning..."

"I'll get it done tomorrow," she said, wrapping her arms around him. "In the meantime, you're not getting away from me tonight. You're not working and you're not getting away."

Katy loosened his tie and took off his jacket and pushed him backward into the armchair. Then she kicked off her shoes and draped herself across his lap, using one hand to play with the small hairs on the back of his neck. "What a terrific sunset tonight... Better even than Saturday."

"I wasn't running from you last night," Donovan said. "I was being noble."

"This is America in the nineties," she said. "The age of nobility is long gone."

He nodded, and said, "It's not even remembered by the expert on the Enlightenment, Tommaso Lucca."

"I don't want to discuss my late husband or his family. He's dead and buried and that's all past. That was then. This is now. Let's talk about you and me."

"There are a few things to get out of the way first."

"Oh *man*," she said, sounding for an instant like Wally Jameson's ex, not Paolo Lucca's.

"Where were you during the day on Saturday?"

"I shopped up and down Fifth Avenue."

"By yourself?"

"Yes. Paolo was at the fucking museum watching something get painted."

"And on Sunday during the day?"

"Paolo went early to the museum and stayed there all day until he came to change and pick me up for the reception. Me, I stayed home and read the papers and rested. I took off all my clothes and swam in the pool absolutely stark fucking naked. William, after we eat let's go back to my place and skinny dip. What do you think of that?"

He smiled. "You were alone?"

"All day. No more questions."

"Only one more. Do you know who Paolo was going to have a special meeting with while the other VIPs were touring the exhibit?"

"Yes. Akbar. The man with the funny gloves who killed him.

Now, that's it for you—no more work. No more anything except paying attention to me.''

"When was the last time you saw Steven?''

"God damn you! At the museum on Sunday. He gave me a hug and nearly made me sick.''

"Before that?''

"One...two years ago. I hated that moment and will see him next in hell. I will hate that moment, too.'' She lowered her lips to Donovan's and pressed a kiss on him. He kissed her back, but halfheartedly. After a moment she broke away.

"Am I *boring* you?'' she asked.

"I want you to stop trying to buy me,'' Donovan said angrily. "I don't want you to buy me apartments. I don't want you to buy me cars or yachts or expensive clothes. I don't want the goddamn fireplace fixed. I like it broken. It keeps the bats out.''

Softened, she touched several fingertips to his cheek. "William, I just want to do something nice for you.''

"Listen to me. You can't buy me half-million-dollar apartments. You just can't.''

"I can do anything,'' she said confidently.

That's it, that's what pisses me off about this woman, Donovan thought. Katy had repeated the mantra that was Marcy's oftspoken assessment of herself: "I can do anything.'' Well, sure Marcy could do anything. She could be black, white, Christian, Jewish, beautiful, an undercover policewoman, and a terrific lover. She was bulletproof. As a policewoman she could even track down two Harlem teenagers who—although drug dealers—were innocent of the crime for which she was after them. She could do anything so well that she shot these kids to death on a Harlem street without stopping to find out they were unarmed. As a result of Marcy's invulnerable attitude two good cops, including T. L. Jefferson, Donovan's longtime partner and onetime best friend, had to cover up for her by planting a gun on the deceased. Then Donovan was put in the position of covering up for the whole lot of them. Marcy never knew about the teenagers' innocence, never knew they weren't armed, never found out any of it, because she was too busy being perfect. She retired from the force still thinking she was perfect and, chanting her mantra, decided to open a restaurant on Broadway. In fact, the only thing that Marcy *couldn't* do was understand why Donovan grew distant.

He thought, *I am so tired of people who think they're above the law. Who think they're bulletproof and can do anything they want because they're young or smart or beautiful or rich.*

Ten or twelve years before, while they were both working on the Riverside Park murder case, Marcy had taken off her clothes and draped herself across Donovan's lap while he was sitting in that very spot and said, "I can do anything."

Well, that wasn't how it had worked out.

"Can *you?*" he asked Katy.

"Can I what?" she asked, undaunted by the strange emphasis.

"Do anything."

She bobbed her head up and down. "Anything I want in the whole world."

Donovan used his right hand to caress her leg. She gasped and her full, sultry mouth fell open as his hand moved up her thigh, under her dress, and over the tight, round swell of her behind. His left hand worked into her silky hair and pulled her parting lips down to his.

"Prove it," he said hoarsely.

"I WAS WRONG about you," Donovan said as she nestled under his arm.

"What?" she asked, lifting her head slightly and looking a bit alarmed. "What were you thinking about me?"

"That you really couldn't do anything you wanted," he replied.

"Oh." She laughed. "I was afraid for a moment you suspected me of killing my husband."

"How could I? You were with *me* then. You're with me now. Hey, do we have to talk about work?"

"I stand corrected," she said, smiling slyly, rolling onto her back and staring at the ceiling. Her left hand rested on his thigh, and she made little circles in his hair with a fingertip. He looked over at her, ran his eyes along the length of her body and back again, then involuntarily rolled his eyes. She saw it and giggled.

"What?"

He rolled toward her and cupped a breast, caressing it with the tenderness that might be accorded a famous piece of sculpture. Donovan had never seen anyone quite like Katy. Every part of her body was perfect. Normally, even with a famous beautiful person you can find a flaw: The nose is crooked, the eyes are too small, the knees are funny-looking. But Katy Lucca was absolutely perfect in every respect. Donovan found himself unable to take his eyes off her, yet each time he looked he smiled.

Finally she could take it no more. "*What* do you find so entertaining, William? Please, God, let me in on the joke."

"It's you. You're like another species. How ever did you get down on this planet in the first place?"

"You know, I was going to say that about you."

"Stop."

"No, I mean it. Me, I'm just another broad."

"Who gets stared at a lot. Do you find yourself in airports and guys can't take their eyes off you?"

"Sure, guys stare. On Madison Avenue this man had his eyes so glued to my boobs that I felt like saying, 'Hi, I'm Katy Lucca, taking the twins for a walk.' Women stare too. I can't tell if they hate me or envy me. When I was on my way to Majorca to do the swimsuit issue a few years back I flew with this gorgeous guy who was doing the shoot with me. The two of us were on the plane and people just *looked,* and you don't know whether to look back or smile or what."

"What do you do?"

"I asked my traveling companion that, and he told me: 'Meet their gazes, honey, but look back at them as if to say, "Yes, I *am* from another planet but I'm letting you gape so long as you promise not to come any closer. However, one more step and I'll pull out my phaser weapon and vaporize you."' He was gay, of course. Probably dead now."

"But you followed his advice."

"No. I married Paolo, and after that I traveled on my own plane. You know what attracted me to you?"

"Beats me. Were you disappointed when you found out that bulge at my waistline was only a Smith & Wesson?"

She laughed and her voice dropped down into that smokey register found in Tina Turner and in women who have smoked too much marijuana. "Whatever that is, honey, it ain't no single-shot. You are the best fuck I've ever had."

"Thank you. It was my birthday recently, and I think I want to believe that."

"How was I?"

"The best."

"Sure, sure. Hey, tell me: Remember when we met?"

"The evening does tend to stand out."

"You asked me how my luck was running lately, and I told you to dial my number and we'll see?"

He nodded.

"Well, my luck has been *great*. You're going to think me a callous bitch—"

"No, I won't."

"—but look at it this way: Paolo was saved a long and agonizing death. I became a millionaire. And I found you. Now if you'd only let me do something for you."

"I suppose this was nothing," Donovan said, sweeping an arm along the length of her body, amazed that, half an hour after the most torrid love scene in human history, her nipples remained erect.

"It wasn't *nothing*. Oh, William, I want to buy you this apartment. It's only—"

"Don't tell me it's only half a million dollars. Please, you're going to make my sick."

"I want to *do* something for you, honey, *please*."

"You really do?"

"Just name it."

"Okay, two things."

"What's first?"

"Let's go out to eat."

"That's *it?*" She laughed.

"Not exactly. It's the grand opening of Marcy's restaurant and I promised I'd be there. All my friends will be there."

"Oh, I see. You want to show me off to your friends. Well, that's cool."

"Hey, wear the wig. Go as Brigid."

"Nah, what the hell. So I get to meet the famous Marcy. At her *opening*."

"I went to Paolo's, didn't I? Where I met *three* of your lovers."

"The man has a point," she said, turning toward him and cupping his balls in her hand. "Tell me: Was Marcy as good as me?"

"I'll answer that question if you tell me if you also asked Steven to tie your arms to the bedposts and talk dirty to you."

She squeezed Donovan's balls. He grimaced slightly and pinched her nipple between his thumb and forefinger. Katy released her grip on him, and her hips churned sensually, as if she were humping the air. She said, "You take my breath away," and licked her long tongue in the air between their faces. He let go of her nipple.

After a moment she said, "Let's not talk about the past. Let's go to Marcy's and eat. What's the second thing you want?"

"If you have enough money you can do anything, right?"

"You want me to prove it?"

"Yes. I never got to see the Treasure of the Silk Road. Neither did you. I want to see it tomorrow night with you, alone."

"Okay."

"There's more."

"Name it."

"I want you to have the museum shut down. The whole god-damn place. I always wanted to be in that building without there being ten thousand kids. At midnight tomorrow, I want you and me to have the whole building to ourselves. Let's take a stroll, hand in hand, down the Silk Road. Can you arrange that?"

"It's yours," she said.

"Let's go eat."

She rolled away from him and got out of bed. "I'll have to fix myself up. It will take a few minutes."

"How'd you know the landlord was after me to buy my apartment?" Donovan asked.

"You left the prospectus on your desk," she said, and disappeared into the bathroom.

No. I crumpled it up and threw it into the garbage in the kitchen, he said to himself. *And, by the way, how did you know there was a terrific sunset on Saturday if you spent all day in Manhattan shopping?* The sunset had been called spectacular as seen from the Canarsie Pier, however.

When he heard the hair dryer going, Donovan got out of bed and went to the closet. He found his tuxedo jacket, the one he'd worn to the museum opening, and reached into the pocket. A three-day-old memory was nagging at him. The memory came with a puzzle that also had been twisting around in Donovan's head. The puzzle was this: If Steven Clark killed Paolo Lucca, how the hell did he get that dagger out of the safe in Kent's office? Sure, bribing the combination out of Di Bello was one way. But when did he actually lay his hands on the weapon? There was another possibility: Katy could have gotten the dagger and slipped it to Clark when they hugged at the reception. She could have hidden it under that stole and slipped it into his inside jacket pocket and nobody would have seen. That was a possibility, Donovan knew as he pulled out what he was looking for, the object that set off the thought.

He walked back to the bedside light and looked at the matchbook she had given him with her number written on the inside. On the outside was the name of a restaurant: Abbracciamento, on the Canarsie Pier. Di Bello's hangout.

Now, what was Katy Lucca doing on the Canarsie Pier if not meeting with the man who knew the combination to the safe?

Is there any way I could be wrong about this? Donovan wondered. *Is there any way she hasn't been stringing me along, spying on me, setting me up? Could it be that Steven Clark won't try to kill me tomorrow night at the museum?*

On a whim, Donovan carried the matchbook into his study and pulled from a shelf the Italian-American dictionary Bonaci had given him one Christmas. Donovan flipped through the pages and, when he found what he was looking for, his eyes gleamed with amazing and cruel irony. In Italian, *abbracciamento* means "to embrace for a moment."

What the hell, Donovan thought. *Let's take the little lady out to eat and wow the folks from the neighborhood.*

THIRTY-ONE

"HE STRIPPED MY GEARS
A COUPLE OF TIMES, TOO," KATY SAID

THE PLACE LOOKED like a cross between a trendy, suggested-in-the-guidebooks restaurant, a neighborhood hangout, and a police precinct muster room. Everyone under the West Side sun had turned out for the grand opening of Marcy's Home Cooking—all of Donovan's old cronies as well as a smattering of very upscale-looking diners.

Moskowitz was there, nattily dressed in a sports jacket and slacks. With him was Michelle Paglia, whose body language caused Donovan to wonder if there wasn't something going on between the two of them after all. Most of the tables were taken, and a few couples waited outside for the moment when Jake Nakima—who was in his accustomed role of doorman—would let them in. Casual noshers milled around between the tables and the bar, carrying drinks and hors d'oeuvres. The whole scene was being taped by Phil the cameraman, while Morty Berman stood at the bar, looking a bit uncomfortable. Berman was halfheartedly helping Richard Marlowe, the Columbia professor, do a crossword puzzle.

Donovan pulled his car up front and walked around to open the door for Katy. When she got out, flashing those eyes and flipping that hair around, Jake nearly fell over. Katy wore her sable over a somewhat more modest dress, this one maroon. She took Donovan's arm and held it tight as he led her across the sidewalk and introduced her to Jake.

"This is Jake Nakima, the only kamikaze pilot to fly twenty-nine missions," Donovan said.

He was struck dumb and merely bobbed his head up and down.

"I saw the movie," Katy said brightly. "You were played by Brandon Lee, weren't you? Pleased to meet you, Jake."

She took his hand and shook it. The man's mouth was still open when Donovan led her into Marcy's. As Donovan and Katy made their way to the bar, the crowd parted for them the way the Red Sea did for Moses. George Kohler was there, in his familiar pose of Paul Bunyan as bartender. This time, though, his usual scowl was replaced by a look of boyish wonder. The last time Donovan had seen that look was when he brought in a Desert Eagle automatic pistol for him to ogle. Leave it to an old Korean War vet to be equally awed by outrageous beauty and massive firepower.

"This is Katy," Donovan said.

"Oh, uh, hi." The few simple words came from his mouth only with the greatest of difficulty.

"Hi." She reached out her hand.

"You said you wondered about her perfume."

Now beet red, George bent to kiss her hand, pausing ever so briefly to inhale her scent. When he straightened up he closed his eyes, took in a deep breath, and expelled it, saying "Now I can die happy."

"That makes you one fuck of a lot easier to please than *him*," Katy said, digging Donovan in the ribs with her elbow.

"What will you have?" Donovan asked.

"Stoli up."

"One Stoli up. I'll take a Kaliber and a table, please. What's good on the menu?"

"Everything," George said.

Marlowe looked up at Donovan and said, "The wild rice with grilled vegetables is the only thing that doesn't have too much salt and fat. You'll like it. Avoid everything else *like the plague*. Hello, Donovan."

"Richard, this is Katy. Katy, this is Richard."

"I loved you in *Questa Notte*."

"Thank you."

While the drinks were being made, Morty Berman pulled Donovan to one side and whispered in his ear, "What gives?"

"What gives is I need a big favor."

"I owe you."

"Get Katy and me on the air. Ask us a few harmless questions. Don't probe. Pretend you're auditioning for *Entertainment Tonight*."

"Three Emmy Awards and this is how I'm spending my old age?"

"Just go with the program. Your payback will be worth it."

"When will it come?"

"Be on call tomorrow after midnight. One way or another, I'll have a story for you."

A few moments later, Phil pointed a camera at Katy Lucca as she stood next to Donovan and with a flotilla of cops clustered around. Morty held a mike to her lips and said, "Mrs. Lucca, you're starting to get out for the first time following the tragic murder of your husband. Are you happy with the pace of the investigation?"

"Very. William is a great detective and I'm confident that soon he'll have the evidence he needs to bring charges against this terrorist Akbar."

A murmur went through the room: *William?*

"Is that true, Lieutenant *William* Donovan of the NYPD?"

Donovan pointedly slipped his arm around Katy's waist. "Let me say only that Mrs. Lucca is being a great help to us in our investigation. She has given us several leads that we are pursuing diligently.''

"That's great. Uh...I see that you're out and enjoying the opening of this fabulous new restaurant owned by former undercover policewoman Marcia Barnes."

"Yes, I've heard a *lot* about her and her terrific new place," Katy answered. "I promised my husband that I wouldn't spend a lot of time mourning him, but would get right on with my life. He insisted on it, and, well, here I am." She laughed and tossed her hair as Berman ended the interview.

As he walked by Donovan heading for the door, Berman whispered, "It'll be on at eleven. Now *you* owe me. I sounded like Don Atherton."

"You'll get another Emmy. Trust me."

"Mmmf," the man said, and left with his cameraman in tow.

"William?" Marcy asked. She had slipped over during the taping and heard the whole thing.

"That's my name," Donovan replied.

"With me your name is mud," she said.

"Aren't you grateful for the publicity? Marcy's Home Cooking will be a big hit now. All you have to do next is cut out all the salt and fat."

"Donovan, you're so predictable. You give and you take away in the same breath. If by chance you bring joy, unintentionally you bring sorrow."

Katy cut in then, saying, "Pleasure and pain, that's him. He's almost Zen-like in that regard. Hi, I'm Katy Lucca."

"Marcia Barnes. Please don't say you've heard a lot about me."

"But I have," Katy replied, taking Donovan's arm and pulling him closer. Then she sipped her Stoli and looked down at Marcy who, while tall by ordinary standards, was still an inch shorter.

Marcy looked at the two of them together, then closed her eyes and shook her head. "Donovan, it's perfectly clear to me now. You're a wonder. Just a wonder. Every time I think you've outdone yourself, you outdo yourself again."

"Yeah, he stripped my gears a couple of times, too," Katy said.

"Now, girls, this could be a long evening. Can we have our table? That and two orders of wild rice with grilled vegetables."

"This way," Marcy said with a sigh.

She seated them at the same table where, a few nights earlier,

Donovan had listened to the commissioner offer him a captain's shield. He held Katy's chair for her and then sat where he could see the crowd. They had begun to settle down and, thankfully, most had stopped gaping at Katy.

"I guess you won't need your phaser weapon tonight," Donovan said.

"I might with *her*," Katy said, nodding at Marcy's retreating figure. "So that's Marcy. Well, she is beautiful. I compliment you on your taste. A bit skinny, maybe."

"She runs marathons."

"Oh God, another athlete. Physical fitness is an epidemic that so far has spared me." She lifted her glass and sipped the vodka. "She does have great skin, though—a complexion many women would kill for. Like cafe au lait, sort of; either that or a *world-class* tan. I have to go to the ladies' room. Is it safe to leave you in the same room with her?"

"Go."

She was barely gone when Moskowitz hurried over, carrying a sheaf of papers, and helped himself to a seat.

"Hey," Donovan said.

"Yo, Lieutenant. I figured it out."

"Good for you."

"The guys on surveillance said that Brigid wore a mink."

"It's a sable."

"Yeah, right. You're something else. Are you shtupping this woman?"

Donovan gave his friend a withering glance.

"Right. You're too noble to tell me."

"What makes you think I'm sleeping with her?" Donovan asked.

"You can start with the phone calls from your apartment at four in the morning."

"Let me see." He grabbed the papers and riffled through them.

"There were four of them from your place to Steven Clark's suite at his casino in Atlantic City."

"Damn. I was hoping I was wrong."

"Why?"

"Now I have to go on paying rent on that apartment. Tell me more."

"The other number, the private line in the Luccas' apartment?"

"What of it?"

"There were a lot of calls from there to Clark, also."

Donovan sipped his nonalcoholic beer. "What about the ashtray?"

"The ashes are from Sherman's cigarettes, all right. And there's more."

"You found prints."

"A decent thumbprint. It's Clark, all right."

"His prints are on record?"

"You bet. The man was fingerprinted when he got a carry permit a few months ago."

"The man is licensed to carry a pistol? What's he packing?"

"A nine-millimeter Spring-Rice. Seven shots in a quick-change magazine."

"That's...just...great," Donovan said. To himself he muttered, *So much for my promise never to shoot or get shot at again.* "Does he know how to use it?"

"Beats me. He's an ex-marine, so I guess so. We also got some saliva off one of those cigarette butts and matched it with blood taken from your bow tie."

"It's the same type?"

"Same type, same person. We ran a DNA comparison. Steven Clark smoked the cigarette you found in the Luccas' apartment. Moreover, he did so over the weekend."

"You talked to the cleaning service."

"Narnia Cleaners did a complete job on that apartment—including all the ashtrays—on Saturday, while Mrs. Lucca was out shopping or wherever she was."

"Possibly on the Canarsie Pier," Donovan mused, looking in the direction of the ladies' room.

"The lady fishes?" Mosko asked.

"I've come to think that hunting is a better metaphor."

"Whatever. Available evidence proves that Steven Clark was in the Luccas' apartment sometime Saturday or Sunday."

"It was most likely Sunday. She said she was home all day, resting."

"More likely she was home shtupping Clark—the man she says she can't be in the same room with."

"Did you run that check on Di Bello's lawyer?"

Mosko nodded. "He's also on retainer with Clark. Sorry, Bill, your lady is as dirty as they come. I see why you named her Brigid after the babe in *The Maltese Falcon*."

Donovan held up his bottle of Kaliber and stared into it. He had suspected this since she'd played Fauré for him on that fancy piano, saying that she guessed he would like it. You might guess that somebody liked Bach, but a relatively obscure French composer who was best known for being Ravel's teacher? No, she'd heard the music while listening at the door of his bedroom that first night. "Somehow it ain't the same staring into your nonalcoholic beer," he grumbled.

"If you wanna fall off the wagon I'll keep you company."

"Forget it. I was wondering if..."

Marcy walked up then, carrying their orders. "I just want you to know that nobody has ever hated anybody more than I hate you right now," she said.

"Is there a pay phone by the ladies' room?" he asked.

"Yes. Go strangle yourself on the cord."

"You don't think she's on the horn to her partner in crime?" Mosko asked.

"I think it's possible. I'll talk to you later. I have some instructions for tomorrow night." Donovan said. He walked back there, certain he would see Katy on the phone with Atlantic City.

Instead he saw Katy standing by, looking irritated, while Jake monopolized the line.

Delighted, Donovan checked his watch, then said, "The Queens number is in."

"*Sí,*" Jake said. Betting information on the Upper West Side was frequently transmitted in Spanish.

"*¿Que es?*" Donovan asked.

"*Cinco quatro uno.*"

"I love my local bookie," Donovan said.

"I was going to call my service for messages," Katy said hurriedly. Unusually for her, she looked flustered.

"Go ahead and call. Jake will be off the phone as soon as he finds out how much money he lost."

"Oh," she said, surprised. "You don't mind?"

"Not a bit. I'll wait back at the table."

"I'll just be a minute, hon," she said.

Jake hung up the phone and gave Donovan a suspicious look. "What did she call you?"

"Hon," Donovan replied, leading Jake away.

"You're letting her make the call?" Moskowitz asked incredulously when Donovan got back to the table. "I'm sure she's calling Clark."

"I'm hoping she is."

"You are?"

"I'm hoping she's telling him to tune in to the eleven o'clock news."

"The man is gonna shoot your ass off with that Spring-Rice," Moskowitz said.

THIRTY-TWO

SEVEN WEBS FROM A BLACK WIDOW SPIDER

IT WAS THE NEXT NIGHT, the night of reckoning, and, dressed to the nines as they had been the night of the murder, Donovan and Katy were alone in the museum, a four-block, four-story cavern of wonders filled with swords, stuffed beasts, ghosts, and eerie noises that came from nowhere and meant danger. "I want to make love to you in the mouth of the blue whale," Katy said, entwining her fingers in his. The gigantic sea beast hung suspended in the core of the building, appearing to take up the better part of two floors.

"Too biblical. Pick someplace less epic."

"Then I want you in the center of the Samarkand market."

"Too dusty. And I thought you were allergic to everything."

"You turn me on and I forget."

She squeezed his hand and nuzzled against him suggestively. But he sighed and said, "After twenty-four hours in bed with you I'm fucked out. You'll have to get yourself a new boy."

"Never. You're the man for me forever. I see it's going to be hard to win you over, but I'll do it. You're stubborn and, I think, have some kind of weird hostility toward people of means."

Donovan cleared his throat and looked up at the figure of Theodore Roosevelt painted on the wall of the rotunda. He was the last

Republican president that Donovan admired. Even though he was, Donovan supposed, one of the fancy people. Come to think of it, after the play Morty Berman had given Katy and him on television the night before, Donovan had to assume that he, too, was one of the fancy people.

"Why Paolo?" he asked.

"Why Paolo what?"

"Why did you marry him? I mean, from what I can see you're attracted to blue-collar guys—Jameson, Clark, me."

"You're not a blue-collar guy. You're an educated man."

"Self-educated. I've read a lot over the years. But I never spent a minute in a college classroom. I taught a few courses in criminology, but that doesn't count. And you met my friends. They're all working stiffs."

"You're gentle with me—sort of. As gentle as I want you to be."

"Was that what you liked about Paolo—he was gentle?"

"I think when I went with Paolo I was reacting against Steven. He was too rough."

"He slapped you around, didn't he?"

"William!"

"So did Wally, I bet. I know you, Katy. I just spent twenty-four hours in bed with you. What was wrong with Paolo? Was he *too* gentle?"

"In a way, yes. He was hyper-educated, and he thought six times about everything. More so even than you."

"Do I question everything?"

"Are you *kidding?*" She laughed. "Let me be blunt."

"When aren't you?"

"More and more every day with you, honey," she said, her voice dripping again into that smoky register. "When a beautiful woman is sucking your cock, don't interrupt to question her motivation. Just lean back and enjoy."

"I did," Donovan said.

"I was making a point. But as for Paolo, his brother is said to be one of the leading humanist scholars in Europe. Some of that was in the blood. Paolo was a lot like him. What I love about you is that you're both tough *and* soft."

"I 'take your breath away,'" he said with a laugh.

"You do, and I want you to take it away forever. Let's run

away, William. Let's get my plane and fly to Rhodes. You'll love it there. There's a little stone chapel where we can get married.''

Donovan led her out of the rotunda and through the entrance to the Treasure of the Silk Road.

He laughed, and said, ''Thank you for letting me know how it feels. I would never have known.''

''How it feels to be what?''

''How it feels to be a beautiful woman.''

''I did that?''

''Sure. You want to sweep me off my feet and take me away to a world of riches and luxury and all I have to do to earn it is be good in bed.''

''I had to put up with that for years.'' She laughed. ''It's someone else's turn now.''

They looked at the exhibit on the Tel Dan inscription. A triangular stone tablet, a fragment of a larger piece, was inscribed with thirteen lines written in Aramaic. An accompanying placard described the writing as being that of Baasha, a ninth century B.C. king of Israel.

''What does ancient Israel have to do with silk?'' Katy asked, pretending interest.

''Israel would be considered the Silk Road equivalent of a soft shoulder,'' Donovan said. ''It's in the neighborhood and it's interesting. Maybe they were the tailors. How much could Paolo put in about the actual Silk Road? Who wants an hour and a half of caravan routes?''

''Not me.''

''Actually, Israel has as much to do with it as does a game of buzghashi, and that's in here too.''

''What's buzghashi?''

''A sort of polo where they use the carcass of a sheep instead of a ball.''

''Ick.''

''Don't worry. They don't play by those rules anymore in Palm Beach.''

She took him by the shoulders, turned him away from the Tel Dan exhibit and pointed him eastward down the road. ''You have got *such* a thing about the rich. What happened, was your mother frightened by a Mercedes-Benz while you were still in the womb?''

"I'm half Irish and half English. Half of me is poor and furious at the rich half. Part of me wants to kill the other part but is too repressed to do it."

"Half of you is drunk and the other half is repulsed," she chimed in.

"Very good, Dr. Lucca."

"You're a seriously disturbed man, William Donovan. I'm more convinced than ever that I love you. Your only problem is you have to loosen up and trust me."

They walked in silence through the Babylonian exhibit. She seemed to stiffen when they strolled by the Phoenician Diorama, behind which Paolo had been killed; Donovan was uncertain if she knew that that was where it happened. But she untensed when they entered the Mesopotamian part of the exhibition. Soon she let go his hand and slipped her fingers into his pants pocket, spreading them out and pressing them against his upper thigh. Perhaps incidentally, the side of her hand brushed the part of his belt holster that held the barrel of his Smith & Wesson.

It was silent, as quiet as a tomb, in the museum after midnight. When they walked Donovan could hear only their footfalls, and when they stood still he could hear Katy's breathing. The air rushed up and down her throat as if through a wind tunnel. At one point he stopped her and pressed her against him and wrapped his arms around her, and she nestled her head against his, the honey hair splaying over both their shoulders. Her breath on the intake hissed through her slightly closed teeth as it did when she was lying in bed, stroking herself and watching the beads of sweat roll down the curve of her breasts. On exhalation, Katy's breath was deep and throaty, like a prolonged *aah* or a climax. Donovan had thought that Marcy was hot-wired; but Katy made her seem like an altar girl. Every step she took seemed like a move she learned in bed.

They stared at the artifacts of Qaleh-i Yazdegerd, a Persian castle that guarded the Zagros Gates, the pass through which Silk Road caravans traversed the Zagros Mountains. It was built in the seventh century by Yazdegerd III, whose ancestor had used his position to persecute, ecumenically, both Christians and Jews. In the display, a fragment of the capital of a column bore a pair of intertwined beasts, Mediterranean in inspiration. In another a nude woman held a pair of dolphins with voluted tails. The commentary said that the castle was, most likely, originally the home of a robber baron who exacted tribute from passing caravans.

Katy was wearing the small black velvet dress that Donovan had practically torn off her the night before. His arm encircling her waist made it ride up her thighs, which were long and dusky in black panty hose. The magnetism of her presence notwithstanding, in between breaths and in the stillness of the massive granite building Donovan thought he felt something change. There was a shift in the wind, as peculiar as that might sound. It was impossible—but Donovan felt a window or a door open and close somewhere in the bowels of the building. It was a fact, however, that Steven Clark had given surveillance the slip a few hours earlier in Atlantic City.

They walked on.

On a stele—a commemorative pillar—from the excavation at Gandhara was a representation of Siddhartha on horseback starting his journey toward enlightenment. Near the pillar was a seated Buddha made of black schist. He was dressed in a toga and wore the somber expression of a Greco-Roman philosopher, another indication of the influence of the Silk Road on the cultures of both East and West. A piece of a wall painting, taken from the meditation cave at Duldur Aqur, showed a goddess with long, slender, curving fingers and sharp nails. She stared off the tablet, bearing a witchy expression.

Donovan heard another sound. He was sure of this one, because it came when Katy had her head on his shoulder and was breathing quietly. The sound was that of metal on metal, machinery working. It was neither heating system nor air conditioning. Nor was it traffic. None could be heard behind those stone walls. The sound was an elevator operating. It was the service elevator, Donovan knew. The sound came from behind, from the direction of the Phoenician Studio.

Donovan's right hand slipped into his pants pocket. His fingers touched the two speed-loaders, each of which carried six spare bullets. Not really reassured—Clark's automatic carried far more ammunition and loaded faster—he walked on.

As they approached the Chandar Diorama Katy tensed up again. Donovan realized that every thought that entered her head was reflected in her body. Perhaps that created a great actress and a terrific lover, but it made for a lousy liar.

"I'm curious: How much did it cost you to get the museum just for us?"

"I gave them the exhibit," she said with a shrug. "I signed it away to the museum's development fund. I hate all this junk and, anyway, I can use the tax deduction."

"You gave them *everything?*"

"The whole goddamn thing. With one exception. I kept a trinket for you. You're going to take *something* from me, whether you like it or not. Since you like to do things on the up-and-up, I even mailed you a letter giving you legal possession." She pointed to the Chandar Diorama.

It was similar to the Oasis Diorama, save for the fact that no wax figures appeared. Instead of a wax Pamiristani bearer unfolding an ancient treasure map, atop a stone block was a swatch of unwrapped leather atop which—lit gloriously to make it gleam like the Star of India—sat the copy of Kublai Khan's dagger.

Surrounding it were other relics of the lost city of Chandar which, located strategically at the midpoint of the Silk Road, contained treasures culled equally from both East and West. A fragment of a wall painting showed two devotees of Buddha, but with aquiline noses, large eyes, and high-necked garments that seemed more Roman than Indian. A gilt-bronze wine goblet from Tang China was decorated with a mounted huntsman. A piece of Sassanian Persian textile, woven silk with a bird motif, sat next to an ancient Greek silver coin, a tetradrachm, which bore the bust of Alexander. These and other objects sat atop and around stone blocks, some of them carved with ancient writings, that Lucca had brought home from the archaeological dig he'd created, in large part, to serve as a cover for oil exploration.

"I love art and history," Donovan said, having forgotten momentarily that money and sarcasm were the lingua franca of the Lucca crowd.

"You do, don't you?" she said, stiffening and taking a deep breath before grabbing his hand and leading him to one side of the exhibit, to the doorway marked "Chandar Studio." She plucked a key from her purse and opened the door. "Come with me," she said, and led him inside.

Another door opened, echoing the sound of the Chandar Studio door. That sound came from a short distance down the hall. Donovan glanced quickly over his shoulder before allowing himself to be led into the studio.

It was like the others he had seen: paint and half-done sculptures. Bits of stone block. Chips of marble and sandstone. Unused fragments of silk. Plans that detailed every aspect of the exhibit, some of them on paper and some of them on a computer-assisted design monitor that had been left untimely on. And of course there was the smell of paint.

She pulled another key from her purse and opened the small, slightly elevated door that led into the Chandar Diorama itself. It squeaked open to reveal, painted on its front, a part of the background for Chandar. There were no human figures in this painting, Donovan noted with some disappointment, only newly uncovered stone walls and ramparts, wine and grain storage pits and, looking down on it all, the towering, white-capped peaks of the Pamirs.

Katy took another deep breath just as she had the moment before. Donovan recognized the move. *She's going on stage,* he thought. "Follow me," she said, stepping into the diorama.

"Where are we going?"

"Into the ancient city."

Looking left and right and ahead, his ears tuned for unexpected sounds, his hand undoing the leather strap that held his Smith & Wesson in its holster, Donovan stepped into the past with the lady.

The artifacts of Chandar were at his feet. He felt like Lucca finding the site; no, he felt more like Roy Chapman Andrews, the genuine article, who taught himself science for the love of it and did it selflessly. Katy put her hand at the small of Donovan's back and urged him to step to the stone block atop which sat the copy of Kublai Khan's dagger.

She picked it up and handed it to him. The gilt bronze dagger, sparkling with its red rubies and blue lapis lazuli against the shimmering gold, might have been the Treasure of the Sierra Madre to him. He held it in his left hand and looked at it adoringly, his right hand—unseen by her—still touching his revolver.

"It's beautiful," he said. "It feels like the real thing."

"It's yours."

"You're kidding."

"You can take *this,* for God's sake. It's only a copy and has only sentimental value. But you're a sentimental kind of guy."

All of a sudden Donovan felt her stiffen again—that "curtain is rising" feel once more—and again take a deep breath. This was the third time. Strike three. She took a big step backward and said, her voice in the low register, "I've been wanting to give it to you for three days."

Donovan said, "I know." Out of the corner of his eye he saw a motion, a man moving, running down the hall directly at him. It was Steven Clark and, in his outstretched hand, a nine-millimeter Spring-Rice: seven shots in a quick-change magazine.

His face was twisted in fury, his movements awkward, ruled by madness. He screamed Donovan's name and began pulling the trigger.

Donovan dropped the dagger and fell to his knees behind the stone pillar, pulling his revolver and trying to shut his ears to the murderous sounds. Katy screamed and lurched away and the museum echoed with seven roars, one after the other in mechanical fashion. The gunshots echoed off the ceiling, the walls, and the glass of the exhibit, which howled with high-tension impacts and the scream of material under stress.

There was a second of silence after which Donovan slowly rose, his Smith & Wesson at the ready, and opened his eyes to look out at the spider-webbing that surrounded seven bullet impacts in the glass. Seven webs from a black widow spider, Donovan thought. Beyond the glass was Steven Clark, his eyes as big as silver dollars, his mouth gaping open.

Filled with triumph, Donovan sucked in his own breath and yelled what he knew, what every one of the millions of ten-year-olds who loved the Museum of Natural History, which had beefed up security in the wake of the Murph the Surf incident, would know. Donovan looked Clark in the eye and yelled, "It's bullet-proof!"

THIRTY-THREE

"IT WAS EASY," HE REPLIED

CLARK STUMBLED backward, three steps, in a panic. He aimed his revolver again and pulled the trigger but the hammer fell on an empty cylinder. He had used the shots in that magazine. Surprised and afraid, he looked at the gun and fumbled for the mechanism that released the magazine.

Donovan turned to jump out of the back of the diorama. As he spun he saw Katy cowering in fear against a tomb carving that depicted a family of silk weavers. "Nice try, sweetheart," Donovan said as he leaped from the display.

When he burst from the studio into the hall, revolver in front of him, Clark was gone. But there was the sound of a man running, and it was clear as a bell in the stillness of the museum after midnight. Clark was heading out of the Silk Road exhibit, back toward the Theodore Roosevelt Rotunda. Donovan started after him.

In better shape and wearing softer-soled shoes, Donovan gained on the man whose every step he could hear clearly. Clark ran into the Rotunda in the shadow of the five-story dinosaurs and, when he entered that cavernous hall, his footsteps echoed fiercely. Responding to the sound, he looked around in panic and, crouching behind the tail of the barosaur, finally found his gun's magazine-release mechanism.

The empty magazine clattered to the floor with a metallic sound that Donovan heard as he flew out of the Silk Road entrance. There followed the quieter clink of a second clip being shoved home. Donovan ducked behind a mammoth pillar just as a shot took a chunk out of it.

"That's one," he counted to himself.

Donovan spun around the other side of the pillar and fired a shot back in the general direction of his adversary. It ricocheted off one faraway wall and then another.

This was like being in a damn pinball machine, he thought. Two more shots came back, but both of them missed and disappeared down the Silk Road.

Donovan counted: Two. Three.

He returned to the first side of the pillar and fired again. This shot clipped a dinosaur vertebra, sending a spray of fiberglass "bone" fragments spraying over Clark, who fired back twice more. Both shots hit the column.

Four. Five.

Clark took off running again, this time across the Rotunda in the direction of the entrance to the Akeley Memorial Hall of African Mammals. Donovan stepped out into the open and aimed carefully. He yelled, "Clark! Freeze!" to no avail. So, tracking the fleeing figure like a hunter tracking a quail in flight, Donovan fired off two shots.

Both missed and ricocheted off the wall just below one of the Roosevelt murals. Above, a "peaceable kingdom" scene had a lion lording over an assemblage of storks, flamingos, antelope, and happy natives on safari.

Donovan took off after Clark, who had made the turn into the African exhibit. Donovan dashed across the rotunda and ducked behind another pillar as a shot sent fragments of stone flying over his head.

Six.

He squeezed his eyes shut and ducked down, then spun around the column and fired twice more. Donovan cringed as he heard his bullets impact a display case. He was out of ammunition, but Clark didn't know that, unless Katy was a gun expert as well as a spy, and Donovan thought that unlikely. He flicked the spent cartridges onto the floor, then realized his mistake: That sound, Clark could hear.

Donovan whipped a speed-loader out of his right pocket and jammed it into the Smith & Wesson. He spun around the other side of the column in time to see Clark aiming at him. A bullet whizzed by Donovan's head and he fired blindly in return, three bullets. All of them ricocheted off walls *someplace*.

Clark was off on the run again, through the Hall of African Mammals, inserting a new magazine as he ran. Donovan heard the spent one clatter to the floor.

Seven. *How many spare magazines does he have?*

Donovan followed the footsteps. It was dark in the African exhibit but the lights glowed softly in the dioramas as Donovan caught a glimpse of two of his bullets. Spider webs graced the glass on the Gorilla Diorama. The dominant male gorilla stood erect, beating his chest, while his family foraged for food and his infant munched wild celery leaves. The volcanic Mounts Nyiragongo and Nyamlagira smoked languidly through the confused tangle of the rain forest, heavy with vines, ferns, and bearded lichen.

Clark ran out a side exit and started up one of the several long flights of marble stairs leading to the third floor. The sounds he made changed distinctively; Donovan was hot on his heels.

The lieutenant ran out the same exit and into the comparative glare of the hallway and stairs. He got to the landing just as Clark was nearing the top. Sighting in on the man, he yelled "Give it up!"

Instead, Clark wheeled and fired two shots wildly. They bounced off one wall of the stairwell and from there to the floor, chipping off some marble and sending Donovan leaping for cover. When he got to his feet Clark had disappeared into the Hall of South American Peoples. Donovan sprinted up the steps, taking them two at a time.

The light was dark and greenish-yellow in the room that housed the Copper Man. In life that unfortunate individual was a pre-Colombian copper miner who died working a shaft in Chuquicamata, Chile. The body was well preserved, at least partly by the copper that oozed with preserved body fluids to create a metallic coating for the corpse. Newly displayed with recreated surroundings that included the stone hammer and shovel and woven collection baskets with which he was discovered, the Copper Man was a striking reminder of the omnipresence of death in that great building filled with stuffed animals and otherwise recreated life. He cast a morbid glow over several adjacent display cases.

Donovan ran into the room, then realized he was silhouetted by the good white light coming from the hall. He dived behind the Copper Man Diorama, but not before three slugs tore up the wall above his head.

One. Two. Three.

He stuck his hand around from behind the diorama and fired once. The slug hit a display case made of ordinary glass, which disappeared in a starburst of splinters. Clark cried out and scrambled to his feet from where he was hiding, behind that wrecked display. In a flash Donovan was after him.

Clark's options included a dead end and a stairway down. He chose the latter. With Donovan forty or fifty yards behind and gaining, Clark ran downstairs and turned to the center of the building, running down the mezzanine balcony that overlooked the blue whale. Clark was now suffering from the excess pounds that Katy had talked about in one of her many attempts to deceive Donovan and the world into thinking she hated the man. His gait had slowed and he was wiping blood from his face—the result of several bits of flying glass. Donovan was catching up.

The ninety-four-foot whale seemed to go on forever, an unimaginably huge beast that spoke of the deep sea, Captain Ahab, and obsessive pursuit. At last Clark made the turn by its tail and disappeared down another stairs. Now only thirty or so yards behind and determined to take Clark alive if possible, Donovan ran steadily and well, breathing regularly as he had learned to do during his near-daily runs in Riverside Park.

Two flights down and on the Seventy-seventh Street side of the building, Clark stumbled past the great Haida canoe, a Northwest Coast Indian canoe of nearly yachtlike proportions, made at the turn of the century, using life casts of native volunteers. Clark was out of breath now but not quite as lifeless as these hollow figures that pondered an imaginary horizon from their lofty perches.

With Donovan closing, Clark half ran, half stumbled toward what he thought was the Columbus Avenue exit. Donovan knew better. Beyond the Hall of Meteorites—and the permanent *Star Trek* exhibit—lay only a securely built dead end that contained the J. P. Morgan Hall of Gems. Relocated since the Murph the Surf mess, *this* display of egregious wealth was not about to be broken either into or out of.

The hall was brilliantly lit and obviously secure. Clark reached the middle of it when he realized that there was no way out but the way he came in, and that was blocked. Donovan stood in the door, breathing heavily but hardly winded. Clark, however, was finished; there simply was no more in the man. He had nothing left except four shots in his automatic plus whatever extra magazines he might have stuffed into the workingman's khaki pants and denim jacket that he'd chosen for his final showdown. His overly long hair was matted with sweat. Blood ran down his cheeks and neck. He finally looked, Donovan thought, like the construction foreman he so much thought of himself as being.

Waving his gun and smiling crookedly, he turned completely around, his eyes catching the rays of light that gleamed off the millions of dollars' worth of rubies, emeralds, and diamonds that glistened from heavily alarmed and brightly lit display cases all around. Donovan had never thought Clark capable of irony. However, the fact that fate brought him to this place seemed to please him.

He smiled, and gasped, "I'll give you anything. I'll make you a wealthy man."

"Your girlfriend already tried that," Donovan replied.

"Married to one another, Katy and I will have it all. We're worth close to *two* billion dollars. Think of it, Donovan, the wealthiest couple the world has ever known."

"I guess she's not planning to give most of it away—like Paolo wanted," Donovan said.

"Of course not," Clark replied.

"That's what this is all about, isn't it? You sent your little slave girl to seduce and marry your dying business partner to get his estate. But the guy surprised you. He decided to atone for his wicked ways by giving most of it away in the few months left him. You couldn't let that happen, could you? God forbid all that money should go to rescue starving people in the less fortunate parts of the world."

To augment his point, Donovan swept an arm around the rich vista contained in the Morgan Hall of Gems.

"To add insult to injury, Paolo was cutting you out of a major share in the oil profits. You wanted all this and more for yourselves. So you stabbed Paolo to death and tried to blame it on the Muslim fundamentalists."

"We'll give you a million dollars. I can make it appear in your bank tomorrow morning."

"I've already turned down half a million. Forget it, Clark. If you want to give me something, answer two questions."

"Will you let me go if I do?"

"I'll think about it. How did you get the dagger out of the safe?"

"Katy couldn't talk Paolo into giving her the combination, so she got it from Di Bello. She slipped the dagger to me under her sable. Two million, Donovan. Three million. What's your other question?"

"Was she there to intercept me from the very beginning?"

Clark lowered his weapon and bent over, hands on knees, catching his breath. Donovan hadn't said no to three million. There was a chance.

"No," Clark said. "We didn't know you were coming. We expected the police commissioner. Katy liked you. She may have been spying on you but you always turned her on. I was pretty mad about that. I mean to speak to her about it."

"Are you going to slap her around?" Donovan asked.

Clark looked at him sharply, laughed, and said: "Do you really care? Five million dollars, Donovan, and all you have to do is walk away. Swiss and offshore bank accounts. My experts can fix it so that no one will ever know. That's my final offer.''

The lieutenant shook his head. ''I'm a pretty happy guy right now. Drop your weapon, Clark, and turn around and put your hands on that display case.''

Clark drew himself up to full height and sighed, then began backing up. But he had taken barely two steps when his back was against a large and gleaming display case, especially well lit and bristling with electronic alarms.

''Don't do it,'' Donovan warned.

''Good-bye,'' Clark muttered, jerking his automatic up and aiming it at the lieutenant.

Donovan pulled the trigger once, firing the last shot in his revolver. It caught Clark in the chest and kicked him backward, draping him over the display case. A thousand alarms went off, drowning out the metallic clink of Clark's gun falling to the hard, cold floor.

Donovan reloaded his Smith & Wesson and walked slowly to the corpse, kicking the automatic out of the way. Clark's face was pressed against the top of the case; blood ran from the corner of his mouth and down the glass, the crimson contrasting with the blue-white glow of the 563-carat Star of India sapphire.

''In the end you're just another thief,'' Donovan muttered as he walked from the Morgan Hall of Gems.

He hadn't gotten far down the hallway when Detective Sergeant Brian Moskowitz walked up at the head of a small army of cops. He had Katy Lucca by the wrist. She was limp and passive, a profoundly wealthy and undeniably gorgeous rag doll.

''Bill, are you okay?'' Mosko asked.

Donovan nodded. ''Poor but healthy. Clark's in there. He's rich but dead.''

Katy let out an immense gasp and her knees weakened. She started to faint again—this time into the arms of a policewoman, who caught her by the armpits and held her up.

''Get these alarms shut off,'' Donovan said, and a moment later stillness again ruled the museum.

''What happened?'' Mosko asked.

''He tried to kill me,'' Donovan said while slipping his Smith & Wesson back in its holster and closing the strap. ''When that didn't work, he tried to buy me off. I wasn't interested, and he tried to kill me again. So I shot the son of a bitch.''

Moskowitz looked past his boss at the body- and blood-bedecked Star of India display. ''Nice mess you made,'' he said.

''Thanks. I worked at it.''

Katy regained her composure and shook off the policewoman's supporting hands. She also tossed her long hair, then pushed some strands of it off her face. Donovan could see that she had been crying. Or maybe that was faked too, along with the sentiment she tossed at him. ''I loved you,'' she said, her voice low and husky.

''You just tried to knock me off,'' Donovan growled. ''Don't make things worse by insulting my intelligence.''

''I *did* love you,'' she protested. ''I mean, I still do. We can make a life together.''

He shook his head slowly and sadly from side to side, then clapped languidly three times. Lazy, sarcastic applause. Then Donovan said, ''I've had enough of this act.''

''I mean it, William.''

She reached out for him, but he took a step back from her and told the policewoman, ''This performance is finally over. Take her away. Be sure to cuff her tightly, though. She'll like that.''

As the handcuffs bound her wrists behind her, Katy Lucca looked at him with misty eyes and said, ''How could you?''

''It was easy,'' he replied.

THIRTY-FOUR

THREE HASH MARKS BENEATH THE RUBY SCARAB BEETLE

''YOU TURNED DOWN *how* much?'' Marcy asked, staring at Donovan across the deserted bar. It was four in the morning, and traffic on Broadway consisted of newspaper delivery vans, garbage trucks, and the station wagons that brought fresh fruit and vegetables to the Korean markets that sprouted on every block. Donovan and Marcy were alone and he toyed idly with the trinket that Katy had left him.

"Five million."

She laughed and shook her head, chopping a potato for the next day's stew. "Do you have any idea what you could have done with that much money?"

"Nope. I can't count that high. I run out of fingers and toes real fast. Besides, who needs it? I'm a lucky guy. I have a rent-controlled apartment and no debts, and I just got a promotion. Look at this."

He showed her the captain's shield that the commissioner had given him an hour before in the Rotunda of the museum, just after Donovan was done giving Morty Berman the scoop of the year.

"I'll be damned," she said. "Captain Donovan."

"The formal swearing-in will be held on Monday at City Hall. You want to go?"

"Are you asking me for a *date?*"

"Yeah, kind of."

She sighed and switched from chopping vegetables for stew to cutting fruit for salad.

"Wasn't Katy Lucca enough woman for you this week?"

He shrugged. "Monday is next week." Using the long, broad blade of the dagger, he moved a grape back and forth across the surface of the bar. He played hockey with it, trying to tap it in between an apple and an orange.

"I have to know: Is she better than me?"

"No one's better than you," he said quickly.

Marcy brightened. "Well, she may be taller and have bigger boobs, but *I* can do anything."

"Don't ever say that again," Donovan said sharply. "No one in this life can do anything they want. Everyone is accountable to everyone else; it's what makes us human."

"All *right,*" she replied. "It's just a saying."

"Stop saying it."

He stopped playing hockey with the dagger and began inspecting it closely for the first time.

"Couldn't you have taken at least *one* million?"

He shook his head. "With a small army of cops outside? Besides, I could never think of ways to spend it."

"I could."

"What for? Judging by the opening night crowd—which *I* helped bring here, by the way, and thank you for acknowledging the fact—Marcy's Home Cooking is a smash hit."

"What about the Lucca fortune? Who'll get the bulk of his estate with Katy on trial for murder?"

"The brother, Tommaso, I guess. At least it will be used to do some good. He seemed pretty comfortable with Paolo's philanthropy. I think he's going to carry on the good work."

"And Akbar, the Muslim. What will he do?"

"He'll give a speech at the U.N. demanding that peacekeeping troops be sent to Pamiristan to prevent the slaughter of his people by the central government. Then he'll get on a plane and fly home—going first-class, this time. Mdivani and Lemovin will also thrive. They have cigarettes and vodka in Cannes."

"Donovan, when you move your office downtown to One Police Plaza I'll never see you again. You'll be all over the city, handling high-profile cases, hobnobbing with celebrities, never in the neighborhood. Just when I open a neighborhood restaurant."

"We never seem to get it right, do we, you and me?"

"Maybe next time," she said. "Sure, I'll go to your swearing-in as captain."

"Great," he replied, beaming and continuing to examine various tiny aspects of the dagger.

"What are you going to *do* with that thing?"

"Keep it as a memento of the case, I guess."

"Oh God, another *tchotchke* to put in an apartment full of them," she said, rolling her eyes. "Donovan, it's just fake junk."

He twisted it around in the light. "It *does* look real, though. Metz did a hell of a job."

"How can you tell the real one?" Marcy asked.

"The real one..." He found the decorative scarab and peered beneath it, and when he did his eyes widened and glazed and his heart started pounding. His voice unsteady, he said, "The real one has three hash marks beneath the ruby scarab beetle."

Donovan was holding in his hand the genuine item, the real dagger that Marco Polo had been carrying to the court of Kublai Khan when it was lost and buried in the sands of Chandar for eight hundred years. The real, *priceless* dagger. There must have been a mixup; Metz had screwed up, putting the real item in the exhibit and the copy in the safe. Consequently, Clark had stabbed Lucca with the fake.

"And the one in your hand has nothing," Marcy said, coring an apple and tossing the scrap into the garbage.

"Not a damn thing," Donovan replied, recovering well enough to use the dagger to spear a grape.

"What will you do with it?"

"I guess I'll put it in the shoe box with my medals. No, the commissioner wants me to be proud of them. Hell, maybe I'll stick this dagger on the mantel *alongside* the medals. Some day it might be worth something. I can sell it and use whatever price it fetches to augment Social Security and my pension."

"You're only keeping that thing to remind you of her," Marcy concluded.

"No," he replied emphatically, smiling broadly. "I'm keeping it to remind myself of the day I traded five million dollars for a captain's shield." And with that he bit the grape off the tip of the dagger and swallowed it.

Take 2 books and a surprise gift FREE!

SPECIAL LIMITED-TIME OFFER

Mail to: The Mystery Library™
3010 Walden Ave.
P.O. Box 1867
Buffalo, N.Y. 14240-1867

YES! Please send me **2 free books** from the Mystery Library™ and my free surprise gift. Then send me 3 mystery books, first time in paperback, every month. Bill me only $4.19 per book plus 25¢ delivery and applicable sales tax, if any*. There is no minimum number of books I must purchase. I can always return a shipment at your expense and cancel my subscription. Even if I never buy another book from the Mystery Library™, **the 2 free books and surprise gift are mine to keep forever.**

415 WEN CJQN

Name	(PLEASE PRINT)	

Address		Apt. No.

City	State	Zip

* Terms and prices subject to change without notice. N.Y. residents add
  applicable sales tax. This offer is limited to one order per household and not
  valid to present subscribers.
© 1990 Worldwide Library.

MYS98

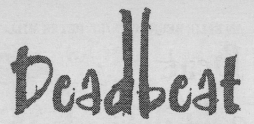

Deadbeat

AN ANGELA MATELLI MYSTERY

Boston is private eye Angela Matelli's beat as well as home to her large Italian family, including a mother who feeds her a steady diet of lasagna and blind dates. But she has little time for either as she investigates a case of credit card fraud.

Cynthia Franklin is a powerful woman. But that doesn't protect her from becoming a victim of a credit card scam. Angela has been hired to discover who has tapped in to her credit line. But her main suspect turns up dead.

Now Angela is hunting down a ruthless killer who's got a score to settle.

WENDI LEE

Available February 2000 at your favorite retail outlet.

WORLDWIDE LIBRARY